dead good editions

In partnership with Sainsbury's

Free story included in this book
plus 50 additional Nectar points on purchase.

Throughout the year Sainsbury's, in partnership with
Dead Good, will be recommending the very best in crime and
thriller books and introducing you to new crime writing talent.
And to celebrate, we're offering you an exclusive
Dead Good Edition that includes a free short story to
enjoy in each book, plus the opportunity to earn Nectar points.

Dead Good is the home of killer crime books,
drama and film and we're dedicated to discovering,
sharing and recommending thrilling crime.

Whether you visit to find out about your favourite author's new
book, to enter an exclusive competition or to find out more about
your favourite crime drama, **Dead Good** is the place for you.

WIN SPINE-TINGLING
CRIME BOOKS AND DVDS!

Enter at www.deadgoodbooks.co.uk/win

Bonus Nectar points offer ends 30.06.16

THE WITNESS

Simon Kernick is one of Britain's most exciting thriller writers. He arrived on the crime writing scene with his highly acclaimed debut novel *The Business of Dying*, the story of a corrupt cop moonlighting as a hitman. Simon's big breakthrough came with his novel *Relentless* which was the biggest selling thriller of 2007. His most recent crime thrillers include *Siege*, *Ultimatum*, *Stay Alive* and *The Final Minute*. He is also the author of the bestselling three-part serial thrillers *Dead Man's Gift* and *One By One*.

Simon talks both on and off the record to members of the Counter Terrorism Command and the Serious and Organised Crime Agency, so he gets to hear first hand what actually happens in the dark and murky underbelly of UK crime.

www.simonkernick.com; www.facebook.com/SimonKernick; www.twitter.com/simonkernick

Also by **Kernick**
_{Simon}

The Business of Dying
Featuring DS Dennis Milne, full-time cop, part-time assassin.

The Murder Exchange
Ex-soldier Max Iversson is hired to provide security for a
meeting that goes disastrously wrong.

The Crime Trade
DI John Callan and DS Tina Boyd uncover a murderous
conspiracy that will take them to the heart of London's
most notorious crime gang.

A Good Day to Die
Exiled cop Dennis Milne returns to London to hunt down the
murderers of a close friend.

Relentless
Tom Meron finds himself on the run, pursued by enemies
he never knew he had . . .

Severed
You wake up in a strange room on a bed covered in blood.
And you have no idea how you got there . . .

Deadline
You get home from work and your daughter is missing.
You know you will do anything to get her back alive –
but time is running out . . .

Target
Rob Fallon is the target of brutal killers. But what do they want?
Either he finds out or he's dead.

The Last 10 Seconds
A man, a woman, a sadistic killer. As they race towards a terrifying confrontation only one thing is certain: they're all going to have to fight very hard just to stay alive.

The Payback
Two cops that haunt them, and a present that could see them both dead. They are about to meet, and when they do, it's payback time.

Siege
A group of ruthless gunmen storm a London hotel, shooting guests and taking others hostage. Only one thing matters: who will survive?

Ultimatum
DI Mike Bolt and DC Tina Boyd have just 12 hours to save London from a major terrorist attack.

Stay Alive
You're being chased by three gunmen, and you know they have killed before. If they catch you, you'll be next . . .

The Final Minute
When the past comes to call, Matt Baron is forced to run to the one person who can help – Ex Met cop, Tina Boyd. But safety doesn't come in numbers and soon they are both on the run . . .

Simon Kernick

THE WITNESS

arrow books

1 3 5 7 9 10 8 6 4 2

Arrow Books
20 Vauxhall Bridge Road
London SW1V 2SA

Arrow Books is part of the Penguin Random House group of companies
whose addresses can be found at global.penguinrandomhouse.com.

Penguin
Random House
UK

Copyright © Simon Kernick 2016

Simon Kernick has asserted his right to be identified
as the author of this Work in accordance with the Copyright,
Designs and Patents Act 1988

First published in Great Britain by Century in 2016
First published in paperback by Arrow Books in 2016

www.randomhouse.co.uk

A CIP catalogue record for this book is available
from the British Library

ISBN 9780099579151
ISBN 9780099579168 (export)

Typeset in Times New Roman (10.81/15.64 pt) by Palimpsest Book
Production Limited, Falkirk, Stirlingshire
Printed and bound in Great Britain by Clays Ltd, St Ives Plc

MIX
Paper from
responsible sources
FSC® C016897

Penguin Random House is committed to a
sustainable future for our business, our readers
and our planet. This book is made from Forest
Stewardship Council® certified paper.

For Janine. You were, and are, an inspiration.

Prologue

Now

The gunshot explodes in my ears, the bullet hitting the door only inches from my head, and, although I'm sitting on the floor, I actually jump, letting loose a terrified gasp.

I'm scared. Jesus, I'm scared.

'Tell me the truth or the next bullet takes you,' demands the gunman. He's standing barely two metres from me, the smoking pistol pointed at my head. His eyes are alive with hatred and anger and I know that he means what he says. He will kill me.

'It is the truth,' I tell him with more confidence than I'm feeling.

'Bullshit,' he snaps, his gun hand steady. 'Last chance. I will kill you without question.'

The room stinks of death. A man lies sprawled against a kitchen unit opposite me, his face and body a mask of blood. He doesn't move. Nor does the woman lying on her side behind the gunman. A pool of thick dark blood is slowly forming round her head where a bullet from the very same gun now pointed at me blew a hole the size of a golf ball in it only a few minutes ago.

I open my mouth to speak, knowing I'm going to have to give this man the information he's looking for, even though it will cost me everything.

And then I hear it. The sound of the back door to the house being kicked open, followed by angry shouts of 'Armed police!' as they come running down the hall.

'I am a police officer,' a man calls out from just outside the door. 'There's no need for anyone to get hurt.'

'It's not what you think,' the gunman staring down at me calls back. 'I'm a police officer too.'

'Then we can sort this out,' says the other man.

The next second they're in the room, two men in plainclothes, their guns pointing at the gunman covering me.

'Put your weapon on the floor now,' says the one on the left. 'Nice and slowly.'

'It's not what you think,' the gunman repeats, his voice tight with tension, never taking his gun, or his gaze, from me.

'It doesn't matter what I think,' says the one on the left. 'You need to lower your weapon now.'

Nothing happens. I have my hands in the air, the expression on my face one of total fear. My heart is hammering away in my chest and I feel like I'm going to faint.

'Drop the weapon. Now.'

The gunman doesn't move.

'I said: drop the fucking weapon.'

The gunman's finger tightens on the trigger. 'If you shoot me, my last bullet takes her out,' he says.

And that's when I know I'm going to die.

Last Night

One

Jane Kinnear

I looked at the two police officers sitting next to my hospital bed and asked if I could possibly have a cigarette. 'I know it's not allowed, but I'm desperate for something just to calm the nerves and I can hardly go outside. Not after . . .' I let my words trail off. It was obvious to all of us I didn't need to finish the sentence.

The more senior of the two officers – an attractive black woman in her early thirties, dressed casually in a neat leather jacket and tight white T-shirt – looked like she was going to say no but then she turned to her colleague, a thin guy about the same age, with slicked-back receding hair. 'Have you got any objection to this lady breaking the law, DC Jeffs?'

'As long as I can have one as well,' he said, throwing me a leery smile.

'I'm afraid I haven't got any,' I said.

'Here, have one of mine.'

DC Jeffs pulled a pack of Silk Cut from his jacket pocket and lit two, handing one to me. I took the cigarette with shaking hands and a murmured thank you, and sucked deep. It tasted good. I blew the smoke up towards the ceiling and took two more long puffs while they waited patiently, before tapping the ash into an empty plastic cup by my bed. Finally, feeling calm for the first time that night, I turned to the black detective, who'd introduced herself to me as DS Anji Abbott.

'Where do you want me to begin?' I asked.

She smiled, placing a tape recorder on the bedside table. 'At the beginning.'

I nodded slowly, steeling myself against what was to come and, with a deep breath, started talking.

'I first met Anil at a hardware shop of all places. I was buying industrial-strength drain cleaner, and he was buying – well, I can't actually remember what he was buying. I was more inter-ested in him. He was a good-looking guy, a little on the short side, and a couple of pounds heavier than I'd normally go for, but he had well-defined features and the kind of face that smiles easily.

'I'll be straight. I was attracted to him. He had nice hands too, which is something I always check out in a man. So I made sure I caught his eye, gave him a big smile, and that was it. We started chatting, exchanged phone numbers, and within forty-eight hours we were out on a date.

'That was two weeks ago. We'd had one more date before

8

tonight, a dinner at a local restaurant, which ended with a kiss on the pavement outside, and which might have gone further if I hadn't stopped myself, remembering my cardinal dating rule: never sleep with a man before date three. If he can't wait until then he's just a player and best avoided.

'Anyway, date three was tonight. I don't drive so we arranged for Anil to pick me up from home in Watford and take me to his place in a little village a few miles from me, where he was going to cook. I think we both knew that we were going to be sleeping together and to be honest I was a little nervous. I've always been a very sexual person. That doesn't mean I'm a maneater, far from it, just that it's important to me that a man knows what he's doing in the bedroom. I've had more than my fair share of sexual disasters and, because I liked Anil, I was really hoping sparks would fly while simultaneously fearing that they wouldn't, if you can understand that?

'The moment he turned up at my house, though, I knew something was wrong. He was tense and distracted, a complete contrast to the other times I'd seen him, and it was clear something was on his mind. I even gave him the opportunity to leave the date for another night, and by God I wish he had, but he told me that no, he was OK, he'd just had a hard day at work. That was another thing about Anil. He was very vague about what he did for a living. Apparently he was a partner in a small family-run business importing boutique furnishings from India but that was about as far as I ever got with it, and it was clear he wasn't that interested in elaborating. But it obviously paid OK because he lived in a pretty detached cottage at the end of a winding country lane backing on to fields. It all seemed very different to the suburb in Watford that I called home.

'"So what culinary delights have you got in store for me tonight?" I asked him as we got out of the car and headed for the front door.

'"Ah, well, there's a bit of a problem there," he said. "It's been a really hectic day with work and I haven't had a chance to do the dish I wanted, but I know a great Thai place that'll deliver for us." He gave me a smile that looked far too forced as he unlocked the door and we went inside.

'It wasn't exactly the most auspicious start to the evening but at least his house was warm and it turned out he had a decent supply of high-quality white wine, which is always a good way of improving things. We shared a crisp bottle of Chablis on his sofa and I think it did the trick for both of us because as he visibly began to relax, so did I. One thing led to another, a second bottle got opened, and we started kissing. I forgot that I was hungry, enjoying the light-headedness that the alcohol provided, and before I really knew it – at least that's what I told myself – he was leading me upstairs to the bedroom.

'I wouldn't say the sex was spectacular but then it rarely is the first time with someone, especially when you've both been drinking. But Anil certainly gave a good account of himself and, as we lay there afterwards chatting about this and that, I remember thinking that the evening was shaping up to be a good one.

'And that was pretty much when it all started to go wrong because the next second I heard the front door opening and a woman calling out Anil's name.

'I knew immediately from her cheery, confident tone that this was either Anil's girlfriend or wife, and the look of utter shock on his face as he shot up in bed just confirmed it. Credit to him though, he knew how to think on his feet.

'"I'm up in the bedroom, babe," he called out, sounding just as cheery. "Be down in a mo." Then he turned to me. "I can explain everything," he whispered, "but please help me and get under the bed."

'"What?" I demanded, flabbergasted by his complete cheek.

'"She's volatile. I'm serious. If she finds you here, she'll kill us both."

'He grabbed me and pushed me off the bed, jumping off himself and flinging the wine glasses and the bottle under it. He kicked his clothes under there after them, making remarkably little noise, as if he'd done this sort of thing before, which I suspect he probably had.

'I could hear the girlfriend/wife coming up the stairs and knew I had to make a decision fast. She hadn't sounded very volatile when she'd called out from the front door, and maybe I should have just stood there and fronted it out, explained who I was while I got my clothes on, before walking out with my head held high. But, naked and in a strange house, and with only a few seconds to make my decision, I went for the easy option and, yanking on my blouse and jeans, I grabbed the rest of my clothes and wriggled under the bed. There was a good foot of space beneath the frame, which was covered by a frilly valance, so it wasn't too difficult to manage.

'"How are you, darling?" he said. "I was just getting ready for bed. I'm absolutely shattered. How come you're back tonight?"

'Jesus, I thought, lying there half naked with my nose almost touching the bed frame. Why are some men such complete and utter bastards?

'And that was the really sad part about it all. The poor woman didn't suspect a thing.

'"I couldn't stick the idea of another night in a hotel," she said, "so I grabbed an earlier flight. I was going to call but I thought I'd surprise you."

'She laughed, and I could hear the crumple of clothes as he hugged her. I wondered if she suspected he was a bit of a philanderer and was just taking the opportunity to check up on him.

'Either way, it didn't seem to worry Anil too much. "It's good to have you back, honey," he said without a hint of fear in his voice.

'God, I wanted to slide out from underneath the bed then and say "No it isn't", but somehow I kept my cool, wondering how long I was going to be trapped for, especially as Anil had announced that he was getting ready for bed.

'It didn't take long for me to get my answer. "Ooh," I heard her say playfully. "You're not *that* tired then . . ."

'Oh no, I thought. Surely not. He's only just done it with me.

'Thankfully I was saved. "Come on, it's far too early to go to bed," she said. "Get dressed and let's grab a drink at the pub. Have you eaten?"

'Anil said he hadn't.

'"No, me neither. And I'm hungry."

'The two of them made small talk while Anil got dressed. He asked her about her trip; she asked what he'd been doing. They sounded just like any other ordinary couple and a part of me was jealous at the casual rapport they had with each other, because I didn't have anything like that, and hadn't for a long time. But I reminded myself that the relationship couldn't be that good if Anil saw the need to be unfaithful, and his wife, who was called Sharon, couldn't spot it.

'Sharon kept walking round the bed as she chatted and I experienced an almost childish frisson of excitement at the fact that I was only inches away from her and yet she had no idea I was there. She was wearing pretty open-toed heels and she had nice feet – dainty and golden, with well-kept, plum-coloured nail polish. For some reason, the sight of them made me feel sorry for her. Here was a woman who looked after herself, who thought she was in a relationship with a decent guy, and who was being betrayed day in and day out, because he wasn't decent at all. He was a piece of shit. I felt a real surge of anger. I wasn't going to skulk away from this any longer. I was going to come out from under the bed and tell her what her boyfriend was really like. I was going to tell her how I met him, how he wooed me over dinner, how I'd had no idea he was in a relationship otherwise I wouldn't have touched him with a bargepole, because I'm not that kind of girl, how—

'"What's that noise?" said Sharon.

'"What noise?" said Anil, opening a wardrobe door.

'But Sharon never got a chance to answer because the next second the bedroom door opened and she let loose a single, surprised gasp. There was a sound like a champagne cork being popped and, after a very short pause, she fell heavily to the floor, landing on her back next to the bed. As I watched dumbstruck, she rolled over on to her side so she was looking straight at me.

She was a pretty olive-skinned woman who looked at least part-South Asian and she was wearing a white dress underneath a black coat. She was clutching her stomach with both hands and I could see the dress staining red with blood. Her dark brown eyes were wide and pleading, and it took all my self-control not to cry out.

'Anil did, though. A terrified "Please, don't shoot".

'There was another sound, like a crackle of live electricity, and I could feel Anil fall back against the bed, the impact banging my nose. The intruder – whoever he was – grabbed a chair from the corner of the room and put it next to where Sharon lay writhing in agony and making low groaning sounds.

'He manhandled Anil into the chair, and used what sounded like duct tape to secure him.

'From the angle I had, I could only see the killer's black boots, although at one point his hand drifted down to wrap duct tape around Anil's bare ankles, and I saw he was wearing a long-sleeved dark top and gloves.

'In those moments, I was the most terrified I've ever been in my life. I was holding my breath as much as possible, snatching some air only when the killer was making a noise, knowing that if he discovered me there he would almost certainly kill me. That was the worst part. Knowing that at any moment my life could be over. I'd once had a brief fling with a detective who'd worked murders, and he used to tell me that murderers were almost invariably hapless fools acting on the spur of the moment, who didn't usually mean to do it and never planned their crimes, so consequently were usually caught very quickly. But this person wasn't like that at all. He – and even though I couldn't see him

I could tell it was a he – was methodical and unhurried, as if he knew exactly what he was doing. He was like something out of a nightmare, and he was barely three feet away from me.

'The fear almost overwhelmed me then and I had to use every ounce of available willpower to hold it in check, knowing that for me it was, quite literally, the difference between life and death.

'Anil was coming round now, making tired moaning noises.

'"What's going on?" he said groggily.

'His question was met with a long silence.

'Then the intruder said, "If you answer my questions truthfully, you die quickly. If you lie, it'll be slow. Do you understand?"

'It was, as I'd suspected, a man. It was difficult to pinpoint where the accent came from – it was quite a neutral sound – and I wasn't really paying that much attention, but I'm fairly sure he was English.

'"Please. My wife . . . she's hurt."

'"If you answer my questions, she'll live."

'I didn't hear Anil's response, but the killer then asked him how many mobile phones he owned.

'"Just one," said Anil, sounding a lot less groggy now.

'The attacker made a sudden movement and Anil cried out in pain and shock, his body shaking in the chair. Any anger I'd felt for him disappeared in that moment.

'"I'm going to cut you to pieces if I have to," continued the killer calmly, "or even burn you alive. But you *are* going to answer my questions."

'"My face," wailed Anil softly as large drops of blood splashed on to the carpet in front of the chair.

'"How many phones?"

'"Two," he said quickly, his voice tight. "One in my jeans. The other in the drawer behind me."

'The killer located the two phones and there was a short delay while I guess he checked them.

'"Next question," he said at last. "What do you know about the proposed attack?"

'"Please. I don't have any idea what you're talking about."

'"Anil, be realistic. I'm here because I know all about you and your secret life, so there's really no point in this charade. Now, are you going to cooperate or do you want me to carve open your other cheek?"

'There was a short pause before Anil spoke, a resigned tone to his voice: "I know the attack's imminent."

'"Who told you that?"

'"Karim."

'"Tell me the details of the attack."

'"I don't know, I promise. I just know that it's going to be a major operation and that it's going to happen very soon. That's all Karim told me. I tried to find out more but he wouldn't say. I'm not even sure he knows the details himself."

'The killer didn't say anything and I heard him turn and exit the room, followed by footfalls on the stairs, leaving a heavy, cold silence behind. All I could hear was Anil's laboured breathing and the continual dripping of his blood on the carpet. It struck me then that Anil might try to get me to free him and I prayed he wouldn't say anything because I knew the killer hadn't left for long.

'"Are you OK?" I heard him say, and I felt a sudden flush of fear. "Sharon, honey, are you OK?"

'Sharon rolled over on to her back. The blood had completely drenched her dress now and her face was pale from blood loss. "Hurt . . ." she managed to whisper, the effort of speaking almost too much for her.

'A minute passed. Or it might have been two. It was hard to tell because time seemed to be moving painfully slowly, and I was terrified that Anil would speak to me and the killer would hear him. But then I heard the footsteps on the stairs again and the killer was back in the room.

'"Please, I've told you everything I know," said Anil desperately. "And I haven't seen your face. I won't tell a soul about any of this, I swear."

'I heard a container being opened, saw the killer's boots again right next to the bed, and then a clear liquid was being poured all over Sharon. It only took me a moment to work out that it was petrol. She coughed and spluttered, trying in vain to wriggle out of the way. Anil was crying and begging now and I could feel my own panic setting in as I realized that I too could be burned alive up there. I almost rolled out from under the bed and made a break for it then, I was that scared, but somehow managed to stop myself, knowing that there was no way I'd make it.

'"Who have you told about the attack?" demanded the killer.

'"MI5 know."

'"What do they know?"

'"Just that there's going to be an attack soon, but they don't know when, where, or who's going to be doing it.'

'"So how have they left it with you?"

'"They've told me to keep pumping Karim for information. To find out everything I can."

'"Have they bugged his house?"

'"Yes."

'"And is he under surveillance?"

'"Yes."

'"Right now?"

'"I don't know, but I would think almost certainly. Look . . ."
Anil hesitated. "Please don't hurt my wife. I've told you everything I know."

'The killer made another sudden movement and once again
Anil cried out in animal pain.

'"Tell me the details of the attack."

'"I've told you all I know, I swear it."

'The killer took a step forward. His boots were no more than
two feet from my body as he stood directly in front of Anil.

'Anil kept insisting that he'd told him everything he knew
but the killer kept repeating the same question anyway, his
demeanour completely calm, as if he was used to doing this sort
of thing; and then I heard the sound of more duct tape being
ripped off the roll and Anil's words became nothing more than
muffled grunts.

'I heard the sound of cutting, and Anil shook violently in the
chair. I don't know how long it lasted – thankfully I don't think
it was more than a few seconds – but eventually Anil's gasps
subsided and the killer took a step back, ripping the tape away
from his mouth. This time Anil didn't make a sound and the
room was suddenly very quiet.

'The killer cleared his throat. "So, Anil, let's start again. What
do you know about the attack? Tell me everything. There are
still other bits I can remove."

'But the only response was Anil's ragged breathing.

'I heard the sound of something else being cut, and Anil seemed to shiver in the chair for a moment before becoming still.

'More blood was now dripping on to the floor and the killer let go of the chair. I thought he'd go then but I felt a surge of terror as he started rifling through drawers and cupboards, knowing he was bound to look under the bed, and then . . .

'I froze. My entire body tensed up. I didn't dare look anywhere but upwards, hoping that if he found me then he'd at least make it quick. I thought of my two sons then, far away across separate oceans, and wondered if I'd ever see them again, and how torn up they'd be if they lost their mother in circumstances like these. That was the thing about the boys. They were both so caring and it would prey on their minds that my last moments were so terrifying.

'And so I waited. And waited. Wondering how much longer I had left. Because the thing about this killer was he didn't seem to be in any hurry. Beside me, Sharon lay on her side, thankfully facing the other way, moaning faintly, the blood from her wound staining the carpet around her.

'I heard a cupboard door shut and the intruder's boots approached the bed.

'He was going to look under. Jesus, he was going to look.

'But he didn't. Instead he strode round the bed, stopped in front of Sharon and shot her twice in the face.

'Her body arched once, her hands falling to her sides, and then she was still.

'I heard the killer walk into the en suite, leaving the door open. He put the gun down on one of the tops before unzipping himself and starting to pee.

'I had a simple choice. Stay there and almost certainly be discovered, or get up and run.

'I've always been impulsive. It's how I ended up married and pregnant at nineteen, so it hasn't always served me well, but I knew I only had a split second to make my decision.

'I rolled out from under the bed on the opposite side to the en suite and jumped to my feet. And then as I turned to run – I couldn't help it – I glanced across at the en suite, barely registering the sight of Anil sitting, head slumped, in the chair. The killer had been wearing some kind of mask but he'd pulled it up over his head so his face was visible. Our eyes met. He stared at me in surprise and, before he could go for the gun, which was sitting on the toilet cistern, I bolted out of the bedroom door, slamming it behind me, ran over to the top of the staircase and took the stairs three and four at a time, so desperate was I to get out of there.

'But he was fast. I could hear his heavy footfalls as he ran through the bedroom, and as I reached the ground floor I could hear him coming through the bedroom door after me.

'I ran through the open-plan lounge to the front door, which I tried to yank open. But it wouldn't budge.

'The killer was coming down the stairs now and any second I was going to be in his line of sight. I knew he was a steady shot too, after seeing the way he'd calmly put two bullets in Sharon's face, so he was going to have no problem putting one in the back of my head.

'Trying not to panic, I saw that the door had been bolted from the inside. Not daring to look behind me in case he was there taking aim, I threw back the bolt, opened the door and then I was outside, a cold bite of fresh air hitting my face.

'I slammed the door behind me to give myself an extra second and kept running, screaming at the top of my lungs. Despite being so close to London, it was countryside out there and there was a field directly opposite, across the road. But it didn't look like it would provide any effective cover so I turned an immediate left where a clump of trees rose in the darkness next to Anil's house.

'Twenty yards of dirt track separated me from their embrace and I ran that distance with a speed I don't think I've ever mustered before, ignoring the sharp tearing of the stones and grit beneath my bare feet, knowing that at any moment I could be brought down by a bullet.

'I hit the tree line at pace and kept going, driven by adrenalin. Through the trees I could see the lights of a house no more than thirty yards away. I couldn't hear the killer behind me but that didn't mean he wasn't there. I had to think fast. Anil's place was in a remote spot. I couldn't even hear any traffic noise. It was highly likely that no one had heard my scream for help. So, if the killer was as cool under pressure as he appeared to be, he still had time on his side, and might well pursue me into any house where I took shelter. Because the problem was, I'd seen his face. It had only been for a split second but that was enough. I could ID him. I could place him at the scene of a double murder. I was a threat.

'I had to hide somewhere. I forced myself to look back over my shoulder but all I could see were trees. Turning sharp right away from the house and keeping low, I ran for another ten yards or so before diving under a tangle of brambles and facing back in the general direction I'd come from. I lay as still as possible, trying to keep my breathing as silent as the trees around me.

'Ten seconds passed. Then twenty. I heard the sound of someone creeping through the undergrowth. It was him. It had to be.

'I pushed myself hard against the ground, seriously relieved that I'd decided to dress in dark clothing for the date, and held my breath.

'He was getting closer but I couldn't see him because I was keeping my face against the dirt so that its paleness didn't stand out in the gloom.

'A twig cracked underfoot no more than five yards away and, as I listened, I could hear his slow, steady breathing. He was hunting me. Slowly and methodically. As if he had all the time in the world.

'"I know you're in there somewhere," he called out in an easy sing-song voice, as if this was a game he was playing with a group of children. "I'm going to find you, and when I do . . ."

'He was close. Jesus, he was close, and the desire to jump to my feet and bolt was almost overwhelming, but I didn't move. Still I held my breath. When I was a young girl back in South Africa I'd been a very strong swimmer and I was used to holding my breath for a long time. Once, aged twelve, I'd even managed two and a half minutes. I'd lost some of that ability with age but I was still able to last a lot longer than most people, which was no bad thing because I heard more footfalls in the dirt and realized he was getting even closer.

'Had he seen me lying there? Was he just toying with me?

'My body tensed. Waiting.

'Another footstep. He was almost on top of me. My lungs felt like they were burning up.

'And then I heard it, somewhere in the distance. The plaintive wail of a siren. It was hard to tell whether or not it was getting closer but that didn't matter because I heard the killer curse under his breath and then he was running back through the woods, away from me.

'I allowed myself to breathe but I didn't move until I heard a car engine starting a couple of minutes later. Then I slowly reached into the back pocket of my jeans and pulled out my mobile. I only had a single bar of signal and, as I dialled 999, still keeping all my wits about me even though I could hear the car driving away, I hoped it was enough.

'It was. The number rang twice and a female operator picked up. I felt a surge of pure relief.

'"Which emergency service do you require?"

'"Police," I whispered, praying that my nightmare was over. "I want to report a murder."'

Two

'Shock's a strange thing. It doesn't always come when you expect it to. After what I'd seen and heard you'd think I'd be near-enough catatonic and yet I was strangely calm as I sat in a warm kitchen drinking strong, and very tasty, coffee with some soothing classical music playing somewhere in the background.

'The couple the kitchen belonged to were called Ben and Diane Miller and they were Anil's nearest neighbours. As soon as I felt safe enough after dialling 999 I'd left my hiding place in the woods and knocked on their front door and, thankfully, they'd let me in. Mr and Mrs Miller were good people – early sixties, both retired and clearly reasonably well off, and I could see they were still very much in love. They'd wrapped me in a blanket and offered me comfort and kind words while we waited for the police to arrive, and their kindness was a real tonic after the savagery of that night. They reminded me of the parents I wish I'd had, and I felt safe in their presence.

'The first police car arrived fifteen minutes after my call, which wasn't particularly reassuring given that I was reporting a recent double murder. Neither cop inspired much confidence either. One was middle-aged and fat and looked like he'd have trouble stopping a clock let alone a determined criminal, while the other was so fresh-faced and dinky it looked like he'd just come straight out of school. They'd come to the Millers' house first to check I was OK and then told me to stay where I was while they investigated. I never saw them again after that.

'Luckily, though, within minutes the cavalry finally began to arrive in numbers. They soon seemed to be using the Millers' house as a mobile incident room because I saw armed cops in uniforms, others in white overalls, and serious-looking detectives in crumpled suits, all trooping through downstairs as they passed in and out. Everyone wanted to know how I was, and they got a doctor to give me an examination. He asked me if I was OK, and able to give a statement, and I told him I was fine but asked whether I could give it sooner rather than later, because I was tired, cold and hungry. "I'm sure someone will be with you as soon as they can," he said reassuringly. But so far no one had come, and the only remaining sign of a police presence was the armed officer standing outside the kitchen door.

'Mr and Mrs Miller had been sitting with me until a few minutes earlier, but Mr Miller had now gone to find out how long it was going to be before I was finally interviewed while a clearly exhausted Diane got ready for bed.

'As I took another sip of the coffee, thinking about how life can hit you with some real broadsides sometimes, a tall man in a suit walked into the room. I hadn't seen him before but his air suggested he was the one in charge.

'"Miss Kinnear," he said, putting out a hand. "I'm DI Alan Clarke, the man leading the investigation. You've obviously had a very traumatic experience. How are you feeling?"

'His tone was measured and calm, and he immediately put me at ease. It was, I thought, comforting to know that the good guys in the world still outnumbered the bad ones. He wasn't bad-looking either, and I had the briefest glance at his ring finger, noting that there wasn't a ring there.

'"I'm OK," I said with a sigh. "It wasn't exactly how I expected the evening to go though."

'"No, I'm sure it wasn't. And it sounds like you had a very lucky escape. Can I ask what your relationship was to Mr Rahman?"

'"I thought he was my boyfriend, but it turns out I wasn't the only woman in his life."

'It embarrassed me to have to go into the details but I knew I had to, so I gave him a very brief version of what I've just told you, hoping he wouldn't judge me too harshly.

'But it seemed he was far more interested in what I'd seen and heard just before Anil had been murdered. "So you were in the room the whole time while the killer tortured Mr Rahman?"

'I nodded. "That's right."

'"So what did he want?"

'"Information. He was asking how much Anil – Mr Rahman – knew about an attack. Who he'd talked to about it." I tried to narrate the whole conversation as I remembered it and, as I spoke, DI Clarke's expression grew grim. It's strange but it was only now that I realized the importance of what I'd heard. Beforehand it had been lost amid the sheer terror of what was going on.

'When I'd finished, DI Clarke made me go through the conversation again. It was clear that the content was worrying him. "I know this is hard for you, Miss Kinnear," he said when I'd finished for the second time, "but if you remember anything else about the conversation – anything at all – please tell us straight away. Now, did you manage to get a look at the killer?"

'I was aware of my situation enough to know that if I said yes then that was it – my whole life would change. I'd be what those cop shows on TV called a material witness, obligated to give evidence in any future murder trial. The fear of testifying – or, worse, of becoming a target myself – would hang over me for months, possibly years. I'm a normal woman leading a normal life, just trying to get on, and, more than anything else, I wanted to forget what I'd just been through.

'So I shook my head. "No, I didn't. I'm sorry. I was too busy running away."

'I took a deep breath, remembering the fear as I'd fled down the stairs, knowing that the sadistic bastard who'd tortured Anil to death was right behind me.

'"You poor thing," said DI Clarke, patting me gently on the arm, and it sounded like he meant it. "I'm going to get a couple of my officers to take you over to Watford police station. You'll be looked after by our specialist liaison people and then, when you're ready, we'll take a proper statement. But you're safe now. It's all over."

'"Thank you," I said, which was the moment the floodgates opened as the enormity of what I'd just experienced hit home.'

Three

'Ten minutes later I was in the back of a patrol car being driven by a cheery female officer and her male companion. They both seemed to want to talk to me, and were obviously trying to make me feel at ease, and I guessed they hadn't been given the full details of what had happened in Anil's house. I wasn't really in the mood for talking and, after I'd made that obvious, they left me alone and carried on yakking together about a colleague of theirs who, they both felt, had been promoted beyond his abilities because of his predilection for kissing the bosses' arses. They clearly didn't like him and were making no bones about it. It always amazes me how quickly people in the front of a car forget there's someone in the back. But their conversation made me feel better. It was good to get back to the normality of everyday gossip.

'I thought about my decision not to tell DI Clarke I'd seen

the killer's face. I now felt bad about not telling the truth, especially in a case like this. I couldn't imagine the killer leaving much evidence behind so a positive ID from a witness might make the difference between a verdict of guilt and acquittal. It wasn't as if I didn't get a good look at him either. I did. I can picture him now. White, around forty, lean muscular build. I'm pretty sure I'd know him if I saw him again.

'I kept thinking about it in the car. I'm not the kind of person who turns away from a confrontation. I might be a normal girl but I've got a tough edge to me too and shirking my responsibilities like this . . . It just wasn't me. I thought about what my dad would advise me to do if he were here now. He'd have said do the right thing, although I'm pretty damn sure he wouldn't have done the right thing himself. Even so, in that moment I resolved to be honest and admit that I'd seen the killer's face.

'But my thoughts were interrupted by the female driver. "Christ, what's this guy doing?" she said loudly, checking her rearview mirror. "Can't he see we're police?"

'A bright glare suddenly filled the car and, as I looked round, I saw headlights bearing down on us fast.

'I knew something was wrong. If nothing else, the horrors I'd seen tonight had put me on my guard, so I cowered lower in my seat so I couldn't be seen.

'"I'm putting the bloody lights on," the woman officer continued, sounding truly affronted. "We're pulling this prick over."

'I remembered how cool and methodical Anil's killer had been. The way he'd walked right into his house and shot Sharon with a single bullet before disabling Anil, all without uttering a word. A man like him was not going to be scared of a couple of unarmed British cops.

'The rational me – and believe it or not, that was usually the dominant side – told me I was being paranoid, that DI Clarke was right when he'd told me this was all over, and I was making a fool of myself my slinking down in my seat like a frightened dog. But that didn't stop the fear from coming off me in waves. I was already a murder witness and we were right out in the country here with trees lining both sides of an otherwise empty road. It was the perfect place for an ambush.

'The other car had pulled out now and was coming alongside. The male cop turned round in his seat to address me. "Don't worry," he said. "I promise we won't be long. But we've got to stop—"

'"Christ, he's got a gun!" yelled the female cop, her voice almost a shriek.

'I dived down in the seat as the windows exploded in a burst of automatic gunfire, spraying me with glass.

'I heard rather than saw the female cop topple over in her seat and the car immediately veered out of control. The male cop cursed, leaning down in the passenger seat and grabbing the wheel as a second burst of automatic gunfire shattered the night air. The patrol car mounted the kerb, bumping heavily over uneven ground as the male cop fought in vain to control it.

'I could feel the car slowing but we were still going at a hell of a pace, the undergrowth scraping the paintwork. Then, without warning, it slammed into a tree with a huge crunch and I was thrown bodily against the back of the front seats.

'The night was suddenly silent bar the moans of the male

cop. I wasn't sure if he'd been shot or not but he looked dazed and hurt. I didn't move or speak. It felt like I was watching a movie and had no control over events. All I could do was watch as the male cop forced open the passenger door and stumbled outside.

'He was wobbling on his feet like a drunk as he looked back in the direction of the road, and I clicked off my seatbelt, knowing there was no point just lying there. I had to help him.

'But as I lifted my body off the seat, more shots rang out. I dived back down and, turning my head, I was just in time to see the cop go down.

'The gunman was still there. I was trapped. With my heart thumping in my chest, I lay as still as I could, face down across the back seats, playing dead.

'I remember seeing a pair of photos on the internet a couple of years back that have always stayed with me. The first one showed a group of blindfolded Iraqi soldiers kneeling in a row before a mass grave while a long line of black-clad Islamic State fighters stood behind them, aiming their assault rifles as they prepared to fire. The second showed the soldiers all lying dead inside the grave, blood pooling under their corpses, while their executioners celebrated. What had chilled me the most was imagining the terror those poor soldiers must have felt as they waited for the inevitable bullet, and at the time I'd thanked God that something like that would never happen to me thousands of miles away in safe, comfortable England.

'And now I too was waiting for that inevitable bullet, knowing that I was utterly helpless. I'd been lucky earlier under that bed, but now it seemed that my luck had run right out.

'A minute passed. I know this because I counted the seconds in my head. But nothing happened. The night remained silent bar the ringing in my ears from the noise of the gunfire.

'I kept counting. When I reached a hundred I began to feel the first glimmer of hope. By the time I hit two hundred I was sure the gunman must have fled the scene. Surely even someone as confident as him wouldn't hang around?

'And then I heard it. The rumble of an engine nearby, followed by the sound of approaching footsteps.

'I lay there, still expecting the worst, right up until the moment I heard the words "Jesus Christ, call 999, they're all dead" through the shattered car window.

'Then I looked up, saw the terrified face of a guy in his twenties, and felt an overwhelming sense of relief.

'The nightmare was finally over.'

I sighed and took a sip of water, bringing my thoughts away from the violence of the night and back to this cramped little room. My hands had stopped shaking and I felt calm as I looked at the two officers in turn.

DS Anji Abbott nodded slowly, her expression inscrutable. 'That's quite a story,' she said at last.

'It seems you're a very lucky woman,' said DC Seamus Jeffs, and something about his tone suggested he didn't entirely believe my version of events, although God knows why.

'Or unlucky,' I said. 'To get involved with someone like Anil Rahman. If I hadn't met him none of this would have happened.'

DC Jeffs nodded slowly, not looking entirely convinced, but I let it go.

'How are the two police officers I was with in the car doing?' I asked. 'Did they make it?'

'I'm afraid not,' said DS Abbott. 'Now there are just a few details of your story we need to go over. Are you OK with that?'

I nodded.

'We're particularly interested in the information the killer wanted from Mr Rahman.' Like DI Clarke back at the Millers' house, she made me go through the conversation again before the two of them questioned me about various parts of my testimony.

'One final thing we need to clarify,' said DS Abbott. 'How many men were in the car that ambushed you on the road tonight?'

'I don't know. I didn't see anyone. I was too busy ducking down in the seat.'

'Was the car being driven erratically?'

'It was being driven fast.'

'That's not what I meant. We're trying to work out whether one person was driving the car while another was doing the shooting, because from what we can gather, the shots to the officers in the front of the car you were travelling in were very accurate, and that would have been extremely hard to achieve for someone who was driving at the same time.'

I thought about this for a moment. 'The car didn't seem to me like it was being driven erratically, so I'm thinking there were probably two people in it.' I shuddered, and took another sip of the water. 'Jesus. I hadn't thought about that. So there could be more than one killer.'

The two officers exchanged glances before DS Abbott replied.

'That seems the most likely explanation. But you only saw and heard one at the house?'

I nodded. 'That's right. There was definitely only one person there.'

The room fell silent for a few seconds while the two of them digested this information.

'So what happens now?' I asked.

'We don't know yet,' said DS Abbott, 'but I've got to be honest with you. This was clearly an organized killing and, as a witness who's seen the face of at least one of the killers, you're a target. At the moment you're perfectly safe. We've got armed officers outside the door, outside the ward, and outside the hospital. No one's going to come for you tonight, but you're going to need full-time police protection going forward.'

I swallowed. 'For how long?'

'For as long as it takes,' said DS Abbott. 'In the meantime, I need to talk to my boss. I'm sorry.' And, with that final apology, delivered as if I'd just been diagnosed with cancer, she and DC Jeffs got to their feet and excused themselves, leaving me alone in the room and, it seemed, in the world.

Four

Ray Mason

There are a million ways to get somebody to talk but these days a police officer's pretty limited in the ones he can use. As you're all no doubt aware, suspects in the UK have all kinds of rights. If you're one of the bad guys you'll know them all by heart, and if by some complete mischance of fate you're still a bit of an amateur and you haven't picked them up yet, don't worry. Your lawyer, who you don't have to pay for, will give you all the info you need. A cop can't hit you; he can't threaten you; he can't coerce you. Shit, he can't even lie to you. We can put you under pressure, of course, and try to get you to cooperate that way, but only if we've got a solid wall of evidence to back our accusations up. Even in these technologically advanced times, with cameras on every street corner, and DNA tests on a single speck of dust that can pinpoint your presence at a crime scene, it's still not that easy to get a result.

As a cop, you've got to learn to be inventive. Which was why I was at the Dungeon of Desire, aka 23 Gladstone Crescent, a rundown end-of-terrace house in an area of Hackney that's so far gallantly resisted gentrification, at half past midnight on a weekday night.

'He's in the room at the top of the stairs,' said Madame Sin, aka Ola Wercieska, the proprietor of the establishment. She was smoking a cigarette and wearing thigh-high black leather boots, black fishnet tights, and a corset that looked like it might explode under the pressure of her girth. She was not a happy woman but then she hadn't been expecting my visit, and wasn't best pleased about the way I'd pushed past her boyfriend, Pietr, who provided the dungeon's security, even though he was all of ten stone and looked like the 'Before' picture in a muscleman ad. Pietr was now sitting with his head down, also smoking a cigarette, and doing his best to avoid Ola's steely gaze.

'You promise you won't bust me, right?' she demanded, turning the steely gaze back on me.

'I promise. I just want to have a chat with him and then I'll be out of your hair for ever.'

'He's a good customer,' she said ruefully. 'But he doesn't smell right.'

'People like him never do. Is he, er, clothed?'

She pulled a face. 'No. Sadly not.'

And so it was with a heavy heart that I climbed the stairs, opened the door and entered the dungeon.

The man I was after was lying naked and spreadeagled on a

bed with stained sheets, his wrists and ankles chained to metal posts at each corner, his whole body shivering with anticipation at the return of Madame Sin. At least I hoped it was him. It wasn't immediately obvious as he was wearing a black PVC gimp mask that covered his whole head, with no eyeholes and just an open zipper across his mouth allowing him to speak, which made a positive ID pretty much impossible. More interestingly, he was also clad in what appeared to be a pair of steel and PVC underpants with a penis-shaped cage sticking out from the groin at a curved forty-five-degree angle, presumably to stifle erection. It made my eyes water just looking at it.

However, since Madame Sin only ran a very small operation, alongside her cousin Katja – aka Dark Mistress – who I could hear administering punishment in the room opposite, I was pretty confident I had my man.

On the far side of the bed, and blocking the window, was a ceiling-high set of shelves that looked like an Ann Summer display, containing whips, dildos, paddles, strap-ons, more whips, and a few things I'd never seen before, with functions I didn't even want to hazard a guess at. Behind the shelves, the window frame rattled as a train came rumbling past on the embankment next to the house.

'Jesus,' I said, stopping at the foot of the bed. 'It actually does smell like a dungeon in here.'

Joe Thomas immediately stopped shivering with anticipation and instead began flailing in his bonds, looking round blindly as he tried to work out what was going on. 'Who the hell are you?' he demanded in a strong northern Irish accent. His tone was belligerent but there was a nervous edge to it.

'Hold on a minute,' I said. 'I'm just taking a photo.'

I lifted my phone and took one of him lying there in all his glory. The train had gone past now and the click of the camera shot was loud in the room. I took a second one for good measure.

'You put that fucking camera away and let me out of here', he called out angrily. 'Or I'll make you bloody sorry.'

'Really?' I said. 'And how do you propose to do that? The great joy, I'm assuming, of being tied up like this is the complete surrender of all control to someone else. But it also makes you very vulnerable, doesn't it?'

I pressed the phone to video, pressed record, and filmed myself unzipping the gimp mask and yanking it off his head, revealing a pale, plump-faced man in his fifties with a neatly-trimmed grey beard and not much hair. He turned his head away from the camera, struggling against his bonds, as I continued filming, but it didn't do him any good.

When I'd got everything I needed, I finished filming and put the phone away.

Joe Thomas stopped moving and stared at me for a few seconds while I stared back.

'Who are you?' he said at last, calmer now.

'I'm a man who holds your fate in his hands,' I replied, locking my eyes on his. 'I know all about you, Joe Thomas. I know where you live, the name of your wife. The names of your children, including the illegitimate one from your affair. I know the names of your friends from your days in the IRA, men who are now dissident republicans actively planning attacks on British soil. And I know you share their views, Tom. You might be an upstanding businessman and important member of your local church on the outside but you're still prepared to help the cause when you can, and I know you're in active contact with them.'

'You can't prove any of this.'

'Maybe not. You're careful, I'll give you that. But then I don't need to prove it, do I? Because I know that if I release these photos and this video with details of where they were taken, your reputation as a hard man, as a family man – it'll be utterly destroyed. You'll be an outcast; a leper. A laughing stock. Your wife and kids will disown you. Your whole life will turn to shit.' I paused, letting the words sink in. 'Unless you do something to help me.'

Thomas's eyes narrowed. 'What?'

'You're going to become my informant,' I told him. 'I know that you know people in dissident republican ranks. People who matter. These guys respect you, they trust you. Most importantly, Joe, they talk to you.'

'I don't know what you're on about.'

'Yes you do. And when they talk to you about what they're planning to do, and how they're going to do it, you're going to get in touch with me. You're going to tell me what's happening and I'll do the rest. If you're truthful and your information's good, none of what's on my phone will ever see the light of day. You have my word on that. If, though, you decline my offer or, worse still, feed me with crap intel, then every tabloid in this country's going to get pictures of you strapped to this bed, along with a complete bio of who you are, and what you represent. It'll be a feeding frenzy. Imagine the headlines. I'll even put up posters at the end of your street.

Be in no doubt, Joe. I will fuck you a lot harder than Madame Sin ever could.'

'You're a copper, aren't you?' Thomas spat. 'I've seen your face before. You can't do this. I have rights, you know. I will report you, and I will have your fucking job, do you understand?'

It's amazing how the so-called enemies of the state – whether they be anarchists, jihadis or revolutionary communists – all use the laws of the state they're so keen to overthrow for protection the minute their so-called rights are breached.

'It doesn't matter whether I'm a police officer or not,' I said. 'The fact is I've got you and there's nothing you can do about it.'

He gave me the kind of look that said, if he ever got the chance, he'd kill me in a second. But he didn't say anything. That was the key.

I approached the bed and stood over him, grabbing his chin in my hand and turning his face towards mine. I stared down at him, my eyes boring into his. My mother used to say she could see auras around people that told her what they were like as individuals and, though I wouldn't say I could see auras, there's something inside me that knows whether the dark or the light is the dominant force in someone's personality. It's a useful trait to have as a detective. Joe Thomas had immense amounts of rage in him. There was a black, swirling evil in there too. I could feel it.

But, most important of all, I could sense the weakness in him. He might have been a radical who supported the use of extreme violence to achieve his ends, but it was only as long as he wasn't putting himself in the firing line. Joe Thomas had always prided himself on being a hard man – someone not to be crossed – but the extent of his action as an IRA operative had been carrying out punishment beatings and kneecappings on compliant victims. Like so many of the extremists I've encountered over the years, he was essentially a coward, and that, along with his predilection for being humiliated by prostitutes, was why I'd picked him.

You may dispute my methods. You may think that blackmail is never justified under any circumstances, particularly when it's being carried out by a serving police officer. You may even be right.

But I don't think so. Joe Thomas was a nasty piece of work. The dissident Republican group he belonged to, though largely forgotten amidst the much bigger Islamic extremist threat, was still deadly serious in its desire to plant bombs on the UK mainland, and had the wherewithal to do it too. All I was doing was using Thomas to keep an eye on them and, in the process, potentially saving lives. And if he did as he was told, then he had nothing to fear from me.

Joe Thomas looked nervous as I tightened the grip on his face and I let the fear wash over him before using my free hand to take a card from my pocket. I dropped it on his chest and let go of his chin. 'There's a number on there where you can always reach me. I want to hear from you once a month at the very least with an update on what you've been doing and what you've found out. Understand?'

He was silent for a couple of seconds as he stared up at me, evidently trying to decide how serious a threat I presented. The expression in my eyes told him in no uncertain terms that I wasn't a man to be crossed, and he saw that.

He nodded quickly. 'All right, all right. What's your name?'

'You don't need my name,' I said, freeing one of his wrists, guessing he'd no longer be in the right frame of mind for his session with Madame Sin. 'Just call that number. There are three people in particular I'm interested in.' I told him their names and was about to give him a final warning not to mess me about when my mobile rang.

I stepped out into the hall and shut the door behind me before checking the screen.

The glowering face of my boss, DCI John Butterworth – a tall, humourless Yorkshireman who liked to run marathons and climb bleak, craggy mountains for entertainment – glared out at me as if he knew I'd been breaking the laws I was paid to uphold and was ready to punish me.

I was taken aback by the fact he was calling. I was off duty for a start, and Butterworth was famous for going to bed ridiculously early in the evening when he wasn't working – eight p.m. if his wife was to be believed – and I knew he hadn't been working tonight. Neither did I think it was possible he could have found out about my visit to Madame Sin's. I'd covered my tracks well but, of course, there was always a possibility that I'd slipped up. If I had, then my career in the Met was finished. If I hadn't, it meant we had an emergency on our hands.

I like emergencies. It's why I work in counter-terrorism. I'm always waiting for that adrenalin rush of excitement when the word goes out that something big's happening.

Dark Mistress was still punishing the poor bastard in the other room and both of them were making enough of a racket to rouse the dead, so I hurried down the stairs, nodded a thank you to

Madame Sin, who was sitting drinking wine with Pietr in the front room and not looking any happier, and was out on the street before I took the call.

'Hello, sir, this is a pleasant surprise,' I said. 'What can I do for you at this hour?'

'You not in bed?' he said, the question coming out as an accusation.

'No, sir, I'm enjoying a midnight walk.'

'You want to watch yourself doing that, with your record,' he grunted. 'Anyway, I'm glad you're awake. We have a situation. A major MI5 informant's been murdered in his home near Watford, along with his wife, and I need you to get up there and secure the scene. We're going to be taking over the case from the locals and I need to get a better idea of what's happened up there.'

'Can't it wait until the morning, sir? If the locals have already secured the scene, I can't see what I can do up there now that can't be done in the morning.'

'There's more to it than just a double murder, Ray. A woman witnessed what happened and the squad car taking her to Watford nick was ambushed by at least one gunman who shot both the accompanying officers dead.'

'Jesus. And what happened to the witness? Is she dead too?'

'No. Thankfully she survived with only cuts and bruises. I've got Anji Abbott and Seamus Jeffs at Watford General with her. The thing is, we've got four murders and two separate murder scenes, and the local CID are swamped. Homicide North are sending in SOCO teams to help, but the whole thing's a mess, and I want you to make sure that everything's being done properly, and give me your take on it. Pick up Chris on the way.'

'I think it might be a good idea if we let Chris sleep. You know, after what happened to Charlotte.'

DS Chris Leavey was my partner, and probably my only true friend. We had history going back a long way, but whereas I'd only had the briefest of forays into marriage a few years back, Chris had wed his childhood sweetheart, had a kid, and should have lived happily ever after. But how often does that happen in life? Five years back, Charlotte had started getting prolonged dizzy spells and having trouble walking. The symptoms had got progressively worse and she'd been diagnosed with multiple sclerosis. Since then she'd gone downhill fast and, though she could still just about walk, it was only a matter of months before she'd be permanently confined to a wheelchair. Two days earlier, while Chris and I were out on a job, Charlotte had had a fall at home and had been unable to get back up again. She'd been trapped like that for fourteen hours, and was dehydrated and semi-delirious when Chris found her on his return. Since then he'd been working shorter days so he could get home to nurse her back to recovery.

'OK, leave Chris behind,' said Butterworth. 'But it means more work for you.'

'I can handle it,' I said, grabbing a pen and paper and taking down the address of the dead informant, whose name was Anil Rahman. 'What can you tell me about him?'

'Not a lot at the moment. He's been working with 5 and I'm waiting for a call from one of their liaison people to give me more info, but my understanding is he was an important asset to them. One other thing. According to the witness, before he killed him, the killer asked Rahman about an imminent terror attack.'

'And what did he say?'

'I don't know, Ray. I still haven't had a chance to read the statement. Anji's only just sent it to me. That's why I need you up there to take an assessment of what's going on. And for now, don't say anything to the locals about the MI5 connection.'

'So what's my reason for being there?'

'It's sorted. The commander's been on to the Herts commissioner and they're expecting you.'

I was exhausted and needed my bed. I hadn't expected Joe Thomas to show up so late at the Dungeon of Desire. Like Butterworth, he tended to hit the sack on the early side. I also didn't want to turn up where I wasn't wanted and throw my weight around. But I also figured I didn't have a lot of choice so I headed to my car, wondering what awaited me across town.

Five

I pulled up on a grass verge behind the long line of emergency services vehicles that ran down to where Anil Rahman had lived, and cut the engine.

Rahman's cottage was slap bang in the middle of what must have been the last stretch of wilderness between Watford and the M1. It looked out on to fields, which themselves looked out on to more fields, before finally you got to the nearest village, which was little more than a collection of houses, a couple of stables and a typical country pub, and then a mile or so beyond that you hit the beginnings of the urban sprawl.

Unsurprisingly, the place was crawling with cops – uniform, plainclothes, SOCO, the whole shebang – but even though several hours must have passed since the killing, they were still very much in the getting-prepared stage, with groups of people milling around waiting for orders, or helping to set up the floodlit cordon round the cottage.

I showed my ID and headed for the front door where two men in suits were talking on the step. As I approached the taller of the two – a solid-looking guy a few years older than me, with the kind of world-weary look that comes of too many years on the force – turned my way.

'Can I help you, sir?' he asked, and I noticed that he looked twice as exhausted as I was. But then four murders on your patch in one night does that to you.

'DI Ray Mason, CT. I believe you're expecting me.' I smiled to break the ice and put out a hand.

He took it, which was a good start, but he didn't smile back. 'I'm DI Alan Clarke,' he said. 'This is my colleague, DC John Howard.'

'Are you *the* Ray Mason?' asked Howard, who was a young, fresh-faced guy in his twenties. He looked pale and a little queasy – never a good sign at crime scenes.

I nodded, not bothering to deny it. 'Yeah, that's me.'

'It's good to meet you,' he said, but he looked at me warily as he spoke.

I tend to have that effect on people I meet, including fellow police officers. Every one of them knows who I am. At least they think they do. To them, though, I'm an enigma. A cop with money, a shadowy past that no one can quite unpick, and a controversial present. A vague cloud of suspicion's always hung over me. There's been talk of corruption and dodgy deals, of mental health issues related to a very public childhood trauma, but no accusation, either direct or indirect, has ever quite stuck, and my many enemies have found me a lot more resilient than they'd like. The problem is, I don't really fit into any of the boxes, which doesn't make me particularly welcome in the new, progressive, forward-thinking Met. I'm pretty good at my job, though, so the top brass tolerate me, and the guys on the ground would like to admire my exploits but can't quite get past the thought that, one way or another, there's something not quite right about me.

To be honest I'm used to it and, at the ripe old age of thirty-eight, it's unlikely I'm going to change anyone's perceptions, so I don't try.

Clarke told Howard to organize the SOCO teams so they'd be ready to start work in the next ten minutes before turning back to me. 'So, to what do we owe the pleasure of CT involvement?'

'I don't know yet. I was told to come up here and find out what's going on.'

'And check that us yokels know what we're doing?'

That's the problem with CT, or Counter Terrorism Command to give us our full, official name. We aren't that popular with our fellow officers, who think we throw our weight about, letting them do the hard work, then whipping their cases from under them and taking the credit when the cases get solved. It happens, but like most things, not as often as most people think, and I didn't want Clarke to think that was what I was planning to do.

I laughed. 'Not at all, and please, I'm not here to get in your way. But my understanding is that CT are going to be taking over this case, so I need to gather information for the SIO.'

'Well, you've got a big case on your hands. I've never seen anything like this and I've been in the job twenty-five years.'

'So what happened?'

He sighed. 'It's an unusual case. From what we can gather, Mr Rahman was in bed with his lover when a woman we've now identified as his wife showed up unexpectedly. The lover's name's Jane Kinnear, and she hid under the bed to avoid detection while Mr Rahman and his wife had a conversation. While they were talking, the wife heard a noise outside the bedroom, and then before she or Mr Rahman could react, the killer entered the bedroom and shot her, but not fatally. The killer then incapacitated Mr Rahman – possibly with a taser – tied him to a chair and tortured him.'

'And the woman under the bed heard it all?'

'Everything.'

'So what did the killer want?'

'This is where it gets worrying – and where I suppose you lot come in. He was after information about an imminent attack.'

'What kind of attack?'

DI Clarke shrugged. 'I don't know. I only spoke to the witness briefly and my understanding is your people have taken a statement from her down at the hospital. I'm also assuming you heard that two of our officers were taking her to the hospital when their car was ambushed by at least one gunman armed with an automatic weapon. It only happened two miles from here so he must have been waiting for the witness, Miss Kinnear, to reappear. When I spoke to Miss Kinnear, she told me she hadn't seen the killer's face, but I think she must have been lying.' He sounded disappointed.

'How did she manage to escape from here in the first place?'

'After he'd finished off Mr and Mrs Rahman, the killer took a leak in the en suite. Miss Kinnear took her chance and made a dash for it.'

'Yet, despite having been seen, he stayed close to the scene of his crime waiting for an opportunity to kill her as soon as she left the police cordon. That's one brazen individual. How do you think he tracked her?'

'Again, I don't know. He could have been listening out for the radio traffic. It's not impossible for someone who knows what they're doing.'

I sighed. 'But Jesus, what a risk. There aren't many criminals with that kind of calmness under pressure.'

'I've never heard of one before.'

'No,' I said, 'neither have I. Do you mind if I take a look around up there?' I didn't want to. I've seen plenty of dead bodies in my time. Starting far too young. It's never pleasant, and it's a whole lot worse when they've died violently, but unfortunately it's all part of the job description and, you never knew, there might be something – just a tiny little thing – that you spot and others haven't. Believe it or not it does happen and, though I'm no Sherlock Holmes, I do know what I'm doing.

He nodded. 'Of course. But I've got to warn you, it's not a pretty sight.'

I followed DI Clarke through the front door and into a quaint but surprisingly spacious open-plan living area. As I followed him up the staircase I noted that it wasn't hard to hear our approach. The stairs creaked like a listing ship, and it made me think that if the killer had got up here while Anil and his wife were talking in the bedroom, then either they were making a lot of noise or he must have been extremely light on his feet.

We stopped outside a closed door on the narrow landing and Clarke turned to me. 'This is the room they died in. So far it hasn't been touched. If you don't mind, I won't come in.'

He stepped aside and I opened the door, feeling the beginning of the black terror that lurked deep inside my psyche and which had haunted me since childhood.

The first thing I saw on the far side of the unmade bed was Anil Rahman's body, strapped to a wooden chair with duct tape. His head was slumped forward with his hair hanging down like a curtain so that it obscured his face. There was a lot of blood. It ran all the way down his shirt in thick rivulets before pooling on the carpet.

It was a truly horrific sight accompanied by the powerful stench of a slow death, mixed in with another powerful smell – petrol. Straight away, gruesome memories from a long-ago night came hurtling back to me, just as I knew they would. I steadied my breathing and counted to five in my head, refusing to take my eyes off his body. To anyone watching me it would have looked as if I was calmly and carefully taking in the scene but, in reality, I was fighting a ferocious internal battle. Years of therapy had got me good at it though, and within a matter of moments the terror had subsided, creeping back into my subconscious from where it could plan its next attack.

I looked around the room. The drawers on both bedside tables and the desk in one corner had all been pulled out, and some of them upended, suggesting the killer had been searching for something. I noticed that there were several framed photos in one of the drawers and I wondered if Rahman had hidden them there when his lover had come round so that she didn't realize he was married. If so, it seemed a very risky thing to do. Just as bringing his lover to the family home was. But then some people like taking risks and I guess if he was an informant working for MI5, he was one of them.

I walked slowly round the bed and looked down at the second dead body, that of an attractive Asian woman in her late thirties lying on her side. Mrs Rahman was still wearing the long black coat she'd entered the house in, with an off-white dress beneath that ended just above the knee, and open-toed shoes, one of which was hanging off. The smell of petrol was stronger here and it was obvious from the way her clothes were clinging to her and how wet her long hair was that she'd been doused in it. She'd also taken a shot to the gut that had bled profusely all over the dress, her legs and the floor, suggesting she'd been alive for a while after being hit. There were two more bullet wounds in her face – one just beneath her right eye, the other in her left cheek. They'd bled far less, suggesting that one or both of them had been fatal.

My first thought was that this was a particularly sadistic killer. Mrs Rahman would almost certainly have been conscious and in a lot of pain while her husband was tortured in front of her. I wondered if the killer had poured the fuel over her while she was still alive, and concluded that he almost certainly had. Bastard.

A few feet beyond Mrs Rahman's body was the en suite bathroom. The toilet seat was up, indicating that a man had been the last one to pee in there – again, tallying with what DI Clarke had told me. I crouched down and looked under the bed. There was just about enough space for someone to hide under there, but it would have been hard for the witness to make it out of this room without the killer taking at least a shot at her. When she rolled out from under the bed, she'd have made a noise, then had to get to her feet and, if it was closed, pull the door open. All without the killer having time to pull the trigger?

It was possible of course, but something about it didn't feel quite right.

I checked the en suite and saw that the killer had flushed, and by the smell from the bowl poured bleach down there as well to kill off any DNA. So he was cool enough to come back from chasing the witness and clean up after himself, even though there was a very good chance she'd raise the alarm.

I walked back into the bedroom, keen to get out of there, but curiosity got the better of me and I stopped and looked at one of the framed photos sitting in the open desk drawer. It showed a South Asian couple in an opulent-looking restaurant somewhere hot. They were both smiling at the camera and they looked happy.

My chest tightened as I picked up the photo with a gloved hand, looking more closely. I frowned, replaced it in the drawer, then went over to the chair where Anil Rahman sat, put my fingers under his chin and gently lifted his head so I could see his face. There was a deep wound in his throat, and his cheeks were virtually hanging off where they'd been slashed. His eyes were closed, but it was definitely the man in the photo. I lifted his right hand and inspected it, immediately seeing what I was looking for.

More recent memories came flooding back to me then. A hot country twelve years ago. A confident, flashy young man in a linen suit who'd been full of superficial charm, who was supposed to net us a big target.

I'd known this man, and we'd shared a secret. One that could never be revealed. He'd just been Anil then; I'd never known his last name. And he'd come close to getting us all killed.

So what, I wondered, had he been up to now?

Six

Jane

When I was a little girl back home in South Africa, my mother always wanted me to be strong and independent. She'd had it hard herself as a child. Although she was white, her skin was dark, like her eyes, and she was bullied relentlessly at school. She didn't want the same for me, which was a good thing. But her way of making it happen wasn't. She told me I had to be the best at everything. In my schoolwork, at sport, even in things that were meant to be fun, like singing and ballet. And when I didn't come top of the class, or first in the race, or fell short in my pirouette technique, I was beaten. Not smacked or shaken or yelled at. Beaten. Like a dog.

I can't remember my exact age when it started but I was young. Six or seven maybe. God, how I would dread coming home with bad news because I knew what was coming. My mother would receive the news with a stony expression on her face, and then I would see the tell-tale tightening of the skin round her eyes and the flash of anger that crossed her features like a black shadow, followed by the words I dreaded the most: 'Go upstairs to the bedroom and choose your belt.'

You see, that was my mother's thing. I was allowed to choose the belt she'd use for the beating from among a row of them that hung up in her dressing cupboard, even though they all hurt exactly the same. I've often tried to work out what her thinking was. Maybe she thought it took some of the responsibility away from her if I was somehow complicit in the beating. Either way, it's difficult to describe the terror I used to feel as I sat at the end of my mother and father's double bed, with the belt I'd chosen next to me, waiting for my mother to come. Sometimes she'd be quick and I'd hardly have time to sit down before I heard her marching purposefully up the stairs. These beatings were generally the worst because I'd be feeling the full force of her rage before she'd had time to calm down. On other occasions she'd make me wait for ages. So you never knew what you were going to get. A lot of the time her righteous anger was already gone and the punishment would be brief and perfunctory, a necessary chore carried out without enthusiasm. But now and again her anger would have built like a storm to immense proportions and the pain would be horrendous.

One time when I was about eight and I'd been waiting for what felt like hours in the oppressive heat of a mid-summer Cape afternoon the fear got so much that I wet myself. When my mother saw what I'd done on her bedroom floor she hadn't just used the belt but had kicked me repeatedly as I cowered on the floor in my own piss, ignoring my desperate cries.

My dad was a good man but he was weak and didn't intervene. And there was no one else to look out for me. No brothers or sisters to share the burden, no close relatives for me to confide in. I simply had to put up with it.

Did it make me strong and independent? Well, I left home as soon as I could and married at eighteen to a man twelve years my senior, much to my mother's disapproval, and my relief. She'd wanted me to travel the world and make something of myself, not become a housewife. You see, the bizarre thing was that she really loved me and was convinced she was doing the right thing by forcing me to be the best at everything. She wasn't, of course, and for a long time afterwards I was emotionally needy, which is never a good position to be in, and doesn't bode well for a long and happy marriage.

What her years of punishment did do, however, was make me resilient. It might have been a long time since I'd felt the crack of one of her belts on my skin, but I still remembered all too well what it was like to suffer physical pain and, more importantly, I was used to feeling real fear. So, sitting here in an unfamiliar hospital bed, having seen four people die tonight, I was holding things together remarkably well. And I guess, in an odd way, I have my mother to thank for that.

There was a knock on the door and Anji Abbott, the black detective, came back in the room, alone this time. 'How are you getting on?' she asked. 'I thought you might be asleep.'

I smiled. 'It's difficult to settle until I know what's going on.'

'I can update you on that,' said Anji, sitting down next to the bed. There was a warmth about her that I found reassuring. 'The good news is that the doctors have said there's nothing physically wrong with you that a few days' rest won't sort out, so you're fit to leave. The less good news is that you're going to be coming with us.'

'OK,' I said, nodding slowly. 'Where to?'

'We're taking you to what we call a safehouse. You're probably familiar with the term if you watch any crime shows on the TV.'

'I know what it is. But I need clothes and other stuff from home. Can we stop on the way? Please. I'll be quick.'

Anji sighed. I could tell she didn't want to. 'Where do you live?'

'In Watford. Only ten minutes from here. I'll be two minutes inside. No more. And there's no way the killer can know who I am.'

'Didn't you leave a handbag or anything at the crime scene?'

I shook my head. 'I must be the only woman who doesn't carry a handbag. I left my overnight bag there, but there's no ID in it. I keep all my ID in a wallet in my pocket.'

'I'll see what I can do,' she said, 'but I'll need to clear it. Obviously we've got a very dangerous killer out there and he's already tried to kill you once. But I don't want you to worry. This whole hospital's being watched from every angle. We've got marked and unmarked police cars on every surrounding street. And no one knows about the existence of the safehouse we're taking you to except two people in Counter Terrorism Command. I haven't even been given the address yet. This way it minimizes the risk of the location being compromised, and therefore the risk to you personally. Now I don't want to go all cloak and dagger on you, but we need you to follow our instructions very carefully. You need to get dressed, then you're going to be wheeled out of here on a gurney with a sheet covering your whole body and face. All we need is for you to stay still and act dead. We'll do the rest.'

She must have seen the look on my face because she gave me a reassuring smile and put a hand on my shoulder. 'Everything's going to be OK, I promise. We've done this sort of thing plenty of times before.'

'Are you armed?'

She slipped a hand inside her jacket and revealed a pistol in a shoulder holster. 'DC Jeffs and I both are, and when we're on the road we're going to be followed by a car containing a team of firearms officers with a lot more firepower than this. They haven't been told our final location so they can't compromise anything but they'll be staying with us at the house to make sure you remain safe.' She smiled. 'I'll give you some privacy so you can get dressed.'

When she'd closed the door behind her, I got up from the bed and inspected myself in the mirror. There was a plaster across one eyebrow where I'd cut myself, and my left cheek was swollen, but other than that I was physically unmarked from my experience that night. I have very dark eyes that have seen far too much in this life, and as they stared back at me in the dirty glass I took a deep breath to prepare myself.

Whatever the next twenty-four hours might bring, I was ready for it.

Seven

Ray

I was at the second crime scene where the police car carrying the witness had been ambushed when I got my second call of the night from Butterworth. He asked me for an update.

'The locals seem to be on top of things,' I told him. 'They've got SOCO at both crime scenes, but it's a mess at the house where the informant was killed.' I didn't mention anything about recognizing Anil Rahman. Right now, that information was best kept under wraps. 'He was tortured, and it looked personal to me. But the killer strikes me as professional, and cool under pressure. He's well armed too. I'm almost certain he used a handgun to kill Rahman's wife, but when he ambushed the squad car, he used an automatic rifle.'

'How many killers were there, in your opinion?' asked Butterworth.

I looked around. I was standing inside the police cordon about twenty feet back from the crash site. It was easy to see where the squad car had left the road and travelled about fifteen metres through some low-lying undergrowth before hitting an oak tree head on. Floodlights now lit the scene and a photographer was taking pictures of the damaged car and the bodies of the two officers.

'The road where the ambush took place is pretty straight, but it's a B-road, so only just wide enough for someone to pull alongside,' I told him. 'Realistically, you'd need a driver and a gunman to be sure you were going to take out the driver of the squad car. My opinion is there were two of them.'

'So,' said Butterworth carefully, 'we're talking about professional killers here?'

'Definitely.'

He sighed. It didn't sound like this was the news he wanted to hear. But then no one wants to hear that they're dealing with professionals as they're always the hardest to catch.

'OK. I need you back here now.'

'Now?' I protested. 'It's a quarter to two.'

'I know exactly what time it is, Ray. And I hate being up this late even more than you. But I've got a man from 5 coming over to give us some background on Anil Rahman and I need you here. That's no problem, is it?'

It was. I was shattered. But I knew that if Butterworth was up it really must be serious and, anyway, I was interested in finding out more about the man they knew as Anil Rahman. 'OK,' I said. 'I can be with you in half an hour. But I'm going to need to talk to the witness too, and soon.'

'Anji Abbott and Seamus Jeffs are taking her to a safehouse in the next hour or so. You'll get a chance to talk to her soon enough.'

'Where's the safehouse?'

'The location's being kept on a strictly need-to-know basis, and right now that doesn't include you or me. Anji's sent me over a copy of the statement they took from the witness, and I've sent it as an audio file to your email, so download it and have a listen on the way here.'

I told him I would and rang off, thinking that this was the kind of case I'd never come across before. To have one such brazen killer was extremely unusual. To have two – and the more I looked at this crime scene the more I was convinced that there were two – was unheard of. I was also wondering why they were so keen to kill the witness when either she hadn't seen the original killer, or if she had it could only have been fleetingly. Even if she had a photographic memory and could make a fairly good photofit of him, it surely wasn't worth the risk of ambushing the police car carrying her only a few minutes' drive from where he'd committed a double murder. More to the point, if the killer or killers were that professional, how had they failed to kill her twice?

As I got back in my car I put a call in to DS Anji Abbott, my colleague and former girlfriend, hoping I'd catch her before she left for the safehouse.

She answered on the fourth ring. 'I'm hoping you've heard what happened tonight and this isn't a very poorly timed booty call,' she said.

'What do you take me for? I respect you far too much for that.'

'I'm glad to hear it.'

'I've been told you have our witness. I've just been to the two murder scenes and it's clear someone wants her dead very badly. What's your take on her?'

'You'd like her. Very attractive brunette. South African living in the UK. She seems pretty shaken up by what happened, as you'd expect, but she's holding it together well. No obvious sign of shock though that could happen any time.'

'Do you believe her story?'

'I can't see why she wouldn't be telling the truth. She said the car she was travelling in was shot up, leaving two cops dead. You've been to the scene – what do you think?'

I looked over at the damaged squad car by the tree. There were at least a dozen bullet holes in the driver's side front and back, and both windows were cracked.

'I think the car was definitely badly shot up and I'm looking at two dead police officers, so yes, it does look likely she's telling the truth.'

'So why do I still detect some doubt in your voice?'

'It just seems she has a knack for extraordinarily lucky escapes.'

'Maybe the people trying to kill her aren't that competent. You know, Ray, I've interviewed hundreds of people – no, make that thousands – over the years. I can spot a liar, and I don't think Jane Kinnear is one.'

Anji sounded a little defensive, which surprised me. We tended to get on well. Our relationship had been pretty casual. We'd ended up having a kiss after a work night out and had gone on a couple of dates, even though we were both sensible enough to know you should never get involved with a colleague. Things hadn't worked out, precisely because we did work together, but we'd stayed friends afterwards and I cared for her.

'OK,' I said. 'That's good enough for me. So what's your next move?'

'We leave the hospital in ten minutes.'

'Have they given you the address of the safehouse yet?'

'No, not yet.'

I looked back at the damaged squad car. The bonnet had concertinaed where it had struck the tree, but the damage didn't look that extensive, which suggested that the ambush had happened very quickly and the squad car wasn't travelling very fast. And yet it was late at night and the road was straight in both directions, so they ought to have been travelling fast.

'I'm still going to need to interview your witness,' I said into the phone.

'Well, you can't right now. We're just about to leave, and I've got a call waiting. I've got to go. Talk soon, Ray.'

'Yeah, talk soon. Take care out there.'

Stifling a yawn, I walked back to my own car. It had been a long night already but, with my meeting with DCI Butterworth still to come, it looked as though it was going to get longer.

Eight

The Met's Counter Terrorism Command has a lot of different offices, and not just in London either. We've got places in all the UK's major ports, as well as outposts in such exotic and far-flung locations as Kenya, Dubai, even Afghanistan. My team's based out of a modern three-storey building tucked away on a side street in Hammersmith which, because it's painted black, looks like a giant shoebox.

On the drive there I listened to Jane Kinnear's statement, which Anji had recorded as it had been given. Miss Kinnear sounded plausible enough, and her version of events made sense, but I still had this nagging feeling that she wasn't telling the whole story. For now, though, there wasn't much I could do about that.

I thought too about Anil Rahman. We'd been brought together for a single, very controversial job back in 2003 while I was still in military intelligence. The details of the job weren't on the record anywhere and, because of the circumstances surrounding it, we'd operated on the basis that the less information we had on each other the better. But during the brief time I'd known Anil Rahman I'd got to know him as a mildly narcissistic, thrill-seeking charmer – a bit like an Asian James Bond – and I could see why people were drawn to him. I hadn't been. I thought he took too many risks that put other people in danger and it had struck me back then that one day this addiction would lead to his coming unstuck, which is clearly what had happened.

The lights were on in Butterworth's office when I arrived and, after swiping my ID at reception, I made my way up there with an industrial-sized takeaway coffee I'd picked up at an all-night petrol station on the A40.

There were two men in the room when I arrived: Butterworth himself, sitting ramrod straight behind his spotless desk – balding, wiry, looking far too much like a fire-and-brimstone Presbyterian minister in need of a good meal – and, across the desk from him, a dapper-looking guy about my age with a hipster beard and sharp suit. The hipster had a certain gravitas about him that suggested a decent public school. Whatever MI5's press releases might say about the changing face of its recruits, its operatives can sometimes be worryingly easy to spot.

'Thanks for coming in, Ray,' said Butterworth in his gruff Yorkshire accent, motioning for me to take a seat. 'Did you get a chance to listen to Miss Kinnear's statement?'

I sat down next to the hipster and told him I had. 'It sounds like she had an eventful night.'

'She's a very lucky woman.'

'Unlike Mr Rahman.' I took a sip from my coffee and put it down on his spotless desk.

'Aye, I heard it wasn't nice what was done to him,' said Butterworth with admirable understatement. 'This here's Tom Hinshilwood of MI5. He's going to be giving us some background on Anil Rahman. We've got a witness to the crime who can ID the killer, which is some good news, but we need to find out why Rahman was targeted in the first place. So, can you tell us what you've got on him, Tom?'

'Of course,' said Tom in the kind of accent that suggested he was trying too hard to hide a very patrician upbringing. 'Anil Rahman has been working for MI5 for more than fifteen years now. At one time he was an actual recruit, but he hasn't been on our books now since 2006. These days he works for us as a paid informant. On the face of it, he's a successful Muslim entrepreneur running a business importing so-called Fair Trade furniture from the Indian subcontinent. But for the past five years he's been developing contacts among a group of suspected Muslim radicals based in north London. It's been a deliberately slow process – a long-term experiment designed to prove his credentials and avoid raising anyone's suspicions.

'In fairness, it hasn't always been viewed as a success. Anil was being paid a lot of money and was providing very little useful intelligence in return, and more than once the op came close to being dropped. I always resisted, though. The really dangerous people are the hardest to gather evidence on, and it takes a lot of time.

'The man Anil has been working hard to get close to for a

long time is called Karim Khan. Khan is a joint British and Pakistani natural who came to the UK from Islamabad in the late 1990s and successfully claimed asylum because his radical Islamic political beliefs put him at odds with the government there.'

I shook my head wearily but didn't bother saying anything. Even after all these years I still found it hard to understand the way politicians played hard and fast with the safety and security of their own people by enacting laws that were so open to abuse, and failing to do anything about them.

Hinshilwood gave a small smile. 'The irony is, we don't actually think he had radical Islamic beliefs at the time. We believe he was an economic migrant on the lookout for better financial prospects. He started a restaurant business and became a Labour councillor for the borough of Enfield, but he got greedy and became involved in the drug trade. He was caught importing a substantial quantity of heroin in 2004 and was sentenced to fifteen years. His wife died while he was in prison, and his four children grew up with other relatives, and when he was finally released in 2012 he claimed to have turned over a new leaf and become a devout Muslim. He helped set up an anti-drugs charity, as well as an Islamic Aid charity, and to all intents and purposes he was – and is – a reformed character. Except he isn't. He's organized aid convoys to Syria twice – once in 2013 and once in 2014 – and he was joined on the second trip by, among others, Anil Rahman. Anil did well in getting close to Khan, and he provided us with intelligence to suggest that on the second convoy Khan visited Raqqa and met with Islamic State officials where he discussed the prospect of getting weapons – particularly automatic rifles and grenades – into the UK for an attack. Anil also gave us the names of several other people on the convoy who potentially posed an extremist threat, one of whom was later convicted of preparing materials for a terrorist attack.

'It's always been Khan we've wanted, though. The problem is, his experience in prison has made him far more careful. He takes counter-surveillance measures every time he walks out of his front door. He never talks on the phone. His home's as good as impregnable to break-ins. He checks every room for bugs constantly and, although we got Anil to plant some very sophisticated devices so we could actually hear what he says inside his house, he hasn't given us anything.

'In recent weeks, though, Khan had finally begun to take Anil into his confidence. Crucially, he told Anil that there was going to be a wave of Paris and Mumbai-style terror attacks in the UK in the coming months, and that he wanted him to be a part of them. Anil, of course, jumped at the chance, saying he'd do whatever it took, but Khan's no fool and before he gave him any details he wanted Anil to prove his loyalty by buying half a dozen AK-47s from a contact in Athens and driving them to Zeebrugge, where his instructions were to hand them over to another contact.'

Hinshilwood paused before continuing.

'As you can imagine, this put us in a very difficult position. A man working for us – albeit in a freelance capacity – would be committing a very serious crime in multiple jurisdictions. If we lost the guns and they ended up being used in a terror attack . . .' He raised his hands in a gesture of uncertainty and eyed us both in turn. 'Well, you can imagine the shitstorm that would have provoked.'

'What did you do?' I asked him, thinking that this was exactly the kind of adventure I could imagine Anil Rahman getting involved in.

Hinshilwood sighed and didn't answer until Butterworth prompted him by letting him know that whatever was said in this room, stayed in this room.

'We took advice from the Home Secretary and she concluded we should run with the op, as long as the consignment of weapons was kept under surveillance at all times. The plan was for a team of authorized agents to rendezvous with Anil before he got to Zeebrugge, so that they could place tracker devices inside each individual rifle. He'd then hand them over to the contact at the port and the weapons would be tracked all the way to their final destination.

'So Anil went out to Athens accompanied by another Islamist sympathizer, who I suspect was only there to make sure Anil did everything he was meant to do, but the contact there didn't have the weapons so they returned to the UK empty-handed, which worked in our favour as it demonstrated Anil's loyalty but without the problem of him having to transport live firearms.

'That was two weeks ago. When he next met with Khan, Khan told him that there was going to be an attack soon in London – in his words, "a spectacular" – and so for the time being they were not to have any contact. At a suitable time afterwards, when everything had died down, Khan said they'd talk again, with a view to Anil being a part of the second wave of attacks. Anil tried to get further details but Khan wasn't giving anything more away.'

Hinshilwood looked at us both in turn. 'That was ten days ago. Anil met with his handler immediately afterwards, and gave him the information he'd got from Khan. He agreed to make contact with the handler again when he had more news.' He paused. 'But he never did.'

'So what have you managed to find out about this attack?' I asked him.

'We've been running surveillance on Khan ever since but it's not anything like as close as we'd like, because we want him to lead us to the people carrying out the attack without raising his suspicions. We've also got surveillance teams on a number of his associates but so far we haven't found out anything to help us identify any of the attackers. Our theory is that Karim Khan is acting as a quartermaster on behalf of Islamic State and that he may not actually know any of the details of the planned attack, or the identities of those who are going to carry it out. He's just organizing the weapons.'

I raised my eyebrows. 'And if he's already organized them, then it sounds like we may not find out anything more about the attack until it actually takes place.'

'There are still leads to follow, Ray,' said Butterworth, 'even without Anil Rahman.'

I took a gulp from my now tepid coffee. The more I mulled over Hinshilwood's story, the less some aspects of it made sense.

'This is what I don't understand,' I said. 'I've just listened to the witness Jane Kinnear's statement, as I'm assuming you both have too.' They nodded. 'She said she heard Anil's killer torturing him to find out what he knew about an impending attack. But if Anil hadn't been given any specific information about the attack like time, location, identities of the perpetrators etc. – and from what your handler says he hadn't been – and if he was doing such a good job of not raising suspicions that Karim Khan confided in him only ten days ago that there was definitely going to be an attack, why did the terrorists suddenly do a massive about-face, decide he was an informant, and then torture him for information they knew he didn't actually have? It just doesn't make sense to me.'

'No,' Hinshilwood agreed. 'On the face of it, it doesn't.'

'The most important thing now is that we bring in Karim Khan,' said Butterworth. 'At the moment we only have Anil's verbal testimony that a terror attack is imminent. But it's clear from the fact that he was murdered that Anil was on to something, and that's why we need to move fast.' He leaned forward in his chair, elbows on the desk. 'The problem we have from a police point of view, though, is that we don't have any significant evidence to bring charges against Khan. I'm trying to organize an arrest warrant based on Anil Rahman's testimony, recordings that were made in which Khan talked about the possibility of attacks, as well as the Syria connection, but it's not a lot to go on and unless there's a mountain of evidence in his house, which we're certain there's not, then there's no reason for Khan to talk to us.'

'Which means that the attack could well happen without us being able to do anything to stop it,' said Hinshilwood.

That was the big problem with UK law. A suspect had every right not to talk, and there was literally nothing anyone could do about it. Not legally anyway. And unless there really was a mountain of evidence against him, it was unlikely Khan was going to be charged with anything. As long as he was careful, he'd walk free, able to carry on plotting more atrocities.

'I'm expecting confirmation that we can make the arrest in the next few hours,' continued Butterworth, 'so, Ray, I want you and your team in place by 6.30 a.m., ready to extract Khan from his home in Enfield. We know he's currently in residence: a satellite tracked him entering the property at 18.45 yesterday and it hasn't picked him up leaving. 5 have got a surveillance team on the scene, and there's an arrest team from CT with them now. So if Khan tries to leave in the meantime, they'll stick to him like glue until the warrant's in place, but he doesn't tend to go anywhere at night, so we're expecting him in situ when you arrive.' Butterworth paused for effect, pumping out his chest like a skinny peacock, which I'd noticed him do before when he was about to say something he considered important. 'We're going in with firearms officers first for full effect. We want to disorientate him completely. Your team go in afterwards, Ray. We want you to personally make the arrest and, if you can, we need you to get a few minutes alone with Khan.'

He paused again, less decisively this time, and Hinshilwood took over. 'We all know the limits of the law, Ray,' he said smoothly, 'and in ordinary circumstances we obey them without question. But these aren't ordinary circumstances. We can't afford another Paris. We need to know when and where this attack is meant to take place, and failing that, the identity of whoever is supplying the weapons so we can search for the attackers that way.'

I gave them both a cold smile. 'You want me to find a private spot in a house crawling with fellow officers and beat a confession out of him, even though we don't have a shred of hard evidence he's involved in anything?'

'No, of course not,' said Butterworth, even though this appeared to be exactly what he and Hinshilwood wanted. 'We don't want any physical violence. Just see if you can get something from him before he gets put in the system.'

'We've known for a long time now that an IS-sponsored attack on UK soil is a matter of when, not if,' said Hinshilwood. 'And the recent chatter we're getting from our people on the ground over in Syria and Iraq is that it's going to be happening very soon – possibly even in days – and that it will be far more organized and sophisticated than the simple lone-wolf op the media have been expecting.'

No wonder they'd kept this meeting small, I thought. Life in the intelligence services isn't like it is in the movies. People play by the rules. They have to. Get caught and you can't do a Dirty Harry and holster your smoking gun, spit out a sneering one-liner to your pinko bosses, and get back to taking out the bad guys. To be honest, I wish it was like that, and I bent the rules myself when I got the chance, as I'd done a couple of hours earlier. But you have to be extremely careful. Any hint of wrong-doing and you lose your job and your pension – and if you get the human rights lawyers on your back demanding restitution, you lose your liberty too. It's a rare individual in law enforce-ment who wants to take unnecessary risks – especially when you're at the very top – so, whatever intelligence Butterworth and Hinshilwood had, it had to be extremely good.

I knew why they were choosing me for this, of course. I was expendable. If the cameras that are always carried by certain officers on high-profile raids caught me threatening a suspect, Butterworth would deny this conversation ever took place, as I'm sure would Hinshilwood. It would be another case of controversial cop Ray Mason taking matters into his own hands. The public and certain sections of the media would be angry if I lost my job. I was a good cop with a good run of cases, and one of the few lower-ranked police officers in the UK with a public profile. Even so, it would make no difference. I'd be gone, and I suspect Butterworth would be secretly pleased. I was too much trouble in an age where presentation, procedures and buck-passing were everything.

'I'll see what I can do,' I told him. 'But don't hold your breath. It doesn't sound like Khan is the type of guy who's going to roll over at the first sign of trouble.'

I saw Butterworth exchange a quick, but significant, glance with Hinshilwood.

'Is there something you're not telling me, sir?' I asked.

For a few seconds there was a heavy silence in the room. Then Hinshilwood answered. 'We've heard from two separate, and reliable, sources that The Wraith may be involved.'

And suddenly I was really interested.

Nine

The Wraith was a legend. Literally. He was one of those mythical figures known only to the upper echelons of international law enforcement – a hired killer suspected of involvement in anything from ten to a hundred murders depending on who you talked to. If you wanted someone dead – and aside maybe from the President of the United States that could mean pretty much anyone, regardless of their level of security – then you tried to make contact with The Wraith. He could make it look like an accident if that's what you needed, or make the victim suffer if you'd prefer. But he always got the job done.

Supposedly.

The reason he was called The Wraith was because he never left any evidence at the scene of his crimes, so you could argue – and plenty did – that he didn't actually exist and was simply a convenient scapegoat for various unsolved crimes. I'd heard mention of The Wraith a few times over the years and preferred to keep an open mind as to his existence. There'd certainly been a number of high-profile deaths in various countries. There was the execution of a wealthy, and famously security-conscious, German industrialist, his mistress and his four bodyguards in a Sardinian villa; the heart attack that a Chinese diplomat, who later turned out to be a spy working for the French government, suffered in a Cannes brothel (the prostitute he was with died of an overdose three days later); the Russian gangster made to watch his whole family being slaughtered before being dispatched himself, without his security detail knowing anything about it . . . All of these operations had clearly been carried out by a highly professional assassin (or assassins), but whether they were linked or not remained a moot point.

However, it now seemed that one of Hinshilwood's people had picked up intelligence suggesting that an individual referred to as The Wraith was doing some work for the bosses of Islamic State. It sounded pretty unlikely, but both Hinshilwood and Butterworth were taking the possibility sufficiently seriously to mention it to me; and since the witness to Anil's murder had claimed the killer was white – and since, for some reason, it had always been assumed that The Wraith was white – both Butterworth and Hinshilwood had suggested that he might be the one responsible.

Like I said, I was keeping an open mind.

The drive back to my place in Fulham only took fifteen minutes at that time of night and it was just short of three a.m. when I pulled into my road, passing the neat rows of whitewashed townhouses until I came to the modern six-storey block at the bottom, which was where I had my apartment. It wasn't the most aesthetically pleasing of buildings – there were too many angles, and too much glass – but it had what I needed most, which was security.

Eighteen months back I'd been living in a loft apartment a few hundred metres behind King's Cross Station. One night I'd returned late from a drink with a friend. I'd parked up as usual on the quiet night street, but as I walked the thirty yards or so to my door I'd had a niggling feeling that something wasn't quite right. Seven years in the army in two separate war zones had helped me hone my nose for danger, so I was already on my guard when I saw the man sitting in a parked car ahead of me. He was trying to look inconspicuous but not making a good enough job of it. I'd never seen him round here before, and it wasn't the kind of road you'd hang about in late at night. I could see he'd clocked me too. The car, a BMW saloon, had blacked-out rear windows but I could just about make out two more figures in the back.

That was my advantage. These people were amateurs.

Afterwards, during often aggressive questioning, I'd been asked why, if I'd seen the three men before I passed their car, had I carried on walking towards them rather than turning and making a run for it. My answer to the questioners had been that I wasn't entirely sure I was right in my suspicions, and didn't want to appear overly paranoid. But that was a lie. I'd *known* that their presence there spelt danger, and I'd deliberately confronted it.

Looking as nonchalant as possible – and I did nonchalant a lot better than the driver of the car – I kept walking. As I passed the BMW I heard doors opening, and swung round fast.

There were two of them with guns. Young guys in their twenties, with hoodies and scarves pulled up over their faces. The one closest to me was still in the process of climbing out, but he was moving fast and waving the gun around. The problem was he wasn't fast enough, and before he could get a decent aim I smacked the gun out of his hand, sending it clattering to the pavement, grabbed him by the hoodie and pulled him round into a tight bear hug, using him as a human shield.

The other gunman looked startled by the speed of my counter-attack but he had enough confidence not to panic and instead pointed his gun at my head from the other side of the car, trying to keep a steady aim as I ducked my head behind his buddy.

'Let him go or I'll shoot!' he yelled in a patois-tinged London accent.

So I let him go, giving him a big shove forward before ducking down behind the car and grabbing the gun that had fallen to the pavement. It was a shabby-looking Browning pistol but easily good enough to kill at close range. As I jumped back up, I caught a brief look at the driver who was still sitting behind the wheel, looking absolutely terrified, and immediately concluded he'd be no problem.

The guy I'd originally tackled ran at me, obviously hoping to wrestle back his gun before I had a chance to use it, so I took him down with two shots to the chest before swinging round and firing another two at the second gunman. Only one of those bullets hit him but it did what it was designed to do, entering half an inch below his right eye, exiting through the top of his skull and, according to the investigating pathologist, killing him almost instantly.

Of the three men in the assassination team, the only one with swift reactions was the driver, who managed to reverse the car into the one behind him to gain an extra couple of feet before pulling out into the road in a screech of tyres – all before the second gunman hit the ground.

But I wasn't letting him get away. Running out into the road, I crouched down and took a two-handed firing stance before blasting away at the rear tyres. It took me three rounds to take out the offside one, another four to do the driver's side. The street I lived on was narrow and when the driver lost control he smacked into a parked van before bouncing off it and burying the front of the BMW in a parked car on the other side.

I raced down the street, gun in hand, and as he clambered, dazed and apparently unarmed, from the car, I hit him with a flying punch, slammed him face down on the tarmac and read him his rights, even though I think at this point he was unconscious. I didn't have to dial for assistance – a few people had already done that. By chance, there was an armed response vehicle patrolling barely a minute away and they were on the scene, sirens blaring, almost the moment the shooting stopped.

As you can imagine, cop or no cop, I was arrested at gunpoint and held in the cells for twenty-four hours while the investigating officers, who had two dead bodies on their hands, figured out what to do. A couple of things worked heavily in my favour. Firstly rope, chloroform and a large samurai sword were found in the BMW's boot, and a search on the three suspects' computers quickly turned up a whole shedload of beheading videos, IS propaganda and – the icing on the cake – messages to each other and to other contacts saying how they were planning to kidnap and behead a prominent police officer, even twice mentioning me by name. Secondly, and more importantly, a witness living in a flat on the other side of the street had heard a commotion and opened her curtains at just the point I'd shot the first suspect. She hadn't been able to see much of what happened as the two of us had been on the other side of the car from her but she'd clearly seen the second suspect pointing his gun at me as I shot him, so, even though the only surviving member of the gang had claimed I'd shot his friends in cold blood, her testimony proved otherwise.

I was eventually charged with reckless endangerment of life, because of the way I'd discharged the gun at the fleeing BMW driver, bailed and suspended from the force (though on full pay, which was a nice touch). There followed a lengthy investigation by the IPCC, and a court case where I convinced the jury that I'd only been trying to stop the third suspect from escaping and knew exactly what I was aiming at when I shot out his tyres, before I was finally reinstated at my previous rank nine months later.

And that should have been that. But the families of the two dead men had continued to make a hell of a lot of fuss, saying that their poor, innocent, would-be-beheader sons had been brutally executed, even though a man with my level of military training could easily have taken them alive. One of those firms of human rights lawyers that only ever seem to be interested in the rights of total scumbags had taken up their case and were now preparing a private prosecution against me for murder, presumably financed by the taxpayer.

Sweet.

I wasn't going to let it bother me, though. My lawyer seemed to think I had a very good chance of beating it and, in the end, I simply couldn't imagine who would convict me for defending myself against men who wanted to kill me, and killing them with one of their own guns. Plus I'm not a worrier.

I am, however, very careful whenever I arrive home, especially at night, and I did what I always do these days and drove round the block, checking for anything out of place, before I made the turn into my building's underground car park. As the steel security shutter opened and I drove down the ramp and past the entrance pillars, I felt a familiar twinge. If anyone was going to ambush me, it would be here. I am far better prepared these days, though. My car windows are bulletproof so no one's going to take a successful potshot at me, and I'm also authorized to carry a firearm at all times now, as the threat to my life from other would-be jihadis is considered serious – although I think the brass would have a collective heart attack if I ever had to use it. But at least I can fight back now.

I was guessing that this was another reason why Butterworth and Hinshilwood wanted me to spend a few quiet moments with Karim Khan, so I could shove my Glock 17 in his face and make him talk that way. They'd never suggest that, of course, not even in the privacy of Butterworth's own office, but I had no doubt that this was their intention.

Would I do it? Probably, if it meant that it would save lives, and I suspect I'd be successful too. Most men will talk if you shove a gun in their face, and I'm the kind of man who looks like he'll carry out his threats. And of course I've killed before, so if Karim Khan had any idea who I was – and he most likely would – then he'd have every reason to think there was at least a chance I'd pull the trigger. Right now, however, the evidence against Khan was looking decidedly flimsy and I had no interest in scaring the living daylights out of him if he was innocent.

I parked the car in my usual spot, took another look round just to make sure I hadn't missed anything, then got out and let myself into the building. I called the lift and, when it arrived, pressed the button to the third floor and let it go up without getting in. If there was someone waiting for me on the staircase, they'd think I'd taken the lift and would try to ambush me when I got out. Call me paranoid, but when you're on an IS hitlist and there's no shortage of disciples waiting to carry out their orders, paranoid's the best way to be. I waited a few seconds before taking the stairs, drawing my Glock and keeping it down by my side, out of sight.

No one was coming to kill me tonight, though, and ten minutes later I was tucked up in bed, knowing I only had a couple of hours before I had to be up again. I closed my eyes, waiting for sleep to take me.

Usually it comes easily, but a lot had happened tonight, and events had dredged up old memories. I thought of the urban legend that was The Wraith and all the murders over the years that had been attributed to him. But I knew of at least one killing he couldn't have carried out, and the reason I knew that was because I was the man who'd committed it.

And the man who'd been alongside me was Anil Rahman.

Ten

'There she is,' said Gaydon. 'Right on cue.'

The 'she' in question was a pretty blonde jogger, no more than twenty, in Lycra running gear and a black headband. She was running slowly along a quiet stretch of country road with her dog, a bow-legged Jack Russell who raced along beside her as if he knew this was going to be his only exercise of the day, which it generally was.

Gaydon and Pryce had been keeping tabs on the jogger for days now, and though Gaydon knew very well that most civilians lacked even a basic awareness of personal security, she was a lot worse than most. For a start, she ran the same route every day at roughly the same time. Yesterday morning she'd passed this spot at 6.38, the previous day at 6.49, and each time, just like today, she wore headphones. It was madness, Gaydon thought, to be out on your own in a relatively isolated spot and deliberately impair your hearing. But then she was too young and naive to realize that to some people – himself and Pryce included – she was nothing more than prey.

They drove past, giving her a wide berth, and Gaydon checked her progress in the wing mirror. 'OK,' he said quietly. 'Five, four, three, two—' He never got to one. She'd already turned off the road, momentarily disappearing from view. Gaydon looked down at the GPS unit in front of him containing a detailed Ordnance Survey map of the immediate area, even though the two of them had reconnoitred the jogger's route the previous day and knew that she was now heading up a steep, narrow path through woodland that connected to a slightly busier road at the top. They'd already decided that they would stop her just before she reached it. 'Right, we've got three minutes,' said Gaydon. 'The turning's one hundred metres ahead on the left.'

Pryce grunted his acknowledgement. He was a quiet man, not given to unnecessary words, which was something Gaydon appreciated. He'd never been a man for small talk.

The turning was sharp and hidden, and Pryce had to slow down fast to take it. As the road – which was little more than a bumpy track – ascended through a pretty beech wood, Gaydon slipped the long-bladed knife from the sheath beneath his jacket and checked the timer on his watch.

At this time in the morning there were few people about. The whole thing was going to be an absolute breeze. It was, thought Gaydon, almost too easy. Seventy-five seconds had passed from the time the jogger had turned up the hill to when they pulled off the track and parked up in the shadow of a beech tree, just out of sight of the road running along the top. The car they were in was a Toyota Hilux stolen to order in Paris with fake French licence plates so, even if it was spotted by a passer-by, it couldn't be traced back to them.

Pryce turned off the engine and Gaydon gave him a nod. That was all it needed. The two of them had worked together so long that they were often able to communicate without words.

Moving in near silence, they jogged down to the path, splitting up to take positions behind separate trees fifteen metres apart.

The jogger was noisy. Gaydon could hear her panting as she approached. A few seconds later she passed the tree he was hiding behind, and he heard the dog slow down and growl warily.

'Come on, Chewie,' she said, pulling on the lead.

The dog growled again but they kept going and Gaydon tensed, silently counted to three, then emerged from his hiding place, moving fast.

They were ten metres ahead of him and he ate up the distance in a few seconds. The dog turned round, its features set in a snarl as it began barking, pulling hard on the lead now. The jogger started to say something to the dog, then caught sight of Gaydon and the words died in her mouth. She was too stunned to react and could only watch as he picked up the dog by the scruff of its neck and cut its throat in one lightning-fast movement that almost severed its head, before flinging the corpse into a tangle of bushes.

Then she ran.

Unfortunately it was straight into the immovable object that was Pryce who'd stepped out directly in front of her. She tried to scream but he slammed a gloved hand over her mouth, swung her round so she was facing away from him, and pulled her into a well-rehearsed chokehold. As he applied the pressure and her struggles grew weaker, Gaydon re-sheathed the knife and kicked the dog's corpse further out of sight under a bramble bush so it wouldn't be seen by the next person coming up here.

The jogger was unconscious by the time he came back. He grabbed her legs and the two of them carried her towards the Hilux. They paused for a couple of seconds in the undergrowth just to make sure there were no inconvenient witnesses in the vicinity. It was only when they were absolutely certain they were alone out there in the woods that they opened the back of the Hilux and placed her in an empty space they'd made earlier behind a fold-up wallpapering table and a few large tins of white emulsion. She wasn't going to be out for long, so Gaydon climbed in after her while Pryce got back behind the wheel and started the engine.

As the Hilux pulled away, Gaydon got to work, using restraints to bind the woman's ankles and wrists and placing a ball gag in her mouth. He then took out a hypodermic syringe from his jacket and gave her a shot of enough diazepam to put her to sleep for the next couple of hours. After that she'd have barely a few hours of life left, all of which would be extremely unpleasant.

Gaydon didn't care about any of this. He looked dispassionately at the young woman lying helpless beneath him, covered her prone form with an old blanket, then climbed into the front passenger seat next to Pryce, got himself comfortable and lit a cigarette.

It was time to get ready for the next stage of the plan.

Eleven

Ray

Police raids are pretty straightforward affairs, if sometimes a little resource-heavy. Once you've identified your target and assessed his threat level you get the warrant. Unfortunately, because of the urgency of the situation and the fact that Butterworth was still in the process of finding a judge who was (a) awake and (b) prepared to grant a warrant on the fairly limited evidence we had against Khan, we'd had to go straight to the next stage of the process, which is to organize your raid team. Because Karim Khan was being investigated for a firearms-related murder we were using two teams from CO19, the Met's specialist firearms unit, and a third team from the Tactical Support Group, who were there to provide back-up and secure the perimeter, as well as a dozen detectives from CT who'd be searching the place for evidence afterwards. In all we had close to fifty officers involved.

An incident room for the Anil Rahman murder inquiry had been set up in Colindale nick, and we'd had a briefing there bright and early at 5.30 a.m. for everyone involved in the raid, which I'd had to give as I was the officer in charge – no easy feat when I'd had barely an hour's sleep.

Then it was just a matter of getting everyone on site.

So that's where I was now, at seven a.m., sitting in an unmarked car staring at a row of terraces in Enfield two streets down from where Karim Khan lived, waiting for the warrant to come through. It was a warm, cloudy, late September morning and next to me in the car was Chris Leavey.

Now I'm a man who has difficulty forming emotional relationships. I always have had – a hangover from my somewhat unusual childhood and the traumatic event that shaped it. I have plenty of acquaintances, mainly from the force, and I was married once – briefly – but it's fair to say that Chris Leavey is the only true friend I have. We've known each other for twelve years, since our early days in the Special Reconnaissance Service arm of military intelligence when we were brought together for a very hush-hush sting operation that should have been straightforward but turned out to be anything but. Five people had been involved in that op. One of those five was Anil Rahman. In those twelve years, neither Chris nor I had ever spoken about what happened that day, either to each other or to anyone else.

Until now.

Chris frowned. He was a shortish guy – five nine according

to him; I reckoned a lot nearer eight – but powerfully built with outlandishly big hands. In our early days together it had been all muscle, but now things were beginning to sag, and his face had taken on a wrinkled, lumpy look. That and the full head of thick hair gave him the appearance of a grizzled but dangerous Shar Pei dog. He was forty-two – four years older than me – but could easily have passed for fifty. Not that many people would dare tell him that.

'So, Anil, that was his real name then,' he said, his voice gravelly from too many cigarettes. 'Anil Rahman. And it was definitely him?'

Back then we'd known him only as Anil. There hadn't been any last names.

I nodded. 'It was him. No doubt about it. Seems he never did get cured of his desire to live on the edge. After what happened back then, you'd think it would have put him off for ever.'

'Some people like to take stupid risks.' Chris looked at me. 'You're one of them.'

'I take risks, but not stupid ones.' Then I remembered last night at Madame Sin's and concluded he was probably right. 'Anyway, it seems he was doing some good work on 5's behalf. You've got to give the guy credit. He had guts.'

'You don't think it was about . . . you know.'

Even now, twelve years on, Chris couldn't refer to the op by name. It was one of those things we liked to pretend had never happened.

I shook my head. 'I can't see why. No one knows anything about it. This is about a terrorism attack, pure and simple. Anil got himself involved with the wrong kind of people. And now he's paid the price.'

I took a drink from my oversized cup of Costa coffee, trying to wake myself up. We fell into a comfortable silence.

'Mind if I have a smoke?' Chris asked eventually.

'Do you have to?'

'Are you going to deny me one of my few pleasures in life?'

'When you put it like that, how could I? Go on then. But open the window.'

He opened it a couple of inches, letting in the cool morning air, and lit up, inhaling with an almost beatific smile on his face before blowing a thin plume of smoke through the gap.

I opened my window halfway to get rid of the smell. 'You know that shit makes you look old.'

'Life makes me look old,' he said, inhaling again.

'How's Charlotte?' I asked him.

Chris's wife was a lovely woman and had always made a real effort with me because of him. At one time I ate dinner at their family home three or four times a year. She was a great cook and took pleasure in feeding me up, and I used to enjoy those times, because it gave me a sense of family that I've never properly had. But then five years ago she'd started getting joint pains and dizzy spells, and then came the MS diagnosis. The disease had moved quickly and now she was housebound and could only walk with the aid of sticks. I visited when I could but I was conscious that it wasn't enough.

'Not good. She hasn't been right since the fall. It really took it out of her. She was lying on the floor for fourteen hours, totally helpless. It's not the physical effects I'm so worried about, it's the mental ones.'

'You should take some time off to be with her.' I didn't want to lose him from the investigation but he looked like he needed it. In the last year he'd aged dramatically. The lines on his face had got deeper and more numerous, and his eyes had lost their sparkle.

'I don't know, Ray. I find it hard to spend too much time with her these days. It's like watching her die.'

I nodded slowly, not sure what to say. I couldn't imagine being in that situation. It's one of the reasons why I've always avoided emotional attachments. I feel safer without them. Seeing Chris like he was just reinforced those feelings, and I realized that, although he loved Charlotte dearly, and I cared for her too, a part of me wished she'd die quickly so that he could move on while he was still young enough.

Once again we fell silent, but this time it wasn't so comfortable. Even though we were good friends, it was still rare for us to talk about personal issues.

He finished the cigarette, chucked the butt out of the window, and looked at me. 'You know I've been thinking,' he said, changing the subject. 'No disrespect to your briefing skills, Ray, but I still don't understand what this is all about. According to 5, the suspect we're going to arrest now, Karim Khan, gave no detailed information to Anil. All he did was tell him that an attack was going to happen in the near future, and yet according to the woman who witnessed Anil being tortured to death last night, the killer wanted to know details about the attack, even though he hadn't been given any. What's that all about?'

I shrugged. 'You're right. It might be that the killer's not connected with Karim Khan. That he's working for someone else. The witness said he was a white male of about forty so it definitely wasn't Khan who killed him, and it's not someone who's a known associate of Khan's. He doesn't have any white convert friends.'

Chris looked puzzled. 'An unidentified white male with no known terrorist connections tortures an informant for information he definitely hasn't got about a terrorist spectacular that may or may not be happening. It all sounds pretty strange to me.'

He had a point. When you boiled it down to its essence, none of it made any sense. The only white male with a possible motive for torturing Anil would be a rogue vigilante secret service agent wanting to foil an attack, but he would already know that Anil didn't have the necessary information and surely he'd be better off torturing the man who did have it – Karim Khan. I hadn't mentioned in the briefing, or to Chris afterwards, about the possible involvement of The Wraith. The waters were muddy enough without bringing rumours into the equation.

'At least Khan should be able to fill in some of the gaps,' I said.

Chris gave a hollow laugh. 'You reckon? From what you said in the briefing, there's not a lot of evidence against him. If I were him, I wouldn't say a word.'

He was right about that too. Khan was canny enough to know we didn't have enough to convict him of anything. Maybe with a gun in his mouth he'd open up but, having slept on it, I'd con-cluded that I wasn't going to risk another lawsuit by threatening to kill him. This time round, the law was going to have to do its work.

And then, as if on cue, my mobile started ringing. It was Butterworth.

'All right,' he growled in his dulcet Yorkshire tones. 'We've got the go-ahead. Go in now.'

Twelve

The first ones in were the armed response units, and such are the wonders of modern technology that Chris and I were able to watch events unfold on his laptop which had a direct feed into the camera on the lead officer's helmet.

Two tactical support officers approached the front door and used an enforcer to smash it open. On a standard door like Khan's, one blow ought to be enough to do it, two at most. But this time it took eight attempts to gain access, and by the time the last blow struck, the door was hanging off its hinges, almost in pieces, which meant he had a lot of locks on it. Straight away this told me that Karim was no innocent. You don't have security like that in place unless you've got something to fear.

While a second firearms team entered the rear garden of the property from the alleyway that ran directly behind it so that Khan wouldn't try to get out that way, we continued to watch as the first team poured in through the front door, immediately setting off a burglar alarm as they moved through the house one room at a time, competing with the alarm's shriek as they announced their arrival with angry shouts of 'Armed police!' just in case Khan was a particularly heavy sleeper.

First they cleared the downstairs, which was empty, then they went charging up the stairs and entered the three bedrooms one by one. They were all empty. The beds hadn't been slept in either. Armed cops yanked open cupboard doors, checked under beds, even opened the wall cabinet in the bathroom which wouldn't have had the space to hide a kid's doll. They scoured everywhere, before finally the lead cop announced over the radio that the house was clear.

The problem was, it couldn't be. We knew Khan was there. It takes a lot of money and paperwork to turn a satellite in the sky so that it's watching an individual house, but the one thing you can rely on is its accuracy and, according to MI5, a man positively identified as Karim Khan had entered that property the previous evening and had not left it since.

But there was no point sitting there arguing with the lead cop's assessment so I gave the order for the rest of us to go in.

We were the first car on to the street, and a few people were already outside their front doors, watching what was going on with bemused expressions. We pulled up behind the firearms cars and Chris and I strode through the busted front door as the Tactical Support Group units came in behind us, sealing the street at both ends.

We were met in the downstairs hallway by a group of slightly confused-looking cops with very big guns.

'Keep looking,' I told them, shouting above the shriek of the alarm. 'He's in here somewhere.'

'We've checked everywhere,' said one of them, looking pissed off as he came down the stairs. 'He's not here.'

'We've got a satellite trained on this place,' I told him. 'He's here.' I pushed past him, heading up the stairs with Chris and shouting down to the rest of my team from CT as they flooded through the door: 'Fan out. Check everywhere.'

In fact, I wasn't entirely sure I was right. This wasn't a big house, there didn't appear to be many places to hide and, as everyone knows, you can't always rely on technology. But I also knew that even trained professionals can miss the obvious. I remember one case a few years back where police searched a suspect's house in the height of a summer heatwave looking for a dead body they were sure was there and missed it on two separate searches, even though one officer got within feet of where it lay in the loft.

The loft.

We got to the top of the stairs and I almost collided with the lead cop – a bodybuilder with a Popeye physique called, amusingly enough, Boner. I'd only met him that morning and I didn't like him. He had a bad aura.

'I don't know where you're getting your intelligence from, sir,' he said, almost spitting out the word 'sir' and getting in far too close to me, 'but he's not here.' I could tell that he'd been a bully in school.

I pointed at the loft hatch. 'No one's had a look up there.'

'He wouldn't have had time to get up there and his bed's not been slept in.'

'It's worth a try,' I said.

'Well, we haven't got a ladder and there isn't one up here.'

This is often the way in policework. You get caught out by the practical things.

'That's fine,' I said. 'Give me a leg up, Chris. I'll take a look.'

'We need to go up first,' said Boner haughtily.

That was the other thing that often caught us out: procedures.

'Don't worry,' I said. 'I won't sue if anything happens to me.'

Chris raised his eyebrows as if to say 'Are you sure you want to go up there alone?', but I gave him a nod and he didn't argue. Bending down, he cupped his hands and gave me a leg up.

Using his shoulders for support, I shoved the hatch aside and poked my head through, which sounds like a braver thing to do than it actually was. I was 99 per cent sure Karim Khan wouldn't be up there with a gun waiting to take a potshot at me. You can divide terrorists into two groups: the doers and the organizers. Khan was an organizer, so the chances of him being armed and dangerous were minimal. Also, he was no fool. He had to know that the evidence we had against him wasn't worth crap, so there was no point in ruining everything by putting a bullet in an unbeliever and going down for thirty years when he could do far more damage as a free man out on the street. Plus, if he did take a shot at me he'd probably miss.

That was my theory anyway.

No shot rang out when my head popped up into the near-darkness, so I clambered into the loft and felt around until I found a light switch. As the light came on, revealing a cramped space with a low sloping roof and a handful of boxes against one wall, I was disappointed to see that it was empty.

'Is there anything up there?' called Chris.

I stood up as high as the roof would allow and opened one of the boxes. It contained a moth-eaten duvet that smelled of mould. 'Not a lot,' I called back, wondering how a satellite could be so wrong, and knowing in my heart that it couldn't be.

I moved past the boxes, crouching like an old man, then noticed that the partition behind them was a slightly different colour from the remainder of the woodwork, and made of plywood. I gave it a tap. It felt hollow. I felt round with my hand, pushing on the wood, before spotting the outline of a small hatch, like a large cat flap, in the bottom corner. I gave that a push and it opened inwards.

I hesitated. I have a phobia for small dark places. I was OK in the main part of the loft because the hatch was open, allowing in light from below, and there was an obvious way out. But I didn't know what lay beyond this little door. I could get Chris to come up and lead the way but that didn't feel right. Even he didn't know of my phobia. No one did.

My mouth went dry and I could feel my heartbeat accelerating.

I took a microlight torch from my pocket and switched it on, then took a deep breath, got down on to my front and crawled through the flap, ignoring the screaming in my head telling me to stop.

My head and upper body came out the other side and into a narrow crawlspace no more than eight feet long and three feet wide, which was clearly part of the loft. I shone the torch around. A single mattress with mussed sheets took up almost the entire floor space. Crawling further inside, I saw a reading lamp next to the pillow and switched it on before taking off my glove and touching the mattress's undersheet. It felt warm. So Karim Khan had been sleeping up here until a few minutes ago, which meant (a) he'd been expecting a visit from us sooner rather than later, and (b), more importantly, he wasn't far away.

There was another hatch the same sort of size on the far side of the mattress that looked like it led into the neighbour's loft. We didn't have a warrant to search the neighbour's place but I figured we had probable cause.

Behind me I could hear someone coming into the loft.

'Where are you?' called Chris, and I had to admit I was relieved to hear his voice.

'Over here,' I called back. 'I think I've found his escape route. Tell TSG to make sure the whole street's sealed off and to stop and search anyone wanting to come out. I don't want this bastard slipping the net.'

'What are you going to do?'

'What do you think? I'm going after him.'

I heard Chris make a noise of disapproval but he knew better than to try to stop me, and I knew better than to try to get him to come with me. I could afford to get into trouble. He couldn't.

'I told you, you take stupid risks,' he said. 'For Christ's sake, be careful.'

I opened up the second hatch and shone my light through it, doing everything I could to beat down the fear. That was the thing with me. I couldn't surrender to it. No matter how terrified it made me feel, I always had to confront it.

Crawling through, I found myself in a very dark and far more cluttered crawlspace. I made my way over a load of junk, still on my stomach, feeling the sweat run down my forehead as my breathing got faster and faster. I had to get out of this place. I just had to. My torch light found the loft hatch that led down into the adjoining house and I crawled over to it, putting my ear to the wood. I could hear the hushed voices of a man and a woman talking on the landing directly below. They weren't speaking English but it sounded from their tone as if they were arguing.

I was confident Karim Khan had come this way only a few minutes before. I was also confident that the fact that he had meant he was guilty of something serious. I shone the light along the loft's far wall. There didn't appear to be any more trap doors hidden away, which meant he must have used this hatch to go down into the neighbour's house, which might also explain why the couple below were arguing.

That was enough for me. The rules of entering a property without permission are complex, and I could get into a lot of trouble if the people below were innocent of any wrongdoing. There'd almost certainly be a lawsuit. Yet another black mark against my name. There are plenty of people out there who need no excuse to bash the police and to make it harder for us to do our job, but as far as I was concerned this was hot pursuit and my philosophy is that the longer you sit around thinking about doing something, the harder it becomes to do.

Taking a deep breath, I yanked up the hatch and came hurtling down, legs first, like a fireman without a pole, almost falling down the stairs in the process and only narrowly missing the couple below. They jumped out of the way in opposite directions and the woman screamed loudly as she tried to cover herself up. She was early thirties, dressed in a long nightgown, and not very happy to see me. The man was also early thirties, dressed in underpants and a T-shirt, and clearly not Karim Khan. He looked even less happy.

'Police!' I shouted as I reached into my jacket for my ID, thinking it might have been easier if I'd had it in my hand before I'd made my dramatic entrance.

The man didn't react well, leaping at me hands outstretched, going for my throat, an incoherent snarl coming from deep within him. I sidestepped, letting the momentum carry him forward, and grabbed his wrist, twisting hard. 'Now, sir, calm down,' I said firmly. But he wasn't listening, and as he swung round to punch me with his free arm I gave him a quick uppercut to the jaw, knocking him back into the wall.

The woman screamed again. She also glanced back quickly over her shoulder, as if she was trying to warn someone in one of the rooms that I was here. Or maybe I was just being hopeful. There were only two doors behind her so if Khan was here, I guessed he was on the other side of one of them.

I yanked out my ID and held it up. 'Police, police! It's OK!'

But she just yelled at me in a foreign language, shooing me away, and as I stepped backwards I saw a little girl of about five with messy hair appear at the bottom of the stairs and immediately start crying. The whole thing had public-relations disaster written all over it, and I imagined Butterworth at a packed press conference apologizing to the whole world for the appalling conduct of one of his officers.

A couple of seconds later a younger man of about twenty

dressed in traditional white Islamic robes and cap also appeared at the bottom of the stairs, putting a protective arm round the little girl's shoulders.

'Who are you?' he demanded.

'Police,' I called back in my most authoritative voice, wielding my ID. 'Stay where you are.'

I'm a great believer in the maxim 'in for a penny, in for a pound'. If Khan wasn't here, then I was in a whole heap of trouble anyway, so I had nothing to lose by going the whole hog and turning the place over trying to find him.

'Excuse me, madam,' I said, pushing the woman out of the way and walking past her along the landing. I opened the right-hand door, revealing a small, empty bathroom.

The woman grabbed me from behind, her shouting almost hysterical now, and I could hear footfalls coming up the stairs. Shrugging her off with a push that was probably a bit harder than needed, and which might well end in another complaint for assault, I opened the door opposite the bathroom and was immediately confronted by a woman in a full-length black burkha standing in the middle of what was clearly a young girl's bedroom.

We stared at each other for a second, and I noticed that she had very hairy hands for a woman. There were nicotine stains on her middle and forefingers as well.

'Hello, Mr Khan,' I said with a sense of relief. 'You're under arrest.'

Karim Khan shook his head and started gabbling away in a foreign tongue, his voice deliberately high-pitched as he tried to get me out of the room.

I had to give him an A for sheer chutzpah. Chris sounded more like a woman than he did but he was giving it his all, to such an extent that I actually had a genuine moment of doubt about ripping off his burkha just in case I was mistaken and it was a particularly manly woman facing me down. That really would give Butterworth a coronary. But I pulled off the hood anyway in one swift movement and, lo and behold, there stood a startled-looking bald man looking very much like the one I'd seen in the photo last night in Butterworth's office.

Khan didn't stay startled for long. He gave me a two-handed shove and tried to force his way past me but I still had hold of his burkha and I pulled him back into a headlock before dragging him across the landing into the bathroom, noticing as I did so that the young guy in the traditional clothes had reached the top of the stairs now, and the one I'd punched was getting to his feet, helped by the angry woman.

Khan struggled wildly in my grip so I just increased the pressure on his neck and that calmed him right down. I locked the door behind me then slammed him into the wall, holding him in place with a gloved hand round his neck. I could see that the expression in my eyes scared him.

There was a commotion outside the door and the young guy demanded to know what was going on as he repeatedly tried to turn the door handle.

I had maybe thirty seconds before someone – whether it be the house's occupants or my colleagues, who'd be here very soon – decided to force it open.

I wanted to get out my gun but it was too risky. If he later said I'd threatened him with it and was able to describe what it looked like accurately enough, then I risked a very long prison sentence. Instead I was going to have to rely on the psychology of fear.

'I know what you're planning,' I whispered, tightening my grip on his throat so his eyes bugged out. 'Give me the name of the man who's going to carry out the attack. Now.' I spoke the words calmly but with a cold menace that my ex-wife had once said came far too easily to me.

I could tell Khan recognized me. For all I know he might have been the man who'd organized the attempted hit on me a year and a half ago. I used this to my advantage as I cut off his air completely. 'Answer me or I will strangle you here and now and tell my colleagues you died in the struggle.'

Someone was banging hard on the door and yelling for me to come out but I zoned out the noise.

His eyes were sticking out like stalks and I could see he was panicking as he fought in vain for breath.

I waited three seconds, my eyes burning into his, the darkness rising within me like a terrible, beautiful warmth. I could feel the darkness in him too. I could tell that his heart was cold and that he was fully prepared to let many people die in pursuit of his cause.

'Tell me.'

He nodded desperately, all kinds of noises rising up from his throat. He was going to break.

I eased my grip.

He opened his mouth to speak, then paused, knowing he was about to commit an act of betrayal.

And then the door flew open as it was kicked off its hinges

and the man I'd punched and the young guy came bundling in one after the other. The one I'd punched was wielding a hammer so I let go of Khan and used my forearm to knock his hammer arm to one side before felling him with another uppercut. I charged into the young guy, wrestling him out of the door and across the landing into the girl's bedroom. He slipped and fell, banging his head on the bed frame, and I turned round in time to see Khan come running out of the bathroom, making for the staircase like the clappers.

He was fast, I'll give him that, especially considering he was dressed in a burkha, and he took the stairs three at a time, holding up the material at the sides to give himself more freedom of movement. But it didn't do him any good. I was right behind him, and when he was two steps from the bottom I jumped on to his back, sending him sprawling. I landed on top of him and he gasped in pain. I couldn't see anyone else so I flipped him round, grabbed him by the scruff of the neck and slammed his head back on to the carpet with a loud thud.

'Give me a name or you die right now.'

I reached into my jacket for the gun, the darkness getting the better of me, knowing this was my last chance.

But it was not to be. Before my hand could touch the metal, Boner and his men and all their guns came smashing through the front door in a wave of testosterone, noise and, unfortunately for us, impotence, almost knocking me over in the process.

Khan smiled up at me. He knew I couldn't do a thing.

And then he started yelling: 'Police brutality! Police brutality! He tried to strangle me!'

I got up, dusted myself down, and read him his rights while

the firearms team looked on, not quite sure what to do. Then with barely a nod to any of them, I walked out of the house, leaving Khan on the floor for them to deal with.

It was time to come up with a plan B.

Thirteen

Jane

I don't tend to sleep late generally so I was surprised when I saw that the bedside clock said twenty past eight. I had that disorientating feeling of unfamiliarity with my surroundings and it took me a good few seconds to remember where I was.

We'd got to the safehouse about three o'clock this morning. It was a long, roundabout drive, mainly down back roads, with a lot of stopping and starting as we picked up and dropped various escort vehicles – apparently no one except those staying here with me and the commander of Scotland Yard's counter-terrorism unit knew where we were going – and I'd spent pretty much the entire journey under a blanket in the back while Anji and her colleague Jeffs, whom I really didn't like, travelled in near silence. Then when the three of us had arrived, along with three uniformed police officers armed with machine guns, I'd been assigned a bedroom and gone straight to bed.

Yawning, I got up and looked out of the window. A medium-sized garden with a climbing frame and built-in, ground-level trampoline gave way to open fields at the bottom, with a line of woodland in the distance. A single-track road ran down beside the house and, as far as I could see, there were no neighbours on the other side, just more field. The only signs of human habitation were a couple of houses and some farm buildings about half a mile away. Take them out and the view probably wouldn't be much different from what it was two hundred years ago, which made me think that I liked England. There was something simple and ancient about its greenery.

I opened the window and breathed in the fresh air, my spirits momentarily lifted. It was surprisingly mild outside but the weather looked broody and thick banks of dark cloud were gathering in the distance. I stood there for a few minutes, allowing myself to relax. I felt no fear about my situation, no real shock after the events of the previous night. You may wonder why I seemed so calm, but if you'd seen half the things I had in my life, then I promise you'd understand.

The bedroom had an en suite shower room. After giving myself a proper scrub, I got dressed in the clothes I'd picked up from my flat the previous night – jeans and a loose-fitting sweatshirt. I put my hair back in a bun, but though I had some makeup in the bag I'd brought with me, I didn't bother putting any on.

The safehouse was a spacious, fully furnished home that had been modernized inside and recently decorated, and I wondered how the police had come to own or rent such places, and how many they had dotted about the countryside.

As I descended the staircase, realizing almost by surprise that I was starving, I saw one of the uniformed police officers – a well-built blond guy in his late twenties, with a baby face that was pretty rather than handsome – sitting in a chair by the front door, drinking a cup of tea, his jacket undone and a machine gun on his lap. He smiled and got to his feet as I reached the bottom of the stairs.

'Hi, I'm Luke. I'm one of the people who are looking after you.'

'I'm Jane,' I said, shaking his proffered hand. 'I'm glad to have you here.'

Although he made an obvious effort to keep his gaze level with mine, I could feel his eyes on my body, so I removed my hand, said I was pleased to meet him, and walked on past.

The other two armed officers were in the lounge playing cards, their guns down by their sides, along with Seamus Jeffs, Anji's detective partner. The two cops didn't look up but Jeffs did, his face forming a leery smile. He was a pretty ordinary-looking guy in his mid-thirties and he'd changed from the previous night so he was now wearing jeans and a linen shirt with one button too many undone, revealing a thin gold chain.

'How are you doing, Jane?' he asked, excusing himself from the card game and coming over with just a little too much enthusiasm.

'I'm OK,' I told him, stepping away to give myself a little space.

'Is there anything you need?'

'No, I'm fine. Thanks for asking.' I gave him a tight smile and turned away, wanting to get away from his testosterone.

I can spot men like Jeffs and Luke a mile away. They spend their lives trying their luck with women, and have an inflated idea of their own wit, charm and good looks. I'll be straight with you here: men go for me. They always have done. Occasionally it can be flattering but for the most part it's not, because the men in question tend to be the predatory rather than respectful kind. When I was young, I'd always be polite and friendly to them, but it didn't take me long to work out that politeness and friendliness are viewed as signs of interest by predatory men, and a pass almost inevitably follows. So now I'm just direct.

'Well, if you change your mind, just let me know,' said Jeffs to my back as I headed for the kitchen and the smell of food.

Anji was at the breakfast bar eating an omelette. She got up when she saw me and gave me a warm smile. 'Can I get you some coffee?'

'Thanks, that'd be great. But I'll get it. You finish your food. Do you mind if I make myself something?'

'Let me do it. You've been through enough.'

I laughed and put a hand on her shoulder, gently pushing her back into her seat. 'Don't worry, I'm perfectly capable.'

I poured myself a coffee from the pot and cracked two eggs into a cup, whisking them briskly, my mouth watering at the prospect of food.

'So,' said Anji, pushing away her empty plate, 'whereabouts in South Africa are you from?'

'Just outside Cape Town.'

'How long have you been over here?'

'Only a few months. I was in the US before that.'

'And you say you've got children?'

'Two sons, twenty-two and twenty. One's back in South Africa, the other's in the States.'

'Wow,' said Anji. 'You don't look old enough.'

I smiled, pouring the whisked egg into the frying pan and letting it bubble. 'Thank you. I need to let them know I'm OK. When will I be able to get my phone back?' Anji had taken it off me and switched it off, citing security reasons.

'I'm not sure. We can't afford to have our location compromised. Because of what's happened to you, and the way the attempts on your life have been so well organized, we're having to be extremely careful. None of us are allowed to use our mobile phones. There's a single secure satellite phone here that only DC Jeffs and I have access to. But I promise you, when I get permission from my boss, you can call your boys.'

'How long am I going to be here for, Anji?' I asked.

She gave me a serious look. 'I don't know. Hopefully not too long. We have a composite artist coming over today. He's going to work with you to try to get an e-fit of the suspect you saw last night, and once that's released to the public you should be in less danger.'

I sensed it wasn't going to be as simple as that. That if they caught someone and I had to testify against him in court then I might need to be in a safehouse until the trial. For months. But I let it go. I knew Anji was doing the best she could.

'Have the police arrested anyone yet?'

She shook her head. 'No. It doesn't usually happen that fast.'

'I saw a TV programme once that said most murders were solved in the first twenty-four hours.'

'Not this one. The man who killed your friend and his wife was a professional.'

'God, that poor woman,' I said, shaking my head. 'What is it with some men? And why do I always find them?'

Anji laughed. 'Tell me about it. I've had my fair share of useless ones.'

'Really?'

'Really.'

'Have you ever been married?'

She nodded. 'That's a story and a half. My husband was a total player and somehow I didn't spot it in the run-up to the wedding. We lasted six months. That's how long it took me to find out he was seeing two other women. One of them was my bridesmaid.'

'My God, you poor thing,' I said, sitting down opposite her with the coffee and omelette.

Anji shrugged. 'I'm long over it. You move on, don't you?'

And God had I learned to move on. I asked her if she was seeing anyone now.

'No. For the moment I've gone cold turkey. How about you? Were you married?'

I nodded. 'A long time back. My mum was a bully. I wanted to escape so I got hitched at eighteen to my first serious boyfriend. He was thirty.'

'That must have pissed her off.'

'It did. I think the main reason I did it was to upset her. The problem was, I ended up marrying a younger version of my dad.

Joel was beautiful to look at, he really was. All my girlfriends wanted him. But he was also weak, jealous, and useless with money. I should have known everything was going to go wrong when he came home early from work one day just after we'd moved in together, burst into tears and got on his knees begging me to forgive him.'

'Forgive him for what?'

'He said his company had gone bust, that he owed hundreds of thousands of rand to the tax people, and that he had to sell the house and both our cars to pay them back.' I sighed, remembering the shock I'd felt seeing the man I loved and respected turn into a wreck in front of me. 'I should have left him there and then, but you know what it's like. I was young. I thought I could change him.'

Anji reached across the table and gently touched my forearm. 'You live and learn, honey. You live and learn.'

'Anyway,' I said, 'he's long gone now. And good riddance.'

'Good riddance to all the shit men in the world.'

Anji lifted her coffee cup in a mock toast and we smiled at each other. I was enjoying this conversation, and I liked the warmth between us. It was a welcome relief from my current situation.

'I've always wanted to go to South Africa,' said Anji wistfully.

'It's a beautiful country,' I replied, remembering how stunning it was.

'Why did you leave?'

I paused, wondering whether I should give too much away.

Anji saw my hesitation. 'Sorry, Jane, I don't mean to pry.'

'It's OK. Telling you might explain why I was able to deal with what happened last night.'

I pushed my plate to one side, took a drink from my coffee and began talking.

Joel might have been a feckless, jealous husband – and a man not averse to having the odd affair – but I know he genuinely loved me, and for the most part those early years of our marriage still rank as the happiest of my life. We had two beautiful sons together, Joel built up a new business, and we moved into a nice family home with a swimming pool in the pretty Cape View suburb of Cape Town. When the kids were old enough to go to school I got a job as a manager in a café just off the beachfront, even though Joel didn't want me to work, and I'll be honest, I even had a casual little affair of my own with a surfer dude who occasionally used to frequent the café. I was settled. The world was good.

And then one hot summer's afternoon in January 2001, everything changed.

I had the day off work and I was looking after the boys, who were about six and eight. The three of us were outside messing about in the pool when I heard a child's cry. It was coming from inside the house next door – Jan and Liesel's place – and it was so faint, I thought at first I might have imagined it. Then a minute later I heard it again. So, after I'd got the boys out of the pool, I looked over the backyard fence. The doors were shut at the back and all the windows were closed which I thought was odd on such a sweltering day. We knew Jan and Liesel pretty well. They were about our age and they had young kids too, a son of about five and a daughter of four. Sweet children. A nice family.

I stood at the fence listening for a good minute without hearing anything more and concluded that everything was fine in there. Maybe they had the air con on. I wasn't unduly concerned. Although the crime rate in South Africa was increasing rapidly at that time, we lived in a leafy cul-de-sac in a secure, gated community with a permanent armed guard. It was a safe family environment. All the children played out on the road in front of the house because we all knew nothing would happen to them.

As I turned away, I heard the cry again. It was the little boy, Deon. And he was saying something. A word. *Assistensi*. It was Afrikaans for help. He sounded scared.

I swallowed, scared now too, then took my own boys, Matthew and Ryan, inside and turned on the television. I told them I was just going to pop next door and collect something from Liesel, and that I'd be about five minutes.

'Can you see if Deon wants to come round and play?' asked Ryan, my youngest.

'Sure,' I said, forcing a smile.

I had a spare key to Liesel's place, just like they had a spare key to ours, so I took it, triple-locked our own front door to make sure that no one got in while I was out, and walked over. I noticed immediately that Liesel's car was in the driveway, which meant she was almost certainly home. People didn't tend to walk very much in South Africa.

When I was outside Liesel's front door I thought I could hear Deon's sister crying, but it was difficult to tell for sure because the sounds were very faint. The road was quiet, but I could hear children playing in one of the other backyards, so I told myself I was wrong to be nervous. Maybe life was so good that I was inventing dramas for myself for a bit of variety.

I rang on the doorbell.

There was no answer.

I rang a second time.

Still no answer.

Liesel wouldn't leave the kids on their own and their maid definitely wasn't here otherwise she'd have answered the door. Even so, I rang a third time before turning the key in the lock and stepping into their spacious hallway.

Nothing looked out of place.

I called Liesel's name and almost immediately I heard the hysterical cries of children coming from upstairs.

'It's Jane,' I called back, hurrying up the stairs. 'Ryan and Matthew's mum. Where are you?'

'In here! In here!' Deon called back in English, sounding scared and relieved at the same time.

I hurried over to the door behind which his shouts were coming from, and could see immediately that it had been locked from the outside. The key was still in the lock so I turned it, told them to stand back, and opened the door.

Crying hysterically, they both ran at me as I appeared in the doorway and I thanked God that they were physically unhurt. 'What's happened?' I asked, bending down to take them in my arms.

'Some bad men locked us in here and went off with Momma,' said Deon through the tears.

'I want Momma,' cried his little sister.

I did what I could to calm them, making sure they didn't see the fear that was tearing me apart inside. 'Stay in this room for a minute,' I told them in as soft and kind a voice as possible.

'I'm going to find Momma, OK? Then I'll bring her back to you.'

It broke my heart to see them look up at me with real relief in their eyes. I knew they thought I would find their mom and then everything would be back to normal.

I left them in the room, keeping the door ever so slightly ajar so they wouldn't feel trapped, then headed along the hall to the master bedroom. Liesel had told me this was where they kept their safe. I had little doubt now that intruders had threatened to kill her children if she didn't lead them to it and give them the combination.

Home invasions are all too common in South Africa. It doesn't matter what your level of security is, you're never entirely safe, not even in a gated community surrounded by high walls and razor wire, with an armed guard on the gate. There are always going to be bad guys out there determined and able to get through, often with the help of those meant to be protecting you. Most people are lucky enough never to cross their paths – it's why a lot of us preferred not to think about it rather than address the issues – but for an unfortunate, unlucky few, the nightmare becomes a reality.

Which was why I stood outside the master bedroom for longer than I should have done, conscious of the silence beyond, before finally opening the door with a shaking hand.

Even so, when I saw Liesel's ruined naked body on the bed, the blood caking the sheets around it, her eyes staring lifelessly at the ceiling, the shock of what they'd done to her still came close to making me faint.

I will never forget that scene. It's etched like a stone carving on my mind. After that, nothing could ever truly shock me again.

'And that was it for us and South Africa,' I said to Anji, finishing the last of my coffee, knowing that I'd given far too much away but strangely not worried about it. 'I just couldn't bring my children up there because I'd have been permanently worried that the same thing might one day happen to us.'

'Jesus,' whispered Anji. 'No wonder you're so good at holding it together.'

You don't know the half of it, I thought. You really don't.

Fourteen

Ray

The search of Karim Khan's house wasn't yielding a whole lot, but then we hadn't expected it to. So far the search team had found three phones in his little hidey-hole in the loft, hidden in a false wall, along with a MacBook Air. The Air had what looked like high-tech encryption software in place hiding the hard drive's contents, which would need to be circumvented. That and the fact that Khan was in possession of three phones served to confirm that he was up to no good; but unless there was something directly incriminating on any of them, such as a series of emails or phone calls to a known terror suspect, then that wasn't going to be much use in getting him to talk.

Khan himself – still in his burkha, and still screeching about police brutality – had been transferred under armed guard to

Simon Kernick

Colindale nick where he'd be checked by a doctor to confirm
that he was physically unhurt and fit to be interviewed. Assuming
he was, we'd be talking to him some time this morning, probably after he'd got himself lawyered up. He'd almost certainly
make a formal complaint against me and might even try to get
me charged with assault. As most people know, prisoners have
a whole host of rights and there's no shortage of ambulance-
chasing lawyers out there to help them file assault charges; but,
given the circumstances of this arrest, and the fact that Khan
had been resisting, I was pretty sure nothing much would come
of it. Although the fact I'd already overheard one wag from TSG
describe me as 'Ray Mason the Burkha Basher' wasn't the most
promising of signs.

'I think it sounds catchy,' said Chris as we stood on the street
outside Khan's house, drinking takeaway coffees and taking a
break from the search, which now involved more than a dozen
CT officers, while half a dozen uniforms kept the scene secure.

'It has a certain ring,' I said, 'although I wish I'd bashed the
bastard more.'

I said these last words quietly and with my head slightly down.
We only had a cordon covering the pavement outside Khan's
place and the house next door where I'd arrested him, so we
were a few yards away from two separate lines of civilians who
clearly had nothing better to do than stand around watching
coppers come and go. Any one of them could have been video-
ing us on a phone and all you need is one comment on film, or
someone who can read your lips, and you're in trouble. I'm not
being paranoid either. This is what happens these days.

It puts a lot of pressure on.

Chris frowned, taking a gulp from his coffee. 'Khan's not going to talk, is he?'

'I don't think so,' I told him honestly.

'So we're left just waiting for a terror attack to happen. Can you imagine what happens if we miss it?'

'If we miss it, we miss it, Chris. We can only do our best.'

'I've got a wife and daughter, Ray. If one of them got caught up in it I'd never forgive myself, especially if I'd had the chance to get the information out of the bastard and didn't.'

'We have got the chance. We'll be speaking to him later.'

'I'd torture it out of him, I really would.'

I stared at him, pleased that he'd said it under his breath with his back to our audience but surprised by his anger. Chris tended to be a calm, unflappable presence who was prepared to live by the rules set out for him.

'Do you really mean that?'

He gave a resigned sigh. 'You know, everyone remembers the fifty-two who died in the 7/7 attacks, but most people forget about the seven hundred injured. A lot of them had terrible burns. Some lost limbs. Add in the relatives and that's thousands of lives torn apart. And the worst part is the world just gets up and moves on. No one thinks about all those left behind. I don't know if it's my experience with Charlotte but the older I get the more pissed off I am with the way we have to operate. One terror suspect's rights are more important than the rights of hundreds of others to live in peace. It's just not right.' He paused. 'I suppose that's what I'm thinking. It's just not right.'

'Well, if it's any consolation,' I said, getting in close to him, 'I half throttled the piece of shit, and yes, he definitely knows something, I'm sure of it. But given we can't put the thumbscrews on him, we're going to have to find out what these guys are planning another way. You know what they say, Christopher. Where there's a will . . .'

I understood Chris's frustration. We all did in CT. The threat level was rising all the time, and the knowledge that at some point the bad guys would get lucky played on everyone's minds. I took a sip from my coffee and looked back up at the house, wanting to get back to business.

'Let's assume Khan's guilty and everything he's been telling Anil Rahman about an impending terror attack is true. He obviously has a role in it. From what we know, this role would almost certainly involve organizing the weapons. So he's got to have been communicating with the people supplying the weapons as well as those carrying out the attack somehow.'

'And you think we might find something on the phones?'

'I don't know. He's no fool. I bet they're all unregistered. But Khan's got to have one he uses for business. He still officially runs a charity, and he's bound to have a number his children can get hold of him on.'

'He's not going to be using that one to organize gun deals though, is he?'

'No, but if he carries it around with him, we can at least see where he's been. That might give us something. Was he carrying a phone when you searched him?'

Chris shook his head. 'No. He just had a wallet with driver's licence, debit card and about three hundred in cash.'

I thought about this for a moment. 'If he thought he was going to escape in disguise and go underground for a while he would have definitely taken a phone with him to keep in contact with the outside world.'

'You reckon? He wouldn't have had any time to think about sorting out which phone to take with him after we came through the door this morning. He'd already have been on his toes.'

'I'll tell you one thing I'm sure of. No one goes anywhere without a phone any more, and criminals are as addicted to them as anyone else. I reckon he must have ditched it after I came through the loft hatch into next door when he knew there was a chance he was going to get arrested. Come on, let's have a look.'

Chris gave me a look that said he didn't think I was on to much of a lead, but he followed me through the next-door neighbour's open front door anyway.

About fifteen minutes earlier we'd been granted a warrant to search the neighbour's house for any clues that might tell us what Khan was up to, but at the moment it was empty. The three adult occupants of the house had all been arrested on suspicion of harbouring a fugitive and assaulting a police officer, three younger children had been temporarily taken into the care of social services, and for the moment the search for clues was centred on Khan's place.

I had the smell of the hunt now. I'm not a patient person. In fact, I'm pretty manic. Those in the know say that the best police officers are slow and methodical, taking their time turning up clues, but I'm not like that. I'm forever trying to get myself into the mind of the suspect. To see the world – albeit temporarily – from his or her point of view. To second-guess them.

I charge around, scouring everywhere for clues, never staying on one train of thought for too long. And when I get a thought in my head, I have to act on it. Like now. I was suddenly convinced Karim Khan had taken a phone with him when he crawled through into his neighbour's loft and, since he didn't have it with him when he was arrested, it had to be somewhere in his neighbour's house. What was more, I felt sure it would yield a clue. This was just a gut feeling, nothing else, but I'm the kind of man who goes with my gut feelings, if only because they make me feel like I'm doing something.

I also had another gut feeling, which was that time wasn't on our side. Careful and methodical was not what was needed today. If necessary I'd tear this place apart brick by brick to find what we were looking for.

As it happened, it didn't come to that. While Chris searched the bathroom where I'd dragged Khan, I searched the kid's bedroom where I'd discovered him in the burkha, and found a Samsung Galaxy 5 that looked at least a year old under the mattress on the kid's bed. It had been switched off, but the SIM card was still intact.

'Bingo,' I said to Chris, switching it on. 'Look what I've found.'

'Are you sure it's his?'

'I don't think it belongs to whoever sleeps in this bedroom,' I said, looking at the screensaver picture on the phone, which was of a group of four young adults, three females and a male, the females all in headscarves but otherwise dressed in western clothes. I showed Chris the picture. 'Now I don't know for certain, but I'm betting these are Khan's kids. I know he's got four.' I looked round the room, then back at the Samsung in my hand. 'This is the phone he wanted to take with him. He didn't get time to stash it properly or remove the SIM.' It was password-protected but that didn't matter. We'd get through the security easily enough.

'Well, it's something, I guess.' Chris didn't sound convinced.

His lack of enthusiasm shrank mine a little. I put the phone in an evidence bag then lifted the mattress again and had another look, just to see if there was anything else he'd stashed there.

'What's that?' said Chris. He bent down and reached under the bed, coming back up with a pocket-sized black notebook with faux-leather bindings. He opened it and flicked through it while I stood beside him. The pages were empty. All of them. Nothing had been written in this notebook at all.

But something caught my eye. 'Look. Some of these pages have been ripped out.' I bent down now, looking under the bed. The only thing under there was a stuffed teddy bear that looked like it had seen better days. I stood up. 'Khan must have dropped this notebook as well. But why? He didn't want us to find it but there's nothing in it.'

Chris continued to flick through the notebook. 'It's what isn't in it. There must be fifteen or twenty pages ripped out. He's been sending notes. That's how he's communicating with the other terrorists.'

I smiled as the truth dawned on me. 'A dead-letter drop. The oldest trick in the book. He never meets them. They never meet him. They just leave notes for each other at prearranged locations.'

'This prick's cleverer than we thought. So how are we going to find out what's been going on now?'

'A lot of legwork,' I said, looking down at the phone and hoping that Khan had been carrying it round with him when he went to his dead-letter drops. If he had, then we had a chance of finding the people he was communicating with. 'So let's get started.'

But as I bagged the notebook, my mobile rang. It was Butterworth.

'Sir?' I said, starting down the stairs.

'We've got a problem,' he growled, which I thought was something of an understatement. Right now we had plenty of problems.

'What kind of problem?'

'Anil Rahman gave us the names of two British-born Muslims who accompanied him and Karim Khan to Syria on their last trip. Rahman claimed they were dangerous radicals who'd almost certainly had some military training. 5 are meant to have been keeping tabs on them, but it seems they haven't been trying very hard, because both men have slipped their surveillance and gone AWOL. Neither of them have been seen for two days now.'

'You think they might be something to do with the planned attack?'

'Could be, and a third man they've been fraternizing with – a Muslim convert who as far as we know hasn't been to Syria but who has been on our watchlists – has also gone AWOL.' Butterworth paused, and I could tell he was worried. 'It may be coincidence, but if it isn't, it means an attack really is imminent.

We need to get boots on the ground looking for these boys as soon as possible.'

'I'll get over to Colindale right now,' I told him, feeling the adrenalin pumping through my system and hoping it would find an outlet.

I needed action.

Fifteen

Gaydon didn't like Pryce's driving. The big man was fine when they were on major highways but, because he was used to driving on the right-hand side, when they were back on regular roads he occasionally forgot which country he was in, and had almost caused an accident at a roundabout on the A31. So they'd swapped seats at a nearby petrol station and now Gaydon was behind the wheel, which was a good thing because barely five miles from their destination they were flashed by a police patrol car.

'OK, keep quiet and let me do the talking,' said Gaydon out of the corner of his mouth as he pulled over.

Pryce kept quiet. He was good at that.

The police car pulled up five yards behind them, its lights flashing. It was after nine a.m. and they were on a semi-rural stretch of B-road just to the west of the town of Alton, and traffic was light. If it came to it, Gaydon was confident he could take out whoever was in the police car with a minimum of fuss, but that was very much a last resort. This whole day needed to run smoothly and two dead police officers and all the unwanted attention that would cause could potentially ruin things. But Gaydon knew better than to show any sign of uncertainty. He'd had plenty of good luck in the past. It was inevitable that he'd eventually get some bad. The most important thing was to handle it properly.

Two police officers – both men – got out and approached on either side of the Hilux in a practised routine. They'd no doubt run a standard check on the licence plates already but that wouldn't have set off any alarm bells. They were good fakes, belonging to an identical French-registered Hilux, and they'd withstand all but the most detailed scrutiny.

The older of the two officers leaned down to the driver's-side window. 'Good morning, sir. We've had a report that your vehicle was involved in a near miss back at the Chawton roundabout on the A31, and that you were driving erratically.'

All of which was absolutely true.

'I'm sorry, monsieur,' said Gaydon in a reasonably good French accent. 'My driving is not as good in this country as it is at home. I will be more careful.'

The officer, a friendly-looking type with silver hair who'd probably seen it all before, seemed mollified by Gaydon's apology, and would almost certainly have let him go without a problem. But then he caught sight of Pryce.

Pryce, it was fair to say, looked like a killer. He was a big, unsmiling man with granite features; a jagged white scar on his chin from an old shrapnel injury; lips so thin and bloodless they were almost invisible; and cold, cement-grey eyes that reminded Gaydon of a lizard's. Pryce scared people, which in their line of business wasn't necessarily a bad thing. The problem was that sometimes – like now – when you needed to keep a low profile, he stood right out.

'Would you mind turning the engine off and stepping out of the car, sir?' said the officer.

'Mais oui, of course, of course,' said Gaydon, looking puzzled as he switched off the engine and removed the keys. This, he knew, wasn't a good sign. He got out without looking at Pryce who remained inside the car. 'Is everything OK?' he asked the officer.

'Just procedure, sir. Would you mind showing me your driving licence?'

As a rule, Gaydon found the politeness of British police officers amusing. In the States, the cops tried to sound polite but their aggressive stance belied their words, while in most other countries they dispensed with the pleasantries altogether. Here, though, they really did sound like they meant it.

He produced the licence from his wallet and handed it over. It was an extremely good French fake bought from an Algerian forger with links to the Ministère de l'Ecologie and cost five thousand euros. Like the Hilux's plates, it would easily withstand a standard check.

'So, where are you and your, er, friend going?'

'He's my cousin. We are decorators. My brother has bought a house in Kingsley. We are here to do some work on it.'

It was the cover story they'd agreed in case of this eventuality and they had the paints and equipment in the boot to back it up. The girl was still out cold under a blanket so the officer wouldn't necessarily see her even if he did pop open the boot. However, that was a risk Gaydon couldn't afford to take. If the cop insisted on seeing inside he was going to have to die. Which meant that his friend would have to die too, and that was going to complicate things.

A car drove past with a couple inside. The woman passenger stared at them and Gaydon had to turn away to avoid her gaze, conscious that anyone passing by now could be a potential witness to a double murder. He was a pretty nondescript individual – early forties, dark hair, medium height and build, the antithesis of Pryce – but even so, he still didn't want to be seen.

The officer scanned the licence, looked at Gaydon. Smiled enigmatically.

Gaydon smiled back, thinking about the half a million dollars he was going to be earning for the work he was doing today, but looking both friendly and bemused. He could tell that the cop didn't entirely trust him.

The officer handed him back the licence. 'Do you mind if we just look in the back of your car, sir?'

'Of course,' said Gaydon, hoping that Pryce had heard the exchange through the open window.

It seemed he had as he emerged slowly from the car, his movements languid. The second police officer took one look at him and unconsciously took a step back. Pryce glanced across at Gaydon, who gave him just the slightest of nods. It was the signal.

Get ready.

Pryce was going to have to kill his man quickly and out of sight of the road.

Another car drove past. This was going to be very risky. Gaydon considered using his hands to break the lead officer's neck but settled instead on getting in very close and using the flick knife with the five-inch blade concealed in his overalls. A quick thrust to the heart and it would all be over. He could put an arm round the cop as he died and manoeuvre him round the other side of the car out of sight. Then, when the road was clear, they'd dump both bodies in the boot alongside the girl and be on their way.

Gaydon found it strange to think that in the space of five seconds this man beside him was going to be dead and gone, leaving behind grieving relatives who'd eventually grow to forget him. It would be as if he'd never existed, and Gaydon felt a little sorry for him that he'd been unlucky enough to run into them today.

They were at the back of the Hilux now. The officer stepped to one side and asked him to open it.

Gaydon complied, tensing a little as he waited for the cop to come in close so he could deliver the death blow, his right hand slipping down by his side, reaching into the overall pocket. The adrenalin was coming now; the excitement of sudden violence.

And that was when the officer's radio crackled into life and a woman's voice came over the line. Gaydon couldn't quite figure out what she was saying but he heard the words 'serious accident' and immediately relaxed. The officer turned away from Gaydon and began walking back to his car, the radio to his ear.

Gaydon shut the boot and glanced over at Pryce standing

casually at the side of the road a metre from the other cop, who was still thankfully very much alive. The lead officer called his colleague over, then turned to Gaydon.

'OK, sir, we need to be somewhere else. Please try to drive more carefully.'

'Of course, officer, no problem.'

Gaydon and Pryce got back in the car, and as they were waiting for the cop car to pull out and pass, there was a moan from the boot. The girl was waking up.

Pryce smiled. It wasn't a pretty sight. 'It seems the devil's smiling on us today,' he said.

Gaydon nodded slowly. Perhaps he was. Perhaps he wasn't. Either way he would surely be pleased with the work they were going to be doing over the next few hours.

Sixteen

Ray

Murder inquiries start methodically. A briefing's held, led by the Senior Investigating Officer – in this case my boss, DCI Butterworth. The team are given their tasks and get on with them, and the murderer, and the evidence against him or her, usually turns up pretty quickly.

Not this time. This was like no murder inquiry I'd ever come across because, although we were hunting the man who'd murdered Anil Rahman and his wife – as well as, it seemed, the two police officers escorting the witness to hospital – we were also trying to stop an impending terrorist attack. Although CT were leading the investigation, we'd had to borrow large numbers of officers from the Met's Area Homicide North to assist us, and we had close to a hundred officers working the case, as well as the SOCO teams at the two crime scenes gathering evidence.

The majority of the inquiry team were concentrating on tracking down the three missing terror suspects. In the briefing, Butterworth had shown us pictures of them. One was black, two were Asian. They all looked very young and fresh-faced. Two were nineteen, the oldest twenty-two. It was depressing to think how they were wasting their own lives while simultaneously trying to destroy the lives of many others.

The problem we had was that Anil's killer was a white man of about forty so none of them could have murdered him, which meant we were hunting, or waiting to question, a number of people who couldn't actually have committed the crime.

Unless, of course, our witness Jane Kinnear was mistaken, which was a theory I put to Butterworth after the briefing, while we were sitting in his office in the Colindale Incident Suite.

'Could it be possible he's a pale-skinned Asian man? I mean, she had, what? A couple of seconds maximum to get a look at him?'

Butterworth shook his head. 'Anji was adamant. Miss Kinnear described him as white, and she must have got a pretty good look otherwise the killer wouldn't have bothered risking everything to go after her afterwards. We've got a lad from an outfit called Evo-fit going over to the safehouse this morning. Apparently their software has had great success in generating useable photofits of suspects, so we'll get a better idea of what our killer looks like when he's finished over there.'

I took a gulp from my fourth cup of coffee of the day, suppressing a yawn. 'OK, so let's assume the killer's white. He must be something to do with this terror cell, which means he was probably hired to carry out Anil Rahman's killing. Which brings us back to The Wraith. You didn't mention anything about him in the briefing. Have you heard any more from 5?'

Butterworth shook his head wearily. 'No. Right now The Wraith's involvement's just a rumour. We can't use it as a basis for a murder investigation.'

I thought for a moment. 'You know, sir, something feels very wrong about this whole thing. The witness's story, as I've heard it, just doesn't make sense. If you're carrying out a terror attack and you think there's a mole but you haven't given him any actual details about the attack, why torture him to ask him what he knows when you already know what he knows?'

'Jesus, you're confusing me now.'

'The point is, I'd like to go through everything with Jane Kinnear myself, just so I've got her version of events right.'

Butterworth sighed. 'I'll see what I can set up but even I don't know where she is at the minute, and I don't want you trying to find out either. I've heard what's gone on between you and Anji.'

'That's the past, sir, and I doubt she'd tell me where she is in any case.'

'OK. Well, I'm told Karim Khan will be ready to be interviewed in half an hour. I want you and Chris to lead it, and lean on him as hard as you can. You won't be surprised to know he's got himself a lawyer. None other than Rupert Elderwood.'

Rupert Elderwood was one of those eminent human rights lawyers who only ever seemed to be interested in the rights of criminals, and generally the nastier the better.

I grunted. 'Great. So I'm assuming Khan hasn't made a complaint against me then?'

'Not yet. But I'm sure he will at some point. How did it go with him earlier?'

'He resisted. I restrained him. And, sadly, he didn't give me anything useful.'

'I didn't think he would. That was good work earlier, though, catching him next door.'

It was so rare for me to get a compliment from Butterworth that I had no idea what to say.

'I think for simplicity's sake,' he continued, 'we're going to have to work on the angle that Karim Khan hired a professional hitman to kill Anil Rahman, but we need some kind of evidence of that, as well as evidence of who he's been meeting in the last couple of weeks. You said you recovered a phone of his?'

I nodded. 'Yeah, it's registered to a charity Khan's supposedly involved with called Without Walls, but we believe it's his main contact phone for family and friends. I've got Chris's team trying to triangulate his whereabouts at the times he slipped his surveillance team.'

'Christ, it's not a lot to go on, is it? Let them keep at it for now and let me know if anything comes up.'

Taking this as a dismissal, I drained my coffee and got up.

Outside Butterworth's office, the incident suite was relatively quiet. Most people were either out knocking on doors or leaning on informants in an effort to track down the three missing suspects, or they were at the two crime scenes searching for physical evidence that might give us the name of Anil Rahman's killer.

Chris and the two people helping him, DC Michelle Frith and DC Rob Mitchell, were clustered in a corner staring at computer screens. Chris stood up as I approached.

'As far as we can tell, Khan kept the phone you found under the bed on him most of the time,' he said. 'Michelle's going back through all the numbers he called or received calls from, but so far nothing suspicious has come up.'

'I didn't think anything would. It's his regular phone. He's not going to want to use it for any of his dodgier dealings. What I'm most interested in is where he went when he lost his surveillance – particularly in the last week. According to the surveillance log, he's unaccounted for for a total of eleven hours.'

'And me and Rob are on that as well. We're going back over all his movements when he had the phone with him. But let's hope the attack isn't that imminent because it's going to take a while, and even if we do find out where he was there's only a slim chance it's going to help us.'

'Maybe we'll get a lucky break,' I said. 'Have you gone through everything for the Khan interview? He'll be ready for questioning in half an hour.'

He nodded, and I told him who Khan had got for a lawyer.

Chris managed a hollow laugh. 'So preparing was a bit of a waste of time then. He won't talk with Elderwood briefing him.'

'You never know,' I said, but actually I did: Chris was right. There was no way Khan would tell us anything. But we still had to go through the process, however farcical.

I hadn't actually had a chance to prepare anything myself but right now I didn't have the energy for it. I needed some shut-eye so I told Chris I'd be back in a minute and made for the toilet.

I don't tend to sleep that well. I dream, and far too often the dreams are dark and disturbing, remnants of a past I don't like to talk about. Consequently, I tend to grab short catnaps when I can, and the best place for privacy when you're in a London nick is the toilet. Colindale's got nice ones too. They're new and the cubicles are comparatively spacious inside. They smell of mid-priced fragrance, which is always a change from the odours of human waste and ultra-cheap air fresheners you still get in most nicks.

I parked myself in the one at the end, settled back in the seat and shut my eyes. It tends to take me no more than a few seconds to conk out and then I'm gone for between five and ten minutes, never more than fifteen, and I can usually set the exact time with my internal alarm clock. This time, though, sleep wouldn't come, which I suppose was no great surprise given my caffeine intake over the last few hours, and the fact there was so much going on.

I gave it a couple of minutes then opened my eyes with a loud sigh. I was going to have to leave it for a few hours and hope another opportunity presented itself. In the meantime, before I left the peace and calm of the Colindale khazi, I took out my phone and checked my personal emails.

There was one from the scuba diving club I never attended reminding me about the liveaboard trip they had planned to Egypt in May which I wasn't going on, and another from Loch Fyne telling me I could get two main meals for the price of one Mondays to Thursdays for the rest of the month at selected restaurants, which wasn't a lot of use either.

I don't get a lot of emails. In truth, I don't have many friends. A lot of the time I prefer it that way, but sometimes the lack of a personal life gives me a twinge of regret, and maybe that was the reason why I opened up my spam folder where I could see I had three unread messages. I was expecting the latest offers of cheap Viagra and penis enlargement, or the chance to make several million pounds helping a Nigerian prince move money out of Lagos and into my bank account. Sure enough the first two messages were obvious scams, but the third was from a numbered hotmail account and it was the text in the subject box that immediately caught my attention: URGENT. FROM ANIL RAHMAN.

Anil Rahman. The man I hadn't spoken to, or had any communication with, in all that time, and who'd been murdered barely twelve hours earlier.

Frowning, I opened the message and read it through twice.

Hello Ray.

Long time no speak. I'm sure you remember me from our trip to the Caribbean. I hope you get this because we need to talk. Like I said above, URGENTLY. Can you meet me tomorrow outside the Coal Hole pub on Fleet Street?

Call the number below and if I don't answer leave a voicemail message saying: got your message matey see you there. Or if you can't make it, say you can't, and I'll come back to you from a different number with alternative dates. You need to hear what I have to say. Do not reply to this email address.

Sorry about all the cloak and dagger but you'll understand why when we speak.

Anil

The message had been sent yesterday at 6.53 a.m., so the meeting was supposed to have been today. Jesus, what had he wanted after all this time? If he'd found out my email address then he'd know I was in CT. Maybe it was to talk about the terror attack, but why to me? Why not his handler?

I sat there for a long minute, suddenly transported to a hot, steamy island all those years ago. A job that couldn't be talked about.

It couldn't be about that. Surely.

I took a deep breath and slowly got to my feet, deciding that, for the moment at least, it was best to keep this information to myself.

Seventeen

Jane

Time passes slowly when you're cooped up in a strange house with nothing to do. I like space. I think it's because of my upbringing in South Africa. I like to breathe fresh air and feel the sun on my face. Sometimes I can walk for miles and miles, relaxing in my own company and mulling over the world, so I'm not the best person to be told she can't go anywhere. I could have lived with it if there'd been books in the house, or use of the internet, but there were neither, and I felt cramped and uncomfortable with all those men around me.

Anji had left a little while earlier to pick up the guy who was going to help me put together a photofit of Anil's suspected killer. Because he couldn't be allowed to know our exact location, he was being collected from a prearranged meeting place a twenty-minute drive away and, according to Anji, he was going to have to wear a blindfold all the way here. 'It's all for your own protection,' she told me. 'No one's going to hurt you while you're under my care.' I believed her too. I could see she was a strong woman.

Although it looked like it might rain, the weather was holding so while I waited for her to come back with the photofit man I paced the garden, occasionally glancing wistfully towards the kids' climbing frame. My boys Matthew and Ryan were men now and I rarely saw them. I missed those early days when they were young children and we'd been a happy family back in Cape Town, before the discovery of Liesel's body on that hot summer's afternoon.

I now regretted opening up to Anji about what had happened. I'm a private person and I don't like to talk about the events that have helped shape my life. I have a therapist I see once a fortnight. She's the only person I talk to in any depth, but even she doesn't know the true extent of my secrets.

No one does.

After Liesel's murder there was no way we could stay in South Africa. Perhaps if it had just been the two of us we might have done, but not when there were kids involved. It was the realization that violent, determined criminals could get to all of us anywhere, even within the gilded confines of our gated community, that made our minds up – an irony, of course, that wasn't lost on me now as I sat here in this safehouse.

Joel was a successful IT consultant and thankfully his skills were in demand in most places in the world. He applied for jobs all over Europe and the States and eventually got one in Florida, paying good money.

It looked like it could be a fresh start for all of us, and I remember feeling excited at the time.

At first, everything was fine. The kids settled in at school and we rented a nice house in the suburbs. I couldn't work, which was a pain. I'm not the sort who likes to do nothing. But I used the time to get fit at the gym and make friends among the moms at school while all the time looking for a place to buy and turn into a real home now that Joel was earning again. In the end, that was all I ever really wanted. To have a home and family.

We'd been in the States over three years, and Joel had left the firm to start a consultancy business with one of his colleagues, when it happened. The company was making pretty good money, I knew that, because I was the one doing the accounts, but even so we were still living in rental accommodation, the purchase of the family home as far away as ever, which should have set the warning signs in motion.

One night Joel came home late from work, long after the kids had gone to bed, and I could tell immediately that something was wrong. The worry was etched deep into his face, seemingly ageing him years in the space of a day. I'd seen him stressed before, but never like this. He looked like a hunted animal.

I asked him what was wrong. He wouldn't say. I knew it wasn't a woman. Joel was one of those men who occasionally felt the need for an affair. I'd put up with it in the past because I had a young family and wanted to keep it together at all costs, and I knew that in his own strange way he loved me and would never leave me for someone else. Consequently we had an unspoken understanding that as long as he was discreet and never brought me any embarrassment, I wouldn't confront him on it.

So it had to be something else. I kept on at him, telling him I knew something was wrong, watching the way the fear seemed to consume him. He kept turning his back on me, demanding that I leave him alone, but eventually, when he could see I wasn't going to back down, he grabbed a glass from the kitchen sideboard, filled it nearly to the top with brandy, and took a huge gulp.

'I owe a lot of cash,' he said, without looking at me.

I took a deep breath, forcing myself to stay calm. 'How much?'

'It doesn't matter.'

'It *does* matter.' My voice was cold. 'How much?'

He sighed, refilling the glass. 'One hundred and fifty thousand dollars.'

The shock was like a physical blow. A hundred and fifty thousand dollars was a lot of money. The company cleared two hundred thousand in profit every year after all the outgoings, split between the two partners. That meant Joel owed a year and a half's salary, and that was before tax.

I rubbed a hand across my face, realizing I was beginning to sweat even though it wasn't a warm night.

'Who do you owe it to?' I asked quietly.

'The kind of man you don't want to owe money to,' was his reply.

It turned out that Joel hadn't been satisfied with what he'd made from his consultancy and had grown greedy. He'd found out somewhere about an investment opportunity in Mexico and become part of a syndicate that was investing in an as yet unbuilt block of vacation apartments in a town on the Pacific coast whose name I don't recall. For a put-in fee of a hundred and fifty grand Joel would own one eighth of the block and would, according to the sales pitch, quadruple his money by the time all the apartments in this supposedly up-and-coming resort sold at the asking price, which he'd been told was an inevitability.

Joel knew that if he'd come to me about it in the first place I'd have bawled him out and told him not to go anywhere near such a risky venture. I was an accountant after all, and not only good with figures but also responsible with money. The bank clearly felt the same way because they pretty much laughed him out of the place when he went to see them about getting a loan, while his partner vetoed any attempt to divert money out of the business into the consortium.

Their reactions should have told Joel everything he needed to know about his supposedly rock-solid investment opportunity. It was a measure of his pig-headed stubbornness and misplaced confidence in his own judgement that, rather than walk away and concentrate on growing his company, he'd approached the worst person possible for a loan.

Frank Mellon was a thug masquerading as a businessman with known links to organized crime. He ran a number of companies, mainly in construction, and Joel knew him because he'd organized IT consultancy for one of them. We'd even gone out for a client dinner with Mellon and his wife one evening during which Mellon had made it known, just by his look, that he wanted to have sex with me. He was a brutal-looking man in his early fifties with slicked-back silver hair and a menacing, almost sexual charisma, and I didn't want anything to do with him. Although I'd had the odd fling, I've always been a one-man woman, and when he tried to make contact with me afterwards I cut him dead. Eventually he got the message. For all I knew Mellon had links with the people selling the Mexican investment opportunity. Either way he agreed to lend Joel the money he needed, taking a 25 per cent stake in our consultancy company as collateral against non-repayment.

It doesn't take a genius to work out the next part of the story. The investment opportunity was a scam. The people behind it, having sent regular email updates on progress for a few months, suddenly disappeared, leaving behind empty offices and no sign of any forwarding address. The land in Mexico – a strip of wasteground just back from the coastline – hadn't been built on and, it turned out, hadn't actually belonged to the company anyway. Joel had been royally ripped off, and now he had to pay back the money.

By the time he'd finished talking we were in the lounge and Joel was on his knees, sobbing his heart out at the foot of the sofa, while I looked on, stony-faced. 'I'm sorry, Janey,' he kept repeating, fighting to control his sobs as he gripped my hands in his. 'I'm so, so sorry.'

He reminded me of my father then. My kind, weak, pathetic father who'd stood by all those years unable to summon the strength to protect me from the tyranny of my mother's belt. I was furious but, in spite of all he'd done, I pitied him too.

I told him he was a fool. He told me he knew that and would never make the same mistake again as long as he lived.

I knew he would. Men like him make the same mistake time and time again. It's as if they take a drug that makes them forget their weaknesses and vastly over-estimate their strengths. They never think through the consequences of their actions because they don't exist in the real world.

But one of us had to and, even though Joel was twelve years my senior, it was always going to have to be me.

'So Frank Mellon takes half our share in the company then,' I said. 'That should cover the money you owe him. You might have to get another job to cover the shortfall in the money coming in, but there's no way round that.'

That was when he gave me another shock.

'The company's in trouble,' he said.

I stared at him aghast. 'What do you mean?'

'We lost a couple of big deals I thought we were going to get and now we've got . . .' He paused, presumably summoning up the strength to continue. 'We've got cashflow problems. The rate things are going we're going to have trouble making any profit at all this year.'

It felt like my whole world was collapsing, all I'd strived for crashing down over my shoulders. I felt upset, humiliated. Defeated.

Joel looked up at me, imploringly. 'I can't believe it's turned out like this. I only wanted to protect our family. What are we going to do, baby? What are we going to do?'

What I should have done was kick him out there and then, and got on with my life without him. By God, I wanted to as well. It would have meant the boys and I having to return to South Africa but that had to be better than being trapped here helpless while the man I married systematically drove us into poverty and debt.

But I didn't kick him out. He played every card in the book, promising he'd change, telling me how much he loved the children and wanted to keep us together for their sakes as much as ours. He was persuasive too, but that was because he'd always been a good salesman, and a charmer too, just like my father. And I have to admit, in spite of everything, he was a good dad to our sons. They needed him as much as they needed me.

I sat there for a long time, allowing myself to calm down and think straight. There's always a way out of any situation, however hopeless it seems, as long as you use your head and don't give in. And I don't give in. Not to anything or anyone.

Finally I broke the silence. 'I'll speak to Frank Mellon. Maybe I can find a way to stall him awhile, while you start thinking how you're going to turn your company around and what other jobs you can apply for.'

'How are *you* going to stall a man like Frank Mellon, Janey?' he asked, with an almost touching naivety.

'I'll find a way,' I told him. 'I'll find a way.'

By rights I should hate men. They've done me a lot of harm over the years, but just like I don't give in to despondency, so I don't give in to bitterness either.

There was a swing attached to the climbing frame and, after pacing the garden awhile deep in thought, I sat down on it, letting myself swing gently as I came back to the present. I saw that the sleazy detective Jeffs was standing outside the back door smoking a cigarette. I wondered how long he'd been out there watching me. When I'm thinking – particularly when I'm thinking about my past – I become completely immersed. It's almost as if I'm reliving events, sometimes blow for blow.

Jeffs gave me a wave and I nodded back without much enthusiasm, hoping I'd made it clear earlier that I didn't want to talk to him. But it seemed he was one of those men whose skins are so thick they either don't know when they're not wanted or don't care, because he strolled over anyway.

He stopped a couple of feet away, just at the limits of my personal space.

'Fancy a smoke?' he asked with a gap-toothed smile.

I should have told him no but I did fancy one, so I took one off him, accepting his light.

He immediately started talking about how unusual this job was for him, this being the first time he'd had to babysit someone since he'd started in counter-terrorism, but I wasn't really listening. Occasionally I made vague noises or gestures to suggest I was, but otherwise I kept my mouth shut and avoided eye contact. Rude, I know, but I'd long ago ceased being a people pleaser.

'There's no need to be so standoffish, Miss Kinnear,' he said abruptly. 'I'm just trying to be friendly, you know. None of us wants to be here.'

He was looking at me sharply as he spoke and I could tell straight away that, behind closed doors, he was a bully. The kind who preys on women by making them feel unsure of themselves.

'I'm not being standoffish,' I told him, getting to my feet and looking him right in the eye this time. 'But I don't feel like talking right now. I witnessed two double murders last night. I'm still in shock. So please, just leave me alone.'

He put his hands up in a gesture of conciliation. 'Look, I didn't mean it like that. I just like to talk, that's all. I'm sorry if I offended you.'

He didn't look sorry at all and I recognized it as an obvious attempt to make me feel guilty. But there wasn't much I could do about it so I told him it was no problem, then finished my cigarette, stubbed it out on the lawn, and picked up the butt.

'You don't need to pick that up,' he said with a leery smile. 'No one's going to arrest you for littering.'

'I'm tidy,' I said, and headed back to the house, conscious that he was walking with me and still talking, explaining that he needed to make a call to his bosses on the satellite phone to give them an update – apparently, either he or Anji had to check in every six hours to let the CT high command know that everything was all right, such was the seriousness of the threat level against me.

'But we're going to keep you safe,' he assured me as he reached the back door and opened it for me, standing aside to let me through. 'You can be sure of that.'

And then, as I stepped past him and he followed me in, getting far too close, I felt a hand brush ever so lightly across my behind.

I'm usually very, very good at keeping my temper in check – and God knows, I've had enough practice over the years. But this was the last straw. It was the utter disrespect shown by someone who so clearly should have known better that pushed me over the edge.

Swinging round in one fluid movement, I drove the heel of my hand into the base of his nose, careful not to strike him hard enough to cause permanent damage, but enough to hurt. At the same time, I grabbed his wrist with my free hand and pushed my thumb into the base of his palm, right on the main pressure point.

Caught out by the explosion of sudden violence, Jeffs staggered backwards, blood seeping out of one nostril, his knees buckling under him as I kept up the pressure on his palm, causing him the kind of pain that left him utterly helpless.

'Leave me the fuck alone,' I hissed.

'Please let go,' he wailed, his eyes wide with a mixture of shock and fear.

The anger left me just as quickly as it had erupted and I released my grip, watching as he staggered back out into the garden, wiping the blood from his face.

'Jane. Seamus. What the hell's going on?'

I turned round and saw Anji standing at the other end of the hall, alongside a nervous-looking man in a suit and glasses. The front door was open behind them. I didn't know if they'd actually seen me strike the blow to the nose but they'd definitely seen the aftermath.

This was not good. Not good at all.

I pulled a suitably distraught expression, looking on the verge of tears as I walked towards her. 'I'm sorry, Anji, I just, er . . .' I ran a hand across my face, letting some tears come. 'We had a misunderstanding. I think I might have overreacted.' I considered saying something else but decided against it. An attractive woman like Anji would know what sort of man Jeffs was, even if he tried to hide it at work.

She glanced briefly in Jeffs's direction, a disapproving expression on her face, then took me gently by the arm. 'You'd better come in here,' she said, steering me towards the kitchen. 'This is Charlie Foulds by the way. He's going to be working with you to build a picture of the man you saw at the house last night.'

I gave Foulds an embarrassed smile, which he returned, but as I was ushered into the kitchen it was DC Seamus Jeffs I was more interested in and I sneaked a final glance in his direction.

He was holding a handkerchief to his face with one hand while rubbing the palm of the other against the material of his cheap suit trousers. But it was the look in his eyes that concerned me. It was no longer one of shock or fear.

It was one of suspicion.

Eighteen

Ray

Minus his burkha, our suspected terrorist Karim Khan was an out-of-shape middle-aged Asian man with pudgy features who looked younger than he did in the photos. He was dressed in an open-necked white shirt with a vest visible underneath. Thick black hair sprouted out from under the sleeves and the collar like some kind of infestation. He was, it has to be said, one of the hairiest men I'd ever seen, except on his head, where only a handful of long greying hairs remained. He was sweating and looked wary.

Rupert Elderwood, on the other hand, looked just as you'd expect a wealthy, privately educated socialist lawyer and occasional TV personality to look. Well groomed; handsome in a debonair sort of way, with a lustrous mane of blond hair that was just beginning to turn a distinguished silver; and utterly pretentious. He smelled nice, though, and his expensive after-shave did a good job of cancelling out Khan's more earthy odour. I also saw he'd put a couple of feet between himself and his client. He might have enjoyed the role of defender of the world's scumbags in the face of the cruel all-powerful establishment – in other words, you and me – but he evidently didn't like to get too close to them.

I'd sat opposite him a couple of times in interviews over the years and had always found him an arsehole of the highest order.

Now I recognize that all suspects have a right to legal represent-ation, regardless of how heinous the crimes they're accused of are, but when someone's obviously guilty – and take my word for it, most of the time they are – I don't see how these defence lawyers can do it and still sleep at night. They're always banging on about a criminal's human rights, but they never seem to give a shit about those of their victims. I remember dating a woman once whose ex was a barrister. He'd represented paedophiles on several occasions, all of whom had ended up convicted due to the weight of evidence against them, and I asked her how they'd both justified it, given that they had kids together. We tried not to think about it, had been her reply. I told her that the kids being raped by her ex's clients probably tried not to think about it either, but that didn't make it any better. We broke up soon after that.

'I'm surprised to see you here, DI Mason,' said Elderwood in his not-very-good mockney accent. 'My client says you assaulted him during his arrest, and we'll be making a formal complaint.'

I smiled. 'Well, I have to say I'm not surprised to see you here, Mr Elderwood. And let's be honest, he would say that, wouldn't he? Now I'm going to do you both a favour and be up front with you. Mr Khan, you're in a lot of trouble. We've arrested you on suspicion of conspiracy to murder, and making preparations to carry out a terrorist act. We also have reason to believe that you've been involved in organizing an imminent attack on the UK mainland.'

'What evidence have you to back these allegations, DI Mason?' demanded Elderwood, cutting straight through the bullshit.

'Plenty,' I said. Which wasn't exactly true, but luckily I was experienced in making a little go a long way.

In interviews, the idea is to build a case against the suspect piece by piece. You only show your cards one at a time, slowly increasing the pressure as you back your suspect into a corner. It can often take hours but you've just got to be patient, even when time's short. Sometimes it works and they break. Sometimes they don't. Looking at Khan right now, I had a feeling that if we played it properly, he'd break.

You start simple. 'Do you know a Mr Anil Rahman?' I asked him.

Khan exchanged glances with Elderwood before answering: 'No comment.'

I feigned surprise. 'It's a simple enough question, Mr Khan. Either you know him or you don't.'

'No comment.'

I looked at Chris, who was sitting next to me, and we exchanged wry smiles, as if we'd been expecting this reaction from Khan and were unfazed by it. In front of me was the file

MI5 had prepared on Khan. The cover clearly identified it as a secret service document, which was deliberate. Next to the file was a recorder with a tape inside containing recordings of those conversations between Anil and Khan that directly or indirectly implicated Khan in the alleged terrorist plot.

I pressed the play button on the tape recorder and for the next half an hour we went through all the evidence we had against him, starting with the innocuous conversations where Khan would ask Anil what he could bring to the cause, whether he'd be prepared to lead a team of martyrs in an attack against unbelievers – what he called 'the kafir' – and where he railed against the decadence of the west and its brutality against Muslims, and spoke of how he would play a part in bringing down the government with a series of strikes that would leave the UK on its knees. Khan also admitted on tape that he'd met with senior IS figures during his last trip to Syria but, though Anil could be heard prompting him for details, he didn't give that much away.

All of this, of course, could easily be construed as the ramblings of a fantasist. But then we moved on to the conversation between Khan and Anil in which Khan instructed Anil to go to an address in Athens and pay twenty thousand euros in cash for a consignment of five AK-47 assault rifles and twelve grenades. Khan then told him to drive the weapons across the continent to an address in Belgium.

'Can you confirm that it's your voice on the tape recording, Mr Khan, telling Anil Rahman that these weapons will – and I emphasize the word *will* – be used in an attack on the kafir?' I asked, knowing that this was pretty damning stuff.

'No comment,' replied Khan for what felt like the hundredth time, but I could see he'd been shaken by the fact that we had him on tape saying all this.

And that was one of the things that had been worrying me during the course of this interview. Although he tried hard to hide it, Karim Khan had looked genuinely shocked when he heard that Anil Rahman was an informant – which suggested he might not actually be the person behind Anil's death.

Chris slipped a piece of paper from out of the MI5 file. 'This is a handwritten note containing the addresses where the weapons were to be picked up from and delivered to, given by you to Anil Rahman. Can you confirm that this is your handwriting?'

'No comment,' said Khan, although he couldn't help glancing at the note as he spoke.

Chris stared him down. Neither of us was playing good cop today. 'It has your DNA on it and the handwriting matches samples taken from your house this morning, so I'm going to ask you one more time. Is this your handwriting?'

'No comment.'

I banged my fist down on the table with enough of an impact to startle both Khan and Elderwood. 'I've had enough of this. Ten days ago, Mr Khan, you told Anil Rahman that a terror attack was about to happen, and that it was best the two of you didn't meet again for a few weeks until everything had calmed down. You stated that you'd be going, and I quote, "off the radar". Because, and I quote again, "the police are going to be after us for this". Now, I'm going to tell you this, Mr Khan,' I continued, pointing my finger at him accusingly. 'If there is a terrorist attack in the next week or so and people die because you refused to cooperate with us, then you are going to go to prison for the rest of your life. No parole. No nothing. All you'll have to keep you company are the four walls of your cell until you finally die old and forgotten, because the world, your family, everyone will have moved on without you.'

'How dare you harangue my client like this, DI Mason,' said Elderwood angrily. 'If you want this interview to continue, then please do your job and ask civil questions rather than make angry, baseless accusations.'

'And remember, he won't be the one going to prison,' I told Khan, pointing a finger at Elderwood. 'He'll be going home in his nice big car to his nice big house while you're rotting behind bars.'

'Stop this or this interview ends right now,' shouted Elderwood.

I stopped. I let my last remark hang in the air for a few seconds, then addressed Elderwood. 'I think it would be a good idea, Mr Elderwood, if you let your client know the gravity of the situation.'

'My client has told me he's innocent of any wrongdoing. That's good enough for me.'

I changed tack, because I could see Khan was rattled.

'Where were you last night, Mr Khan?'

'At home,' he said, looking surprised and actually answering a question for the first time.

Elderwood put a hand on Khan's shoulder – a silent warning to watch what he was saying.

'Alone?'

'Yes. Yes.'

You've got to throw the cat among the pigeons sometimes. 'Who did you hire to murder Anil Rahman?'

Khan stared at me aghast, then turned to Elderwood. 'I didn't kill anyone. I didn't know Anil was dead. I—'

'It's all right, Mr Khan,' said Elderwood firmly before addressing me. 'Are you saying that Anil Rahman, your MI5 informant, is dead?'

'Yes. He was murdered alongside his wife last night.'

'You know the rules, DI Mason. You should have shared that information with me. And what evidence do you have to suggest that my client was involved?'

I had a dilemma now. If I told the two of them about our witness, and what she'd seen and heard, then I put her in even more danger. It might even be that she had to spend the rest of her life in witness protection, and I wouldn't wish that on anyone. But right now I figured I didn't have much choice.

'We have a witness to the murders who overheard the killer questioning Anil Rahman on what he knew about an impending terror attack, the attack we strongly believe your client is involved in organizing. The attack your client will be held personally responsible for if he doesn't tell us what he knows, and it goes ahead.'

I watched Khan out of the corner of my eye as I spoke and saw that he was making a gargantuan effort to maintain an inscrutable expression, and doing a pretty good job of it. He was still sweating though.

Sweating a lot.

Elderwood gave me a look that managed to be dismissive,

haughty, sceptical and amused all at the same time, which was no mean feat. 'Can you tell me something, DI Mason? If MI5 has been expending so much effort on finding evidence of wrongdoing by my client he has presumably been placed under surveillance. Would that be correct?'

He had me there. We can't lie in an interview. Do that and it doesn't matter how guilty your suspect is, he's walking. 'He has been placed under surveillance, yes, although he's been employing a variety of sophisticated anti-surveillance techniques.'

'Was he under surveillance yesterday?'

'As far as I know, yes.'

'So was he at home last night?'

'We believe he was, yes.'

'Then he's obviously not your killer. Is he?'

'He may not have pulled the trigger, Mr Elderwood, but that doesn't mean he wasn't involved.' But I was floundering, and we both knew it.

'In light of these new allegations, I need a few moments alone with my client. Can you suspend the interview please?'

I nodded to Chris, informed the interview recording tape of the time and what was happening, and we got up and left the room.

When we were out in the corridor, Chris looked at me.

'I don't think that went very well,' he said, with admirable understatement.

I sighed. 'The problem is we've got no hard evidence against him for anything. I'm telling you something else as well. I don't think he killed Anil or his wife.'

'He looked shocked when we told him Anil was dead, didn't he?'

'Yeah, and he wasn't putting it on either. I'd bet money he didn't have anything to do with it.'

'So who the hell did?'

I tried to put the pieces of the puzzle together in my head. 'Logically, the murder's got to be something to do with Anil's work for MI5 and what he'd found out about the terror attack. The witness specifically said that Anil's killer was questioning him about it.' I gave a grunt of frustration. 'We're missing something.'

'Whatever it is, Khan's not going to tell us.'

I made a decision. Looking round to check that there was no one else in the corridor, I leaned in close to Chris and said, 'I heard from Anil.'

Chris frowned, surprised. 'What do you mean? When?'

'He sent me an email. Two days ago.' Keeping my voice low, I gave him the details. 'I can't for the life of me think what he wanted to talk to me about. If he'd found out anything about the attack he'd have told his handler at 5 about it, not me.'

'But what else could it be about?'

'Christ knows,' I said.

Chris frowned, the worry lines etched deep into his face. 'I can't afford for what happened with Anil and us to get out, Ray. It would kill Charlotte, and if I ended up behind bars, who'd look after her?'

'Don't worry,' I said quietly, 'nothing will get out. No one's seen the email. It's in my spam folder.'

'But you'll look like a suspect if it does and you don't say anything.'

I shrugged. 'I'll just have to risk that.'

He still looked anxious so I gave his arm a gentle squeeze, suddenly feeling protective of him and his family. 'It's going to be all right, mate. Let's just forget about it and get on with the case.'

He gave me a half smile but I don't think he was entirely convinced.

But then he had so much more to lose than me.

Ten minutes later we were back in the interview room with Khan and Elderwood, and straight away I knew we had a problem. Khan had composed himself and looked far more confident. He'd even stopped sweating. Obviously Elderwood had managed to persuade him not to cooperate. The lawyer gave me one of his supercilious smiles, which was another bad sign.

'My client would like it put on the record that he has nothing to do with any planned terrorist attack on either UK soil or in any other sovereign country. Yes, Mr Khan's been to Syria twice, but both times as part of aid convoys on behalf of the registered charity he's involved in, Without Walls. During those visits, his work involved distributing food and other essential supplies to refugees, and he categorically denies meeting with any figures, senior or otherwise, from Islamic State. He may have spoken in anger to your informant about getting weapons to carry out attacks but I'm afraid Mr Khan is something of a fantasist. He has no contracts with any terror organization, nor access to weapons of any description.'

I smiled. 'Well, that's very nicely put, Mr Elderwood, as befits a man of your education.' I turned my gaze on Khan. 'Is that a fair summation of your position, Mr Khan?'

He nodded. 'Yes.'

'So tell me, just out of interest. Why are you sleeping in your loft with at least three mobile phones? And why did you escape through a specially designed hatch into your neighbour's house and then attempt to flee in a burkha when the police arrived to question you?'

'Because I was scared,' he said belligerently. 'I knew the police were following me. I thought they were out to get me. And after the way you tried to throttle me, can you blame me?' He motioned theatrically to the near-enough non-existent marks round his neck where I'd been strangling him earlier. It made me wish I'd finished the job.

It was all bullshit too. At the very least Khan was guilty of helping to organize a terrorist attack. And the thing was, everyone in that room knew it. Khan himself, that conscience-free slime-ball Elderwood, Chris, me. But bullshit or not, I knew we weren't going to get any further, so I suspended the interview – ignoring Elderwood's predictable demands that we either charge his client or let him go – and stood up, pointing a finger at Khan. 'If any act of terrorism occurs in this country at any time in the coming months, I will look for any connection, however tenuous, with you, and I will find it. And then I will fucking bury you for it. You understand?'

Elderwood was on his feet in an instant, his face red with righteous anger. 'How dare you speak to my client like that! I will have you suspended for this.'

I turned my gaze on him, and he momentarily flinched because he could see that I wasn't afraid, and whatever power he possessed had reached its limits. 'And I'll bury you as well,' I told him. 'Be absolutely certain of it.'

Nineteen

The year was 2003. The location was East Cay in the Turks and Caicos Islands.

I was still a soldier working in military intelligence operating out of a base in Cyprus when I was seconded to MI6 to take part in a classified operation.

It was a sting, and a delicate one at that. It had come to the attention of the US and British intelligence services – already working flat out in the aftermath of 9/11 – that a minor member of the Saudi royal family, one Zayed bin Azir who was always referred to as 'the Sheikh', was a secret al-Qaeda sympathizer interested in buying a quantity of military-grade nerve gas for use in a terror attack against the west. He'd made some very discreet contacts with various sources and let it be known that money was no object if the right product was available.

This was where Anil came in. As far as I knew at the time,

The Witness

Anil worked directly for MI6, but this was never actually spelled out for me. Anyway, he was posing as a shady Eton-educated Qatari businessman with links to corrupt officials in the Syrian government who could supply a limited quantity of sarin in aerosol form. All undercover operatives require a legend – a plausible backstory that can be checked by the criminals he or she is targeting, and which stands up to detailed scrutiny, so that the target can feel confident they are who they say they are. I don't know what kind of legend 6 had provided Anil with but it was obviously a good one, because he and the Sheikh had already met twice before I became involved. The third meeting was arranged for the Turks and Caicos Islands, a British territory in the Caribbean, where they were to discuss the final terms and Anil would supply a sealed sample of the gas in aerosol form as a demonstration of intent. The reason the Sheikh had chosen the Turks and Caicos for the meeting was the lack of border security, allowing him to sail in and out with little risk of customs checks.

Because of Saudi Arabia's position as an ally in the war on terror, and the fact that the Sheikh was connected to the Saudi ruling family, everything had to be set up very carefully and only a handful of people knew the details of the sting itself. The plan was for Anil to rendezvous on the Sheikh's yacht, bringing with him a fake sample of sarin – because of its toxicity the Sheikh would be unable to test it outside a sealed lab so he would have no idea it was fake until it was too late – in exchange for ten thousand dollars in cash. Because Anil had been searched thoroughly for recording devices both times he'd met the Sheikh, another way had to be found to gain the evidence needed against him, and this was supplied by the CIA.

In the previous month, the Sheikh had befriended a high-class French escort girl in Marseilles and she was now travelling with him on his yacht (it never ceases to amaze me how many fundamentalists give in to the sins of the flesh without actually acknowledging the hypocrisy of their actions). Except she wasn't an escort girl. She was a deep-cover CIA agent we only ever knew as Alpha, and she'd managed to smuggle a miniature camera attached to a tape recorder on to the yacht. Because the tape recorder wasn't actually transmitting anything live it meant that it wouldn't be picked up by even the most sophisticated bug finder. All that was needed was for the agent to hide the tape recorder and camera in a place where they weren't going to be found in a detailed fingertip search, but where they could provide audio and video of the whole meeting, and then retrieve them at some point afterwards.

Once the authorities had received word that the evidence was there and the Sheikh's yacht was back in international waters, it would be discreetly intercepted by the US Navy, and he'd be secretly detained away from the prying eyes of the media while the US and Saudi Arabia decided what to do with him.

My role was to act as one of Anil's two bodyguards for the sting which, because it was taking place on British territory, would be British-run.

The whole thing should have been simple and straightforward. Of course, it turned out to be anything but.

East Cay is a largely uninhabited stretch of barren rock peppered with tiny bays and inlets sitting in crystal-blue waters twenty kilometres south-east of Grand Turk Island, making it a perfect location for a clandestine meeting. Anil had been given the use of a six-berth motor yacht to make him look like a successful businessman and he clearly enjoyed playing the part. He was, as I said before, something of a narcissist but he also had a lack of fear about what he was doing which was either rank stupidity or true bravery. Looking back on it now, I think it was probably the latter.

The meeting was set for 8.30 in the morning, and the mercury was already pushing twenty-eight. I remember that it was a truly glorious day without a cloud in the sky. In fact, I was feeling pretty good as I drove the boat through the crystal-clear waters of the Caribbean. Because of the sensitivity of the target, the secrecy of the op, and the desire to avoid a confrontation at all costs, it was decided we would all be operating without guns. I'd never been on a job like this before, particularly in such incredible surroundings, but I wasn't unduly nervous, even without a gun, because there was no reason to suspect that anything would go wrong.

As we came round the headland into the bay where the meeting was to take place, we saw a solitary double-decker yacht about twenty metres long anchored a little way offshore.

'It's smaller than I was expecting,' I said to Anil, who was standing next to me, dressed in a white linen suit and suede loafers, looking like something out of a Wham! video from the 1980s. In his right hand was a small attaché case containing the fake sample of sarin.

Anil laughed. 'That's just his runaround,' he said, and I thought that even his accent – a mix of Gulf Arab and mid-Atlantic

English – made him sound like some kind of international playboy. 'It goes on the back of the main yacht. The one over there.' He pointed to what looked like a small cruise ship anchored a couple of miles further out to sea. 'This guy's got serious money, I promise.'

I was wearing a headset through which I had a direct line to the op's controller, a senior MI6 executive with the slightly unnerving name of Simon Pratt, who was running things from a poky office back in Grand Turk. 'The meet looks set to be on the smaller vessel,' I said into the mike. 'Can you confirm that Alpha has it wired for sound and visual?'

'Affirmative,' said Pratt. 'Main cabin has both.'

'We're two minutes from destination so we're going off-line imminently.'

That, I suppose, was my only concern. The fact that no one would be able to listen into this meeting. That we would be completely on our own.

I removed the headset and stowed it in a cubbyhole beneath the wheel, slowing up as we approached the boat. I spotted Alpha lying on a lounger on the sun deck at the rear of the boat, dressed in a red bikini. I'd never met her before and I gave her just the briefest of glances as we came past. She didn't acknowledge me so I have no idea if she was nervous or not, but seeing her made me wary because I couldn't understand why the Sheikh would bring his new lover to a highly illegal business meeting. Why not leave her on the main boat? It didn't make sense, and even then I didn't like situations that didn't immediately make sense.

'What's she doing here?' I whispered to Anil out of the corner of my mouth.

'I've no idea,' he said. 'It's not our problem.'

I wasn't so sure about that but I didn't say anything. We were too close now.

A big Arab guy in a suit appeared at the front of the boat and I cut the engine and threw him the rope, waiting while he tied it. Two more Arabs in suits appeared behind him, one of whom was smaller and older than the other two with an undertaker's grim demeanour. He looked to be the one in charge.

'Hello, Anil,' he said. 'Good to see you again.'

'Good to see you too, Rashid,' Anil replied with a big mega-watt smile. 'Is the boss on board?'

'He is. You know the routine.'

One of the big Arabs helped him on to the boat and immediately patted him down while the other ran a handheld RF bug detector over his clothes.

'I need my bodyguards with me,' said Anil, pointing at us.

'Why?' demanded Rashid. His face was like stone. 'This is a private meeting. The Sheikh doesn't want any outsiders knowing his business.'

Anil was smooth but insistent. 'I'd just prefer them on board, Rashid. They don't have to be in the room. The Sheikh has you guys, I need mine. And I trust these men with my life.'

Rashid eyed us suspiciously, and we met his gaze. It wasn't essential we were on the Sheikh's boat with Anil. Obviously it was preferable so we could see what was going on, but we'd agreed beforehand that if they didn't want us there, we wouldn't push the matter.

'Are they armed?' Rashid asked Anil.

Anil shook his head. 'No, course not. Are your guys?'

Rashid shrugged, ignoring the question. 'Sure, they can come aboard as long as they stay out here.'

With that agreed, the other bodyguard and I stepped up on to the boat where we were both frisked in turn and given the de-bugging treatment. One of the Arabs took our phones.

'You both stay here,' Rashid told us, giving me a look that let me know in no uncertain terms what he thought of me.

I don't enjoy being treated like dirt, but I'm also a professional. To me this was just a job and something I therefore had to put up with.

'I'll come out in fifteen minutes, just to let you guys know it's all OK,' said Anil. He was smiling as he spoke but it looked a little strained.

He gave me a final nod and then Rashid flicked a switch on the cabin wall and a pair of tinted double doors opened, releasing a blast of artificially cold air. Beyond the doors, I just had time to see a spacious yet dimly lit inside area done out in expensive mahogany before Anil, Rashid and the two Arabs disappeared inside and the doors clicked shut behind them.

My fellow bodyguard's name was Chris Leavey. We'd only met two days earlier, although I'd seen him a couple of times before back on the base in Cyprus. He was four years older than me and, as a sergeant, was the senior of the two of us. He walked over to the tinted glass and looked inside.

'I can't see a damn thing in there,' he said.

'I think that's deliberate,' I told him.

'So what are we meant to do?' he said, stepping away. 'Just stand here?'

'I guess so,' I said, looking out across the turquoise sea and thinking I'd love to have a boat like this one and sail it round the Caribbean islands. 'There's not much else we can do.'

So that's what we did. Stood and waited.

Five minutes passed. Then ten. Then fifteen.

Anil didn't emerge.

Chris and I exchanged glances.

'I think it might be time to go in,' I said.

But before we had a chance to do anything I heard movement and two of the Arab bodyguards appeared from separate sides of the boat so that they had us penned in, except this time they were holding guns. They kept a safe distance away, pointing the guns at our heads.

I'd been in the military for five years at that point in time. I'd been trained with the best of them, had taken part in dangerous reconnaissance missions in Kosovo and Afghanistan, but I'd never fired a shot in anger, nor faced down a man with a gun. I'll be honest: I was terrified. Especially as the guy pointing his weapon at me had the dead eyes of a killer. I knew Chris had seen more action than me – he'd told me about a firefight he'd been involved in in Afghanistan the previous year – but he wasn't moving either. We'd been caught off guard and we were paying the price.

The gunmen didn't say anything, not a word, and I remember I could hear my heart beating in my chest. Suddenly the beauty of this place no longer mattered. Nothing did. Except staying alive.

The double doors opened and Rashid stood there, his expression tense. There was no sign of Anil.

'Come in,' he said in English, before barking an order in

Arabic to the gunmen. I knew a little Arabic from my time in intelligence but I didn't catch any of it.

The gunmen ushered us inside, following behind as the doors closed. Rashid led us into a spacious lounge area with a huge plasma TV on the far wall and sofas running down both walls.

Anil was sitting in a large tub chair with a third gunman standing behind him, pushing the barrel of his gun – a SIG Sauer semi-automatic – into the back of his skull. He was visibly shaking and staring straight ahead. He had one hand down by his side but the other – his right – was resting palm down on the table in front of him. It took me a second to spot that a knife had been driven straight through it, pinning it to the table. Also on the table was the foot-long aerosol cylinder can that supposedly contained the sarin gas. It was on its side. The locked seal at the top had been broken, and since everyone in the room was very much alive – at least for the moment – it was obvious that it contained not a drop of anything harmful.

Opposite Anil on a long curved sofa that looked like it cost a year of my wages, a bearded Arab man of about thirty-five dressed in an open-necked shirt and suit trousers reclined. He had a thick gold chain round his neck and another round his wrist and he was smoking a cigarette. His expression was sadistically playful.

'Welcome, my friends,' he said, waving an arm as we were led up to the table. 'Come over, come over.'

When we were standing opposite him, behind the table, just a few feet from Anil, Rashid moved to one side.

'Do you know who I am?' asked the Sheikh, still smiling as he approached the table.

We both said we didn't.

'Well, let me tell you. I'm a man who doesn't like to be treated like a fool. And that's what your employer's done. He has tried to sell me something that is fake. And I'm trying to work out why he's done that. He says it is because he's a liar and a cheat, and now he's very, very sorry and can I let him go, now that he's been punished. But I'm not so sure.' He pulled on the cigarette then stubbed it out on Anil's prone forearm, smiling as Anil let out a strangled moan through the corner of his mouth, trying hard not to cry out. The Sheikh smiled again before turning to us. 'Do you know what it is your employer's trying to sell me? Do you?'

'We're just bodyguards,' I told him. 'We do a job and that's it.'

'And yet this guy' – he pointed at a shaking Anil – 'this piece of fucking shit, he says he trusts you with his life. So you know what I'm thinking? I'm thinking you're all in on this.'

We had a choice now. We could bluff, say we were police, or we could continue to act like we were the hired help.

Chris spoke first, opting for the latter. 'I don't know what you lot are doing here but it's got fuck all to do with us. Why don't you give us our phones back, we'll leave and that'll be that?'

The Sheikh glanced across at Rashid, and I saw Rashid give a barely perceptible shake of the head.

That's when I knew we weren't getting off this boat.

'Listen, Zayed,' said Anil desperately. 'It's not what you think. I was told this was the right stuff. I've been duped. I'll get you some more—'

'I don't give a fuck!' screamed the Sheikh, banging his fist down on the table. And then he was looking beyond us, to the men who were still pointing their guns at our heads, his face a snarl of spoilt anger. 'Do it!'

But it was Chris who reacted first. He swung round in a blur of movement and I saw him yank the gun arm of the man behind him and duck down at the same time, slamming his head into the guy's chest.

A gunshot echoed round the confines of the cabin, shockingly loud, and then I too was swinging round, acting entirely on instinct. Thankfully the gunman behind me had been shocked by the suddenness of Chris's resistance and had swung his weapon round to point at him. He'd already pulled the trigger by the time I leapt on him, grabbing him by the wrist of his gun hand and slamming my head into his face.

The whole room seemed to erupt in noise then as shots came from everywhere. I knew I was a target so I used my weight and momentum to send the two of us crashing to the floor, wrestling the gunman round so he was between me and whoever else was firing, trying to use him as a human shield.

It took me a second to realize that he wasn't resisting. The gun dropped from his hand on to the floor and, though he was still alive, I saw he'd been shot in the neck and was losing blood fast. I didn't give him a second's thought. This was all about survival. Keeping his body in front of me, I felt around on the floor for the gun, grabbed the handle and swung it up in front of me as my finger found the trigger.

Everything was happening incredibly fast. I could see that Chris had been hit in the leg. He was lying down a few feet away, while the gunman he'd been grappling with was no longer moving. The third gunman, the one who'd had his gun pointed at the back of Anil's head, was standing almost directly above Chris. It looked as if he'd been about to fire but had spotted my movement in his peripheral vision and he was now bringing the gun round to face me. Anil himself was crouching down beside the table, his right hand still attached to it with the knife, and I could see the Sheikh scrambling on his hands and knees along the floor trying to get out of the firing line. His sidekick, Rashid, had disappeared.

I computed all of this in the space of a second – maybe not even that.

Then I was pulling the trigger, one-handed, the gun kicking wildly as it spat out bullets.

The first shot missed the third guman and he fired back, the bullet striking the guy I was hiding behind, before passing through him and bouncing off the varnished-wood floor inches from my head.

I hit the gunman in the shoulder with the second or third round and, as he swivelled slightly, I steadied my aim, remembering my training, and put two more in his chest. At the same time, though wounded, Chris grabbed a gun from somewhere and sat up, pumping several more bullets into him as he fell backwards, the bullets ricocheting violently round the room, before he hit the floor with a thud I felt rather than heard.

After that, everything just stopped. The room was completely silent except for the incessant buzzing in my ears. Thin clouds of smoke hung in the cold air and there was a strong yet not unpleasant smell of burning. For a long time, possibly as long as ten seconds, nobody moved, as those still alive realized with a sense of utter relief that they'd survived this sudden yet terrible flash of violence. Finally, I took a deep breath and heaved the gunman's body off me. He was no longer breathing and I saw that the last bullet that struck him had been a shot to the forehead that was still smoking. I got to my feet unsteadily, looking across at Chris who was wincing in pain and holding his leg with his free hand.

I asked him how badly he was hurt.

'I've been a lot better,' he told me, 'but I don't think any arteries have been severed.'

I crouched down and inspected the wound. Blood was dripping out steadily but it didn't look life-threatening.

I got back up and looked around.

'Thanks, I'm fine,' snapped Anil, who clearly thought I should have been paying him more attention.

'I'll be with you in a minute,' I told him, scanning the room to make sure there weren't any more gunmen hanging about.

The first thing I spotted was the Sheikh lying on his front on the floor near the far door. A pool of blood was already forming under him and, as I watched, he moved very slightly, trying but failing to lift himself up. It didn't look like he was armed.

I turned away, and that was when I saw Rashid – the guy who less than twenty minutes earlier had been talking to me like I was a piece of shit. He was crouched in the corner behind another table, a terrified expression on his face.

He slowly put his hands up in a gesture of surrender as I bore down on him, gun outstretched. I felt good. I'd survived a firefight and killed a man. It gave me an intense burst of power that didn't feel at all healthy.

'Get up,' I told him, waving the gun.

He did as he was told. 'Don't kill me, please. I'm nothing to do with this.'

I got him to open up the first-aid box and apply a tourniquet to Chris's leg while I dealt with Anil.

'This is going to hurt,' I told him, placing my hand round the knife handle.

'Just do it,' he hissed.

So I did, and Anil yelped in pain as the blade slid free and blood poured out of his hand. While Rashid was applying a dressing to this wound I asked Anil where Alpha, the deep-cover agent, was.

'She's down in the hold.'

'She's unhurt,' said Rashid, although I'm sure that fact had nothing to do with him. I told him to shut his mouth and asked Anil what had happened.

It turned out that the Sheikh was a lot more cunning than anyone had given him credit for and, once he knew he was going to be obtaining sarin gas, he'd had airtight seals placed in one of the hold cabins, along with a separate state-of-the-art air filtration system so that poison gas could be pumped in and pumped out without affecting the rest of the boat. With the most lethal nerve gases, like VX, this wouldn't have worked, as they liquefy and stick to surfaces, sometimes for months on end, but sarin disperses easily. The Sheikh was also cruel enough to use a woman he assumed was just some hooker who wouldn't be missed as a guinea pig to test the viability of the product he was buying. So, when Anil had produced the gas cylinder, the Sheikh had taken him down to the hold where there was a viewing area into the room where Alpha was being held. Rashid, it seemed, was the technical man and he was the one who'd pumped the contents of the cylinder through the filtration system.

Sarin works extremely fast. A two-litre dose of the weapons-grade product that Anil was supposedly providing delivered into a confined space would take barely a minute to leave Alpha unconscious, and no more than three to kill her. Unfortunately for Anil, after five minutes Alpha was still very much awake and suffering no discernible effects, which was when the Sheikh knew he'd been duped. Anil had been taken back upstairs and tortured in an attempt to get him to reveal whether he was just a simple conman or actually working for a western government. The Sheikh had become convinced it was the latter, despite Anil's protestations, and had obviously decided it was safer to get rid of us rather than risk letting us go.

When Anil had finished talking I looked across at Rashid, who was literally shaking with fear.

'You deserve to die, you know that, don't you,' I told him, pointing the gun at his face.

Rashid wet himself then, the urine soaking his right trouser leg and dripping on to the floor.

I felt sick. I wanted to kill him for what he'd done, and there was little doubt the world would be a better place without him in it. But the fact remains I'm not, and never have been, a cold-blooded murderer, and seeing his abject terror took the sting out of my anger.

'Show me where the woman is,' I said, motioning with the gun towards the hold.

He nodded frantically, a desperately ingratiating look on his face, and led me down a flight of wooden steps and into a long corridor of the same varnished mahogany as the main cabin, with doors on either side. At the end of the corridor was a tinted glass door that looked newly installed. He pressed a button on the wall next to it and the door hissed open, revealing a small bare room lit by a single fluorescent light. Alpha was stood in the corner, still in her red bikini. She looked relieved when she saw me.

'Jesus, you guys took your time,' she said. 'I didn't know what the hell they had planned for me when they took me down here. Did you blow my cover?'

I told her what had happened as we made our way back up the steps, and when she saw the carnage, she cursed. 'This is not what was meant to happen.'

'We know that,' I said evenly.

'Don't tell me the fucking Sheikh's dead,' she said, crouching down to feel for a pulse. The pool of blood beneath him had grown in size and he was no longer moving. 'Worse,' she said, standing back up. 'There's still a faint pulse. He's dying.'

'Then we need to get him to a hospital,' I said.

'Are you the police?' asked Rashid uncertainly.

No one answered him. Instead, Alpha walked up to where the third gunman had dropped his gun and picked it up. She ejected the magazine and pushed it back again, still cursing under her breath. 'We've got a real problem, gentlemen,' she said, and then, without any warning whatsoever, she stepped in front of Rashid, lifted the gun and shot him in the eye at point-blank range.

It all happened so fast, and yet was done so calmly, that no one had a chance to stop her.

I jumped out of the way as Rashid hit the floor but I hadn't even raised my gun by the time she'd lowered hers. Chris had managed to get himself on to one of the sofas and he just sat there, still holding the gun he'd fired earlier, his mouth open. Anil, meanwhile, hit the deck, landing on his bad hand.

'What the hell?' I said, staring at Alpha.

And do you know what she did? She shrugged. Then, as cool as you like, she walked over to where the Sheikh lay, leaned down so that the end of the gun was two feet from the back of his head, and pulled the trigger.

When the echo of the gunshot had subsided, she turned back to the rest of us. 'Sorry, gentlemen, but there's no way we could have left these guys alive. It would have been a major diplomatic incident. This is damage limitation.' She reached down behind one of the sofas, retrieved a tiny screwdriver, used it to unscrew one of the electricity sockets, then removed a box-shaped device barely an inch square. 'The only record of what happened is on this little thing here. We're going to go back to Grand Turk, give it to the controller and let the bosses handle the mess. And then I think none of us should ever speak of this again. Agreed?'

So that's the story of how I met Anil Rahman and how we got involved in what Alpha quite rightly pointed out would have been a major diplomatic incident if the details had ever been made public. Instead, Anil and Chris were flown to a US naval vessel further off the coast where they received medical treatment, and I was sent back to the boat to get rid of the evidence.

Naturally, we were all sworn to secrecy, and Simon Pratt did a fine job of covering things up, though whether this was with or without the cooperation of his bosses I don't know. The newspapers reported that the incident was an act of piracy carried out by persons unknown, who'd then set the boat on fire. The Saudi government expressed their anger at what had happened and demanded that the British authorities leave no stone unturned in their hunt for the killers.

No one was ever brought to justice and the incident was slowly forgotten.

Until, it seemed, now.

Twenty

I had to report back to DCI Butterworth after the interview. While Chris went to check on his team's progress, I gave Butterworth a brief rundown of my thoughts, which went something like this. One, Karim Khan was definitely involved in terrorist activity on an organizational level. Two, he wasn't going to tell us about it and knew that our evidence against him was thin to say the least. Three, it was very possible he hadn't known that Anil Rahman was an informant and therefore hadn't had anything to do with his murder.

'Ach,' was Butterworth's growled reply. 'Then who on earth killed him?'

'Well, that's the big question,' I said.

Butterworth sat with one arm crooked in the other, drumming two fingers against the side of his face, the sound audible from ten feet away. It was a habit of his when he was thinking hard, and it always made him look mildly insane.

'We'll keep Khan for the next twenty-four hours while we search his house and all his computer equipment, just in case anything turns up, but if it doesn't, we're going to have to let him go.'

'Any sign of our three terror suspects yet?' I asked.

'Nothing. But we believe the older one, Danesh Kashani, is the leader and, according to people living nearby, he's just bought himself a silver Ford Focus that he's been driving for the past week. It's nowhere near his flat now so we're contacting local auction houses, car dealerships and trade mags to see if we can get a number plate for it, then we can track it via ANPR. We've got the whole of the Met looking for them so they're not going to be able to stay anonymous for long.'

It struck me that they didn't need to stay anonymous for long – at least not if they had weapons. But I didn't think it would be helpful to mention that right now.

'Anything turned up at the Anil Rahman crime scene?' I asked him.

He shook his head. 'Nothing yet.'

'According to her statement, the witness said the killer was taking a leak when she made a break for it. He's going to have to have left some trace of him behind.'

'Apparently he poured bleach down the toilet.'

'Yeah, I know. What kind of killer chases his victim for several minutes then, unable to find her, returns to the scene of the crime to clean a toilet?'

'Someone who's OCD,' Butterworth mumbled.

'But that's what I can't understand. Why didn't he just burn the place down and make sure he got rid of all the evidence that way? He'd already poured petrol over Mrs Rahman's body.'

'You know what killers are like, Ray. They're just the same as anyone else. They don't always operate with rhyme or reason. Not even the pros. And everyone makes mistakes.'

Which was a fair enough point, but this time round I wasn't so sure.

I made my excuses and left Butterworth's office, and was just on my way to the toilet with a view to trying to get that power nap when Chris collared me and told me they'd found out something interesting on Karim Khan's movements.

'What have we got then?' I asked, walking over with Chris to where DCs Michelle Frith and Rob Mitchell were sitting in front of their PCs.

Michelle looked up as we approached and I could tell that she'd been the one to uncover the lead, which didn't surprise me in the least. She was one of those up-and-coming young cops, a tech-savvy graduate with plenty of intelligence, idealism, and a belief in the rules, who'd probably end up being commissioner one day. She tended to keep her distance from me, recognizing that I wasn't the person to impress if she wanted promotion, but she looked pleased to see me now.

'I've been checking Karim Khan's phone against the MI5 surveillance log,' she said, 'and those times he's slipped surveillance he either doesn't have the phone with him or he switches it off. Yesterday he had it on him but he switched it off at 16.31 and switched it back on at 17.19. According to the log, he was seen by the surveillance team leaving his house at 16.04. He was driving and they tried to follow him, but he used a number of counter-surveillance techniques, including a dangerous U-turn, and they lost him at 16.22 and didn't pick him up again until he arrived back home at 18.45. I don't think he'd have made those efforts to get rid of any tail unless he was meeting someone he didn't want anyone to know about. Or maybe delivering or receiving a message.'

'That sounds logical,' I said.

'Show him what else you've found out, Michelle,' said Chris encouragingly.

She gave him a quick smile, and I could see the respect she had for Chris. There was nothing between the two of them, I knew that, but she looked up to him, and it struck me then, not for the first time, that Chris was much more of a people person than me. The thought made me envious.

Michelle turned to me. 'Khan turned off his phone while he was driving. The last signal was picked up on Grange Road in Tottenham but I've been on to ANPR and they've tracked his movements using his plates. He parked his car in a car park just off the Tottenham High Road at 16.40. The car didn't move again until 17.59 so I got in touch with the council and got them to send over their CCTV footage of the high street for that time. And if you look at this . . .'

I looked over her shoulder as she pressed a button on the keyboard. Her screen lit up, revealing a still picture of the High Road looking north at 16.49 the previous afternoon. Both pavements were relatively busy with pedestrians, as was to be expected at that time of day.

'This is Karim Khan here,' she said, tapping on a figure in a tan jacket with his back to the camera. 'I checked what he was wearing with the surveillance team,' she added by way of explanation before tapping the keyboard a second time.

I watched as Khan walked away from the camera, covering a distance of about ten metres before turning sideways on to the camera as he slowed down to enter a building. He then swung round quickly as if he'd been startled, looking back up the street. Michelle stopped the footage and zoomed in until his upper half filled the screen.

'I know the quality's not brilliant but that's him, isn't it?'

The quality wasn't very good and I had to look closely for several seconds before I could tell for sure. 'Yeah,' I said, 'that's him.'

Michelle started the film again and we watched as Khan entered the building. She zoomed out to full street view.

'The place he's just gone into is a Turkish-run café called Mehmet's. I can't see what he gets up to in there but he leaves after fourteen minutes. He then goes into a fruit and veg shop further down the street and makes some purchases, then into an Asian-run supermarket where he makes some more purchases. The camera then loses him for six minutes when he turns into the Florence Hayes recreation ground at the northern end. I'm trying to track down any cameras that cover the ground because he comes back on to the High Road at the point he left it, still carrying his groceries, and returns to his car.'

I thought about what Michelle was telling me. 'Does Khan employ counter-surveillance techniques like the one he used before he went into the café when he goes into the fruit and veg shop and the supermarket?' I asked her.

She shook her head. 'No. He just goes straight into both places.'

'So if he's meeting someone, or doing a dead-letter drop, the chances are he's doing it in the café or when he goes missing in the recreation ground. That's good work, Michelle,' I told her, then turned to her colleague Rob, who was looking mildly pissed off that she was getting all the plaudits. Get used to it, mate, I thought. He was a reasonable cop but something of a plodder. Still, plodders have their uses. 'Rob, I need you to chase the council for any footage that covers those six minutes when Khan's off the radar. Tell them it's an emergency, and make sure you get the footage fast. Then I want you to go down to that café, show them your warrant card, and find out if they've got security cameras inside their premises. If they have, seize the footage, and don't take no for an answer. If Khan was meeting anyone in there, I want to know who it was.'

He nodded and said he'd get on to it.

I turned back to Michelle. 'We need to go through the footage from the street camera that covers the entrance to the café, starting from an hour before Khan arrives until an hour after he left. I'm interested in who goes in and comes out during that time. I want to see if any of them are people of interest. Can you do that?'

'Sure.'

She pressed a few more keys and thirty seconds later she had an image of the front of the café at 15.50. I told her to start playing the footage, sceptical that this would get us anywhere. But we were lucky. The café hadn't been that busy yesterday. On average, an individual or a group came in or out every four minutes. Michelle would then zoom in and save an image of that individual's face before continuing the film. The customers were overwhelmingly male and of either Middle Eastern or Asian origin, but there was no one there I recognized – not that this was any great surprise. At any one time, CT has a database of no fewer than two thousand people of interest – individuals who are playing an active role in either planning or supporting terrorism – and I was never going to know them all. But we'd be able to use high-level facial imaging to compare the photos of the café patrons with those on the database, and if there was a match we'd find it.

It was time-consuming work, though, and after half an hour Chris and I went off to grab a sandwich from the Colindale canteen.

It was strange how we'd become friends after the Turks incident. I suppose it was the fact that we'd both met in such violent and traumatic circumstances, and almost died together. Something like that – whether you can talk about it or not – creates a tight bond. I also felt like Chris had saved my life, having swung round when he did on the Sheikh's boat, before that first shot was fired.

We'd kept our distance at first, once we were back at base in Cyprus, and the brass had made sure we were kept apart, although it was highly unlikely any of them knew what had happened that day. Slowly, though, we gravitated towards each other and we'd both left the military the following year. We'd stayed in touch back home, both joining the police, and had become very good friends over time, although we hadn't started serving together until three years ago. Now we were like an old married couple. We even played battleships together on breaks in the canteen or on particularly dull surveillance ops. We had a game going at the moment but I didn't think it would be appropriate to play today so we ate in silence.

When we returned to the incident suite twenty minutes later, Rob was nowhere to be seen, having presumably gone to the café to check for security camera footage, and Michelle was looking excited.

'What have you got?' I asked, hurrying over.

'I've got a man going into the café at 16.26. That's just over twenty minutes before Khan arrived. What makes him interesting is that he looks around before he goes in, to check he's not being followed. And he doesn't stay inside long either. He buys a takeaway drink and he's in and out in five minutes. The only problem is he doesn't match anyone on the database.'

She brought up an image of a big man with a bald head and a small, neatly trimmed beard. He was dressed in a muscle T-shirt and jeans and, as Michelle zoomed in on his face until she got the best image, I saw that he was in his mid-thirties. He looked Caucasian, or possibly southern European. Turkish at a push.

I stared at the screen for a good ten seconds, then very slowly a smile formed on my face.

'What is it?' asked Chris.

'I recognize him.'

'Are you sure?'

Five years ago, I took a break from counter-terrorism and went to work for the Serious and Organized Crime Agency in their organized crime division. I guess I just wanted a change and thought it might be an exciting new challenge. It wasn't. It was a lot of legwork with no results. I lasted eighteen months, which I'd always thought of as a waste of time. Until now, that is.

I kept staring at the image just to make sure I was absolutely right.

'Yeah, positive. I remember him from Soca. His name's Dokka Aliyev, and when I knew him he used to work for a guy called Bula Ruslan. And that's the interesting part. Ruslan was a Chechen businessman with some very nasty ways of doing business. He was also a suspected gunrunner.'

Chris stared at the screen. 'Do you reckon it's possible that Karim Khan's a good actor and that he did know all about Anil? And he hired this guy to kill him?'

'It's more likely he'd be involved in supplying weapons, but Aliyev's certainly got the credentials,' I replied after thinking about it for a while. 'He's been in the UK about ten years but before that he was suspected of being in one of the Chechen Islamic militias fighting Moscow, so it's almost certain he's killed before. And if you got a fleeting glimpse of him – and that's all the witness did get – then he could pass as white, and the age isn't too far off. So yeah, he could be the killer. The timing's coincidental to say the least. Let's get a decent image together and get it across to the witness. This could be a real lead. Well done, Michelle. You've done a brilliant job.'

I don't know if she was pleased by the words of praise or not because I was already turning away and recalling my days in Soca. I'd come across a lot of very nasty people during that time, and the fact that it had been so hard to put any of them away was ultimately the reason why I'd left. Of those I had met, though, they hadn't come much nastier than the Chechen gang that Dokka Aliyev belonged to.

I needed information on what these guys were up to now, and I knew just the person to call.

Twenty-one

Jane

Charlie Foulds was a nice guy, handsome in a bookish way and, to start with, a little nervous around me. Obviously witnessing me taking down DC Jeffs wasn't the ideal way of making my acquaintance, so I had to put my charm on full-throttle. It worked, and we were soon getting on fine.

Anji was another matter. She'd been shocked by what I'd done to Jeffs. And angry too. We'd only managed a brief talk earlier on in the kitchen. I'd explained what had happened, looking suitably shocked myself at what had gone on, and she'd demanded to know where I'd got my, in her words, 'fighting skills' from. I told her I'd done self-defence classes, having been on the wrong end of unwanted, sometimes physical, attention from men too many times in the past.

'I need to speak to DC Jeffs,' she said, 'and if he's assaulted you he *will* be suspended as soon as this is over. But in the meantime, I don't want you to have anything to do with him, and don't pull any tricks like that again. Understand?'

'I promise I won't. That was the first time I've ever used any of my self-defence skills in anger.' This was a lie of course, but I hoped a believable one.

For the last hour and a half I'd been sitting on the sofa in the lounge next to Charlie, his laptop between us, while we tried to come up with a picture of the Anil Rahman murder suspect.

The Evo-fit software worked very simply. I gave Charlie a basic description of the suspect. He fed this information into the computer and the software generated a series of random facial composites. I picked those among them that had a likeness to the suspect, and the software then mixed together the images I'd picked, using them to generate a new set of images. I then repeated the process, picking the ones that most resembled the suspect, the idea being that we slowly built up a likeness.

It worked more effectively than you'd think and the software had developed quite a good likeness to the picture of the man in my head, but it wasn't entirely right and the process wasn't exactly exciting. As a consequence, my mind began to drift and I thought back to the time I'd first taken self-defence classes.

It had started when I made the decision that I was never going to be able to rely on anyone else to look after me again – and that was when I'd started sleeping with my husband's loan shark, Frank Mellon.

When I'd first mooted the idea of sleeping with Mellon to Joel as a means of clearing the debt, I thought he'd go crazy.

For all his many faults, Joel was protective of me, and he was a macho territorial man, not the kind who'd want to pimp out his wife. But he didn't go crazy. He was hurt at the suggestion, I could see that, but there was relief in his eyes too and it was clear that the idea had crossed his mind more than once. That was what really hurt me: the knowledge that he was prepared to do anything, even humiliate the mother of his children, to repay that debt.

And after all that he still didn't have the mental strength to make the decision himself. 'What do you think?' he'd asked me. 'Do you want to go for it?'

'Of course I don't want to go for it,' I told him. 'But I'll do it for us as a family.'

'But how will it clear the debt? He won't let us off it.'

He looked and sounded like an overgrown boy. My husband. The man I'd looked up to, who once upon a time I'd actually thought would be my saviour.

'Let me deal with that,' I told him.

I knew Mellon would be interested. I'd seen the way he looked at me when we were out on that client dinner, and he'd gone to a lot of trouble to make contact with me afterwards, so when I called out of the blue a few days later, he bit immediately.

We met for a drink in a suitably anonymous bar just outside Fort Lauderdale. I remember the way he came into the room, dressed in a sharp suit and open-necked shirt, exuding confidence and power. I'd been doing some research on him. He was worth at least ten million dollars by most estimates, so what we owed him was chickenfeed, but for Frank Mellon, it was the principle. He'd got to where he was in the pecking order through a combination of good business sense and sheer ruthlessness. Twice in the early part of his career he'd been arrested on suspicion of murder but both times had been released without charge through lack of evidence. He wasn't a man to be trifled with, and I was in no doubt that he could destroy my family if he chose to.

I was dressed in a black off-the-shoulder dress that showed off my legs and boobs, and five-inch heels. I'd spent a long time doing my hair, my eyes and my nails and I was looking the best, and the sexiest, I'd looked in a long time. I stood up to greet him, allowing him to kiss me on both cheeks. He lingered long enough for me to notice he smelled of expensive cologne.

'You're looking good, honey,' he said, staring at me greedily as he took a seat opposite. 'To what do I owe the pleasure?'

I'm not a person to beat about the bush so as soon as we'd ordered our drinks, I laid my cards directly on the table. 'I know my husband owes you a lot of money and I'm here to make you an offer. We can't pay you back in cash right now but . . .' I paused and stared at him, my eyes saying everything. 'You can have me.'

Mellon didn't say anything, just watched me with traces of a smile on his lips, so I told him how I wanted it to pan out. For the duration I was seeing him, the loan would be fixed at its current value with no further interest, and I would be available to him as and when he wanted me, although sometimes I'd need a day or two's notice. Every time I spent a full night with him a thousand dollars came off the loan amount. When it was just a quick meeting, the rate would drop to five hundred. When Joel and I had raised enough money to pay him back, the arrangement would stop and we'd all be free to go our separate ways.

I didn't feel any emotion as I spoke. Just a deep, deep empti-
ness where my emotions should have been. This was simply a
job that had to be done.

'You're quite the businessman, lady,' he said when I'd finished.
'But I'm not exactly short of offers. What makes you think
you're worth so much?'

I flinched inside from the blow but on the outside I smiled
slowly and seductively. 'I could do things to you you can only
dream about,' I said, leaning in close to him so he could smell
my perfume, my dark eyes fixed on his, knowing I had to close
this.

My fingers touched his inner thigh, moving gently upwards.
He looked down at my hand with a dismissive expression and
I realized I had to play this better. Needy wasn't going to work. I
brushed my hand against his cock, felt him stiffening, then sat
back up in my seat and faced him down.

'That's my offer,' I said with a lot more confidence than I
felt. 'Take it or leave it.'

He stared at me for several seconds, his features inscrutable.
Then he laughed. 'I've got to give it to you, baby. You've got
cojones. But you're going to have to let me try out the goods
first.' As the waiter served the drinks – a Coors for him, a lime
and soda water for me – he reached over and squeezed my
breast. The waiter turned away and I didn't react as Mellon
turned his attention to my other breast, squeezing the nipple
with his thumb and forefinger through the material of the dress.
'If I like the quality, then we've got a deal. If I don't, then
you and your old man still owe me a hundred and fifty grand.
And if I don't get it back in full by the end of next month, I

start adding a ten per cent monthly vig until I do. Capeesh?'
He pinched my nipple hard enough to make me flinch then sat
back in his seat, viewing me like a king views a subject who
needs bringing into line. 'And don't ever think about trying to
flee the state, or the country. I've got a long reach. I'll find
you.'

I felt sick then as the full realization of what I was getting
into hit me, but it was already way too late to pull out.

We did it for the first time a week later in a Palm Beach hotel
room. I fucked like I'd never fucked before. I acted like a whore.
I did everything he wanted me to do, and he wanted a lot. He
was rough, though thankfully not as rough as I'd been expecting,
and afterwards when he lay spent beside me on the bed, his arm
round my shoulders as if we were just a pair of regular lovers,
he laughed out loud, the sound like a hungry hyena, and told
me that Jesus, yes, I was as good as I'd been making out, and
I'd got myself a deal. And I remember thinking that I was unsure
whether to thank God or throw up.

In the end I did the latter, pretty much as soon as I got
home and saw the haunted, beaten expression on Joel's face.
I threw up and he cried. But at least we owed five hundred
bucks less.

Mellon and I saw each other at least once, sometimes twice
a week after that. It never got any easier but I looked at it as
something I had to do to protect my children and keep my family
together, and I learned to tolerate it. By this time, Joel had wound
up the company and got a job working for another IT outfit. He
was on his best behaviour and had given up drinking. Even the
affairs had stopped. The problem was, I'd lost all respect for

him now that he could no longer protect our family. That part was up to me, which was how I got into self-defence.

I became obsessed with being physically strong and able to take down anybody, however big. I went to the gym every day and took up the Israeli self-defence technique of Krav Maga which teaches you how to act and react in real-life hand-to-hand combat situations. I trained three times a week. My instructor told me I was a fast learner – one of the fastest he'd ever seen. He called me brutal, and I took it as a compliment. Slowly, in spite of everything, I began to feel better about life as my self-confidence grew and I saw the first chink of light at the end of the tunnel, because one way or another I was going to clear that debt and then the kids and I were going to start a new life somewhere far away.

But that's the fairytale, isn't it? And one thing I've learned is that life never works like that. Not mine anyway because, four months after my business relationship with Frank Mellon had begun, and with the debt now teetering around the hundred and twenty grand mark, Mellon took me in his arms one day after we'd had sex in the bolthole he occasionally took me to in Palm Beach and told me he loved me.

I should have seen it coming. I'd seen signs of a change in him for a while. He'd become far more affectionate. He'd begun to talk more, and open up about himself and his life. Under different circumstances I might even have found him attractive. After all, he wasn't bad-looking and had a certain charisma about him. And Jesus, he would have done a hell of a lot better job of protecting the boys and me than Joel had ever done.

But this was business, pure and simple.

First Joel had fucked things up. Now Mellon had.

'I love you, babe,' he'd said a second time, kissing me tenderly on the lips. 'I genuinely do.'

That was when I decided I was going to have to kill him.

I came back to the present with a start. I was aware of Charlie talking to me. He was asking which of the faces on the screen most resembled the killer.

I took a deep breath. 'Sorry about that. I was miles away.'

He smiled. 'I could see that. I get like that sometimes. And I know that this process isn't all that stimulating.'

I looked at the laptop screen. A dozen faces stared back at me, each of them resembling the man I was trying to picture in some way.

'Take your time,' said Charlie.

Which was exactly what I did as I inspected them each in turn. One by one I removed them until only a single image remained. He looked like the suspect just a little bit more than the previous shortlisted image. We were getting there.

'That's really beginning to look like him,' I said.

Before Charlie could respond there was a knock on the door and Anji came in holding a piece of A4-sized paper. 'Do you mind if we have a minute, Charlie?' she asked. 'You can wait in the kitchen.'

Charlie nodded and left the room. When the door had closed behind him, Anji thrust the paper in front of my nose. It featured an upper-body shot of a bald-headed man, and it was obvious it had been taken on some kind of security camera as the face was partly in profile and it looked like he was walking away.

'Is this the man you saw at Anil Rahman's house last night?' she asked me, barely suppressing the excitement in her voice.

I stared at it then shook my head. 'No. It's not him.'

'Are you absolutely sure?'

'Yes,' I said. 'I'm absolutely sure.' I saw the disappointment in her face. 'Who is he?'

Anji sighed. 'Just a possible suspect. I think we were all hopeful. It would have been a real break.'

'I'm sorry, Anji.'

'It's OK. Policework's all about false alarms. Listen, I spoke to DC Jeffs. He claims he didn't touch you and he was just trying to be friendly.'

'He wasn't. I know exactly what he was doing, and I've got to be honest, I'm very disappointed he'd pick on someone who's been through what I have.'

Anji sat down on the corner of the sofa next to me and leaned in close. 'Off the record, I know DC Jeffs can be overfriendly with women. He's tried it with me before. Now he's under direct orders not to speak to you again, and to keep out of your way, and when all this is over I'll be speaking to my boss about what we do about him. In the meantime, if he bothers you in any way again, please don't go all ninja on him. Just come to me and I'll sort it out, OK?'

I nodded. 'I will. I promise.'

'You know you could have really done some damage to him.'

'I know, and I'm sorry.'

We looked at each other for a long moment and I could tell she thought I was an enigma. An attractive mother of two and freelance accountant who'd married young with the kind of self-defence skills you rarely saw on someone without military training.

'Look, Anji,' I said, 'I've been through a lot. I've had to learn how to survive.' Which, in essence, was the truest thing I'd ever said to her.

'I know,' she said, her face breaking into a warm smile.

She was, I thought, a beautiful woman, and I wanted to touch her, to take her hand in mine and feel her warmth. I think she sensed it too, and we were silent for a couple of seconds, and the moment passed.

'How's the e-fit coming on?' she asked.

'This is what we've come up with so far.'

I turned the laptop screen round so she could see the latest image.

'Wow,' she said.

'What?'

'That doesn't half look like my boss.'

I laughed. 'Really? Is he the sort who'd have anything to do with this?'

Anji laughed too, but interestingly she didn't answer my question.

Twenty-two

Ray

Sam Verran knew as much about eastern European and Russian crime gangs and their impact on the UK as any British police officer. He always seemed to have a handle on what was going on and, like a lot of cops, he was prepared to talk off the record. I knew him from my time in Soca. We hadn't spoken in a few years but I knew he'd remember me. People do.

I still had his number so I went back to my desk in a quiet corner of the incident suite and called him.

'Bloody hell, Ray Mason, is that you?' he said, answering on the first ring.

'How are you doing, Sam?'

'Not bad. I heard about your run-in with those would-be

jihadis. You did a good job there. You've got a lot of support among the people over this way.'

'Thanks. I appreciate that.' Not that their support would count for anything in a courtroom. 'It's never a good day for justice when you're prosecuted for defending yourself against a bunch of loons who want to kidnap and behead you, but that's just the way it seems to go these days.'

'Too right. All this kid-gloves treatment of criminals and shitting over decent cops is never going to end happily. What can I do for you, Ray?'

'Dokka Aliyev. Chechen thug. Part of Bula Ruslan's outfit. He's come up as a suspect in a murder investigation we've got running at CT. Do you know what he's up to these days?'

'Ruslan's outfit is still operating and, as far as I know, Mr Ruslan's still at the helm. They've supposedly gone legit, but that's bullshit of course. These guys are way too ruthless ever to be legit. As far as I know, Aliyev is still working for the outfit as a hired thug. He's not much use for anything else, and he's lucky to be still in the country. He served three years between 2009 and 2012 for a hit and run he did while driving uninsured. The victim was a female pedestrian – young girl, early twenties – and she was lucky to survive. When the case got to court there was evidence of jury tampering and pressure on the victim to change her story, but there were so many witnesses to the accident and Aliyev was so blatantly in the wrong that he got sent down anyway. He should have been deported afterwards, but he used the old Human Rights Act to scupper that.' Verran sighed. 'These bastards – Aliyev, Ruslan, their whole crew – are a law unto themselves, but at the moment they're not even under investigation. We just haven't got the manpower.'

I knew exactly where he was coming from. People don't realize quite how short-staffed we are these days. We're fire-fighting, all of us. CT, the NCA, even the coppers on the beat, and the flames keep shooting up everywhere. They might not be overwhelming us yet but sometimes it feels like just a matter of time.

'Yet you still know all about these guys, Sam,' I told him. 'You're a walking criminal encyclopaedia.'

'Not much point knowing it all if you can't put them away.'

'Maybe I can help you there. We've picked up Dokka Aliyev on CCTV and we believe he may be in contact with a suspect on a terror case we're working on, and that the suspect might have hired Aliyev to kill an informant.'

Verran grunted. 'From what I know, Aliyev doesn't work alone. Certainly not as a hitman. He's still very much part of Ruslan's outfit, and Ruslan keeps a tight rein on his people. He wouldn't want Aliyev getting involved in a hit, especially not now he's pretending to be legit.'

I took a deep breath, thinking about this. 'Now this is where you really prove what an expert you are on the criminal under-world. Do you know which prison Aliyev served his time in for the hit and run?'

He was silent for a couple of seconds, then: 'Pentonville, I think.'

'Our suspect was in Pentonville around the same time. His name's Karim Khan. Does that name ring a bell with you?'

He said it didn't.

'Well look, we're sure Khan and Aliyev were in contact yesterday. Four hours later the informant in Khan's group was murdered at home along with his wife. She was shot dead but he was tortured to death. It was pretty gruesome.'

Verran didn't say anything for a couple of seconds. 'Look, if you're asking me if Aliyev could have murdered those people, I'd say it's possible, but unlikely. It's not his style.'

That blew one theory. But I'm nothing if not determined so I pressed on. 'We believe our suspect, Khan, has also been trying to source weapons for a terror attack. Is it possible he could have been buying guns from Ruslan's crew? I remember there was talk at one time they were bringing weapons into the country.'

'They've got access to weapons, we're pretty certain of that, but if they were ever gunrunners, they're not now. The money you make gunrunning is far outweighed by the risks, and Ruslan's always been a businessman at heart.'

'Great.' I sat back in my plush new seat, balancing on the rear wheels, and sighed loudly, beginning to get frustrated.

'Word is, though,' continued Verran, 'that Ruslan's found God. Or Allah, anyway.'

That made me sit back up. 'How long's that been going on?'

'I don't know. I just heard it on the grapevine a while back. I mean, he was a Muslim anyway, coming from Chechnya, but in his early days he fought in one of the militias for the Russians against the mujahideen, so he obviously wasn't that devout. But if he's making up for the sins of his past then he might be helping people like your man with his expertise, and maybe his weaponry. Who knows? But it's a thought.'

It was more than a thought. It was a real lead.

'Have you got addresses for Ruslan and Aliyev?'

'Probably not current ones. You'd have to look them up on Holmes. But I do know that Ruslan's HQ is a recovered oil plant out in Essex, near Billericay. That's where he conducts a lot of his business from. It's well out of the way and very hard to get close to for surveillance teams.'

'What the hell's recovered oil?' I asked him.

Verran chuckled on the other end of the line. 'Have you ever wondered where all that fat from chippies and kebab houses and KFCs and cheap Chinese restaurants ends up?'

'No, can't say I have.'

'Nor me before Ruslan got involved in it. What happens is his company comes and collects all the used oil from these places in big trucks and takes it back to the plant, where it's reheated in huge great chimneys and converted into biofuel. I don't know the technical details but it's a lucrative business, and because it involves cheap retail outlets much of it is cash-based so there's a lot of opportunity for money laundering.'

'You say it's well out of the way and hard to watch. So if you were going to do an arms deal, would you do it there?'

'It's as good a place as any, I suppose.'

'Can you text me the address?'

'Sure. Are you going to put a team together to watch the place?'

'That's the plan. Thanks for your help, Sam.'

As we said our goodbyes, Chris came out of Butterworth's office and walked over to my desk. He looked deflated.

'Don't tell me,' I said. 'The witness says Dokka Aliyev isn't our killer.'

He frowned. 'How did you know that?'

I gave him a brief rundown of my conversation with Sam Verran. 'He didn't think it was Aliyev's style to carry out a freelance hit, especially one as messy as that one.'

'So we're no nearer catching the killer?'

'But at least we've got a lead on the terror attack. We need to get a surveillance team in place at that oil plant and see if our three suspects turn up there.'

'Butterworth won't go for that, Ray. We haven't got the resources.'

'We'll see,' I said.

But Chris was right. When I told Butterworth what I wanted, he turned me down flat. 'We've got no evidence, Ray, so I can't justify putting a team in place when they could be there for days.'

'Khan met one of Ruslan's people yesterday. It can't be a coincidence.'

'But according to Jane Kinnear, the man on the CCTV is not Anil Rahman's killer.'

'No, but he could be selling the guns for the terror attack.'

'Could be, Ray, but that's not good enough. I need you here.'

'To do what? I'm just sitting around waiting for the search teams to come up with leads. Let me go over and see if Bula Ruslan's there. I used to know him, so if he's there, I'll talk to him. I don't expect him to roll over and admit anything, he's not that kind of guy, but if he is planning on selling weapons to Karim Khan, and if he knows we're on to him, he's not going to go ahead with the deal. And right now the most important thing is to keep the guns out of the hands of these terrorists.'

'What if he's the subject of a separate investigation? We could be ruining it.'

'He's not. I've just talked to the NCA. He's not on any watch-list at the moment.'

Butterworth still didn't look convinced.

'How dangerous is this lad Ruslan?'

'He's a serious player but he's not stupid. He won't hurt me.' Although I wasn't entirely sure Butterworth would be too worried about that. 'Come on, sir, I'll be gone an hour and a half, two hours tops, and we might actually save some lives.'

Butterworth sighed. 'Go on then,' he said at last. 'But I don't want you going alone. Take Chris with you as back-up and report back as soon as you've spoken to him.'

'Of course. Thanks, sir. By the way, have you spoken to the commander yet about the possibility of me going to the safehouse and talking to Jane Kinnear? There are quite a few things I want to go over with her face to face.'

'I put in a request earlier. I haven't heard back yet. I'll let you know when I do.'

I thanked him again and headed out of there quickly before he changed his mind. To tell the truth, what I was doing was a lot more dangerous than I was letting on. Whether he was trying to go legit or not, Bula Ruslan was, at heart, a sadistic brute, albeit one with a flair for business. Since arriving in the UK after the first Chechen war at the tail end of the nineties he'd made his money in people trafficking, prostitution and drugs, before branching out into more legitimate concerns, and had avoided prison with a potent combination of bribery, cunning and brutality. He didn't tend to kill people who crossed him – although I recall he was suspected of involvement in at least two murders – he preferred to torture them instead. That way they learned their lesson and, more importantly, they kept their mouths shut. Toe and finger amputations were his speciality.

'What did Butterworth say?' asked Chris when he saw me.

'Grab your jacket,' I said. 'We're going to pay a visit to the lion in his den.'

Twenty-three

Gaydon tasted the chicken Thai red curry simmering in the pot. It tasted a little too sharp so he added a touch more sugar, gave the liquid a stir, and had another taste.

Perfect.

Food was Gaydon's greatest pleasure. Even on jobs like this one, when they were going to be in and out of the country in the space of a few days, he always made sure he sourced good ingredients and ate well. They now had less than eighteen hours left in the UK. By that time they would have left behind a trail of murder and destruction that would stun the British public and frustrate the police, who would never know the truth of what had happened.

Gaydon had to admit it was an ambitious plan and not something he would ever have been able to come up with himself. There were risks involved, more so than Gaydon would ordinarily have liked – he'd done well in his profession by always minimizing his risks – but, by God, it was ingenious. And lucrative too. The money he'd receive for this would fund his retirement, and not before time. Murder was an inherently unstable career, however good you were at it.

He spooned boiled rice into four bowls and added generous portions of the curry into two of them, which he put to one side. He then poured the contents of a small glass vial into the pan containing the remaining curry and gave it a good stir before adding the mixture to the other two bowls.

Pryce gave him a strange look as he set the first two bowls down on the kitchen table, and picked up the two contaminated ones. 'What's the point in feeding them?' he asked. 'They'll be dead by the end of the day.'

They were holding two women here. The one they'd abducted this morning, and a prostitute in her late thirties they'd picked up three nights earlier.

'I've put in enough diazepam to keep them quiet for a while,' said Gaydon. 'And we need them quiet.'

Pryce didn't bother responding. Instead he attacked his late lunch with something close to anger, as befitted a man of his size and temperament. It looked as if he took no pleasure at all from the meal, which irritated Gaydon, who took great pride in the quality of his cooking.

The girl they'd taken this morning was in the basement lying spreadeagled on the bed in her jogging clothes, gagged and blindfolded. Two steel spreader bars with restraints attached that had themselves been chained to the bed kept her hands and feet in place.

She turned her head anxiously when Gaydon switched on the lights and came down the steps. It smelled of mildew down here and something else too. The girl had soiled herself.

Wrinkling his nose, Gaydon approached the bed and put the food down on the floor. He took a mobile phone from his pocket. It belonged to the girl herself and he used it now to film her lying there, getting a close-up of her face so that, even behind the gag and blindfold, it was possible for a close relative to identify her. Gaydon slipped a knife from his waistband and, still filming, held the blade close to the girl's face. He then slowly moved it so that it was millimetres from her throat. She sensed something was happening and made a high, scared sound behind the gag. Gaydon made a sudden cutting gesture for the benefit of the man who was going to see the film before pressing the stop button, replacing the knife in its sheath, and removing the girl's gag.

'I've brought you something to eat,' he told her. 'But if you cry out, or try to do anything stupid, I will hurt you, and I don't want to have to do that.' He made his words come out soothing even though he felt nothing for her.

'Why are you keeping me here?' she asked nervously.

'I'm afraid I can't talk about it, but I promise you'll be released soon.'

'Please don't hurt me. I haven't done anything wrong.'

'Then nothing will happen to you,' he lied, unlocking the restraints on her wrists so that she could sit up on the bed, and placing the bowl and a spoon in her lap. 'Don't remove your blindfold, because if you see my face, I'll have to kill you. Do you understand?'

She said she did, and Gaydon believed her. This one was going to be compliant. You could always tell.

He watched her in silence for a few moments as she ate the food, gulping it and the crushed sleeping tablets down ravenously; and then, because he couldn't resist, he asked her what she thought of it.

She told him it was delicious, and he could tell she meant it. He thanked her for the compliment and, beaming with professional pride, headed up the stairs. There weren't many chefs who could elicit culinary enthusiasm from a kidnap victim.

After he'd delivered the food to the prostitute, who was being kept in one of the upstairs bedrooms and who, having been their prisoner for three days, had learned the hard way that there was no point playing up or trying to escape (she'd never complimented him on his food either), Gaydon headed back to the kitchen and joined Pryce at the table.

'Is it time yet?' Pryce asked him, pushing aside his empty bowl.

Gaydon didn't answer until he'd finished his own food, savouring the subtle flavours of the curry, trying without success not to hurry. Finally, he looked at his watch and got up from the table.

'Yes,' he said, confident as ever, even though this next stage of the plan was the riskiest. 'It's time.'

Twenty-four

Ray

The recovered oil plant belonging to Waystone Holdings, a company with known links to Bula Ruslan, was set on a thirty-acre plot that had once been a farm in a semi-rural stretch of south Essex. The Google Maps aerial view of the site showed a central fenced compound containing the old farmhouse and a couple of adjacent buildings and Portakabins, surrounded by a stretch of wasteground and grassland with a lorry park, half a dozen large chimneys, and a sprinkling of outbuildings. A long winding track led down to the central compound, protected by two high steel gates topped with barbed wire at the entrance to the plot. Cameras on top of the gateposts surveyed the area in front of them and thick hedges on either side made it impossible to see anything beyond from ground level.

Chris was driving, and he slowed the car as we passed.

'That's a lot of security for a place storing chip fat,' I said.

'So what do we do?' he asked. 'They're not going to let us in if we ring on the doorbell, are they?'

'There's a track a couple of hundred yards down here on the right,' I said, looking at the satellite map of the area. 'Park up down there and we can approach over a field from the west. We'll be able to get close to the central compound that way.'

'Then what are we going to do?'

'We'll think of something,' I said, although I wasn't quite sure what.

Chris sighed but didn't respond. I noticed he seemed miserable today. Miserable and preoccupied. I wondered if it was something do with Charlotte. I couldn't even begin to imagine how hard it must be watching the woman you loved deteriorate bit by bit in front of you, knowing it was only ever going to get worse. I couldn't live like that. It was far safer not to get involved.

Chris took the turning, and when we were about a hundred metres down it I told him to park up where he could. He found a passing space and stopped the car. To our right, a thick hedge about head-height still blocked our way to the plant. We walked along it in silence, looking for a gap we could get through, eventually finding a short stretch where it thinned out just enough for a man to crawl under it.

'We're not going under there, surely,' Chris said when I stopped and crouched down.

I chuckled. 'Come on. It'll do us good to get a bit dirty. We don't do enough of it these days.'

He didn't say anything. Nor did he crouch down.

I looked up at him. 'What's wrong?'

'I'm thinking of quitting, Ray,' he said.

That stopped me dead. I stood back up. 'You're joking?' But I knew he wasn't. I could see it in his eyes.

'I'm sorry. I've been meaning to talk to you about it for a while. You know I did some work in cybersecurity? A company's offered me a job in the same field.'

'What about the pension? You're only a few years off your thirty.'

'It's a lot better money, and it's less unsociable hours. It'll be easier with Charlotte.'

I felt deflated. 'Do you want to do it?'

'I need a break from all this. It's wearing me down. And this thing with Anil . . . You know, what we did that day in the Turks? No one supported us. No one gave a shit. I need to think about my family for a change. About me.'

'Then you should do it,' I said, and it hurt me to utter those words. I'm a man who's alone a lot of the time and maybe I need people more than I like to admit because I felt a real sense of loneliness then. It was a relief that for the moment at least I had something to concentrate my mind. 'But right now you still work for CT, and you still work for me. And that means we're going to take a look at this place. Come on.'

I got down on my belly and crawled slowly through the gap, ignoring the thorns scratching the back of my head and the thistles that clawed at my front. When I emerged on the other side there was a fresh cowpat directly in front of me and, though I managed to keep my face out of it, the arm of my jacket got caught as I rolled away, leaving a dirty stain on the elbow.

I clambered to my feet as Chris crawled through behind me, muttering under his breath.

'Mind the shit,' I warned him.

'Oh, for Christ's sake,' he cursed, just about managing to avoid it. 'What's that smell?'

I'd noticed a strange smell in the air when we'd got out of the car but it was stronger now, and more pungent. It wasn't difficult to identify it as rancid animal fat.

'I'm guessing they're reheating all the old chip shop oil in those,' I said, pointing to the cluster of concrete chimney stacks, each one a good hundred feet high, a hundred yards distant.

He wrinkled his nose. 'Jesus, it stinks. How can you work with that smell all day?'

'I don't know, but I bet it does a good job of keeping unwanted visitors away.'

'You're not wrong there.' He brushed himself down. 'You know, this doesn't put me off changing careers.'

We were standing on a stretch of scrubby grassland with extremely sparse cover that ran down directly to the chimneys. The smell seemed to be getting worse the longer we stood there.

I pulled out a pair of binoculars and had a quick look. There didn't seem to be any activity around the chimneys and another hedge cut off the view of the central compound, so it didn't look like we could be seen.

'Come on,' I said. 'Let's get closer.'

We moved across the grass, keeping low. It reminded me of the old days when we used to do long-term surveillance of suspect properties. I remember once, when I was with Soca, digging in and watching a house in the country from an observation post under a holly bush, waiting for a shipment of stolen gold bullion to turn up. It was without doubt the most boring three days of my life. I was never patient enough for surveillance, which was why I'd already decided what I was going to do now.

When we were about twenty yards short of the chimneys, we crouched down in a slight dip. From here we could see the front gates and a portion of the track running down to the central compound. There were about a dozen red lorries with Waystone Holdings printed in big yellow letters on their sides parked in a row in front of a building next to the chimneys, but there was no one around. To the left of the chimneys, partly obscured by another hedge, was the central compound. It was surrounded by a chain-link fence about twelve feet high and ringed at the top with two lines of razor wire. I could see two single-storey buildings inside, which looked like converted barns. Two of the windows in one of them were open but there was no obvious sign of life.

I was just about to hand the binoculars over to Chris when a man in a leather jacket walked into view from behind one of the buildings in the central compound smoking a cigarette. I focused in so that only his upper half was visible, immediately recognizing him.

'What is it?' asked Chris, seeing my smile.

'I'm looking at our man from the CCTV footage yesterday, Dokka Aliyev.'

I followed Aliyev with the binoculars, watching as he reached into the inside pocket of his leather jacket and pulled out a phone. I thought I caught a glimpse of a gun in a shoulder holster beneath but I couldn't be sure. As Aliyev talked into the phone, looking agitated, he turned and walked back behind the building, disappearing from sight. I gave Chris a running commentary on all this except for the part about the gun. There was no point complicating matters.

'So what's the plan now?' he asked. 'We can't just sit here and wait for something to happen.'

'I figure we've got two choices. We go back to the main entrance, ring on the bell and announce who we are. Chances are they won't let us in without a warrant but at least that way we let them know we're on to them, so if they are intending to supply the terrorist cell with weapons and they haven't actually handed them over yet, they're almost certain to call off the deal, and there'll be no attack.'

'OK,' said Chris. 'That sounds like a possibility. What's the other choice?'

I looked at him. 'I go in. Alone.'

'Oh no. We're not doing anything stupid.'

'Hear me out. I'll go in, flash my warrant card. They'll be pissed off and angry but remember, these guys are business people. They're not going to hurt a cop. I know them from the past. If Ruslan's there, I'll speak to him. I'll give him a warning. If he's involved in arming a terrorist cell and they commit mass murder then I'll promise him that we'll concentrate every resource we have on bringing him to justice. I'll scare him out of giving them a single gun. And if he's already supplied them, then I'll know. I'll be able to see it in his eyes.'

'Jesus, Ray. Going in there's way too risky. You know that.'

It was, and I did know it. But something inside me craved the excitement of the confrontation. I was angry with these guys.

I remembered Ruslan and his crew well. They were violent thugs who'd come to the UK thinking they could act with total impunity, and so far, events had proved them right. I have a burning desire for justice. Sometimes I think it's the only thing that truly motivates me, and more than once in my career I've let it get the better of me. Like now.

'I told you, Chris, they won't hurt a police officer. Not on their home ground. You stay here. I'll message you in ten minutes, and then every ten minutes after that. If I'm more than two minutes late with a message, call the cavalry.'

'But how the hell are you going to get through the fence?' demanded Chris.

I always bring a briefcase containing various bits and pieces – most of them non-regulation – into whichever office I'm working in that day, and I'd taken a pair of wire cutters and a set of lock picks from it before coming here.

When Chris saw the wire cutters, he looked very unhappy. 'I can't let you do this, Ray.'

'I'm not asking your permission, Chris. I just need to stir up the wasps' nest a bit, that's all.'

He shook his head angrily. 'You know, this is why I don't want to work for you any more. You're a good bloke – you mean well – but you're a glory hunter. You don't do the job properly. You'd have done better sticking in the army. At least that way you could take out all the bad guys you want and not have to worry so much about the paperwork.'

His words stung me, essentially because they were true, but I didn't let him see that. Instead I took out my phone and put it on to vibrate. The clock said 15.16. 'I'll send you a message at 15.26. Then at 15.36, and so on. Remember, if I'm any more than two minutes late, call for back-up.'

'You could lose your job over this.'

I thought about the impending private prosecution I faced for double murder. The complaint that Khan was about to make for police brutality. I shrugged. 'I'll take my chances.'

He looked at me and there was a sadness in his eyes. Over the years he'd been there for me plenty of times, and I could tell that now he thought that maybe all his efforts had been wasted. That, when it came down to it, I really was a hopeless case.

To be honest, I couldn't disagree.

Clutching the wire cutters, I got to my feet.

The central compound fence was partly covered by old leylandii and I circumnavigated it until I found a spot where the hedge had thinned out enough to give a view of the buildings beyond.

It wasn't too hard to cut through the fence. The cutters were good and the wire was thin. The distance to the first building – an old Portakabin – was no more than twenty yards across an empty car park. I wasn't wearing any camouflage but that wasn't a problem. I was expecting to get spotted. I wanted to be. That way I could get to Bula Ruslan – assuming he was here – and say my piece.

I felt the reassuring presence of the gun in my jacket and wondered if I'd be feeling quite so brave if I wasn't armed. Probably not. Right now, though, I felt invincible, as if nothing could hurt me. I didn't want to have to draw my gun. I was as aware as anyone of the legal repercussions of pulling a police-issue firearm – and, God forbid, using it – especially when I'd already broken the rules by entering a premises without a warrant or any kind of probable cause. But if I had to, I would draw it.

Because, you know, what had I really got to lose?

When I'd made a hole that would fit me comfortably, I crawled through on my belly and got to my feet. It was almost 15.26 so I sent a two-word message to Chris – 'All OK' – then started walking purposefully towards the nearest Portakabin, trying not to dwell too much on the insanity of what I was doing.

The smell of rancid fat was terrible this close to the chimneys. It seemed to get into every pore, eating up every ounce of fresh air, so there was no escape. It was, I had to admit, a supremely effective way of keeping unwanted visitors, police or otherwise, away and it took all my willpower to stop myself from gagging. Keeping my breathing to a minimum, I pulled out my warrant card so there'd be no doubts as to who I was.

It was worryingly quiet in the yard. I couldn't hear any voices or sounds of activity, nor see any cars. But I had seen Dokka Aliyev, so there was at least one person round here.

When I reached the Portakabin, I peered in the window. The place was empty. I rounded the corner into the main courtyard and, with the old farmhouse on my left, walked rapidly over to one of the converted barns.

That was when I spotted two men standing about thirty yards ahead of me at the main entrance to the compound. They had their backs to me and it was clear they were guards, but what worried me was the machine pistol one of them was holding.

I immediately froze as the sudden realization that I'd stepped into something out of my depth took hold. I'm not a stubborn man. I can admit when I'm wrong, and I'd been wrong to break in here; but now that I'd seen an illegal firearm being brandished, we had the evidence we needed to raid the place. Chris and I could easily claim we'd seen the guard with the gun through the binoculars. The problem I had, though, was that Chris wouldn't be able to see the armed guards from the position he was in, so he wouldn't call for back-up.

Which meant I needed to get out of here.

I took a step backwards, then another, moving as quietly as possible on the flagstones.

And then I heard movement behind me.

'Who are you? Put your hands up. Now!' The accent was foreign, probably Chechen, and there was an undercurrent of nerves in it.

Ahead, the two guards turned round and looked our way. The one without the machine pistol pulled a gun from inside his leather jacket, and the two of them started to walk over.

'I'm a police officer,' I said to the man behind me, lifting my warrant card along with my hands and turning slowly round.

'Don't move!' he hissed, but I was already facing him.

He was a small wiry guy in dire need of a shave, probably no more than twenty-five and dressed in jeans and a black leather jacket, which seemed to be the standard uniform for a lot of these Chechen guys. He was holding a semi-automatic pistol, but he didn't look entirely comfortable with it in his hands. This guy was low-level, and unlikely to pull the trigger.

'I'm here to see Bula Ruslan,' I said. 'We're old friends. And like I said, I'm a police officer, so you're committing a very serious criminal offence by pointing that thing at me. Put it down please.'

He looked hesitant but didn't lower the gun. Behind me I heard the sound of footsteps. One of the approaching guards called out something in Chechen to the guy pointing the gun at me, and he yelled something back.

I told him to put the gun down again, repeating my mantra that I was a police officer. 'Please, take a look at my warrant card. Then you can see I am who I say I am, and you can put that thing down and save yourself a lot of prison time.'

The guy's gun hand was shaking a little, but he wasn't going to back down, not with his friends coming.

As cops, we're always taught to be calm. Not to raise our voices and let our emotions get the better of us. That way we project a sense of authority that automatically generates respect. Most days it works.

Today wasn't one of them.

The other two had arrived now, flanking me. The one holding the submachine gun – a Heckler and Koch that looked like it had been fired a few times – came close and pointed it at my head. He was older and had the blank, brutish face of someone who doesn't waste time on other people's feelings. He looked familiar too; I thought I remembered him from my earlier days investigating Ruslan's crew. But if there was any recognition on his part he didn't show it, and when I started to explain that I was a police officer and that I wasn't here alone, he told me that if I said another word he'd kill me.

I'm not a complete idiot. I shut up.

The third one grabbed the warrant card out of my hand, gave

it a cursory glance, and the three of them had a hurried, tense conversation in Chechen. It was clear my arrival had riled them and they weren't entirely sure what to do. The guard pocketed my warrant card and gave me a rapid, not-particularly-professional pat down. Even so, he quickly discovered my Glock and my phone, along with the wire cutters and the lock picks. He threw the cutters and picks across the courtyard but pocketed the gun and the phone, and they continued their conversation.

I noticed that the guy holding the submachine gun was sweating and angry, and a thin pool of saliva was forming at the corner of his mouth. The way he spat out his words, and the way the weapon's barrel shook ever so slightly in his grip, made me think he wanted to kill me there and then. I felt my heart beating hard in my chest as I realized, almost as an afterthought, that actually I didn't want to die.

'What's going on here?' came a heavily accented voice from behind me. 'Who's he?'

'He says he's a cop but he's carrying a gun and cutters,' said the one who'd searched me, in English. 'He broke in.'

I felt myself being swung round and suddenly I was facing Dokka Aliyev at very close quarters.

He was a big, intimidating man, my height but a good stone and a half of muscle heavier, with a shiny bald head, narrow, rodent-like eyes, and the kind of welcoming expression that made babies cry and men turn the other way quickly. He recognized me instantly, and he didn't look happy.

'Shit,' he said, looking at the others. 'He *is* a cop.'

'Look, Dokka. Can you tell these guys to stop pointing their illegal weapons at me? I've come here to have a quiet word with your boss. Then I'll be on my way.'

But that was the problem. I couldn't just go. Not now I'd seen all these guns.

I remembered Dokka Aliyev as a hard man, not easily rattled, but he was looking worried now, and I knew that wasn't a good sign.

'Who are you here with?' he demanded.

'We've got the place surrounded,' I said with a lot more confidence than I felt. 'You've been under surveillance here for weeks.'

Aliyev's eyes scanned the perimeter fence before turning back to me. 'Then why haven't they come in to help you?' he asked, but he didn't sound entirely sure of himself.

'They will do. Mark my words.' I paused, then took a gamble. 'We believe you are planning to sell weapons to terrorists, and I have to tell you, Dokka, that unless you want to spend the rest of your life in prison, then that's a very, very bad move.'

Aliyev flinched and I knew I was on to something. He knew I knew it too.

'What's your name again?' he said, his face inches from mine. 'You weren't important enough for me to remember it before.'

I held his gaze. 'Detective Inspector Mason to you. And you want to remember who you're threatening.'

'Well, Mr Mason, *you're* the one who's made a very, very bad move, my friend, because you know what? I don't believe you've got this place surrounded.'

I started to say something, knowing I had to keep the dialogue going, but he responding by punching me hard in the gut. I doubled over in pain, holding my stomach and resisting the urge to drop to my knees and throw up. I let the pain ease a little then forced myself to stand back up.

Aliyev was eyeing the perimeter, and it must have been as clear to him as it was to me that the cavalry weren't on the horizon. I stole a glance at my watch. Nearly twenty-five to four. A couple of minutes before Chris was expecting a message from me, less than five before he called for help; but we were a long way out of town so help wasn't going to be just round the corner.

'Come with me,' he said. 'It's time to see the boss.'

'That's all I actually wanted to do,' I said as he grabbed me by the arm and dragged me across the courtyard, followed by the other three. I was hoping that Chris would catch a glimpse of me and see that I was in trouble but I couldn't remember whether the route we were taking was visible from his position.

There was a side entrance to the old farmhouse, and Aliyev stopped outside and knocked three times, waiting for a shout from inside before opening the door.

This was my chance. Bula Ruslan might have been a thug of the worst order but he was still a businessman and he wasn't going to like his men manhandling a senior detective so, as I was dragged inside, I began to protest at my treatment.

Until I saw that the man sitting behind the desk facing me wasn't Bula Ruslan. Instead I was looking at a small bearded guy dressed in an open-necked shirt with his sleeves rolled up. I'd put him at about fifty, and there was an air of cold authority about him that would disconcert most men. He inspected me with black, flinty eyes through the smoke from the cigarette in his hand.

I felt his aura immediately and it was dark. Very dark.

Aliyev had come in behind me with two of the other men. He went over to the man behind the desk and handed him my gun, phone and warrant card, talking to him in Chechen.

The man listened in silence, never once taking his eyes off me.

'What are you doing here?' he asked in heavily accented English, putting my belongings in one of the desk drawers.

'I'm here to see Bula Ruslan,' I told him.

'And do you have a warrant to be on these premises?'

Like all organized criminals, even ones fresh to these shores, he knew the limits of the law.

'No,' I told him. 'I'm just here for a friendly chat.'

'And how did you get in?'

'There was a hole in the fence.'

'You don't knock on the door like everyone else?' His face cracked a smile. It wasn't a pleasant sight. 'I think that in your country that is called trespass, is it not? And I understand you're carrying a gun too? So I'm thinking you are here illegally.'

One of the most important lessons a police officer learns is never to let the person you're talking to think he's in charge. You have to assert yourself, however nervous you're feeling – and I was feeling very nervous now.

'I'm here to see Bula,' I told him. 'I understand this is his business. Where is he?'

'Not any more it isn't. Bula's gone. The business belongs to me, and you're trespassing.'

'I just came to give him a friendly warning,' I said. 'We've had word he might be supplying weapons to terrorists, and if that's the case then he, and any of his associates who are involved – you and your friends here included – are going to go to prison for a long, long time, particularly if those weapons end up being used.'

The smile died on his face and the black eyes narrowed. 'I don't know what you're talking about.'

But he did. I could see that.

'And I don't know what Bula's doing either. Maybe that's his scene, I don't know. Maybe you need to go ask him.'

'Maybe I'll do that.' I exhaled loudly. 'Well, thanks for your time.'

I started to turn but stopped when I felt the barrel of a gun being pushed hard into the small of my back.

'You're not going anywhere,' the man behind the desk told me, a worrying firmness in his voice. 'Because if you do, I know you'll tell all your colleagues about all these guns you've seen, and that's not going to happen. My friend Dokka here says you're a famous police officer. That you shot dead two jihadis?'

So Aliyev *had* remembered who I was. And knew about the incident outside my apartment eighteen months ago, even though my identity was supposed to be a secret.

'Look, I'm not prepared to discuss any of this. I want to leave. Now.'

'He also says you've been in trouble at work for breaking rules and that you are the kind of man who would turn up here and break in without the knowledge of his superiors.' The smile came back again. 'That they might not even know you're here.'

'They know.'

The man shook his head. 'I don't think so.' He turned to Aliyev. 'You know where to take him.'

It's at moments like these that you either react or you acquiesce, and there was no way I was going to acquiesce. I'm not a hero. I feel fear just like everyone else, especially with a gun in my back. But I don't avoid a fight.

'Fuck you,' I told him, trying to pull my way out of Aliyev's grip.

The sad thing is, I never stood a chance. A fist slammed into my kidneys and I was pulled down to my knees, my hands forced behind my back. I started to struggle but I got a blow on the back of my head from one of the guns, and I grunted in pain. Thankfully it was only a glancing one, delivered without much force, but it was enough to slow me down while my hands were tied.

I was dragged out of the door by Aliyev's henchmen and taken round the back of the building, definitely out of sight of Chris now. There was no comforting sound of approaching sirens. Just a grim silence.

'You're making a big mistake, Dokka,' I told him over my shoulder as I was led to a dilapidated-looking shed.

'No, man,' he replied, with, I thought, a hint of regret in his voice. 'It's you who's made the mistake.'

I didn't bother commenting. It was hard to argue with that assessment.

Aliyev pulled a bunch of keys from his pocket and opened the door, revealing an old workshop with counters on either side and largely empty, cobweb-strewn shelves lining the walls. The room was dark and smelt of mould and age, which was a considerable improvement on the smell outside. Aliyev went in first and pulled up an old rug from the middle of the floor.

That was when I saw the wooden hatch about three feet square set into the concrete. It was secured in place by two heavy bolts. Aliyev barked an order and one of the men released the bolts and yanked open the hatch, revealing nothing but darkness below.

'Please,' I said, staring into the hole and feeling the panic building. 'Not in there.'

I struggled like a madman, feeling a renewed strength born of pure fear, but it was too late. The three of them forced me into a position where I was standing on the edge, and I felt my legs being kicked from under me.

I'm not afraid to tell you I cried out in terror as they let go of me and I fell into the darkness.

I landed almost immediately on a hard stone floor. I kept my footing and raised my arms skywards in an effort to stop them shutting the lid, but I was too late. It closed with a loud thump, plunging me into total darkness, and I heard the bolts being pushed across, followed by the rug, then the sound of footsteps moving away.

I was all alone in the pitch black, and the terror came at me in crushing waves as I was dragged back to a terrible night many, many years ago.

Twenty-five

Gaydon stood at the top of a hill overlooking fields and wood-land, the hazy buildings of London in the far distance. He took a deep breath then took out the phone he'd used to film the girl they'd abducted this morning and dialled a number, taking a deep breath when it started ringing.

Chris Leavey looked at his watch. 15.40. Ray should have texted him four minutes ago to let him know he was OK.

He cursed. It was typical of Ray to put him in a position like this. He'd always been a difficult guy to work with but since the night eighteen months ago when he'd shot dead the two men outside his apartment he'd become increasingly unhinged. By rights, Ray should have been invalided out of the force. He was psychologically damaged and unpredictable, but the fact remained he was also highly experienced, and in these days of manpower shortages and ever-increasing threats, that counted for a lot. At one time he and Chris had been good friends, but that time had gone now. Chris felt sorry for him. Pitied him really. But he was no longer close to him and, in truth, he would have preferred it if the two of them no longer had anything to do with each other.

Which was why it was a relief for Chris to know he was now leaving the force. He would write his resignation letter this evening. See out the current security threat, then be gone to a place where he could work eight-hour days for twice the money, and where he didn't have to risk his neck or have to face down hardened criminals ever again.

He checked his watch again. 15.41. What the hell was he going to say when he called in for back-up? That Ray had decided to go walkabout with a pair of wire cutters and was now AWOL? Butterworth would go ballistic, and with good reason.

But Chris knew he had to make the call. If nothing else, Ray knew how to look after himself and if he wasn't texting it meant he was in trouble.

He lifted the phone to punch in the numbers.

And stopped.

The main gates to the plant – the ones he and Ray had driven past earlier – had opened, and a car was driving through the gap, moving slowly. Chris lifted the binoculars Ray had left with him and looked through them.

The car was a silver Ford Focus – apparently the most popular make and colour in the country. It was also the car that witnesses had suggested one of the three terror suspects, Danesh Kashani, was now driving. Chris focused the binoculars. From his position he could just about make out that there were three men in the car. He couldn't see the driver but he had a direct view of the two passengers. He looked at the one in the front seat, recalling the photos of the three suspects he'd been shown earlier that day, getting in as close as the binoculars would allow.

The car disappeared behind a bank that ran along the far side of the chimneys and he heard it stop as it pulled up, out of sight, at the central compound's main gate. But Chris had seen enough. His heart was beating faster now, and the reason for that was because he was 95 per cent sure that the front-seat passenger was one of the terrorists.

In a moment, his opinion of his one-time friend Ray changed. No longer was he the maverick idiot. He was the man who'd come up with the clue that had led them to this place and ultimately to the terrorist cell they were looking for.

'Jesus, Ray,' he whispered. 'You sure know how to pull a rabbit out of the hat.'

But where the hell was he?

As Chris lifted his phone a second time, it started ringing. He looked at the screen. It was his daughter. She didn't often phone and ordinarily he'd have taken the call, but not right now, in the middle of this. He pressed decline and put in an immediate call to the incident room, getting transferred straight through to Butterworth.

He told the boss what he'd just seen.

'Are you sure?' said Butterworth.

'Not a hundred per cent but they're driving a Focus and the one I saw looks a lot like suspect two, Youssef Ali.'

'We'll be there as quickly as possible. If they leave before we seal off the place, get the registration on the car they're in and follow too if it's safe to. Where are you positioned?'

Chris gave his location and was told to keep his phone line free. Butterworth then ended the call without asking where Ray was, which was perhaps just as well.

He took a deep breath, thinking that he needed to get closer to the action so he could get a better view of what was going on. There was no activity round the chimneys so he got up and ran between them, ignoring the intense stench of fat they were emitting. Beyond the chimneys was a rubbish tip piled high with all kinds of industrial junk tucked into a large man-made bank where earth that had been quarried when they built the lorry park had been piled.

As Chris reached the bank and started to climb up it, his phone rang a second time. Once again it was his daughter, and this time he was concerned because it was obviously urgent.

'Hey, honey, how are you doing? Long time no hear.'

'This is not your daughter,' said a cold, male voice. 'But she is here with us.'

Chris felt his stomach clench. For a couple of seconds he was too shocked to speak. He crouched down on the bank, conscious that he was exposed out here.

'Please keep calm, DS Leavey,' said the caller. 'Are you alone?'

Chris took a deep breath. 'Yes.'

'Is there anyone in earshot?'

'No. I'm outside. Who are you? And what do you want?'

'Don't start throwing questions at me. I'm the one in control here. We have your daughter. We took her this morning from near her university and she's being kept unhurt at a secure location.

As soon as this call ends I'm going to send you a short video of her that we took an hour ago.'

The caller wasn't using a mechanism to disguise his voice and Chris detected an accent that he couldn't quite place.

'What do you want me to do?' he asked, keeping his voice calm, his tone reasonable.

'A woman called Jane Kinnear is being kept in a safehouse provided by your organization, Counter Terrorism Command. We want its location.'

Chris's breath caught in his throat. Jesus. So this was something to do with the Anil Rahman murder.

'I don't know its location,' he said. 'Only the head of CT knows that.'

'Then find out. Now. Or your daughter dies.'

'Look, I'm not privy to that information. I can't just get hold of it.'

'With respect, DS Leavey, that's your problem. I'm going to call you back within the hour from a different phone. You give me the address, and when I'm satisfied it's the right one, your daughter will be released along with her phone.'

'I can't do it in that time.'

'I don't think you're hearing me. If you ever want to see your daughter alive again, you'll do it. And, DS Leavey? Do not go to your bosses for help. As you should be able to tell by now, we will find out. Also, do not try to trace your daughter's phone. It will do you no good. I'm speaking to you on it miles from where she's being kept.'

'How do I know she's even alive?' demanded Chris, but the caller had already rung off, leaving him staring at the screen.

He was still staring at it ten seconds later when his phone bleeped to tell him he'd received a WhatsApp message from Amber.

Amber. His gorgeous nineteen-year-old daughter. The apple of his eye. His only child and the most important person in his world. They hadn't always seen eye to eye. She'd been a sweet child who'd turned into a wild teenager, and they'd had more than their fair share of fallings-out, but their relationship had settled back down since she'd started uni. He'd even arranged to go down to visit her in Brighton with Charlotte the weekend after next.

And now she was being used to blackmail him as his work clashed with his personal life in dramatic style. It was hugely unfair that it had to happen now when he was on the verge of leaving the force after more than twenty years. A few more weeks and Amber would have been safe and life could have carried on as normal – or at least as normal as life can ever carry on when your wife's slowly dying of MS.

The WhatsApp message was a video, as the caller had told him it would be.

He closed his eyes for a second, steeling himself. Chris Leavey was a strong man. He'd had to be to do his job these past two decades. He'd seen things that no one should ever see. The charred corpses of a young mother and her two tiny children after a house fire; the library of horrific kiddie porn on a suspect's laptop; the immediate aftermath of the Edgware Road bomb on 7/7. He'd managed to cut himself off emotionally from all of it because it was his work. But he couldn't cut himself off from this.

He watched the video for five seconds; ascertained that yes, these people – whoever they were – did indeed have his beloved Amber, and were fully prepared to kill her; and then he switched off and shoved the phone in his pocket.

He felt dizzy, nauseous, and a cold, damp sweat formed on his brow as the anxiety took hold. But he ignored all that, because he needed to think.

And he knew he didn't have much time.

Twenty-six

Ray

I'm afraid of the dark. I have been ever since a night thirty-one years ago when I was only seven years old. It was the night that defined my whole life and made me what I am today, both bad and good.

Crouched down in this small black space smelling of damp, not knowing what was going to happen to me, fighting the terrible panic that kept coming at me in waves, I was transported right back there.

Let me start at the beginning. I was brought up in a wealthy household, the middle son of three. My father had inherited from his own father, a successful businessman who'd run a thriving furniture company. My father didn't have the same entrepreneurial drive. Put bluntly, he was a lazy alcoholic. He drifted through life living off his inheritance, and met my mother when he was in his mid-forties. She was almost twenty years younger, and it wasn't a happy union.

My father was a charmer, good-looking too, and, although I'm not sure of the whole story, it seemed he swept my mother off her feet. By the time she realized what a philandering arsehole he was, she was married and pregnant. He didn't bother changing his behaviour afterwards and appeared to use my mother as a glorified cleaner and baby machine. He bullied her, I remember that. Bullied all of us. I learned at a very young age to keep out of his way – not to cry in front of him, or upset him in any way, just to keep myself to myself – but it wasn't as easy for my mum. She was constantly in the firing line.

In the end, my father broke her spirit. Turned her into a husk of a woman. She would still put food on the table for my brothers and me, make sure we got off to school on time and did our homework; but, although she was there physically, emotionally she'd disappeared for good. She never told me she loved me, and yet I still have a picture of her in my mind smiling down at me as I lay in her arms, no more than two years old, and there was still something close to love in her eyes then, I'm sure of it. I cling to that image, I always have done.

And then all my memories of them ended one cold February night.

It was a Sunday and my father had been away for at least two days. No one knew where. I hadn't even bothered asking. He did it all the time. What mattered was the effect his absence had on my mother. Usually she just accepted it and carried on as if it was the most natural thing in the world, but I remember vividly how differently she'd been behaving that day. She was agitated and angry. Muttering to herself. She'd disappear into her bedroom for long periods of time, leaving my brothers and me alone, and when I went up to find out what she was doing, she shooed me away. I found out later she was packing. She was going to leave the three of us with my father and make her own way in the world. She'd had enough of life with all of us.

That night, when my father came crashing noisily through the door, Olly and James were in the lounge watching TV while I was upstairs in my bedroom reading a book. I stayed where I was. I'd learned that when my father made a lot of noise coming into the house, it meant he was drunk and best avoided. I could hear him talking loudly downstairs but couldn't make out what he was saying.

And then I heard him and my mother screaming at each other, their voices raised to almost hysterical levels. I tried as hard as I could to shut out the noise, but it was impossible. The shouting didn't go on for long – a couple of minutes at most – and was followed by a single cry from my mother. It sounded like a cry of pain. I'd heard such cries before because he'd sometimes hit her to bring her into line, but then, instead of tears and recriminations, there was just silence.

I was already in my pyjamas, and I put down the book and got up from the bed, padding lightly over to the bedroom door. I opened the door a crack and listened. All I could hear was the sound of the TV coming from the lounge.

I remember feeling a cold sense of dread heading up my spine. It was the very first time the sixth sense I've had ever since came into play. Before then I'd been an innocent child. Not a happy one – never happy – but at least unaware of the true extent of darkness in this world. Now I was about to discover it in its entirety.

The silence was unnerving. My father was never quiet. My mother yes, but not him. I wanted to call out to see if everything was all right but something stopped me. Instead, I opened the door wider before creeping down the stairs as my natural curiosity got the better of me. We lived in the country in a big, rambling house that dated back to the early 1800s. It would have been a good place to be a kid if our home life had been happier. Now, with each stair making an angry creak as my feet touched them, the house felt dark and foreboding.

Across the entrance hall, the kitchen door was slightly open and there was a light shining from inside. I crept over to it, my footfalls quietened by the thickness of the Persian rug. The TV was still blaring away in the lounge and I wondered if my two brothers had heard the argument and, if so, whether they'd simply zoned out.

I listened at the kitchen door.

I could hear breathing. Thick, rasping breathing.

It didn't sound right.

The dread climbed up my spine and my hand was shaking as I slowly pushed open the door, terrified but desperate to know what was inside.

At first I saw nothing. The dining area to the right was empty and my view of the main kitchen area was blocked by the work unit to my left. The breathing was louder. It was coming from inside the main kitchen. I stepped further into the room, trying to be as silent as humanly possible, then stopped at the end of the unit. Very, very slowly I peered round it.

The Witness

My mother was sitting on the floor, her back supported by a kitchen unit. She was dressed in a white top and jeans. I can picture her now. Perfectly. Her face and hair were drenched in blood and it had leaked down on to her top. When she breathed, the blood made little bubbles that popped audibly. One eye was shut but the other was staring straight ahead. There was no expression in it at all.

I didn't make a sound or say a word. I simply stood there staring at her. I don't even think she knew I was there. I doubted she would have cared if she'd seen me. My mother didn't love me. I knew that. But I felt something for her then, I just wasn't sure what.

I heard a noise and looked towards where it had come from.

My father stood at the sink, dressed in a long coat. He was unshaven and his hair was a mess. He looked like some kind of wild man, and he was breathing fast and heavily. There was something in his hand too, although I couldn't see it.

I crouched down. I didn't think he'd seen me.

I heard him call my mother a bitch under his breath. Then louder. 'You bitch!' He made a sudden movement and I heard him jump on her, even though I knew she must have been badly hurt, and then a sound like a melon being sliced.

I peered round the kitchen unit. I couldn't help myself. My father was all over her like some kind of immense spider, the long carving knife bloody in his hand as he drove it into her time after time.

Without even thinking about it I screamed and ran for the door, the shock surging through me.

'Wilf!' I heard my father call out. 'Come here, boy!'

Wilf had been my name then. Wilfred Piers Webster.

I slowed down. When my father shouted for you to come, you went if you knew what was good for you. But then, as I saw him come after me, dressed from head to foot in black, his face contorted in an expression of pure madness, I knew without a doubt that he meant to kill me.

I was out of the door and across the entrance hall in a flash, yelling and screaming for my life. I didn't even think about making for the front door. For me, safety was the upstairs.

As I ran up the staircase, taking the steps two at a time, so frightened I could scarcely think, the lounge door flew open and Olly came running out. 'What's going on?' he cried, and then, as he saw my father, the words died in his throat. He was wearing pyjamas too. Superman ones.

In one sudden movement, my father swung round and fell on him too. The knife arced through the air, I saw blood, and Olly crumpled to the floor with barely a sound. From inside the lounge I heard Jamie scream as my father rushed into the room crying and shouting and howling as if he was battling some cruel and malevolent spirit inside him, and losing.

I kept running, fear and confusion coursing through me. Some people would have shut out the memories of that night in order to cope with what they'd seen but it was the reverse with me. I can remember every thought that ran through my head as first I ran into my bedroom, looking around desperately for a place to hide and realizing that this would be the first place he'd look, then set off down the landing corridor towards the back of the house and the spare rooms, trying to keep as quiet as possible, wondering why my father was doing this to my brothers and me because we hadn't been bad and we didn't deserve it, and wondering too whether I was going to go to heaven after he killed me.

I stopped when I got to a small, rarely used bedroom near the end of the hall and went inside, closing the door behind me as quietly as possible. The room was full of boxes of junk but there was enough moonlight coming in through the open curtains for me to make my way through it without making any noise. There was a large antique cupboard against one wall and I climbed inside, closing it gently behind me before crouching down in the darkness and covering myself with old coats and dresses. Wondering whether there was a better hiding place anywhere else. Hoping I'd chosen well . . .

I waited.

Time passed. It was probably no more than a few minutes but it felt so much longer. The darkness in the cupboard was welcoming, acting as a camouflage, and I figured that if I waited long enough then I was going to be OK.

And then I heard it. Footsteps coming down the hall in my direction, accompanied by heavy breathing.

It was my father.

'Wilf, where are you?' he called out. 'Come out and see me. I'm so sorry. We can sort this out. Just tell me where you are.'

He sounded genuinely apologetic and I wondered for a moment if what I'd just witnessed had been a horrible dream and now I'd woken up. I wanted to go to him. God, I did. No young child wants to believe that his dad would deliberately hurt him. He'd hit me before, of course, although only occasionally, and usually a single slap round the head or body just to keep me in line. But never anything like this.

I sat up inside the cupboard. I'd dreamed it. Surely I'd dreamed it.

But some deep-seated instinct kept me from calling out.

I heard one of the other doors opening across the landing. 'Are you in here?' he called out. 'Where are you, Wilf? Come out now otherwise your dad's going to be very cross, and you really don't want to make me cross.'

A minute later another door opened, closer. It was the room next door and I could hear my father looking around, and cursing under his breath. He didn't sound sorry any more.

I could have run, I suppose. Made a break for it while he was in one of the other rooms. But I was seven years old and scared out of my wits. I lay back down under the clothes in the fetal position, praying for this terror to end. Hoping that the police would somehow have found out what was happening and already be on their way here to rescue me and put my father in prison.

The door to the room I was in opened. Very, very slowly.

And then he was inside, only feet away from me. I heard the light being switched on and him coming closer.

I held my breath, my whole body stiffening, praying over and over in my head to God, asking him to protect me, telling him that I'd be the best boy ever just as long as he let me live.

'I know you're in here,' he growled, 'and you're really making me angry now. Come out, you little bastard.' I could hear him grinding his teeth in frustration and could imagine the anger on his face. The bloody knife in his hand.

The cupboard door opened and, even though my eyes were shut and I was hidden under all the coats, I could feel the light flooding through.

He was going to find me.

I didn't move a muscle. My lungs felt close to bursting. I have never been so scared in my life. Because at that moment I felt utterly alone in the world.

I could hear him feeling around clumsily inside the cupboard. He patted the pile of coats and dresses I was hiding under, and I heard him grunt with exertion as he bent down and prodded it with the knife. Once, twice, three times. Harder each time. He pulled aside one of the coats, stabbed the remaining pile again, and I felt the sharpness of the blade on my leg but not enough to break the skin.

Somehow, miraculously, I had the strength of will not to cry out, but I knew I was going to have to breathe soon. I couldn't keep it in much longer.

My father cursed, kicked the pile then shut the door hard in frustration.

I exhaled, inhaled, almost in one movement. Prayed he hadn't heard.

I heard him moving around the room. 'Why don't you come out wherever you are, Wilf? Come out and see me. Come out!' He howled out the last two words, and then just as suddenly his whole body was racked with desperate sobs. 'Oh God. What have I done? Forgive me . . . forgive me . . .'

I wanted to forgive him too – to break free from my hiding place and tell him it was OK.

Again, instinct stopped me. I forced myself to stay silent and unmoving as he left the room and walked off down the hall, still sobbing and crying.

I waited. And waited. I could no longer hear anything. I kept asking myself, is it a trick? Is it a trick?

Then I smelled it. Strong and acrid. Smoke. Growing stronger all the time. I coughed. I couldn't help it. It took me a few seconds to compute that my father had set the house on fire. I didn't know what to do. If I stayed, I died. But if I left my hiding place I risked dying too.

It was getting progressively harder to breathe, and that was what made the decision for me. Pulling off the coats that covered me, I tried to push open the cupboard doors.

Nothing happened. I pushed again. Hard. For some reason, they simply wouldn't open.

Panic flooded through me. Trapped in the dark and struggling to breathe, I'll never forget that feeling of utter meltdown. I kicked. I struggled. I screamed. I no longer made any effort to conceal myself. I didn't care if my father was standing right outside with the knife raised above his head ready to strike. Anything was better than this.

Smoke was pouring in now. Choking me. Soon I wouldn't be able to breathe at all. I was going to die. Burnt alive. It was over. But still I lashed and screamed, pushing and shoving the doors to no effect, unable to think straight, the panic infecting every nerve ending in my body.

I don't know exactly what happened but somewhere in the midst of my wild, seemingly impotent struggles I lashed out with a kick that connected in exactly the right place and one of the doors flew open.

The Witness

My father had switched off the light but I could see the thick smoke in the gloom and hear the crackle of fire coming from somewhere outside the door. But it didn't matter. I was free.

I ran to the bedroom door, opened it, and recoiled from the intense, almost painful, wave of heat. A huge cloud of black smoke enveloped me, burning my eyes. There was no way out. Coughing uncontrollably, desperate for fresh air, and almost completely unable to open my eyes, I ran over to the bedroom window. It was one of those big old-fashioned sash windows and luckily I knew how to open it. With trembling hands, I yanked open the lock and pulled the bottom pane upwards, letting in cold beautiful air. I clambered on to the ledge, throwing one leg over so I was balanced half in, half out.

It looked a long way down. It probably wasn't, but it felt it, and I was only seven years old. I hesitated. Wondered whether I should wait for the fire brigade or the police to come and rescue me.

And then I looked back and saw him come running into the room, his long coat in flames, eyes wide open and utterly mad, as if oblivious to the smoke, the knife high above his head ready to strike. It was the final image I had of my father. A demon made flesh, screaming his hatred at the whole world.

This time I didn't hesitate. I jumped.

It was over. And yet at the same time it had just begun.

Twenty-seven

I looked at my watch, the dial barely illuminated in the gloom. 15.49. I should have sent a text to Chris confirming I was OK at 15.36, meaning he should have called for back-up about ten minutes ago. I was confident he would have done. He might have been pissed off with me but he was totally reliable.

I wondered why this new boss had put me here, and what he and his comrades intended to do with me. It was clear that this was some purpose-built dungeon, the kind I remembered seeing in medieval castles during school visits. Still struggling to control my terror, I felt round in the darkness and worked out that the place was no more than ten feet across. There were old rags on the floor, an upturned plastic bucket in one corner, and a lingering smell of damp and piss. The only way to reach the trap door was if I jumped up, and there was no way out that way anyway.

I was utterly helpless, just like I'd been in that bedroom

cupboard all those years ago. Even if the police turned up, they wouldn't find me. For all I knew the Chechens might have abandoned the place already, leaving me here to rot unseen. That way there'd be no evidence against them for any crime. No one would ever find me. I'd starve to death . . .

I shut my eyes, slowed my breathing. Told myself to stay calm and be patient. I'd long ago learned that you have to remain positive whatever the circumstances. The police would search this site from top to bottom to find me. I'd hear them when they were nearby and then I'd be able to make enough noise to alert them to my presence. It might take a while but they'd find me.

Stay positive. Stay positive. Stay positive.

And then I heard something. Movement directly above the trap door. The bolt was being pulled across.

I stood up as the trap door slowly opened, letting in welcome daylight.

The man staring down at me was the small wiry guy who'd been the first to stop me earlier. He had a quick look round to check there was no one about before lowering a short stepladder into the pit.

'You must be very quiet,' he whispered. 'I am going to get you out.'

I took the stepladder, steadied it and clambered out with a huge sense of relief.

'Thanks,' I whispered as he helped me to my feet. 'I owe you one.'

'Then help me by not reporting me to anyone,' he said, shutting the trap door and replacing the rug on top. 'I am leaving with you. I want no part of this.'

Simon Kernick

'No part of what?'

'Of what is going on. The new boss is supplying weapons to jihadis. I heard the others talking about it. And now the jihadis have turned up here to collect them.'

Jesus. So I'd been right.

'They want to kill you too. And I don't want to get involved in killing a cop. It's way too much trouble.'

I grunted. 'Thanks for the concern.'

'The boss says you're here on your own. Is that right?'

I shook my head. 'No. My colleagues know I'm here, and they're going to be here soon. You've got a gun, right?'

He could hardly deny it, seeing as he'd stuck one in my back fifteen minutes earlier, but he was clearly reluctant to hand it over. 'I'll keep the gun,' he said, pulling it out and flicking off the safety in a way that suggested he knew how to use it. This guy was clearly no innocent but he'd made the right call. If you were a budding gangster, it was all about making money. There was no reward or future in getting involved with terrorism. He could keep the gun if he wanted. Frankly, I just wanted to get out and make sure we rounded up our three suspects who were planning the attack.

'Lead the way,' I told him. 'Is there a back route out?'

He shook his head. 'No, and the front's covered. The only way out is the way you came in. If I help you, you're not going to arrest me, right?'

'You've got my word. I'll forget we ever met.'

He nodded, and we crept out of the shed and headed round the back of the farmhouse, keeping low so we couldn't be seen from inside, and remaining close to the perimeter fence.

'Where did you get in?' he whispered.

'I cut the fence on the other side of the car park, near where the bins are. How many of you are there here?'

'Only the ones you've seen. Four of us altogether, and the boss. Plus the three guys buying the guns. The plant's closed today.' He turned to me. 'I don't know what he thinks he's doing getting involved in something like this. It is bad for us all.'

Like I said, most criminals just want to get on with the business of theft, extortion and murder rather than concern themselves with more lofty ideals. And this one was no different. You could almost feel sorry for him.

Across the courtyard, the guard with the MP5 stood outside one of the converted barns, looking the other way. Parked a few feet in front of him was a silver Ford Focus, which I had no doubt was the one our three terrorist suspects were driving. So we had everyone we needed in one place.

I listened out for any sirens but couldn't hear anything.

There was a twenty-yard gap across a further stretch of courtyard, which we had to cross with no cover and the possibility of being spotted by the guy with the gun before we could get behind a line of wheelie bins in the car park. From there it was only another fifteen yards and we were at the hole in the fence, and freedom.

I looked at the man who'd rescued me and he stared back at me. On closer inspection, he was probably only in his early twenties. He held the gun tightly in his hand and I guessed that he'd never fired a shot in anger. I motioned for him to give it to me but he shook his head adamantly.

I wanted to argue. I had full confidence that, if I had to, I could shoot dead the guy with the MP5, even from ten yards away, but I didn't have a clue whether this guy would be able to, or even if he'd have it in him to pull the trigger.

It was too risky for us to remain where we were. We were just going to have to try to sneak across and hope the gunman didn't spot us. I peered round the end of the farmhouse again. He was in the process of lighting a cigarette, with his back to us.

'Come on,' I hissed, 'let's go. Nice and quiet. Make for the bins.'

I grabbed him by the arm and gave him a push, making sure he stayed between the gunman and me. If he insisted on keeping the gun, then he had to be the one in the firing line.

We walked as slowly as anyone can when they know that every second they risk losing their life in a hail of bullets. My rescuer kept his eye firmly on the other gunman, his own gun hand outstretched, ready to fire.

The gunman took a long drag on his cigarette, turning round so he was now in profile but still not looking our way. I was conscious of the loudness of our footfalls on the concrete. Twelve yards, eleven yards, ten . . . Soon we'd be beyond his line of sight.

Which was when my rescuer tripped slightly on an uneven flagstone and his boot scraped on the concrete.

The gunman heard it. I saw him cock his head. He turned round and saw us.

My rescuer cursed but had the presence of mind to start firing. He got off two shots before they were answered by an intense burst of automatic weapon fire. My rescuer took the full force of it. He took a step backwards, stumbled and then collapsed, dropping the gun in the process and sending it clattering across the concrete.

The whole thing happened so fast that I didn't have a chance to make a break for the bins. Instead I dived on to the flagstones, getting myself behind my rescuer's body so I could use him as cover, and scrambled on my front towards the gun as another burst of bullets erupted through the air, several of them striking the body, causing it to judder and shake as they threw up gobbets of blood. The air was full of noise and violence. I could smell the cordite, feel the eruption of adrenalin that coursed through me as my hand reached out and found the gun. Bullets spat up dust only inches from my arm but I didn't even think about them. This was all about survival. I started firing in his general direction without even looking, hoping to throw him off kilter, before rolling on to my back and taking aim two-handed.

My first shots had caused him to jump back behind the building for cover. As he came back out now, firing off another burst, I pulled the trigger three times in rapid succession.

I hit him at least once, somewhere around the groin, and he staggered backwards, his gun arm swinging wildly as the MP5 kept spewing its bullets into the air. I took a better aim and shot him twice more in the upper body, and he fell to his knees, dropping the weapon.

Almost immediately, Dokka Aliyev appeared at the office door, a pistol outstretched in hand, resembling some sort of cut-price Terminator as he looked round angrily for a target to shoot. He'd obviously been in the UK too long and it had made him over-confident. As he turned my way, finger tensing on the trigger, I fired first, cracking off a much-deserved double tap to his chest. He never even got a chance to return fire. His eyes widened in shock and he staggered backwards. Unfortunately, though, he didn't go down. Instead, to my amazement, he steadied himself and took aim back at me, the shock on his face immediately turning to anger. The bastard must have been wearing a flak jacket.

I felt a surge of panic as he fired his first shot. I swear I heard it whizz past my ear, but I steadied myself for long enough to take aim at his face, knowing that legally at least I was only ever going to get one chance to put a bullet in a piece of shit like Dokka Aliyev. Squinting down the sights, I pulled the trigger. A shot rang out, but when I pulled it a second time nothing happened. I'd used up my last bullet. It had been a good one, though. All that training paid off as the round slammed into the bastard's ample chin, sending a fine cloud of blood flying out the back of his head.

He managed to crack off a final wild round then fell back against the side of the barn just as the third gunman stuck his head out of the door, pistol in hand.

I pointed my gun at him and he jumped back inside, giving me time to jump to my feet and run like Usain Bolt towards the bins. By the time the next shots rang out I was already level with them, crouching down and using them as cover as I kept going across the car park, not daring to look back as I tried to remember the spot where I cut through the fence.

I heard panicked shouting coming from behind me, and another shot rang out, but it didn't come anywhere near me. I spotted the hole, and let the gun clatter to the ground as I made a final sprint, diving head first through it, scrambling behind the leylandii and out of sight.

From somewhere in the distance came the first wail of sirens.

I was safe.

Twenty-eight

As shot after shot rang out, Chris Leavey tried desperately to decide what to do. His view of quite a lot of the plant's central compound was obscured but he'd managed to pinpoint Ray through the binoculars – distinctive in his suede jacket, lying on his back as he fired a gun towards an unseen target while the body of a man in black lay a few feet away.

It all seemed almost irrelevant to him now that he might never see his daughter again. He couldn't understand how the kidnappers had managed to snatch Amber so quickly. It was only eighteen hours since Anil and his wife had been murdered. Yet in that short space of time the kidnapper had managed to work out that Chris was on the investigating team and therefore might know the location of the safehouse where the witness to the murders was being kept; found out that he had a daughter and where she lived; and then successfully abducted her before finding a place to keep her secure. They even knew the witness's name. It meant they had to have some high-level inside help. Even so, Chris's detective radar told him that something still wasn't right about this.

Right now, though, that was the least of his problems. He had to get Amber back. Nothing else mattered.

Except it did. As Chris watched through the binoculars, trying to keep his hands from shaking, he saw Ray leap to his feet and start running for his life, rapidly disappearing from view. Forcing himself to act, Chris put a call through to the incident room and hurriedly told them that a number of shots had been fired and there was at least one person down. 'Get armed support here now!' he shouted, before hanging up.

He heard a car start up and he crawled forward to the edge of the hillock trying to get a better look at what was going on. His view was blocked by several buildings but through the central compound's perimeter fence he could just about make out the Ford Focus belonging to the suspects. As he watched through the binoculars he saw the three suspects rush over, looking scared, and jump in. One of them was carrying a black holdall and Chris wondered if it contained guns.

The Focus pulled away at speed. It momentarily went out of sight, and Chris heard it accelerate.

Amber. Oh, Amber. Lying helpless on a bed, a knife being held to her body . . . Chris felt sick with anxiety. He had to get her back. If anything happened to Amber it would kill him. It would kill Charlotte too, and God knows his wife had been through enough . . . they all had. They didn't deserve this.

In the distance he could hear the first sirens. Now that shots had been fired, reinforcements would be racing towards them without the need for stealth, but they sounded like they were still some way away.

The Focus came back into view, racing towards him and nearing the plant's outer gates.

Chris was unsure whether or not the men were armed but he knew he had to stop them. Not because they were about to embark on a terrorist attack that would inevitably leave many dead. Right then, he didn't care about that. What he cared about was finding out where his daughter was and, because her kidnapper had linked her abduction with the terror attack, he was banking on these guys providing some answers.

The car was thirty metres away and was going to have to pass directly below him. There were some broken lumps of concrete amid the junk at the foot of the bank and Chris scrambled down, grabbed a piece about a foot across, and ran back up. He wasn't a particularly fit guy these days – not like Ray, who was forever in the gym – but the trauma of what he was going through had pumped him full of adrenalin. As he reached the top of the bank, he hurled the rock with all his might, just as the Focus was passing below.

It hit the windscreen with an immense crash. The shatterproof Perspex was no match for gravity and the rock exploded through on the driver's side. The Focus left the road at speed, bumping wildly over the uneven ground and into the lorry park where its nearside bounced off the back of one of the stationary lorries with a loud crash, sending it into a spin that turned it round a hundred and eighty degrees before it finally came to a halt in an angry wail of tyres.

Chris had no idea whether these three men knew where Amber was being kept but at that moment they were his only potential lead so, ignoring the fact that they were probably armed, he sprinted across the grass towards the car.

He could see the driver slumped, unmoving, in his seat, while the front-seat passenger was slowly opening his door. It was the convert who'd been identified as Youssef Ali. He was bleeding from the forehead and he looked dazed.

Chris charged straight at him. Realizing the danger he was in, Ali tried to heave himself out of the car. Behind him, the driver was now stirring in his seat but he didn't look like he was capable of doing anything. Chris couldn't see if either man was armed or not. Ten yards separated them. He roared out a battle cry.

Then Ali kicked the door fully open. He was reaching inside his bomber jacket, trying to pull something out.

Without breaking stride, Chris slammed into the car door using all his considerable body weight. The window hit Ali full in the face while the bottom edge trapped his shins with a painful crunch. But Chris wasn't finished. In a fit of rage, he opened the door a second time and began slamming it again and again on Ali's legs. He heard something crack, then reached into the car, punched Ali in the face and dragged him out by his jacket collar, letting his head strike the doorframe en route. Chris yanked Ali's hand out of his pocket and, when it came out empty, he threw him to the ground, took a step back, and kicked him so hard in the stomach that his whole body was actually shunted back a few inches.

'Where's my daughter?' he screamed, pulling Ali to his feet

again and slamming him back against the car. 'Tell me, you fuck! Tell me! Where's my daughter?'

Ali stared at him, his eyes glazed, blood dripping from the side of his mouth, but Chris wasn't giving up and he screamed the question again, so engrossed in the moment that he didn't even hear the rear door open on the other side of the car, or see the third terror suspect emerge.

Twenty-nine

Ray

I was running back to the place where I'd left Chris when I saw the Ford Focus come hurtling out of the central compound making for the main gates. I picked up my pace, my heart still beating ferociously from the bloody encounter I'd just had. I spotted Chris up on the top of the bank with his back to me about fifty yards away, partially obscured by one of the chimneys. He was holding something in both hands and, as I watched, he threw it.

There was a loud smash followed by a screech of tyres and the Ford Focus came hurtling into view across the lorry park next to the chimneys, hitting a lorry before spinning to a noisy halt. I could hear sirens but I didn't want the three terror suspects getting away on foot, so I kept running, even though the adrenalin was beginning to seep out of me now that I was safe. I knew I was going to have to answer questions about what I'd just done. I'd shot two men. I was pretty certain they were both dead, and the frightening thing was, the thought I'd killed them pleased me. They were both amoral thugs, Dokka Aliyev especially. He'd committed crime after crime, torturing rivals, forcing young, vulnerable girls into prostitution, crippling a cyclist in a hit and run and never giving her a second thought. Now he was supplying weapons to those intent on mass murder. Dokka Aliyev was evil. Neither the government nor my colleagues in the police had had the stomach for ending his life, but I had. And at that moment, for the first time in many months, possibly years, I felt truly happy.

Ahead of me, I saw Chris making straight for the Focus. He reached the front passenger side door just as one of the suspects – the black guy, Youssef Ali – started to get out. The next second Chris was using the car door on him like some kind of battering ram, then pulling him out and kicking the crap out of him. He was yelling stuff as well and acting like a madman. I was shocked. Chris was usually the calm, collected one, patient enough never to have to resort to violence. Maybe he'd become more frustrated than I'd thought? But he was going to have to be careful too. I might be able to talk my way out of shooting two men on the argument of self-defence, but you couldn't use that justification when you'd just beaten a man to death.

I was about to yell out when the rear passenger door opened on the far side and the third suspect – the youngest of them, Rani Hussain, only eighteen years old and apparently ready to die – emerged. As he came round the back of the car, I saw that he was carrying an AK-47 assault rifle that looked far too big for him.

By this time I was no more than twenty yards away from the Focus, but he didn't see me. Instead, his attention was focused on Chris. I saw him raise the rifle to hip height and take aim at him. It took a second for Chris to see him and then the two men turned and faced each other while Youssef Ali fell back against the car as Chris let go of him. The two of them – Chris and Hussain – were less than a car's length apart. There was no way Hussain would miss if he pulled the trigger now, however crap a shot he was. A blind man couldn't miss. And I was unarmed and still too far away to save Chris. Any second now he was going to die, leaving his dying wife a widow, and his daughter an orphan.

He'd saved my life once. I could never forget that.

There was a rubbish tip to my left, providing immediate cover. I could have hidden behind it and waited for reinforcements, and no one would have been able to blame me. But I also knew I'd never be able to live with myself if I did that. If I had to die, at least I was going to do it on my feet and facing in the right direction.

'Armed police!' I yelled at the top of my lungs. I pointed my right hand straight out at him, using my middle and forefingers to make a fake gun the way kids do it, hoping that he'd be too panicked by my rapid approach to work out that it wasn't real.

Hussain did look panicked too as he turned my way, but not quite panicked enough. He kept the assault rifle trained on Chris as he watched my approach and it took him barely a second to work out that I didn't have a gun at all, and I was on my own.

At the same time, Chris dived round the front of the Focus so he was out of Hussain's sight, leaving me as the only viable target. Hussain swung the assault rifle round in my direction, an angry snarl on his face. I kept running, virtually on him now, not even thinking about the price of failure, even as I saw his finger squeeze the trigger.

I gritted my teeth, tensing against the impact of the bullets, recognizing in that single tiny flash of time that I was about to die.

Except I didn't. No shots rang out.

I charged into Hussain, knocking the rifle to one side with my arm and launching a headbutt straight into his face. The force of the blow, coupled with my momentum, sent him flying backwards into the side of the Focus. He went down like a sack of potatoes, a look of shock and – I think – disappointment on his face.

Panting with exhaustion, I took a step back and picked up the AK-47. I checked the safety. It was off. Then the magazine. Fully loaded. And yet it hadn't fired. I sighed with relief as the full extent of my good fortune hit me. The rifle was shaking in my hands and I had to force myself to breathe steadily and calm down.

Chris got back to his feet and came striding towards me. His eyes were wide and he looked terrified.

'It's OK now,' I said. 'It's over.'

He stopped beside me, his whole body shaking intensely, and stared down at where Rani Hussain lay, dazed but still conscious. 'It isn't over,' he whispered.

I frowned. 'What do you mean? We've got them.'

Chris stared at me, and the pain in his eyes was palpable. 'Someone's kidnapped Amber.'

'What?'

'He wants to know the location of the safehouse where we're keeping the witness.'

I shook my head. 'That doesn't make sense. You don't know it. None of us do.'

He leaned in close. 'I know that, but a man's just made contact with me on Amber's phone while you were gone. He sent me a video of her . . .' He stopped, took a breath. 'Of her blindfolded and tied to a bed and him holding a knife to her. It was her, Ray, and it's no joke. The kidnapper even knew the witness's name.'

'Shit.'

I felt for him. Jesus, I did. But I felt something else too. Another kick of adrenalin. The excitement was continuing.

Chris motioned towards Hussain. 'If any of these pieces of shit know anything, we need to get it out of them now. I can't lose my daughter, Ray. Not after everything else that's happened.'

The sirens were loud now, and there were a lot of them. They were out on the main road, closing in, but they'd still have to break through the front entrance. I guessed we had two or three minutes before they were on us and Hussain and his buddies passed into the black hole of the criminal justice system where they'd have defence lawyers, all kinds of rights not to answer questions, and nice comfortable cells from which to dream of creating more mayhem. And no one would give a shit about whether or not a mid-ranking police officer's daughter died a lonely death and left a welter of grief behind.

But Chris cared. And I cared.

Chris's mobile was ringing. He pulled it out and switched it to silent. Looked at me.

I stood over Hussain and pointed the AK-47 down at him, the end of the barrel lingering a foot above his face. I noticed almost as an aside that my hands had stopped shaking. I was back in the zone.

'Where's his daughter?' I said coldly, my finger tensing on the trigger.

Hussain's eyes blazed with defiance. 'Fuck you. I don't have to say a word. That thing doesn't work.'

I laughed without humour. 'It works fine. It's just that the trigger guard's tight. You need to give it a good squeeze, and then it'll fire perfectly. Answer my questions or I'll shoot you in the balls and leave you alive, so by the time you get to paradise there'll be nothing but a hole for those seventy-two virgins to play with.' I moved the rifle so it was pointing at his groin.

'You wouldn't dare,' he said, but the defiance in his eyes had gone.

'I just shot two men dead. What's to stop me shooting you? I'll say we were wrestling with the gun and it went off and you were the one who got hit. Chris'll back me up. Won't you, Chris?'

Chris stared down at Hussain with utter contempt. 'Absolutely.'

'And no one's going to have any sympathy for a murderous jihadi who loses his balls before he gets a chance to massacre a load of innocent civilians. Most people will think good riddance, and no one'll be able to prove otherwise. So you answer my questions right now, or I pull the trigger.'

I shoved the end of the barrel hard into his groin, gave him the look that told him I meant what I said and asked him again where Chris's daughter was being held.

'I don't know,' he said, shaking now and motioning towards Chris. 'I don't even know who this guy is.'

'Last chance,' I said, leaning down on the barrel, pushing it even harder into his groin, watching him wince in pain.

'I'm telling the truth, I swear it. You've got to believe me.'

The problem was, I did. He was telling the truth.

Beside me I heard Chris take a deep breath as he fought to hold in his emotions.

The sirens, loud and insistent, were static now and I guessed that the whole convoy of reinforcements was gathered at the front gates, trying to get through. Soon they'd have helicopters at the scene. I needed to hurry.

'Who organized the attack you're meant to be carrying out?' I said, my finger tightening on the trigger once again. 'Who's your handler?'

'Karim Khan,' Hussain said quickly, clearly wanting to co-operate.

'Why did he have Anil Rahman killed?'

Hussain looked confused. 'What are you talking about? Anil's dead?'

'You knew him?'

'I was with him out in Syria one time. I didn't know he was dead, I swear.'

I heard several loud bangs and then the sound of the gates opening, followed by cars roaring through in our direction. From off to the west, a helicopter was approaching fast.

'Do you know a white convert, a man of about my age, who's joined the cause? Tell me now.'

But Hussain knew the police were just seconds away and I could see he wasn't going to talk.

The fear and frustration that were always inside me came tearing up to the surface, almost uncontrollable in their intensity. I truly wanted to kill Hussain then. In cold blood. To rid him from this world.

He saw it in my face and began shaking once again.

I smelled shit. He'd soiled himself.

It took the edge from my emotions and I stepped back, still training the weapon on him as the first armed response vehicle skidded to a halt ten yards away and three armed uniforms piled out, shouting at us to place our weapons on the ground and get down on our knees with our hands behind our heads.

My eyes met Chris's.

'Don't say anything, Ray,' he whispered. 'Please. I've got to sort this alone.'

'No,' I told him, gently laying the AK-47 on the ground. 'We do this together.'

Thirty

Jane

I wasn't able to improve the e-fit of the man who'd killed Anil and Sharon Rahman and by now it was nearly four p.m. and I was getting tired, so Charlie agreed to call it a day.

'So, how close do you think we've got?' he asked, bringing up an image of a dark-haired man with a lean face and strong jaw on his laptop screen.

I shrugged. 'It does look like him but you've got to remember I saw this man for no more than a second and then I was running for my life.' I looked across at Anji who was sitting on the opposite sofa watching proceedings. 'I think it's the best I can do,' I told her.

She gave me a warm smile. 'That's fine. Charlie will leave you a copy and if you can think of anything that needs changing on the picture then I'm sure you'll come back, won't you, Charlie?'

'Of course,' he said.

He printed off a couple of copies of the image and put his laptop away before getting to his feet. I got up too, and he put out a hand.

'Thanks for your cooperation, Jane. I think you're very brave, and I hope you don't remain cooped up here for too long.'

I smiled bravely. 'My sentiments exactly, but I'll try to make the best of it.'

'If you want to go and wait in the car, Charlie, I'll be out in a few minutes,' said Anji. She waited until he left the room, then turned to me. 'I'm going to take Charlie back to his car then I've got a few errands to run. I won't be gone long. An hour, an hour and a half maximum.'

I told her it was no problem.

'And don't worry about DC Jeffs either,' she said. 'I think he's scared of you. He's been sat outside smoking most of the afternoon. He's going to be replaced tomorrow. Me too, probably, and the response team.'

'Then what happens?'

'You'll get exactly the same number of officers, and I may well be back in the next couple of days. Then it's just a matter of playing everything by ear. If it's not deemed safe for you to go home, we'll collect the rest of your belongings, bring them here, and organize things so you can call work, your sons, et cetera. Hopefully this'll all be over soon.'

'Sure,' I said noncommittally.

She looked down at the printed copy of the suspect e-fit in

her hand. 'I can't believe how much this picture looks like one of my colleagues.' She said it with a smile on her face but the smile looked forced.

'You don't actually think it's him, do you? Why would he do something like that?'

'He wouldn't. But it's an uncanny resemblance.' She took out her phone and began scrolling through her photo collection. 'Don't worry, it's on airplane mode,' she told me, 'so it's not transmitting a signal. Here's one of him.' She handed me the phone.

The photo was of a handsome dark-haired guy in his mid to late thirties with a strong jaw, and dark eyes the same colour as mine. I looked at it for a good five seconds. 'I don't think so,' I said eventually. 'But you're right, he does look similar.'

'You don't sound so sure.'

I handed the phone back. 'No, I'm pretty certain it's not him.'

She took a deep breath. 'Well, I hope not. I went out with him for a while.'

'Really? And what happened?'

'He was too intense for a relationship. His wife committed suicide a few years back and he's got . . .' She paused. 'Quite a troubled family history. He's a good guy, just not the easiest person. But not the sort to torture innocent people either.' She replaced the phone in her pocket. 'I'll see you in an hour or so. And stay out of trouble while I'm gone, please.'

I lifted my little finger. 'Pinkie promise.'

I watched her walk down to the car and pull away. The two older armed response officers – Jack and Trevor – were sitting in the lounge in separate chairs, like an old married couple. Jack was reading a book while Trevor was messing about on his phone. They weren't wearing their flak jackets, and their machine pistols were nowhere to be seen. Neither of them looked particularly battle-ready but that wasn't much of a surprise. The day was surprisingly warm and the house felt stuffy and airless.

Both men glanced up as I passed. Jack gave me a curt nod but Trevor just stared for a moment then returned to his phone. Neither man was much interested in me. They were here because they had to be.

The third armed officer, the younger one who'd introduced himself to me earlier as Luke, was in the kitchen fixing himself a sandwich when I went in to get myself a glass of water. We'd had a brief chat at lunchtime when he'd not so subtly managed to let slip the fact that he was single.

Men. They can be so predictable.

He asked me how I was doing.

'Tired. I didn't get much sleep last night. I think I need a nap.'

'I heard what you did to that DC earlier,' he said, leaning back against the countertop, making a pretty desperate effort to look cool. He'd taken off his flak jacket as well and was wearing a too-tight white T-shirt. 'What happened there then?'

I sighed. 'He was being sleazy. When he grabbed my arse, I snapped.'

'Where did you pick up those fighting skills?'

'Self-defence classes.'

'You definitely got your money's worth. Good on you for standing up for yourself. I suppose you must get a lot of unwanted attention.'

He was looking right into my eyes as he spoke, letting me know in no uncertain terms he was interested, and I wondered whether the irony of his words was lost on him, or whether he was trying to be clever.

'Too much,' I said.

'Listen, you get any more trouble from him, let me know and I'll sort it.'

'I can manage,' I said, 'but thank you for thinking of me. It's nice to know there are a few gentlemen out there.'

I smiled, and deliberately held his gaze for a couple of seconds, watching as he filled up with pride and pleasure, clearly thinking he might have a chance with me later.

Like I said. So predictable.

I told him I'd see him in a while and retreated to the bedroom. I took off my shoes and lay down on my bed in just my jeans and T-shirt, leaving the door open. I shut my eyes and concentrated on my breathing, allowing myself to slip into a gentle state of meditation.

Sometimes I can empty my mind completely of all conscious thoughts, but now wasn't one of those times. Instead, I found myself heading once more back into the troubled waters of my past.

So there I was in Florida with a useless husband, a big debt and two young children, pimping myself out to the man we owed money to: Frank Mellon, gangster and loan shark, and the man who had now told me he loved me.

Love complicates everything and I knew that Mellon's feelings spelt real trouble. But one of the best lessons I've ever learned is never to give your true feelings away. At least not until you're absolutely ready. So when he told me he loved me, I smiled and replied that we needed to take things one step at a time.

'Do you have feelings for me?' he asked, his expression almost touchingly needy. Here was this brutal thug – a man I know had killed on more than one occasion, and who was feared by a hell of a lot of people – and all he wanted right then was for me to say I had feelings for him.

'I like you,' I said, thinking the only feelings I had for that prick were ones of disgust. 'We have fun. But I'm a married woman.'

'How about you split from your old man, I let you off all your debts, I set you and your boys up in a nice house some- where, then we start dating properly?'

I knew that even if I went along with Frank's fantasy vision of the future it wouldn't work. His wife would never let him leave and he'd tire of me soon enough. I was also pretty sure that he wouldn't let Joel off the debt either.

I asked Frank for a little more time before we started making such huge decisions. He was like a big impatient kid and I knew he'd never stop hassling me until he got his own way, but on that night at least he reluctantly agreed to my request.

When I got home the following morning I told Joel what Frank had said to me. Joel was shocked and once again clearly unable to work out what to do, so I sat him down and told him what was going to happen. The relationship between Frank and me couldn't continue. If we tried to leave without paying him what Joel owed, he'd follow us to the ends of the earth for revenge. So we were going to have to kill him. There was no way round that. And when we'd killed him we were going to head to Panama or Venezuela, or anywhere where we could start a new life with the boys.

Joel didn't argue, as I thought he'd might. Instead he asked me how we were going to do it.

'Don't you worry about that,' I told him. 'I know exactly what to do.'

And I did.

Frank had bragged to me that he knew a guy who could produce top-quality forgeries of pretty much any document, and a little bit of digging quickly got me his name. I got Joel to visit the guy and buy a fake driver's licence with a fake name, and then sent him to Miami – far enough away not to arouse suspicion – where he used the licence to buy a semi-automatic Heckler and Koch USP pistol with silencer. Now we had our murder weapon.

I was seeing Frank a couple of times a week by this time, always staying overnight. Our meeting place was a pretty art-deco villa owned by one of his front companies situated on a quiet stretch of road just in from the coast at Palm Beach, and a long way from any prying eyes. The villa had lush gardens dotted with statues and water features, and a beautiful swimming pool hewn from granite and marble in the style of a natural pond. It was the one place where Frank claimed he could truly relax. Apparently, not even his wife knew it existed.

Frank took his security very seriously. High walls topped with razor wire surrounded the property and a caretaker/bodyguard lived permanently on site with a Rottweiler called Caesar who wasn't quite as majestic or as fearsome as his name suggested.

The villa was the obvious place to carry out the killing, and I knew that the longer we put it off, the more fraught our situation would become. Frank was already beginning to push hard for me to leave Joel. Every time we saw each other he'd tell me repeatedly how much he loved me; how every moment we spent apart hurt him. And he wasn't going to take 'I'm thinking about it' for an answer for much longer.

Joel and I decided to do it on a Friday evening about two months after Frank had first declared his love. Friday was a favourite time for Frank to meet me. At the end of a hard week he liked nothing better than a night's fucking to get him in the mood for the weekend.

The plan was simple. Joel and I made sure both the boys were out on sleepovers for the night and I drove to the villa as I always did, except this time I had Joel concealed in the back under a blanket along with the HK. Now that it was actually happening, he was scared. He asked me twice if I was sure I wanted to go through with this, saying that there were always other ways of sorting our problems out, but when I asked him to name one, he hadn't been able to come up with anything.

'I've got the hardest part,' I told him. 'You just do your bit and let me worry about the rest.'

He'd looked at me strangely then as if he couldn't quite work out whether the change he was seeing in me was a good or a bad thing. I think he thought it was probably bad but I could tell that he was also relieved that he'd been stripped of responsibility and was deferring to me. You see, I was confident. More confident than I'd been in a long time. I knew what I had to do to protect my children and I was going to do it.

When we got to the gates, I pressed the buzzer on the pad – Frank might have claimed to love me but he was no fool, and he still didn't trust me enough to give me the combination – and was let inside by Sal the bodyguard. As I parked in the driveway, Sal approached with Caesar on a lead. He was a big guy about the same age as Frank, with a stoop and a hangdog face not dissimilar to James Gandolfini's. He was dressed in a garish tracksuit that I think was a luminous blue, although it was difficult to tell in the near-darkness, and he had a pistol hanging from a shoulder holster.

As I got out of the car, Caesar wagged his tail. He was always pleased to see me. I'd made a point of being friendly to him these past few weeks and giving him a doggy treat when I arrived.

'No treats for him tonight, all right?' grunted Sal as I got out and started making a fuss of him.

'Come on, just one,' I said, pushing into Caesar's mouth a treat filled with enough temazepam powder to knock him out for a good few hours, then walking past him in the direction of the house.

'Hey, not so fast,' Sal shouted. 'I need to check you out.'

Frank was a stickler for security. He didn't trust anyone and had a fear of being recorded saying anything incriminating. So Sal always had to run a cheap bug finder up and down my person to make sure I wasn't wearing one, although he knew better than to get in too close. It was a hot night and I was wearing a light dress so it only took a few seconds. Then he asked for my handbag, rummaged through that and handed it back to me with an expression of distaste.

Sal didn't like me and made no secret of it. He knew he

couldn't be too rude to me because of my relationship with his boss, but I had the feeling that if Frank and I ever ended acrimoniously and he got orders to throw acid in my face, he'd do it with far too much enthusiasm. Sal was not a nice guy.

He escorted me to the villa's front door, unlocked it, and followed me inside. The building was single-storey and not particularly big inside. Sal had his quarters at the front so that he could be on hand immediately in case of any security breaches, and he disappeared into his room where a TV was blaring some sports game, leaving me to wander down the hall to Frank's huge open-plan lounge and bedroom where he was sitting waiting for me, dressed only in a Hugh Hefner-style silk dressing gown, and sipping from a tumbler of whiskey.

He repulsed me, and it was with a combination of ecstasy and fear that I realized this was the last time we were ever going to see each other.

The evening took its usual course. We kissed a little until Frank was hard then he led me to the bed and did his stuff. When we'd finished he told me he loved me and asked whether I'd thought any more about his offer.

'I think I want to go for it,' I told him with a smile. 'I'll talk to Joel this weekend.'

The key's always to keep your enemy off-guard. That way they never get the chance to focus on the fact that they might be being played.

He laughed. 'That's beautiful news, babe. We're gonna celebrate tonight.'

I ran a finger through his thick mesh of chest hair. 'I'm looking forward to it.'

One of the more predictable things about Frank was his bladder, and a few minutes after we'd finished making love he excused himself to go to the bathroom. 'When I come back, I've got a surprise for you,' he said.

Not half as big as the surprise I've got for you, I thought.

I fluttered my eyelashes and looked excited. 'Really? I love surprises.'

As soon as he'd shut the bathroom door behind him, I opened the bedside drawer and took out the loaded revolver he always kept in there. Moving quickly, I ejected the cylinder and emptied the bullets into my hand before putting the gun back. I scattered the bullets out of sight under the bed then called out to Frank that I was going to use the other bathroom.

'I'll be out in one second,' he called back, a belligerence in his voice.

Frank was a control freak. He didn't like me doing anything which displayed the tiniest bit of independence, even using the other bathroom, but I pretended not to hear, put on my gown, and headed out of the bedroom door.

When I was safely inside the other bathroom, I locked the door behind me and opened the top window. This was the only time when my heart was really pumping and that was because I was relying on Joel. I'd told him to wait exactly twenty minutes after I'd left the car to allow time for the temazepam to work on Caesar then come out quietly – I'd already made sure on a previous visit that there was no CCTV feed in Sal's quarters, so he wouldn't be seen. He was then to make his way round to the back of the house, and use duct tape to secure the pistol and a pair of surgical gloves to the exterior wall just in reach of the window. After that I told him to wait in the nearby bushes, within earshot, in case I needed him. I'd drawn him a map and gone over with him a hundred times which window he had to go to because if he got the wrong one, and was hiding in the wrong place, the whole thing was off.

I climbed up on the toilet, stuck my hand out of the window, and felt around outside. Nothing. My first thought was that my husband truly was a useless arsehole, but then I felt round the other side, and touched metal. It was there.

Breathing steadily but quickly, my adrenalin kicking in now, I brought the HK with silencer attached inside and closed the window to keep the noise of any gunshots inside the building. I removed all the tape and put the gun in my gown pocket. Then I pulled on the gloves and checked the gun. It felt heavy but comfortable in my hand. I'd fired plenty of handguns at the range back in South Africa, including HKs, so I knew what I was doing. The magazine had a full clip of fifteen rounds with one in the chamber. I took a deep breath to steady myself, left the bathroom and walked back down the hall, moving silently in my bare feet, keeping the gun down by my side.

As I passed the door to Frank's bedroom I heard him inside popping a champagne cork as he prepared to celebrate his good news. I kept going, heading for Sal's room, my breath coming faster now as the fear began to kick in.

Stay strong, I told myself. Stay strong and everything will be all right.

I stopped outside Sal's door. The blare of the sports game he was watching seemed artificially loud in my ears and my finger tensed on the pistol's trigger.

What if he'd locked the door? What if he'd already heard me and was reaching for his gun?

I stopped thinking, cast the doubts aside, and turned the handle.

The door opened immediately and I walked into the room. Sal was sitting on the sofa opposite, a bowl of popcorn on his lap, Caesar flat out asleep by his side. My gown was partially open and, even though it must have been abundantly clear he was in danger, Sal couldn't help but stare at my cleavage.

I raised the gun in both hands and fired my first two shots without hesitation. Even with the silencer, both sounded loud to my ears. They caught Sal on the upper body. His eyes widened and he gave me a shocked yet curiously defiant look, so I took aim more carefully this time and, as the popcorn fell off his lap and he lurched forward in his seat in a vain effort to escape, I shot him right between the eyes. The HK's a powerful gun and the bullet tore a huge chunk from the back of his head, depositing it on the wall behind. What was left of Sal's head tipped to one side as if he'd nodded off and he slumped on the sofa, no longer any kind of threat. There wasn't a peep from Caesar.

I strode back down the hall, feeling an incredible confidence now that I'd killed Sal, and flung open the door to Frank's room, taking a step backwards just in case he tried to ambush me. He didn't, but he must have heard the shots because he was scrabbling for his gun in the bedside table drawer.

As I walked towards him with the pistol outstretched in my hands, he turned back round, holding his revolver in his right hand but making no move to bring it up into a firing position. Instead he stared at me, his mouth literally hanging open like some oversized plankton-feeding fish, naked and vulnerable.

'What the fuck?' were the only words he managed to utter before I shot him, first in the belly, then in the chest.

He stumbled back against the bedside table, knocking it over as he grabbed on to the wall for support. He tried to raise the gun but he didn't seem to have the energy and it fell out of his hand and thudded uselessly on to the ten-thousand-dollar Persian rug. Slowly he slid down the wall before landing with a bump on his arse.

'Please,' he whispered as he looked up and saw the cold expression in my eyes.

I smiled down at him. 'Fuck you, Frank. And just for the record, you always repulsed me.' I pulled the trigger a third time, and he juddered once and was still.

I took a couple of deep breaths as the enormity of what I'd just done took hold, but I only allowed myself a few seconds to reflect. There was still plenty of work to be done. Placing the HK carefully on the bed I ran back to the bathroom I'd been in earlier, opened the window and whispered Joel's name. 'Come over here,' I hissed. 'I need you.'

A few seconds later he emerged from the bushes and approached the window.

'What's wrong, darling? Is everything all right?'

'Have you got your gloves on?'

'Yeah, course I have. Look.' He held up his gloved hands. 'Did you do it? I heard gunshots.'

'Were they loud?'

'No, not really. Did you do it, baby? Did you sort it?'

I nodded. 'Yup, I did it. But I need some help. Come in through this window.'

I opened it as far as it would go, then got out of the way so he could climb through. He started to ask me why he couldn't just come in the back door but I ignored him and waited while he squeezed himself through the gap and slid down head first using his hands to balance himself on the toilet seat.

'What's going on, Jane?' he asked as I led him back through the house. 'We need to get out of here.'

'I want you to see something first,' I said, heading back into Frank's room.

'Jesus,' he said, his voice filled with awe as he stared at Frank's naked corpse. 'You did do it. I, er . . . I didn't think you'd . . .' He was stumbling over his words now, his eyes fixed on the grisly sight in front of him. 'How did you . . . how did you kill him?'

'Like this,' I said.

The pistol was already in my hand. I'd picked it up from the bed while his attention was on Frank, and now I pushed the barrel against his right temple and squeezed the trigger.

Joel died instantly, which was a blessing really. After all he was the father of my sons and, although it was him who'd got us into this whole sorry mess, I was pleased that he hadn't had time to realize the full extent of my betrayal. If there's a heaven and Joel's up there – neither of which I think is very likely – I suspect he's forgiven me. He always loved me through thick and thin, and do you know what? Now and again I still miss him.

But unfortunately for him he was a hell of a lot more use to me dead than alive, and I didn't even give him a second glance as I placed the murder weapon in his right hand, gently moving his forefinger so it was resting against the trigger. I then picked up Frank's revolver and reloaded it before putting it back on the floor. I was working methodically now, remembering the details of the plan, knowing that it was essential I get everything right.

I removed my gloves and fed them and the duct tape through the waste disposal unit in Frank's kitchen that turned everything that went through it into tiny scraps. Just in case they pulled out the bin and checked it, I fed through the contents of a couple of tins of food and most of the fruit in the fruit bowl to disguise it better. I then went back into the bathroom where I'd let Joel in, climbed out the window and punched a hole in the glass from the outside using a stone next to the patio. I replaced the stone, climbed back in through the window and returned to the bedroom.

When the police checked the footage from Frank's security camera they would see me being searched before I entered the house so they would know I was unarmed. They would then see Joel emerge from his hiding place in the back of the car, hopefully carrying the gun. I of course would say I hadn't known he was there. Why should I have done? I was there to see my lover. I certainly didn't want my husband coming with me, and the car was a big station wagon so he could easily conceal himself without me knowing.

Frank could be amazingly loose-lipped when he was in the bedroom so I knew that there was a second camera pointing at the back of the house. This was why I didn't want Joel coming in through the back door. Crucially there wasn't a camera covering the side of the house where the bathroom was so it would look as if Joel had broken in through the bathroom window before running amok in a jealous rage, killing my lover and his bodyguard before finally turning the gun on himself.

There was just one more thing to do. I walked to the far end of the bedroom, away from the carnage, placed both hands on the wall to steady myself, then drove my face into it with all the force I could muster. I stumbled backwards, my vision temporarily blurring, the pain searing through me. I closed my eyes tight and thought of my sons and the new life I was going to give them, and slowly the pain subsided. I looked in the mirror above the bed. There was a cut just above my left eye oozing blood, and my forehead was already turning a nasty red. I rehearsed what I was going to say to the police.

I couldn't believe it. We were in bed and I heard these three loud pops and then before either of us could do anything the door flew open and Joel came running in holding a gun. He had this terrible look on his face. I've seen it before but only when he's very, very angry. Frank had pulled a gun out of his bedside drawer. He was determined to protect me but he never got the chance. Joel just . . . He just shot him. A couple of times in the body. Frank sort of half fell, half sat down, and Joel went over to him and shot him right in the head. Just like that. I couldn't believe it. The entire thing was surreal. It was like it was happening to someone else.

Then he grabbed me by the hair and dragged me out of the bed. He hit me, then threw me down on the floor. I knew he was going to kill me. I could see the look in his eyes. He was calling me a whore and a slut, and saying I didn't deserve to live. I begged him not to kill me. Not for my sake but for our boys', Ryan and Matthew. He couldn't leave them without a mom.

And I think then, you know, he realized what he'd done, and the anger seemed to leave him . . . And then . . . then without another word he put the gun to his head and pulled the trigger.

The story worked too. The cops believed me. Sure, it had a few holes in it, but the most important thing was that it was plausible and, let's face it, not many people were going to miss a man like Frank Mellon.

So I got away with it. At least for a few weeks until I got a visit from a man who it turned out was Frank's boss. The police might not have known what had actually happened but this man did, and he was someone no one crossed. So I'd jumped out of the frying pan and into the fire.

But the man admired my guile and my coolness under pressure and he gave me a choice. Come work for him and earn good money, or he'd kill my sons in front of me and force-feed me their hearts.

It wasn't really much of a choice.

And after that?

That, my friends, is another story.

Thirty-one

Ray

Within five minutes of the first armed response vehicle arriving, the whole plant was crawling with police. Two helicopters hovered overhead in ever-widening arcs as they searched for any more suspects, and Chris and I were quickly released after we'd shown ID to prove who we were.

The first detectives to approach us were local guys from Essex CID who both looked like they were about to faint from the stench of fat. I introduced myself and Chris to the most senior of them – a big DCI called Lomax with a thick head of iron-grey hair that resembled a helmet – and gave him a brief rundown of what had happened.

'And you shot two suspects?' he said to me, raising his eyebrows. 'From what I hear, you seem to be making a habit of that.'

'In self-defence, sir,' I told him. 'They were both trying to kill me at the time. One of them also shot a third man – the one who was trying to rescue me.'

'If I didn't know who you were, I'd think you were telling fairy stories. And those are the three terror suspects we're all after, are they?' He nodded towards the Ford Focus where Rani Hussain lay on his front with his hands cuffed behind his back while paramedics attended to Youssef Ali on the ground next to him. The driver, Danesh Kashani, had now been lifted out of his seat but didn't appear to be conscious.

'That's right.'

'And they were resisting arrest, were they?'

'They had guns and we didn't. We did what we had to do to stop them.'

The ambulances were coming in now, a line of four of them with lights flashing and sirens blaring, temporarily stopping our conversation. At the same time, an armed uniform came jogging up to Lomax.

'It's clear in there, sir,' he said. 'We've nicked one suspect, and there are three people down with gunshot wounds.'

'There's a fifth guy in there somewhere as well,' I told him.

'If he's hiding we'll find him,' said the uniform.

Lomax turned to me. 'Right, I've got to sort all this out. Don't go away, either of you. We're going to need to take statements. Although you're allowed to get out of range of this stench.'

He tried to waft the worst of the smell away from his face, which was never going to work, then asked for my phone number. I gave it to him, watching as he marched off with the uniform.

I looked at Chris. He hadn't said a word and the tension was coming off him in waves.

'What am I going to do, Ray?' he hissed. 'What the fuck am I going to do?'

I put an arm round his shoulder and led him away from the access road and out of earshot of everyone.

'What are your instructions?'

'The kidnapper told me to find out the address of the safehouse and said he'd call back from another phone with more instructions. I give them the address and then, when they've confirmed the location and done what they have to do, they release Amber with the phone and she calls me.'

'What kind of accent did the kidnapper have? Was it local? Asian? Caucasian?'

'It wasn't local, but I couldn't pinpoint it, and I think he was white. This fella was a pro, Ray. He warned me in no uncertain terms not to talk to my bosses. And he's definitely got Amber. There was a video.'

'Let me see it.'

He unlocked the phone and gave it to me with a shaking hand.

I brought up the video while moving away so that neither he nor anyone else could see it. It lasted thirty seconds, and I watched in silence. Sometimes these things can be doctored if you have access to the right technology, but this one wasn't. It was genuine.

I walked back to where Chris stood, his body visibly shivering. 'We've got to talk to Butterworth,' I told him. 'We can't do this alone.'

'This man knows exactly what he's doing, Ray. He told me he was calling from a location well away from where they were keeping Amber and was going to shut off her phone, so we wouldn't be able to use it to track him. If we pull in the kidnap teams, we waste time. And we haven't got any of that.' He shook his head as if trying to rid his mind of the anguish I could see he was feeling. 'They'll kill her if they find out I've gone for help. I can't do it. She's my daughter.'

'OK, OK. Keep your voice down.' I stopped myself from telling him the kidnapper would probably kill Amber anyway, even though I was certain he already knew that. 'Amber's at Sussex uni, right? Have you checked she's actually missing?'

'No.'

'Call her friends and give them some bullshit reason why you need to speak to her. Then find out when she was last seen.'

'OK. But how's that going to help?'

I stared down at the ground, thinking. 'Something's all wrong here. Rani Hussain – the man I just threatened with an AK-47, and who literally shit himself in fear – didn't know anything about any kidnap, or even that Anil Rahman was dead. And Karim Khan didn't know that Anil was dead either when we spoke to him this morning. But within hours of Anil's death, a man manages to identify that you're on the team investigating his murder, find out you have a daughter, then organize her abduction, film her tied up somewhere secure, and contact you. The timing doesn't work.'

'But Anil's killer asked him about the terror attack. And we know there was actually going to be an attack because we've just stopped it. And the kidnapper wants to know where the witness to Anil's murder is. So Anil's death, the attack and Amber's abduction are all linked.'

'I don't believe that anyone could organize a professional kidnapping this fast.'

'So what are you saying happened? You've seen the video. It's genuine. They've got her.'

I shook my head in frustration. 'I need to think. Look, make the call to Amber's friends.'

Chris looked on the verge of tears. I'd never seen him so vulnerable before, and it hurt me to see it.

'I'm going back inside the central compound to get my gun and phone. Meet me back at the car, and stay calm.'

'That's easy for you to say. You haven't got kids.'

'Don't use that on me, Chris. I've had loss. You know that. More than most people.' I put my arm round his shoulders. 'We'll sort this,' I said with far more confidence than I felt. 'If the kidnapper calls you back, tell him you've got the location but you're not going to give him any information until you've seen Amber in person. Then they can let her go and take you instead.'

'No way, Ray. They could just as easily take both of us. Then what?'

'They won't. I'll be there. Right behind you.'

'On your own? Because I can't afford for anyone else to get involved in this. You know what it's like. There are procedures to follow, arses to cover. And if the kidnapper gets one sniff of what's going on, he'll kill my daughter. I need you alone, Ray. Please.'

What choice did I have? Chris was my friend, and I didn't have many of those.

Simon Kernick

'I'll help you,' I told him. 'But we need to get away from this lot and avoid having to give a statement. You get back to the car and wait for me. I'll be there in about ten minutes.' I gave his shoulder another squeeze then walked away, moving quickly.

298

Thirty-two

Jane

I don't know how long I'd been lying on the bed for when I heard the sound of footfalls on the stairs.

I opened my eyes and sat up, watching as the younger armed cop, Luke, appeared on the landing.

He saw me and smiled, coming to the door but staying outside.

'How's it going?' he asked. 'Did you manage to get some shut-eye?'

'I don't think I had time,' I said, taking a drink from the water by my bed and stretching. 'But I feel better. Where are the rest of you guys?'

'Jack and Trevor are still lolling about in the lounge. They're not the most dynamic pair. I've got to admit – no offence to you – this isn't one of our more interesting assignments.'

'No, I bet it isn't.' I got up from the bed, my eyes lingering on him for a couple of seconds. 'To be honest, I'm pretty bored too. I could do with some excitement.'

He gave me a look like a lusty dog and stepped inside. 'What kind of excitement?'

'I think you know exactly what kind,' I whispered, closing the door behind him and running my fingers along his T-shirted chest.

He murmured with pleasure. 'I think I do . . . But we're going to need to be quiet. I'll be sacked if anyone catches me.'

My lips brushed his. 'Don't worry. No one will.'

We kissed. Passionately. He wasn't a bad kisser – a bit over-enthusiastic, but better than a lot of men – and I let myself slip into the moment. He pushed me against the wall, running his hands up and down my body, his breathing coming faster as he rubbed me through the material of my jeans, whispering things to me I couldn't quite make out. I felt the urge to fuck rise in me. I love sex. It's such an incredible release, and I wanted it right now.

But in the end, business is business.

I pulled away from the kiss. 'What's that noise?'

'What noise?' he said, looking confused. 'I don't hear anything.'

The jet knife I'd concealed in the back pocket of my jeans had been specially made for me two years before. Ultra-thin, and with its four-inch blade concealed in the plastic handle, it was extremely easy to hide. And very, very sharp.

I pulled it out now, put the end of the handle against Luke's unprotected chest and released the trigger. The blade – high-tensile steel with a diamond tip – could cut through bone as if it was butter, and it shot straight through Luke's heart. He gasped in shock, his body tottering, and I placed a hand firmly over his mouth, silencing him. Slowly I went with him down to his knees, removing the blade and stabbing him a second, then a third time in the heart, keeping my body at an angle so that I wouldn't get spattered with any blood. I felt him move his hand to his holster as he tried to go for the gun, but his strength was ebbing away far too fast for him to be able to do anything.

A stab wound to the heart is always quick and fatal, and it didn't take long for Luke to die. Perhaps a minute, if that, and it was a very easy death, with no major blood loss to worry about.

When I was certain he'd gone, I moved him out of sight behind the bed, cleaned the knife on his T-shirt and replaced it in my pocket before removing the pistol from Luke's holster. It was a Glock 17, another weapon I was familiar with. I gave it a quick check then placed it in the waistband at the back of my jeans, before putting my jacket on over the top to make sure it stayed hidden.

I took a quick look in the bedroom mirror. There were no obvious signs that I'd just killed someone. In fact, I looked good. I rearranged my hair in a ponytail, then turned and left the room.

It was time to go to work.

Thirty-three

Ray

The access road was chock-a-block with emergency services vehicles parked wherever they could find space. They'd even sent a fire engine in. An ambulance came out of the central compound gates with its lights blaring, dodging through the traffic, and I wondered whether the young guy who'd rescued me was the one who was in it. I hoped he'd survived. He'd done me a huge favour getting me out of that hole in the ground.

Although there were plenty of cops on the scene, things were still fairly disorganized, and I went through the gates unchallenged. Armed police were everywhere, including ones with dogs, as they scoured the site for any remaining suspects. Next to the nearest converted barn was the skinny bearded man who'd taken over the business from Bula Ruslan. He was lying on his front with his hands cuffed behind his back while two armed uniforms looked on. He saw me coming and glared, so I winked and gave him a wave.

'I told you my colleagues were on their way,' I said. 'Enjoy your time in prison. It'll probably be a nice change from this place.'

He let loose a few expletives but I was already walking past him.

Up ahead I could see two paramedics attempting CPR on a man I immediately recognized as Dokka Aliyev. Good luck with that, I thought, remembering the way the last bullet I'd fired had exited the back of his head, taking a fair amount of his brains with it.

You may think I'm sounding as cold or ruthless as the people I'm trying to put away – and maybe I *am* closer to them than I'd like to think – but I'll tell you this. I've never hurt an innocent person in my life. Only the guilty have anything to fear from me.

A few yards beyond where Aliyev was being treated lay the body of the man who'd got me out of the hole. A blanket covered him so that only his boots were sticking out, and two plainclothes guys with their backs to me – one of whom I immediately recognized by his mane of hair as DCI Lomax – were looking down at him. So he hadn't made it after all.

I hurried over to the end of the farmhouse to the office where I'd been taken when I was first captured, not wanting to be spotted by Lomax. This whole area was a crime scene and, whether I liked it or not, I was a potential suspect, so by rights

I shouldn't have been anywhere round here. Still, right then, that was the least of my misdemeanours. The paramedics didn't even look up from what they were doing as I passed. I glanced down at Dokka Aliyev. His eyes were closed and he looked dead.

The office was empty and the door open. The desk drawer where my belongings had been put was locked but the key was in the lock so I turned it and pulled the drawer open, pleased to see that my gun was still inside. I shoved it into my shoulder holster, covering it with my jacket.

It was good timing because the next second Lomax stepped inside, looking extremely pissed off.

'What are you doing?' he demanded.

'They took my phone and warrant card,' I said, taking them both out of the drawer. 'I was just picking them up in case you needed to get hold of me.'

'You shouldn't be in here. You know that.'

'I'm sorry, sir. I wanted to get them before the whole place was locked down.'

I came back round the desk, keeping the card and phone in my hand so he could see them.

Lomax was sensible enough not to take me at my word and he checked the warrant card and then the phone, asking me for the code to unlock it. I thought that was a bit much but I gave it to him anyway. As the home screen appeared, the phone started ringing. A photo of a very angry-looking man appeared on the screen. For once it was good to hear from Butterworth.

'That's my boss,' I told Lomax.

'Well, you've got plenty of explaining to do to him,' said

Lomax, deadpan. He handed me the phone. 'Don't run. As soon as the scene's secure, you, me and your colleague are off down the station.'

I told him no problem and left the office, putting the phone to my ear.

'Hello, sir. How are you?'

'What the hell's going on?' Butterworth barked. 'I hear we've got multiple casualties.'

'All bad guys, you'll be pleased to hear.'

'I'm not pleased to hear it. It means IPCC investigations, lots of paperwork, and unneeded media attention. What I want to see is a nice collar.'

'We stopped a terrorist attack, sir. Chris and me. Singlehandedly.'

Butterworth sighed. 'I'm aware of that. But I've also been told that two of our three suspects have been seriously injured, one of whom was hit with a large rock.'

'They resisted arrest, sir.'

'But there's such a thing as proportionate force, Ray. And that's what we have to use. And I've been informed that you shot two people as well?'

'Not with my own gun. I used one of theirs.'

'Thank God for that. What happened?'

I told him the truth.

'Christ, Ray. I swear your antics are why I'm fucking grey. You can't keep shooting people, whatever the provocation. It happens too often. People are going to be saying you're some trigger-happy Dirty Harry. You're going to have to hand your weapon in.'

I could have argued but I didn't see there was much point.

'I'm going to be taken in for questioning about the shootings,' I told him.

'That's inevitable, and it's a pity. Because I'd just got permission from the commander for you and Chris to interview the witness to Anil Rahman's murder. However, in the light of current circumstances, that's now been rescinded.'

'I still want to talk to her,' I said.

'Well, she's not going anywhere fast, so if you can get through the questioning all right you may get another bite of that particular cherry. And by the way, Karim Khan's lodged a formal complaint against you for assault, and his lawyer's making one against you for harassment.'

I didn't much care about all the black marks building up against my name. I had a clear conscience and I could handle any flak coming my way. I was far more concerned with what was happening with Chris. I'm usually decisive. It's one of the reasons I'm good at my job. But on this, I was torn. Whoever had kidnapped Amber wasn't going to let her go until he'd got the information on the location of the safehouse, and had acted on it. In fact, if he was that ruthless, he wasn't going to let her go at all. So what the hell were the two of us going to do?

I could understand why Chris didn't want to get CT involved officially. Even with all our resources it was unlikely in the extreme that we'd be able to locate Amber, and it was almost certain that the kidnapper would get wind of it. Maybe the safehouse location wouldn't be compromised but Amber would die. That was the harsh truth of it. And I knew I had to try to stop that happening.

I'd hardly seen Amber at all these past five years, but I remembered that when she was younger she'd been a sweet kid. Pretty; polite; a little shy. I once bought her a huge pink teddy bear I'd seen in a toyshop window for her birthday, when she was about eight. It was the only time I've ever bought her anything but I remember she called to thank me, we had a lovely chat, and I vowed I'd buy her a gift for every Christmas and birthday.

But of course I never did.

I felt a wave of regret as I remembered that phone call from all those years ago, Amber's tiny soft voice saying how much she loved her teddy. Tears stung my eyes and I had to force them back. I couldn't weaken. Not now.

There were two more messages on my phone from Butterworth plus a missed call from Anji Abbott's mobile. I wondered why she was using her mobile when she was meant to be keeping it switched off, and what she wanted.

I spotted my set of picks on the flagstones where one of my captors had flung them and picked them up on my way out. When I'd passed through the central compound gates and turned away from the access road in the direction of Chris's car, I dialled Anji's mobile.

'I thought you were meant to be guarding our witness,' I said. 'It sounds like you're out shopping.'

'I am. I've managed to sneak away from the house so I can pick up some bits and pieces in town. That's why you can get me on my mobile.'

'How's it going?'

'It's been interesting,' she said. 'For one thing our witness Jane beat the shit out of Seamus Jeffs when he got a little too friendly.'

In spite of myself, I laughed. 'Seriously?'

'Seriously. And this girl's good. I saw it all. She took him down in the space of a few seconds. I know Seamus isn't the biggest of guys but even so, he didn't have a chance. She says she picked up the skills on self-defence classes.'

'Do you believe her?'

Anji sighed. 'Well, I can't see any reason not to believe her.'

Neither could I. 'Any other news?'

'Jane spent several hours with the man from the Evo-fit company and managed to put together a picture of Anil's killer. And guess what? It looked just like you.'

'You're joking?'

For two heartbeats, there was a silence on the end of the line.

'Blimey, Anji, you don't think it *was* me, do you?' But even as I spoke the words, I experienced a deep-seated unease.

'Of course not,' said Anji. 'I showed her a picture of you, and she said she didn't think you were the man she saw last night.'

'That's hardly a ringing endorsement. And as it happens, I know I wasn't. I have an alibi.'

Except I didn't have one.

'Anyway, the reason I'm calling is that I've been told that you and Chris have got permission to interview our witness, Jane Kinnear.'

It struck me then that Anji hadn't been told yet about what had happened here at the plant and the fact that suddenly all the plans had changed. But I wanted to speak to Jane Kinnear even more now, given that she'd suggested the killer looked a lot like me, because something about that really didn't smell right.

'That's right,' I said. 'Have you got the address?'

'No one's in earshot, are they?'

'No, and I'm sure no one's listening in either.'

She gave me the postcode and I immediately memorized it. 'It's a detached redbrick cottage at the T junction, and it's the only building in the vicinity so you can't miss it.'

'Thanks, but I'm not sure when I'm going to get the chance to get up there.' I told her about the events of the last hour.

'Well they're not going to let you interview her now, are they?' she said, sounding annoyed. 'You're going to be stuck in IPCC interviews for days. Why did you make me give you that address?'

'I didn't. And don't worry, I'm not going to tell anyone you told me and I'm not going to do anything with it. But there's no reason why I can't see your witness anyway. I didn't actually do anything wrong, and we also managed to stop a terror attack, so there's no way I'll get suspended.'

Anji sighed. 'I think you're being optimistic. Did you get any clue as to who killed Anil and his wife?'

I thought of Chris. Then Amber, trussed up on a bed, a knife held to her face by the man who also wanted the location of the safehouse. The man who was most likely Anil's killer. 'No,' I said. 'You didn't really think I'd killed Anil Rahman and his wife, did you?'

'No, of course I didn't.'

'You don't sound totally convinced.'

Anji sighed. 'I know you wouldn't do anything like that . . .'

'I can feel a "but" coming on.'

'But you've got demons, Ray. When I was with you, you used to cry out in your sleep at night, have these horrific nightmares. Things happen around you. It's why we split up. You're just a . . . you're *different*.'

'I'm a good man,' I told her, but though my head believed it, my heart wasn't so sure.

'Yes,' she said. 'I know you are.'

But if I truly was a good man I would have told her that there was a dangerous individual trying to find the woman she was guarding, and that both Anji and the witness were in real danger.

But I didn't.

'So I suppose I'll see you when I see you,' she said.

'Count on it,' I said, thinking that, whatever happened, I was going to get to talk to Jane Kinnear. I had a strong feeling she knew a lot more than she was letting on.

In the meantime, though, I had other, bigger fish to fry.

Thirty-four

Chris Leavey paced up and down the track next to the car, waiting for the next phone call, praying that it would come, even though it might simply accelerate the death of his only child. He cursed himself for not leaving the force earlier. He cursed a God he didn't believe in for giving him such horrendous ill fortune even though he'd always tried to do the right thing.

He'd called Amber's housemate at uni, Anna, and she'd told him that she hadn't seen Amber all day, although she didn't seem unduly worried, which suited Chris fine. He didn't want anyone down there raising the alarm in her absence and calling Charlotte. It struck him that he should call his wife now, that she would want to know what was going on, however traumatic the news. They'd been married for the best part of twenty years and they'd been close through all that time. Theirs wasn't like so many other police marriages that fall apart because of the pressures of the job. He and Charlotte discussed everything: they were a partnership. Even with her illness she was still a rock to him, as he was to her.

But if he called her, what would he say? What *could* he say?

In his jacket, the phone rang.

He pulled it out. It was a number he didn't recognize.

'Hello?'

'Hello, Chris.'

It was him.

'I hope you haven't talked to anyone about our previous conversation because that would be a very foolish move.'

'I haven't told anyone.'

'Good. And do you have the information we asked for?'

'Yeah. I've got it.'

'Give it to me then.'

Chris swallowed hard. 'No.'

'What did you say?'

'I said no. Not until I see my daughter in person.'

'That's not going to happen.'

'I'm willing to exchange myself for my daughter. When I see that you've let her go, you can take me and I will give you the information you need. But not until then.'

The caller laughed. It was an unpleasant sound. 'You think you've got all the cards, don't you? Well I'm telling you something now, Mr Detective Sergeant Leavey, you don't. We've got your daughter, and we'll start taking bits off her and sending you footage of it unless you give me the information I've asked for right now.'

Chris felt his guts clench. Why was he following Ray's advice?

What the hell was he doing full stop? He didn't even have the information this man wanted.

'I'm willing to give myself to you in exchange for my daughter,' he repeated. 'That's my final offer. If you hurt her, I'll tell my bosses what's happened and you'll never have a chance to get to the safehouse or the witness.'

'You wouldn't do that.'

'Fuck you, I would. You lay one finger on her and this is over. All of it.'

'And you'll risk never seeing your precious girl again? What does Charlotte think about that? Do you think she'll ever forgive you?'

Chris felt himself weakening. He forced himself to stay strong.

'I want to see Amber go free,' he said. 'If I don't, you don't get your information. Do we have a deal?'

There was a silence on the other end of the phone. He could hear the caller breathing. He remained silent himself, resisting the urge to say something. There was nothing to say.

'I'll be phoning you back soon,' said the kidnapper ominously and cut the call, leaving Chris staring at his phone.

Thirty-five

Ray

I found the spot where I'd crawled under the hedge earlier and went back through on my belly, emerging the other side to see Chris about twenty yards down the track standing next to the car holding his phone. He looked ashen.

'Are you all right?' I asked.

He rubbed a hand across his brow. 'The kidnapper just phoned. I did what you said and told him that I'd only give him the location of the safehouse if he accepted me in Amber's place.'

'What did he say?'

'He hung up.'

'That means he's thinking about your offer.'

'Or he's torturing Amber so he can send me footage of it. He threatened to do that, Ray.'

'He won't. There's no way he'd phone you from the place he's keeping Amber, just in case his phone's being tracked. It's too risky.'

'Then maybe he's on his way back to torture her now.'

'Then perhaps it's a good idea for you to talk to Butterworth and get the heavy mob involved.'

Chris shook his head vehemently, running his hand across his face again, hard enough to leave a mark. 'No. No one else. Not yet. Oh shit, Ray . . .'

'You've got to hold it together, Chris.'

My phone was ringing again. I didn't recognize the number. It was probably Lomax wanting to know where the hell I'd got to. I switched it to silent.

'One way or another we will free Amber. She will survive this day. I give you my word.'

We stared at each other and I saw tears forming in his eyes. There was no way I could guarantee getting his daughter back but I knew I'd do everything in my power to make it happen.

I hugged him then. I'm not a man who expresses emotions easily, particularly round other men, but I held him for a few seconds before pulling away.

Chris managed a smile. 'I'm glad you're with me, Ray. I wouldn't want anyone else.'

A helicopter flew overhead in a tight circle and I had no doubt that news of our whereabouts would get back to Lomax soon.

'Right, we need to get out of here,' I said.

But as we got back in Chris's car, his phone rang again.

He looked at me. 'It's the kidnapper's number.'

'Take it.'

Chris put the phone to his ear and listened. The conversation lasted no more than thirty seconds, with the kidnapper doing most of the talking.

'He's texting me a postcode,' he said as he came off the phone. 'I've got to drive there alone and await further instructions.'

I nodded. 'Well, I'm coming with you. We'll work out a plan en route.'

Without another word he switched on the engine and turned the car round.

I checked my phone and saw I had a voicemail. I'd guessed right: it was Lomax wanting to know where I was.

I replaced the phone in my pocket, wondering if I'd still be in a job by the end of the day.

Wondering, too, if I'd still be alive.

Thirty-six

Anji Abbott was feeling tired as she pulled up outside the safe-house. It was gone five o'clock. She'd called HQ and been told she and Seamus weren't going to be relieved for another twenty-four hours minimum. It didn't matter that it seemed that Ray and Chris had actually foiled the terror attack: the main suspect in the Anil Rahman killings was still at large, which meant Jane Kinnear wasn't safe, although having seen the woman in action, Anji wouldn't give any killer that much chance against her.

She thought back to the account Jane had given her last night about her ordeal at Anil Rahman's house. Anji had felt sorry for her, but now somehow she felt less so, as if someone with Jane's self-defence skills was never going to be in too much danger, even though she knew that such an attitude was unfair.

But Anji liked Jane too. She was a survivor, like Anji herself. She didn't put up with the shit that life so often seems to throw up, and Anji was looking forward to finding out a bit more about her. She'd bought a couple of bottles of Sauvignon Blanc in Sainsbury's and was hoping they could share a glass or two later. Drinking on duty might be strictly forbidden but Anji felt she'd worked hard enough over the last twenty hours to warrant a break, although she'd have to watch Seamus because she knew that after what had happened with Jane earlier, and her complaint over his sexual harassment, he'd report her the minute he saw anything untoward, just to deflect attention away from himself.

As she got out of the car and went to the front door, Anji smiled to herself. It was funny sometimes how things turned out. As far as she was concerned, Seamus had thoroughly deserved the beating he'd got from Jane. Seamus and Anji had history too. When they'd first started working in the same department two years earlier he'd politely asked her out for a drink, and she'd just as politely declined. All had been fine for a couple of months until one night the whole team had been out for drinks and Seamus had begun coming on a little too strong. He was subtle enough to make it look like he was just being friendly – a pat on the shoulder; an occasional bump at the bar; moving in too close when he spoke to her – but it had made Anji seriously uncomfortable and she wasn't the sort to put up with it, so she'd politely but firmly told him to stand further back when he spoke to her. He'd acted all innocent and hurt, making it out as if she was wildly overreacting, but he'd backed off.

However, over the next few weeks she heard that he'd been badmouthing her behind her back, telling colleagues that she was one of 'those women' who couldn't take banter, that she was up her own arse and, most insidious of all, that the only reason she was on the team was because she was black and female and so fulfilled all the right quotas. Anji knew she couldn't let this crap slide so she'd confronted Seamus about it, told him that if he ever spoke like that about her again she'd kill him. Coward that he was, he'd backtracked, apologized, and said it would never happen again. Since then, Anji had been promoted and there'd been no recurrence of the rumours. Seamus had kept his nose clean, as far as she'd heard, but even so, his behaviour around Jane hadn't surprised her. Jane was one of those women who simply oozed sex appeal. Even Anji, who was rigorously straight, had felt the charge coming off her.

And that was another thing that bothered her about Jane. She just didn't seem vulnerable or naive enough to have got herself mixed up with a married man like Anil Rahman and ended up in a situation like the previous night's. That was why Anji would have liked a second opinion on her from Ray.

Ray was good like that. He could see right through people, whoever they were. This was a fantastic gift to have in a profession capacity, because it was very difficult for someone to hide their lies from him, but it had been too much for Anji as his girlfriend. Ray was an intense, driven man with a past so dark it seemed to seep from every pore, and sometimes she wondered just how much it had affected him. He acted like one of the good guys, and in truth he'd never been anything other than a gentleman to her, but the way violence always seemed to seek him out, and the way he appeared to embrace it, scared Anji, even though she was certain it was a coincidence that he looked like the e-fit of the suspect in the Anil Rahman murder. She knew he couldn't have done it and felt guilty that she'd even had a momentary suspicion that he might have been involved.

On the way back from the shops, Anji had received a call from Butterworth on her mobile telling her that Ray and Chris wouldn't be interviewing Jane now, at least not for the time being. Anji had decided to come clean and she told Butterworth that she'd already given Ray the safehouse location. Butterworth hadn't been too pleased, even though all Anji had done was follow the orders he'd given her, and he told her to phone him immediately if Ray showed up unannounced. Anji had told him she would.

The first thing she noticed when she stepped inside the house and put down the shopping bags was the silence. No music, no TV, no talking.

She yawned, then called out, 'Anyone home?'

No response.

She shrugged to herself. Clearly they were all otherwise occupied. Picking up the shopping bags, she started down the hallway, pausing to poke her head round the lounge door.

She froze.

There in front of her, sitting in armchairs a few feet apart, just as they had been for most of that day, were the two older firearms officers, Jack and Trevor. Jack, who was nearest the door, had a neat bullet hole in his forehead from which a long, thin line of blood ran down the middle of his face, bisecting it perfectly, before pooling in the crook of his neck. The book he'd been reading was still on his lap. It was clear he'd died first. Trevor had turned in his chair so he was looking away from the door. He hadn't been wearing his flak jacket and the chest area of his white T-shirt had two small round bloodstains the size and colour of roses on it. There was also a bullet wound on his temple and his face was splattered with blood, as was the coffee table next to him.

Anji had been a police officer long enough to know that the shots that had killed both men had been fired by a professional – the type of man who'd killed Anil and his wife, and the two officers escorting Jane to hospital.

Behind her she heard the lightest movement, so light it was almost as if she'd imagined it. Except a sixth sense told her that she hadn't.

Anji dropped the bags just as her head was jerked back by the hair. She felt the hot touch of a blade against her throat and braced herself for the death blow, feeling a moment of regret that her life should come to an end like this.

But instead she felt the touch of warm breath in her ear and the smell of soft, subtle perfume.

'Hello, Anji.' Jane's voice was at its most seductive. 'Sorry to creep up on you like this but I need your help.' Jane's grip on her was strong and confident and Anji remained stock-still. 'It's just you and me now, Anji. And if you want to be the only one to stay alive then you need to do exactly what I say.'

'I understand.' Anji didn't, but what else was she going to say? 'What do you want me to do?'

She could almost hear Jane's smile. 'You're going to deliver me Ray Mason.'

Thirty-seven

Ray

I was hunched up in a fetal position on the floor behind the rear seats of Chris's old Audi estate so it looked like he was alone. The rear windows were tinted so I couldn't be seen unless someone physically got into the car and had a proper look round, which I didn't think was very likely.

I'd been in this position for the past five minutes as we made the final approach to the location Chris had been ordered to drive to. It was a stretch of country road surrounded by woodland near the Surrey/Hampshire border west of Guildford. Surprisingly, getting here on the M25 hadn't been that bad, although when we did hit a stretch where there was a jam Chris had put on the blue light and raced up the hard shoulder.

My phone had been going crazy all the way here. I now had

three more messages from Lomax, three from Butterworth, and even one from Commander Pugh, the head of CT. I hadn't listened to any of them. There didn't seem much point. By fleeing the scene of a triple shooting, where I'd already admitted that two of the victims had been shot by me, I was in breach of every regulation going, and if any of my bosses had a clue what I was doing now I'd be out of a job immediately, and possibly behind bars as well.

'ETA two minutes,' Chris called from the front. His voice sounded shaky.

We were approaching the moment of truth.

'Is anyone following us?' I called back.

'No. The road's quiet and I've been watching behind.'

'So when we get there, you just wait. Is that right?'

'That's right.'

I thought about this.

'I think there may be more than one kidnapper,' I said. 'It would be a lot easier taking Amber if there were two. One of them could be with her now while the other watches you arrive, so as soon as you park, we stop speaking.'

'If I see one of them, I'll get hold of the bastard and I'll make him tell me where Amber is.'

'Chances are you won't see him, Chris. And anyway, leave that shit to me. They're going to tell you to abandon the car. They may make you take a walk into the woods. They may even pick you up in another car. The most important thing is to drop your keys nearby so I can use this car if I need to follow you. And remember, if they send you into the woods, leave a trail so I can follow.'

We'd stopped at a service station en route and bought a dozen small packs of KP peanuts, which Chris had stuffed in his jacket pocket. If he was told to leave the car and head into the woods he'd drop a pack at regular intervals so I'd have an idea where he was going. It was hardly a foolproof plan but it was the best we could come up with in the time available.

'If they see you following me, they'll kill Amber.'

'I'll be careful. And they won't touch Amber until they have the information they need. You don't have it, but they don't know that. And that's your trump card.'

But as soon as I spoke the words, I could hear how empty they sounded. This whole thing was a bad move. It had been from the word go. We should have called in all the resources of CT. They could have tracked Chris the whole way, massively increasing the chances of getting Amber – and indeed Chris himself – back alive. I could do nothing except react to events as they happened and hope for the best. Yes, as a last resort I could give them the postcode of the safehouse, but knowing criminals like these as I do, that wouldn't save any of our lives – in fact it might hasten our deaths. I cursed myself for my gung-ho behaviour. I should have persuaded Chris to go for the right option. But I hadn't, and now the responsibility for what was happening fell squarely on my shoulders.

I felt a wave of anxiety. My hands were beginning to shake. I wondered if it was the onset of shock after the events of this afternoon. Whatever it was, I couldn't afford to weaken now. Not with the life of my only friend and his daughter at stake. I pictured the teddy bear I'd bought Amber all those years ago, remembered that conversation on the phone and the emotion it stirred in me.

For her sake – for both their sakes – I had to stay strong.

'All right, we're here,' said Chris. 'The road behind and in front is empty.'

He started to slow down.

I wanted to wish him luck, to tell him that he was one of the few people I truly cared about, that I counted him as my one true friend. But I didn't say any of this. Instead I told him to make sure he left the keys where I could find them, then fell silent as the car stopped and he cut the engine.

We'd been there barely a minute, waiting in silence, when Chris's phone rang.

This wasn't a good sign. Someone was definitely watching.

Chris picked up immediately. The call lasted ten seconds and Chris only said yes once. He then turned on the engine and drove forward another hundred metres or so, going slowly, before making a left turning, pulling up on the side of the road and cutting the engine.

Thirty seconds passed. Neither of us spoke. Then the phone rang again.

This time the call lasted longer, and it sounded like Chris was listening to instructions. I heard him throw the phone down on the passenger seat when the call ended.

'Got to go one hundred metres left of car and grab phone taped to tree,' he hissed in my direction. 'Got to leave my phone here. They're checking.'

'I'll follow in one minute,' I hissed back. 'Try not to go too fast.'

Chris didn't reply but instead got out of the car and slammed the door behind him, leaving me in silence.

I looked at my watch, kept my eye on the second hand as it ticked steadily round, feeling the pressure. If I moved too soon then I might be spotted leaving the car, and that could ruin everything. For the first time, I thought seriously about calling Butterworth and letting him know what was going on. I was sure he could get a helicopter here fast if it came to it. I even reached into my pocket and grabbed my phone.

But I didn't make the call.

Thirty-eight

Chris walked quickly through the trees. He was conscious of the fact that Ray needed time to follow, because if he lost Ray then he lost the chance of getting Amber back alive, but the caller had told him that he had thirty seconds to get to the other phone. The caller also told him not to look round as he walked but to go in a completely straight line inwards from the postbox by the side of the road, keeping his eyes straight ahead.

He wondered if he was being watched but didn't dare look. The woods were dark and thick, and there was a smell of damp in the air. He pushed brambles out of his face as he kept to the line, listening out for any sound but hearing nothing.

If he ever got his hands on the man who'd done this to Amber, he would beat him to death without mercy. He would tear him limb from limb. Chris had always prided himself on keeping a calm head in a crisis and not overreacting to situations and suspects as Ray was sometimes prone to do. But right now he was in danger of losing complete control.

Somewhere up ahead, a phone was ringing. Chris quickened his pace, breaking into a run, tore through a thick fern bush and saw the phone – a cheap throwaway Nokia – taped to a tree a few yards in front of him.

He ripped it free and put it to his ear.

'There's a fence fifty metres ahead of you,' said the caller. 'When you reach it, turn right and follow it for one hundred metres. A gate with a sign saying "Private Property" will be open in front of you. Go through it and lock it behind you. Walk ten metres forward. Then await the next call. You've got one minute.'

The call was disconnected the other end. Chris wanted to look round, to see if Ray was following him, but didn't dare. Instead he reached into his pocket as surreptitiously as possible, let a pack of peanuts fall to the ground, then set off at a jog, clutching the phone.

He dropped another two packs of peanuts before he got to the fence then a fourth as he reached it, knowing he was taking a big risk. He was nothing like as fit as he'd once been. He worked long hours and his spare moments these days tended to be spent helping Charlotte. He couldn't remember the last time he'd been in a gym and it showed as he ran alongside the fence, his breathing getting more laboured. He dropped a fifth pack of peanuts at roughly the halfway point, no longer resisting looking round. The wood was thinner here, the thick pine trees giving way to beeches and oaks. Consequently, there were fewer places to hide. But he couldn't see anyone.

The Witness

The gate appeared in front of him. It was just a regular farmer's gate, no more than stomach high, with a prominent sign in its centre saying 'Private Property: Keep Out'. It was open a few inches, and a chain with an open padlock attached was looped round one of the bars. Chris went through the gap, reattached the padlock behind him, dropped a sixth pack of nuts, then walked forward ten metres along the rutted track that meandered through the trees.

He stopped, conscious that the only sounds he could hear were his rapid breathing and the wind passing through the trees and shaking the leaves. Like Ray, he was struck with the unwelcome thought that everything seemed far too slickly organized to have been set up in the last few hours. For one thing, how would the kidnapper have known about this place? It was at least forty miles from the site of the murder the previous night, and a good forty from where Amber went to uni. It had to have been set up beforehand. But how?

And, more to the point, why?

His thoughts were interrupted by the sound of the phone in his hand. Still breathing heavily, he answered.

'I can see you,' said the kidnapper.

Chris looked around furiously, saw nothing.

'Remove your jacket, throw it on the ground, then pull the linings out of your trouser pockets so I can see they're empty.'

Chris did as he was told.

'If you've brought anyone with you, Mr Leavey, or you're not being entirely truthful, I will kill your daughter.'

'I've come alone. I just want Amber back. You can do what the hell you want with me.'

'Take your shoes off.'

'Come on. Please.'

'Off.'

Again, Chris did as he was told.

'Now run down the track until you come to an empty can of Coke on the ground. Then stop. You've got one minute to get there or my colleague cuts her finger off.' The call was ended before Chris got a chance to respond.

Trying desperately not to think about anyone hurting Amber, he started running, praying that Ray was there somewhere and still keeping him in sight because now that he'd been forced to leave his jacket behind he had nothing to leave a trail with. Out of the corner of his eye he thought he saw a shadow moving in the woods, and he had a terrible feeling he was being led straight into a trap. He slipped on the mud, steadied himself, his breathing coming in angry pants now. He had no idea how far he'd gone but he'd turned a corner now and there were still more woods ahead. He turned another corner, the track got wider, and he saw fresh tyre marks in the mud. Somewhere high above him a plane passed overhead, its occupants blissfully unaware of the life-or-death drama going on beneath them.

Chris almost missed the Coke can as he tried once again not to lose his footing in the mud, and failed, falling over on his side. It was straight in front of him, five feet away. Exhausted and in pain, he clambered to his feet and walked over to where it sat at the side of the track.

That was when he saw her. His Amber.

She was bound to a tree about ten yards in from the track, wearing nothing but a T-shirt and jeans, her feet only just touching the ground. Two lines of rope secured her legs, two more her body. She was blindfolded, and her mouth was gagged.

An animal wail rose in Chris's throat. He didn't even have time to think. He just ran towards her.

Which was when a huge hooded man stepped out from behind an adjacent tree and put a gun to her head.

Chris stopped, then heard movement behind him followed by an intense, immediate pain. He gasped in shock and his strength ebbed from him like air escaping from a balloon. He took a few steps forward, sheer willpower driving him towards his daughter, only feet away from him now. But then, just as suddenly, his legs were kicked from under him and he fell to his knees. He looked down, saw blood seeping through the material of his work shirt, and realized that he'd been stabbed in the side.

A second hooded man stood over him, a bloodied knife with a blade about four inches long in his hand.

Chris stared at him, putting a hand to his side in an effort to slow the bleeding, knowing the wound was serious.

'I'm not going to let you know the location of the safehouse unless you let my daughter go,' he said with as much strength as he could muster. 'Whatever you do.'

The man nodded slowly, then leaned down so that his mouth was close to Chris's ear. 'Let me let you into a little secret,' he whispered. 'We already know the safehouse location.'

Thirty-nine

Ray

My theory was that there was a maximum of two kidnappers. Amber's abduction had been highly professional, and professionals tend to keep their numbers as small as possible, particularly when committing serious crimes like kidnap. Therefore even if one of them had been watching Chris's car arrive, he'd have been gone as soon as Chris headed into the woods.

I might have been wrong, but in the end you've got to go with your gut, and mine told me that events were going to move very fast. The kidnappers weren't going to want to be hanging around a wood in one of the most populated parts of Europe for long. They'd want to be in and out with the minimum of fuss.

My only fear was that, rather than a watcher, they'd left a camera in the vicinity to check that no one followed Chris to the rendezvous. After all, the kidnapper had been very specific about where Chris parked. So before I got out of the car I'd sat up slowly in the back and looked round to see where they might have planted one. We were parked at the side of a single-track road surrounded on both sides by thick walls of pine trees. About five metres in front of the car, and partially shaded by one of the pines, was an ancient-looking red mailbox. If I was one of the bad guys I'd have planted a camera there, because it gave good coverage of the road without looking too conspicuous. Which meant my exit from the car was going to be difficult.

I'd got out my picks and used one of them to flick open the boot's internal catch. I'd slowly opened the boot until there was enough room for me to squeeze through the gap then rolled out, hopefully out of sight of any camera, and gently closed it behind me. I had then run low and crab-like a few yards back from the car before darting inside the woods and setting off at a sprint, less than a minute after Chris had gone in there.

I'm fit, and I'm fast too, and it hadn't taken me long to get Chris in my sights. I'd seen him up ahead talking on the phone before running further into the woods. I'd waited to make sure he wasn't being followed, then taken off after him, gun in my hand, keeping as quiet as possible.

I'd lost him at the fence but followed it and picked up the peanuts trail, and seen him go through a gate marked 'Private Property' that led on to an old track where he'd taken a phone call and then removed his jacket and shoes. I'd stayed back out of sight at this point, hiding behind a tree and watching as he took off up the track at the kind of pace I hadn't seen him employ in years, almost going arse over tit in the mud in the process.

That was when I saw something move in the trees about twenty yards to the right of where Chris had taken his gear off. It was a man in military fatigues and a camouflaged hood, only just visible against the background. Almost immediately he disappeared from view back into the trees. I slowly scanned the tree line, tracking in the direction Chris was heading, and I thought I saw the man again running through the undergrowth. By the route he was taking, it looked like he was trying to cut Chris off.

I gave it a few seconds then broke free of my hiding place, climbed over the gate and cut into the trees at the side of the track, following the route Chris had taken as quickly and quietly as possible, every part of me attuned to the surroundings. Fear, excitement and anger swirled through my insides, fighting for supremacy. I pushed them down, willing myself to remain calm and ready.

You're not a frightened little boy any more.

You're a killer.

And then I heard Chris's anguished wail ripping through the trees, the pain in it hitting me like a physical blow.

The distance was thirty metres. No more.

I slowed right down, slipping further into the woods away from the track. I was creeping rather than walking, using the individual trees for cover.

I heard voices and, as I rounded an oak tree, I froze.

The sight I witnessed will haunt me for a long time. A woman I can only assume was Amber was tied to a tree. A huge hooded guy in fatigues stood on the other side of her, a gun to her head. A few feet in front of her, Chris was on his knees, swaying like a punch-drunk boxer while a second hooded man stood above him, a bloodied knife in one hand. The second man's hand was outstretched, holding a phone, and it looked like he was filming Chris.

I was right in the line of sight of the big gunman so I crouched down on my haunches, moving a little way to the right so he wouldn't be able to see me. I was still too far away to get an accurate shot in so I crept slowly forward, step by step.

The knifeman started speaking to Chris. I had to strain to make out his words but I managed to.

'You're going to watch your daughter die now, Mr Leavey,' he said. 'Have you got anything you want to say to her?'

'Please don't do this,' I heard Chris beg.

'Do you think we should do it quickly with a nice head shot?' The knifeman chuckled. The bastard was enjoying this. 'No, I think we're going to use the blade and watch her bleed out for a bit. You know, during the Rwandan genocide the Hutu Interahamwe used to cut the arms and legs of Tutsi children in front of their parents. Maybe we should do a little bit of that here.'

I saw him nod in the direction of the big gunman who took a step back and started to remove something from his fatigues.

Sometimes you have to make a snap decision, and I made one then. I jumped to my feet, gun in hand, and fired two rapid shots at the big gunman, careful to keep my aim away from Amber, the bullets cracking through the silence.

I was off balance and missed, and the gunman immediately returned fire, jumping back behind Amber so I couldn't get a shot at him.

'Armed police!' I screamed at the top of my voice, diving to the ground and firing two shots in the direction of the knifeman's upper body and two more into the space between Chris and Amber as more bullets came flying back in my direction. I was no longer trying to hit anyone, I just wanted to panic them, and it seemed to work. From my position in the undergrowth I saw the knifeman's camouflaged legs disappearing into the trees away from me. I fired two shots at them but again I missed.

I held my fire then and looked around for the big gunman, knowing he was the most dangerous of the two. I didn't think he was behind Amber any more so very slowly I got to my feet, gun still outstretched in front of me. I'd fired eight rounds so I had seven left. It was enough.

But the woods were silent. Nothing moved, and I felt my heart sink when I saw Chris lying in a crumpled heap on the ground.

I took a step forward, then another, expecting an ambush at any moment. I looked around, still keeping low. Up ahead, I heard a car start up. The kidnappers were leaving.

Chris was writhing on the ground making desperate choking sounds and I rushed over to him, crouching down.

'Oh Jesus,' I whispered.

At some point in those few seconds of shooting the knifeman had cut his throat. Blood was pouring from his severed carotid artery and his face was ghostly white.

I turned him on to his side and tried to close the wound with my fingers in a bid to stall the bleeding. But it was too late. It was always going to be too late. Chris's eyes rolled up in his head, his breathing stopped and his body went slack.

'No, don't die, Chris,' I whispered. 'Do not die on me. Please do not die.'

All the trauma of that terrible night all those years ago when I saw my brother cut down by my father in one fell swoop came hurtling back to me. My only friend was dying. I felt for a pulse, unable to keep a lid on my emotions. Tears stung my eyes as I realized there was no pulse there. Nothing. I rolled him on to his back, tried CPR, refused to give up. But the blood was everywhere. It drenched his clothes and the ground around him. It was all over my hands. I kept going. No response. No response. No response. Nothing. He'd bled out completely. He was dead. He was gone. It was over. I was alone.

I stopped, wiped the tears from my eyes with my jacket sleeve, and stood up.

That was when I heard the whimpering coming from Amber. In these last few desperate minutes I'd forgotten about her, and I felt a surge of relief as I realized she was still alive. I rushed over to her and untied the gag.

'What's happened to Dad?' she said urgently. 'Can you tell me what's going on? Who are you?'

'It's Ray. Your dad's colleague. You remember me. You're safe now.'

I started untying the ropes.

'Please, get this blindfold off me.'

One of the ropes came free. 'Just give me a moment.'

'What's happened to Dad?' she repeated.

I told her the truth. 'I'm afraid your dad didn't make it, Amber.'

Her face crumpled with defeat. 'Get this blindfold off me now. I want to see him.'

'Amber, sweetheart, you don't,' I said, struggling with the next knot.

'Why? What have they done to him? Tell me.'

She was starting to get hysterical but I didn't want her to see her dad's body, especially while she was still tied to a tree.

'Are you hurt at all?' I asked her.

'I can't hear much out of my right ear. The shots were very close to my head.'

'Your hearing'll come back in a minute,' I told her as the final knot came free and I helped her away from the tree. 'Come on,' I said, turning her away from her father's body as she yanked off the blindfold.

But she struggled free from my grip. 'I want to see my dad. Let me see him!'

I tried to hold on to her but it would have meant using force and I wasn't prepared to do that so I let her go and watched helplessly as she ran over to her father and fell to her knees beside him, sobbing as she held his lifeless, bloodied body in her arms.

The men who'd murdered Chris were animals. They deserved death. And yet they'd escaped when I had my opportunity to kill them. I'd had no choice but to act. I'd opened fire because I was certain the big gunman was about to kill Amber, and almost certainly Chris very soon afterwards. And yet Chris couldn't have told them what they needed to know – the location of the safehouse – because he didn't know it, so why kill Amber before they'd got that information? It didn't make sense.

Unless somehow it was all a ruse. Maybe they were never after the safehouse location. Instead they were using Amber to get Chris where they wanted him.

But why? What motive could they possibly have for going to all this trouble just to kill him? And to make him suffer like that too?

It had to be revenge.

And that, of course, was the moment when everything, at last, began to make sense.

I pulled out my phone and dialled 999, identified myself as a police officer, explained that there were two casualties, one deceased and the other with minor injuries, and gave the location as the postcode Chris had been given by the kidnappers.

There were more messages on my phone from the usual suspects, Lomax and Butterworth. I knew I was never going to be able to explain away what had happened in the last two hours to the bosses. This, I was fairly certain, was my last night on the job. As of tomorrow, I was going to have to think of something else to do with my life.

Right then, though, I didn't care. My friend was dead. I'd failed to save him. The fact that Amber had been freed largely unscathed was a welcome development but scant consolation for what I'd just lost.

I took a deep breath and looked over to where Amber still cradled her father in her arms, her sobs quieter now. I waited for a few minutes with my gun drawn, just in case the kidnappers decided to come back. Only when I was satisfied that they were gone for good did I gently lift Amber to her feet. This time she didn't resist but fell into my arms.

'Who did this?' she said. 'Who'd do that to my dad? He's a good man. And why did they take me? Why?'

'I don't know,' I whispered, although I was beginning to get an idea. 'Let me get you down to the car. We can wait for the ambulance there.'

'But what about Dad?'

'The paramedics will take care of him. Don't worry about that. The important thing is you're safe now.'

I held her close, feeling a powerful pang of emotion as we walked slowly and in silence through the trees.

'I know about you, Ray,' she said when we'd reached the road and could hear the approaching sirens. She looked at me as she spoke the words and there was a fierce expression in her tear-stained eyes. She looked so different from the gawky teenage girl I'd last seen five years ago, just after her mum's MS had been diagnosed. Now her innocence had gone, just as mine had, never to return.

'What do you mean?' I asked her.

'I know you've killed before.'

'Only when I've had to.'

'I want you to find the men who did this.'

'I'll do everything I can.'

But she wasn't listening. 'And when you find them, I want you to kill them. I want those bastards dead. Promise me you'll do it.'

'It doesn't always work like that, Amber,' I said, hating the fact that she saw me this way.

Anger flared on her face. 'Promise me.'

'If I get the chance to, I will kill them. I promise you that.'

It was the only thing I could say, and it was the truth too, although the chances of me ever seeing these men again were slim at best.

She nodded slowly and her body began to shake as the tears came again.

I held her in my arms, rocking her gently, until the ambulance arrived. I showed the crew my warrant card and waited while they took Amber inside. A second ambulance arrived, and I used the maps section on my phone to locate Chris's body for them.

The police would be here soon but I didn't want to hang around for that. I'd give myself up soon enough but not yet.

I walked hurriedly back to Chris's car, finding the keys where he'd dropped them just inside the tree line. With the sound of more approaching sirens ringing in my ears, I got in, started the engine, and entered the postcode Anji had given me earlier into the maps section. It was a forty-five-minute drive to the safe-house, and it would be my one and only chance to talk to this witness before I lost my job. Something was going on, and the witness was the key to it all. I was looking forward to meeting her.

I memorized the route then switched off the phone so I couldn't be traced before turning Chris's car round and pulling away.

Forty

Jane

So now you know. I'm a killer. A professional one too. I go by a number of different names – Jane Kinnear's just one of many – but the one I enjoy the most is The Wraith. There's something mysterious and ethereal about it that suits me perfectly.

Are you shocked? Are you surprised?

Sure, the story I told Anji and DC Jeffs at the hospital about what I was doing at Anil Rahman's house was a lie, but I think you've guessed that by now.

The story I told you, though? About the beatings my mother used to give me as a child? Of having to choose the belt she was going to use? Of the rape and murder of our neighbour in South Africa while I was playing with my children next door? The humiliation that my husband heaped upon me with his infidelities, his debts, and finally his turning me into a whore with another man? No. All that was real. All that shaped me. Perhaps I could have taken a different path, put it all behind me and gone to work for an orphans charity, but then I would have risked losing my sons. No, the moment I killed Frank Mellon, I was doomed. I had no choice but to go and work for his boss – a mysterious man with a hundred times more power and ruthlessness than Frank ever had. A man I couldn't turn down. A man who recognized my talents and transformed me from a single mother with few prospects to a woman possessing true and immense power.

I'd still be working for him now if he hadn't died of cancer two years ago, giving me the opportunity to form my own team of people and go freelance. The job I was on now was the most lucrative I'd ever been involved in and would provide enough money to keep me and my sons financially secure for the rest of our days. It was that thought that drove me now.

Anji was on her knees in the corner of the kitchen, handcuffed to the oven door, looking scared behind the gag. Sitting against the worktop opposite her was DC Seamus Jeffs, the sex pest. His hands were cuffed behind his back, and his ankles and lower legs were bound with household string. I'd gagged his mouth with one of his socks to stop him from making a noise as I'd cut pieces off him. Whatever else my sins, I'm not a sadist. Hurting Jeffs was the only way to ensure Anji's cooperation. He was still alive but only just and it wouldn't be long until he was out of his misery.

'You know, Anji, I actually like you,' I told her. 'It's a pity you were in the wrong place at the wrong time. But if you do what you're told, you'll get out of here alive, I promise you that.'

I pulled the gag down so she could speak. I thought she might start bombarding me with questions but she didn't. Instead she looked me in the eye. The fear had left her face, replaced with something that might have been defiance.

'You're never going to let me out of here alive,' she said.

'Why not?'

'Because I can ID you for a start.'

'Tomorrow, when I leave this country, I'll look completely different,' I told her. 'I have a dozen appearances, a dozen names. I'm a chameleon. It's why I'm good at what I do. The fact that you can picture me as I am now won't help you at all.'

'I don't believe you.'

I gently touched her cheek. 'I'm many things, Anji, but I'm not a liar. I always keep my promises. You have one more task. Do it right and I guarantee that you'll live.'

I could see the doubt in her eyes. The poor thing wanted to believe me so much.

I looked at my watch: 6.45 p.m. It was time. Keeping the Sig trained on her, I released one of Anji's hands and handed her her mobile.

'Call Ray.'

Forty-one

Ray

The traffic was horrendous on the way to the safehouse, so I used the hard shoulder and the siren where I needed to. I also had time to think. To try to work out what was happening.

So had it somehow been a ruse? And if so, what was this whole thing really about?

Chris had only one link with Anil Rahman. The Turks and Caicos Islands and the death of the Sheikh, Zayed bin Azir. The man who'd wanted to buy sarin for al-Qaeda. Could someone really have come back after all this time seeking revenge? The Sheikh's family had deep pockets. It was possible one or more of them could have found out what had happened to him. The problem with this was that the witness had claimed that Anil's killer wanted information about an impending terror attack, and the attack had been real. We'd only just foiled it. Yet the conversation the witness had described had never sounded quite right. None of the terror suspects, including the organizer, Karim Khan, had known Anil was an informant. And, according to MI5, Anil himself had never been told any details about the attack either, so there was no point in the killer torturing him for information.

In the end, everything kept coming back to the witness.

When I was only a few miles from the safehouse, I pulled off the M25 and into a petrol station and turned on my mobile. Once again there were more messages from Lomax and Butterworth. I'd run out of excuses now. I was officially AWOL and, even without listening to their messages, I knew that soon there'd be a warrant out for my arrest.

There was another message too. This one was from Anji's mobile. I'd had three missed calls from her: the first was at 18.46, the second at 18.49, and then the one with the message at 18.58, nearly half an hour ago. I wondered where she'd been phoning from given that she wasn't meant to be using her mobile at the safehouse. I pressed play, and her voice filled the car.

'Hi, Ray, hope you're OK. Listen, our witness, Jane Kinnear, has specifically requested that you come here. She's got important information that she only wants to relay to you. She'd prefer we didn't do it officially either so don't say anything to anyone. I know this sounds very cloak and dagger but she seems to think it's very important. Can you call me back as soon as you can and I'll give you the address?'

The message ended. I listened to it a second time, just to check that I hadn't made a mistake. I hadn't. Anji wanted me to call her so that she could give me the address of the safehouse, even though we'd had a conversation less than three hours ago in which she'd already given its postcode to me. She hadn't sounded her usual self either. There'd been an undercurrent of tension in her voice. It didn't make sense. I wondered what the hell the witness wanted to speak to me about. Or how she even knew who I was.

Once again, something didn't feel right. Anil dead, Chris dead. The fact that Anil had emailed me out of the blue the day before his murder. And now the witness – his supposed lover – wanted to see me, and Anji needed me to keep it quiet. I thought back to the op in the Turks. I didn't have the real name of the female CIA agent, Alpha, the one who'd set the Sheikh up, but Simon Pratt, the guy from MI5 who'd run the op, might have it. I hadn't spoken to him since the chaotic debrief afterwards when it had been agreed by everyone involved to keep the whole thing quiet, and I had no idea what had happened to him afterwards. I had an urge to speak to Pratt now, though, let him know what was happening here, and see if he could shed any light on things.

I Googled him on the phone. It was an unusual enough name, I thought, there weren't going to be too many Simon Pratts out there. The first results were Linkedin and Facebook, but then I spotted the name in conjunction with a news story further down the page. The headline read 'Former Spook Goes Missing in Thailand'.

I clicked on the link and read in silence.

The story was from November the previous year. Pratt, it seemed, had retired from the security services to live in Hua Hin, Thailand, with his Thai wife, a woman some twenty-five years his junior. According to his wife, he'd gone for a swim one morning on the local beach and had never come back. He hadn't taken his credit cards, his passport or his phone, and at the time the story appeared he'd been gone for five days. The local police chief was quoted as saying that a full search was ongoing and it was possible that he'd drowned. I looked for further articles on the story and had to trawl for several minutes before I found another one from a local ex-pat paper, dated a month later, which simply stated that Pratt was still missing and was now presumed dead. Drowning was thought the most likely cause, although the author of the piece pointed out cryptically that the waters of the local beach were generally calm and that this would be the first drowning there in almost ten years.

There was no way this was a coincidence. Three of the five people from the Turks op were dead. For all I knew the American CIA agent was dead too. I might be the only one left. It wasn't a comforting thought.

I switched off the phone, knowing that it was only a matter of time before Butterworth and co. used it to track my movements. They'd have found out about Chris's death by now and there'd be an absolute clamour to get hold of me. I'd give myself up soon enough. But not yet.

Forty-two

Five minutes later, as the trees gave way to fields on both sides, I found a spot in front of a farm gate and pulled the car up there. Night was falling fast and there was a chill in the air as I got out and started up the road, taking my gun from its holster and slipping it into my jacket pocket for easy access. I had no idea what to expect but my instincts were telling me to be careful, and I wasn't going to ignore them.

The redbrick cottage was on its own at a T junction where two quiet rural roads met. Its lights appeared in front of me and I stopped at the edge of the driveway, keeping close to the hedgerow so I couldn't be seen. All the curtains were closed, which wasn't a surprise: the occupants wouldn't want to be advertising their presence to any passers-by. Two cars were parked in the drive. I recognized one – a battered Nissan saloon that reflected the constant budget cuts the Met was making – as a station pool car. The other was a Land Rover, which presumably belonged to the armed escort.

I decided against knocking on the door until I'd checked everything out. Instead I passed the cottage on the other side of the road, making sure I wasn't spotted, before turning left at the junction so I was moving parallel to the back garden. A fence about my height, screened by a row of apple trees, marked the border of the property. I peered over it. The curtains were all pulled at the rear of the cottage too and several of the lights were on. I was as aware as anyone how risky it was for an armed man to approach the back of a safehouse where at least three heavily armed police officers were protecting a vulnerable witness, so I waited several minutes, scanning the garden for any movement, and only when I was satisfied that it was empty did I heave myself up and climb over the fence.

I crept over to the back door and peered through the glass into a long hallway running down past a staircase to the front of the cottage. The light was on but nothing moved. By my reckoning there were six people inside, yet they were being remarkably quiet for this time in the evening. Clearly they hadn't gone anywhere because the cars were still out front, but it was anyone's guess what they were all up to.

That was when I saw something on the carpet, a few feet inside the door. Two dark, uneven stains the size of two-pence coins. There was a thin dark smear on the lower skirting of the wall next to them.

It looked like blood.

I could hear my heart beating faster as my body released a powerful dose of adrenalin. Blood. And not just a little bit either.

I tried the door, my touch gentle. It was locked. The lock was easy enough to break but again I hesitated. If I'd made a mistake and there were cops inside with guns at the ready, they'd shoot without asking too many questions and I'd be a dead man. It would be a damn stupid way to die too. Shot by my own side because I couldn't ring the doorbell like everyone else.

So again I waited.

Five minutes passed. Still no movement.

I didn't trust the witness. Her story about Anil had never entirely held water; she was, according to Anji, some kind of martial arts expert who'd taken out Seamus like he was nothing when he'd upset her; and now from out of nowhere she'd specifically requested to see me and, crucially, wanted our meeting kept quiet.

I gave it a little bit longer then looked at my watch. Eight minutes since I'd arrived at this door and there hadn't been a single sign of life in that time. It was time to make a decision.

With a deep breath, I reached down and got to work on the lock. I was rusty, and I only had a basic set of picks, but I still had the door open in the space of a couple of minutes and, most importantly, I did it quietly.

Very slowly I pushed the door open and stepped inside. The silence was loud in my ears. No music, no TV, no voices. I shut the door behind me, bringing out my warrant card so I could be easily identified and keeping my other hand on the gun in my jacket pocket.

I heard movement behind the nearest door, the sound of a woman clearing her throat, and the next second the door was open and a pretty brunette was standing there staring at me with a shocked expression on her face.

'Jesus!' she screamed. 'Help!'

Startled myself, I held up my warrant card and took a step towards her. 'It's OK, I'm a police officer.' My other hand left my pocket without the gun as I instinctively tried to make her feel at ease.

It all happened so fast I didn't have time to think straight. When I see a frightened woman I immediately try to make her feel calm. By the time my brain started to process that there was no one responding to her screams and this might be some sort of ruse, she had a gun pointed in my face.

She was that fast.

'Raise your hands straight above your head,' she snapped, moving out into the hall to put a bit of distance between us.

I had the feeling that most of the people in this house were dead and that it was this woman who'd made them that way so I did as she said. She had her hair tied back in a ponytail and was wearing no makeup but she was still strikingly attractive, and her deep brown eyes were alive with intelligence. And, I think, something else. Ruthlessness.

'You're early, Ray,' she said in a mild South African accent. 'I wasn't expecting you for a while yet.'

'Sorry to disappoint you. I can always leave.'

She smiled, showing perfect teeth. 'I don't think so.' Her dark eyes scanned my body. 'You definitely don't look pleased to see me so I'm assuming that's a gun in your pocket. Move your right hand very slowly inside the jacket and take the gun out by the handle, using just your thumb and forefinger to hold it. And please don't try anything. I know your reputation as a man who takes risks, and it wouldn't be a good move. I'd prefer you alive, but I'll accept you dead.'

'Where is everyone?' I asked, following her instructions and removing the gun with my thumb and forefinger.

'Not in a position to help you, I'm afraid. Put the gun on the floor.'

It struck me that this was the second time I'd had to give up my gun today under duress, which wasn't a very good record, but I didn't see what else I could do so I placed it very carefully on the carpet, trying to work out my next move but knowing that my options were limited in the extreme, and getting more limited with every passing second.

'Kick the gun over to me. Then step back against the door.'

Again I obeyed, looking for an opening when she reached down to pick it up, but she was watching me like a hawk. I could see that I was in the presence of a real professional, and in the criminal world you don't often see that.

She removed the magazine one-handed, emptied out the bullets and scattered them on the floor before flinging the gun over her shoulder.

'So you're the witness who saw Anil die,' I said. 'I'm guessing it was you who killed him.'

'I'm not interested in a conversation. Step into the kitchen.'

With a sigh, and my hands still ramrod straight above my head, I walked through the doorway she'd come out of and into the kitchen.

The breath died in my throat. I don't know what I'd been expecting but what I did see will stay with me for ever. Seamus

Jeffs propped up against one of the work units, his upper body and face drenched in blood. More blood pooled on the tiled floor around him, and just the briefest of glances told me he'd died slowly and in pain.

Opposite him Anji crouched on the floor on one knee, her wrists cuffed to the handle of the oven, a gag covering her mouth. Her face and body were splattered with blood but it must have come from Seamus because she looked unhurt. At least physically. Mentally it was clear she'd been through a horrendous ordeal. Her eyes were wide with fear, and she didn't even seem to acknowledge me.

There was a kitchen stool in the centre of the room and the witness – or whoever she really was – told me to sit on it.

'What are you planning to do to me?' I asked over my shoulder, knowing that if I sat down it was highly unlikely I'd be getting back up again. I tried not to look at Seamus's body but it was etched in my mind, just like the memory of Anil's ruined corpse. This woman had tortured both men. She would almost certainly torture me the same way. If it came to it, it would be better to be shot. At least it would be quick.

'Sit down.'

I got on to the stool, looking back at her. Ten feet separated us. It was too far.

'Don't even think about it, Ray.'

She lowered the gun a little so it was pointed at my chest then crouched down beside Anji. Still keeping her eyes on me, she untied Anji's restraints before hauling her up by the hair.

'Tie his hands behind his back,' she demanded, handing Anji

the restraints and giving her a push in my direction before moving off to one side so she could keep the gun trained on both of us.

Anji stared at me, and I saw a sudden flicker of fire in her eyes. She might have been traumatized by her ordeal but she wasn't beaten yet.

She took a step towards me, then another.

I tried to think how I could get out of this, knowing it was my only chance. I couldn't risk hurting Anji, or using her as a shield, but if she tied me up now then I was certain the witness would kill her, and I'd be helpless. I had to do something. Had to . . .

Anji took another slow step forward. Then, in one sudden movement, she swung round and lunged at the witness, keeping her body low to make herself as difficult a target as possible.

Jane Kinnear might have been caught momentarily off guard but she reacted fast, turning the gun on Anji and firing twice in rapid succession. She was already turning the gun back towards me when Anji fell into her, carried forward by her momentum.

Kinnear stumbled backwards, her gun hand momentarily knocked off balance as she shoved Anji aside.

That was all the incentive I needed. I launched myself off the stool and charged straight at her. She swung her arm back round, already pulling the trigger, and I felt something hot sting my side as I grabbed her gun hand by the wrist and yanked it upwards before launching my head at her face.

She tried to turn away at the last second but she wasn't quite fast enough and I caught her in her upper cheek. Her head hit one of the kitchen cupboards with a bang and I butted her a second time before she could recover properly.

She went down and my thumb found the pressure point in her palm. I pushed down hard and she yelled in pain, letting go of the gun. I knocked it out of reach and rolled off her as she struggled beneath me.

But this girl was fast. Even though she was hurt, she was on her feet in a moment. Her eyes flashed as she saw the gun and my hand reaching towards it, and she launched a kick at my head. She caught me a glancing blow but it wasn't enough to knock me off my stride and my finger found the trigger guard. I brought the gun up in front of me, firing a wild shot to stop her attack.

It worked. She jumped back, thankfully not hit, and I pointed the gun straight at her chest, slowly getting to my feet. I felt my side through the jacket. It was wet. I'd been hit but I was still standing and for the moment adrenalin was masking the pain. I reached under the jacket and explored further. There wasn't much blood. The bullet had only grazed me, although I still felt a little nauseous as the day's bloody events and my part in them began to take their toll.

Jane Kinnear glared at me, her cheek already reddening from where I'd struck it, blood leaking from a cut on her cheek.

'Get down on the floor,' I told her. 'Now.'

For a few seconds she did nothing. There was defiance in her eyes but surprise too. I could tell she wasn't used to being in this position.

My finger tightened on the trigger. 'You know who I am, so you should know what I'm capable of. I don't know how you've done it, but one way or another you're responsible for the death of two people dear to me today, and I'm itching to get revenge for that. So either sit down in that corner there or I will shoot you in the gut and watch you squirm. Your choice.'

She sat down on the floor against one of the cupboards, only a few feet from where what was left of Seamus Jeffs slumped motionless in his own blood.

Without taking my eyes off her, I crouched down beside Anji. She wasn't moving and I saw she'd been hit in the head. There was an exit wound the size of a golf ball at the base of her skull, leaking blood. I felt for a pulse and couldn't find one. She was dead.

I stood back up, my eyes cold. 'No one knows I'm here. It's just you and me, and we've got plenty of time. Answer my questions and you might just end up in a prison cell. Refuse, and I promise that you will die slowly.'

We stared at each other. Her dark eyes glittered and I could see she was trying to control me with them. It didn't work. I was dead to her charms – I was dead to everything right then – and she could see it.

'This is about what happened in the Turks and Caicos, isn't it?'

'I'm impressed. How did you know?'

'Things never quite added up with your story. So who hired you?'

She didn't answer.

I aimed the gun at her belly. 'Answer me.'

'The brother of the man you killed, Zayed bin Azir.'

'I seem to remember he had more than one. Which one?'

'His name's Mohammed – aren't they all? But you'll never prove anything against him. I never even met the man. It was all done through go-betweens.'

That was the way it always worked when you were dealing with organized criminals, and I had no doubt she was right. There'd be no way of proving anything against him.

'That operation in the Turks was top secret. Hardly anyone knew anything about it, so how did he find out who was involved?'

'My understanding is it took a long time. The best part of a decade. My client never believed the official story that his brother was killed by pirates, mainly because he knew what Zayed was involved in.'

'And he set this whole thing up?'

She raised an eyebrow. I had to give her full marks for coolness under pressure. 'Of course he didn't set it up. He's a rich man with good connections but he's no organizer. I did it.'

'And who are you? The Wraith?'

'Call me what you want. I'm just someone who gets things done. When the client found out who was responsible for his brother's death, he wanted you executed one by one, and he wanted the killings to be personal, and where possible filmed. The first two – the undercover CIA agent, Janine Wheeler, and the controller, Simon Pratt – were easy enough to carry out without raising suspicion. Anil Rahman was easy enough too, given his status as an MI5 informant trying to infiltrate terror groups. But you and Chris Leavey still worked together after all these years. If you both disappeared, or ended up being tortured to death, it would raise all kinds of suspicions. So I had to come up with a more challenging plan.'

'You had a contact in MI5, didn't you? Someone very high up who gave up our names, and presumably told you about Anil Rahman's role as an informant.'

She nodded. 'You have to remember my client has major resources. You can buy anyone if there's enough money on offer.'

'Who's the insider?'

'I don't know.'

My finger tightened on the trigger and I pointed the gun at her torso. 'Believe me, I can still get answers out of you, even with a round in your gut.'

'I honestly don't know. I didn't need that information. I just needed to know that Anil Rahman was an informant.'

'But the terror attack itself. How did you know it was planned?'

'The insider in MI5 knew what Rahman was up to. He told my client. We always thought it best to carry out the killings of you and Chris Leavey as close as possible to a terror attack because it would deflect attention from what was really going on.'

I sighed. 'So you did all this. Got caught deliberately, set up Amber's kidnapping—'

'It was a challenge. I like challenges.'

'It was an insane risk.'

'A risk, but not an insane one.' She shrugged casually. She didn't seem remotely scared by the consequences of being caught.

'How did you plan to escape? You couldn't just walk out of here leaving behind a pile of dead bodies. There'd be a huge manhunt.'

She didn't say anything, but there was something arrogant in her expression that even now told me she had something up her sleeve.

'Answer me.'

'I'm good at disguising myself, Ray. I look different now from the way I did an hour ago.'

I didn't believe her. No amount of disguise would get her away from here. There was something else she was relying on.

I pulled the trigger, the shot exploding round the room. She gasped and her body jumped. Smoke rose from the hole in the wood six inches from her head. Now she looked rattled.

'Tell me the truth or the next bullet takes you.'

'It is the truth.'

'Bullshit. Last chance. I will kill you without question.'

She opened her mouth to say something but never got the words out before there was a crash as the back door was shoved open followed by tense shouts of 'Armed police!'

Still keeping my gun trained on Jane Kinnear, I turned towards the door as the shouts grew louder. They were coming down the hallway, more than one of them, and then I heard one of them call out from behind the door: 'I am a police officer. There's no need for anyone to get hurt.'

'It's not what you think,' I called back. 'I'm a police officer too.'

'Then we can sort this out.'

The next second they were in the room, two men I didn't recognize, dressed casually in jeans and jackets, guns trained on me.

'Put your weapon on the floor now,' said the one on the left, the smaller of the two. 'Nice and slowly.'

In front of me, I could see that Kinnear had raised her hands and adopted a frightened expression.

'It's not what you think,' I told them, making no move to comply.

'It doesn't matter what I think,' said the cop. 'You need to lower your weapon now.'

He had an accent. Not very much of one, but enough to set the alarm bells ringing.

That was when I knew that neither of these men were police officers. They were the kidnappers. One was a huge guy with a scar on his chin, the other was shorter and leaner, ordinary-looking, but the same build as the man who killed Chris.

So The Wraith wasn't one person. It was a team. These three were in this together and I was caught in the middle. But it was obvious they wanted me alive, otherwise I'd have been shot down by now. I remembered the scene in the woods. The way the smaller of the two kidnappers had been filming Chris, capturing his pain – for the benefit of their client, so he could get off on his revenge.

I had no doubt I was going to be taken away from here to an undisclosed location where I'd be tortured to death, slowly and painfully, all of it captured on film. I'd seen this woman's handi-work. I knew what was in store. That still didn't explain how she planned to disappear and not get caught for what had happened in this place, but that was no longer my problem.

My problem was far bigger than that. I was trapped.

'Drop the weapon. Now,' said the smaller guy.

I continued to point the gun at Kinnear's face. I thought of Anji; I thought of Chris; I thought of my mum and my brothers – of all the people I'd lost. If I had to die then it was going to be on my terms. I wasn't going to go out like an animal for the viewing entertainment of some cold-hearted arsehole in the desert. I was going to go out fighting and I was going to take at least one of the two bastards who'd killed Chris with me, as well as the cold-hearted bitch currently in my gun sights.

'I said: drop the fucking weapon.'

I was sweating, the sound of my heart roaring in my ears.

'If you shoot me,' I told him, 'my last bullet takes her out.'

'Drop it!'

I stayed utterly still. The silence in the room was like a never-ending scream. Someone was going to pull the trigger at any moment. I was about to die. The end.

I couldn't have it. I had to have revenge.

The groan was like something from the dead. Loud and tortured. For just that half a second it broke the spell.

It was Seamus. His leg twitched. He was still alive.

The smaller gunman's eyes darted towards him.

I made my move without thinking. Launching myself backwards in a twisting dive, I swung the gun round, opening fire in a tight arc. I hit the floor shoulder first as bullets cracked around me. The smaller guy fell backwards as I hit him somewhere in the torso, momentarily getting in the big one's way. The big gunman kept firing anyway, hitting his colleague, and I concentrated my fire on him, pulling the trigger again and again. The big gunman stumbled as I hit him in the chest, then fell as a round took him in the mouth.

Jane Kinnear had leapt to her feet by now and was running for the door, moving fast. I tried to get her in the gun sights, realized she was getting away, and fired again. But she'd already gone, and I heard her running down the hall in the direction of the front door.

I couldn't let her go. Not after everything she'd done. Operating on the last of my adrenalin, I got up and started after her, jumping over the body of the smaller gunman and charging into the hall, keeping low just in case she was preparing to ambush me.

But she was at the front door, one hand on the handle, just about to pull it open. She looked back at me as I raised the gun. She was in my sights – still a good twenty feet away, but I could take her and she knew it.

We stared at each other.

'Are you really going to kill me in cold blood?' she asked, her voice remarkably calm.

I didn't say anything. She really was a beautiful woman and her dark eyes glittered with a fire that came close to entrancing me, and I thought then that it was a terrible pity that someone so attractive could have such a rancid heart.

A smile crossed her face. There was no coldness in it, or arrogance. It was just a pleasant, almost sweet look, and I wondered what had made this woman the way she was.

'I don't think so,' she continued. 'I don't think you're that kind of man. I think you're better than that.'

She turned the handle. The door opened a couple of inches.

I've never shot a woman, or even come close. I'd never expected to be in a situation where I was going to have to do it either. It just didn't seem right.

The door opened further. She was going to bolt.

I thought of Chris.

I pulled the trigger.

Nothing happened.

She actually laughed. 'Take care, Ray. Consider yourself the one who got away.'

And then she was gone. Out of the door and into the night.

I ran back into the kitchen, grabbed the gun the smaller of the two gunmen had dropped when he'd fallen, and started after her again. But I'd lost valuable seconds and by the time I'd crossed the driveway and was out on the road she was nowhere to be seen. Somewhere in the distance I heard a car start, and then I saw headlights as it drove away at speed. I was never going to catch her now.

I stood where I was for a few seconds, still coming to terms with what had happened, allowing my breathing to steady, then walked back inside.

The kitchen was a charnel house with bodies everywhere. I felt Seamus's pulse. He was still alive. Just. I had to get him help. Pulling out my phone I dialled 999 and gave my location.

Out of the corner of my eye I saw the big guy roll over on his side. He had a bullet wound in his throat but he too was still alive. I walked over to where he lay and stood above him.

He looked up at me, making strange rasping noises. 'Help me,' he managed to croak, slowly lifting an arm.

It was my professional duty to offer first aid to a shooting victim, even if he was a murderer.

But I wasn't feeling very professional right then.

'Fuck you,' I said, and shot him in the head.

Forty-three

Jane

As I pulled up outside the rented Surrey farmhouse I'd been using as a temporary HQ with my associates, Pryce and Gaydon, I felt deflated. I'd been truly scared back there when Ray Mason was pointing a gun at me, and I was disappointed with myself. Disappointed with everything.

So much planning, and still things hadn't quite worked out, which was bad news for me. With Ray Mason still alive I forfeited the million-dollar bonus I was supposed to receive for killing all five of the individuals involved in the murder of Zayed bin Azir in the Turks and Caicos Islands all those years ago.

It was a real pity because my plan for Ray Mason had been perfect. The idea was for him to turn up at the safehouse where Pryce, Gaydon and I would be waiting for him. He'd be overpowered then taken to the farm where he'd be tortured to death as the others – with the exception of Chris Leavey – had been, the footage filmed for the client to view later. To avoid any suspicion falling on me, Pryce and Gaydon had abducted a prostitute approximately my age and height a few days earlier. They'd brought her with them to the safehouse. The plan had been for them to kill her and then we'd set fire to the safehouse and leave her body in it with all the others. Since no one had taken a DNA sample from me, the investigating officers would think that I'd died along with the police guarding me. With no sign of Ray Mason, and the fact that he bore an uncanny resemblance to the e-fit I'd produced of the suspect in the Anil Rahman killings, suspicion would fall on him as the murderer. The email I'd sent to Mason from Anil's hacked email account requesting a meeting would further muddy the waters. Obviously the police would never be able to come up with a viable motive as to why Mason had killed Anil, but with that much circumstantial evidence against him they were unlikely to look much further.

It had been a risky plan – 'an insane risk', as Mason himself had called it – but it had come extremely close to working, even with Mason turning up before we expected him. At least I'd managed to escape in one piece. I'd found the Toyota Hilux Pryce and Gaydon had been using easily enough, parked round the corner from the safehouse. The keys were still in the ignition, the prostitute still tied up in the trunk. I'd turfed her out and driven like the wind back here without any problems.

I got out of the car and went inside, badly in need of a drink.

When I emerged tomorrow morning, my hair would be cut short and dyed a sandy blonde, and I'd be wearing blue contact lenses, to match the photo in one of my fake passports. Then I'd be on a plane back to Miami and freedom.

But I wouldn't forget Ray Mason entirely. I wanted that million dollars, so one way or another I'd be back for him.

Ten Days Later

Forty-four

Ray

Someone once told me that human beings have only two natural fears. Loud noises and being left alone.

I've always been able to handle the first, but never quite mastered the second. But today, sitting in my front room staring out of the window on to a cloudy London morning, I felt totally alone in the world, and Jesus, it was a horrible feeling. As was the sense of listless boredom that had hung over me ever since I'd been released from hospital, having been treated for the bullet wound I'd received – my first – courtesy of Jane Kinnear. Although the injury wasn't serious, the bullet had cracked a rib and my abdomen was currently tightly bandaged, meaning there was no way I could return to work.

Not that it mattered. I was suspended anyway while the

IPCC investigated the three separate shooting incidents I'd been involved in that day. Add to that the private prosecution brought by the families of the two jihadis I'd killed the previous year and the official complaints brought by Karim Khan and his lawyer, and it was unlikely I'd be returning to work any time soon, if ever. Khan himself had since been released due to lack of evidence against him, despite Rani Hussain naming him as his handler, and I had little doubt he'd be back planning further atrocities soon, just being even more careful about it next time.

One up for the bad guys then.

As for the good guys, my team in CT had taken significant losses. Chris and Anji were both dead, and although Seamus Jeffs survived his ordeal, he was still in hospital being treated for what were described as life-changing injuries, and there was no doubt he'd be invalided out of the force. They were losses CT, already short of experienced manpower, could ill afford and which on a personal level had cut me deeply. I hadn't been able to face Chris's wife Charlotte or Amber since that day, even though I'd been told they both wanted to thank me personally for what I'd done to save Amber's life. Frankly, I was finding it hard to face anybody.

The men who'd kidnapped Amber, and who I'd shot dead at the safehouse, still hadn't been identified, and Jane Kinnear, or whatever her name really was, had not been caught. It seemed she'd disappeared off the face of the earth. Apart from some grainy CCTV footage from the hospital and witness descriptions of what she looked like, she had left no clues behind. I doubted she'd be found now. She might have been a monster but she was also a very clever and resourceful individual. The police attending the safehouse that night had found a woman, later identified as thirty-nine-year-old prostitute Leonie DesChamps, wandering in the road nearby. She told the officers that she'd been abducted on the street four days ago and kept at an undisclosed location before being brought in the back of a car to where she'd been found. It seemed she was roughly the height and build of Jane Kinnear and it didn't take long to work out that Kinnear's plan was to kill the woman at the safehouse and then burn the place down so that it looked as if the witness herself had been murdered along with the police officers protecting her. The Wraith would have struck again and the legend would have grown.

You almost had to admire her. Almost, but not quite.

I wondered if I'd see Jane Kinnear again. After all, she hadn't yet finished the job, and I was fairly certain that there was a big reward on offer from the client if she finally got to me. She was the type of person who'd try it too. She was like me in that respect. She took big risks. I was going to have to be on my guard, although a part of me relished the opportunity to face her again. I owed her for what she'd done.

As for the client himself, Mohammed bin Azir, there was no way he could be charged with anything, or even questioned, since there wasn't a shred of evidence linking him to what had happened. So he went scot-free and probably would remain so until either he stepped on the wrong toes or, more likely, died of old age. I would have loved to know who it was in MI5 who'd betrayed the five of us to bin Azir, the man or woman who'd effectively sentenced us all to death, presumably just to line his or her own pockets. But there was no way I was ever going to find that out.

Three days earlier, though, while I was sitting in the park near my home, I'd been joined by a smartly dressed man in late middle age. He hadn't identified himself but had simply said that he appreciated what I'd done to prevent a terror attack and that he'd be grateful if I didn't say anything to anyone about any work I may or may not have done for the security services in the past. It was all suitably vague, although I assumed he was talking about the Turks. I told him that someone within MI5 had definitely betrayed us and he'd nodded and replied that he knew that, and that the situation was being dealt with. He also told me that there were people who were watching my back and that I shouldn't worry too much about my current trials and tribulations. Then he'd got up and left, leaving me unsure about whether justice would be done or not.

In the end there was nothing I could do about it anyway, so I'd let it go, wondering if there were actually people watching my back or whether it was all bullshit. I suspected the latter, though I would keep my mouth shut about the Turks op anyway.

I sighed. It was strange to think that there was a line of people probably a mile long who wanted to put me either behind bars or in the ground just because I'd spent my career trying my best to take bad people off the streets. The irony of it was that I didn't even have to work for a living. I'd never had to. When my father murdered my mother and brothers he'd been a wealthy man, and when I came of age that money had been passed to me. The best part of three million pounds. I could have lived the life of a playboy, just like my old man had done.

Instead, I'd changed my name to Ray Mason – it was the toughest name I could think of – joined the army and put the money in the bank. Some shrewd investment decisions over the years meant that the three million had turned into five, and I now had an apartment in one of the nicer areas of London with no mortgage. It had struck me more than once over the last few days that I could afford to leave the UK tomorrow and travel the world incognito. Let those arseholes track me down and bring me back.

But I knew I wouldn't do that. Just as I knew I'd never commit suicide – even though, I'll be honest, there have been times when I've seriously considered it. Because in the end if I did either of those things it meant that the bad guys had won, and I couldn't have that. I just couldn't. I owed it to my mother and brothers. I owed it to Chris and Anji. I owed it to Chris's wife Charlotte, and to Amber, who now had the chance to live her life. I owed it to all of them not to give up. Not to bow out of the fight.

Outside the window, the sun appeared through the clouds, its rays warming my face through the glass. I finished my coffee and put the mug down on the table, suddenly feeling better.

It was time to face the world again.

dead
good

If you enjoyed *The Witness*, read on for a thrilling race-against-time short story from Simon Kernick.

ONE BY ONE

Six ex school-friends have been brought together on a remote island.

They haven't all been in contact since a fateful night twenty-one years ago, when their friend Rachel Skinner was found dead. The man arrested for her murder has now been acquitted, and the seven friends are fearing for their lives.

But are they hiding from the right person? Or have they fallen into a deadly trap?

Join the conversation on:

Before
Prologue

As he parked the car and walked down the narrow path to the deserted jetty, breathing in the crisp sea air, Charlie Williams should have been a supremely happy individual. At forty-two, he had everything a man could want: an attractive wife eight years his junior, who doted on him; two extremely photogenic young children – one of each; several million pounds in the bank as a result of a number of successful business decisions; and now a stratospheric career in politics that had already seen him rise to the rank of junior minister in the current government, with the Westminster gossip suggesting that he could be PM one day.

But as he approached the boat that was going to take him out to the island – his island – he felt a deep sense of foreboding. Dark clouds were gathering and if he didn't act decisively, he risked being enveloped by them entirely.

Pat was already standing at the wheel – grim-faced and stoic as ever, dressed like he should have been working the nets on a fishing trawler. He turned, gave a grunted 'Hello, sir' and helped Charlie aboard.

'Hello, Pat. Good to see you,' Charlie lied. He always found himself slightly uncomfortable with Pat, unless the two of them had been drinking together, which had happened a few times over the years. Even so there was little familiarity between them.

Frankly Pat gave him the creeps. It was his eyes. They were totally expressionless. He was ex-army, and had served in Afghanistan and Iraq, where clearly he'd done, or at least seen, things that had affected him deeply, and of which he would never talk. Still, he'd worked for Charlie as the island's caretaker for more than three years, and in that time he'd always been completely reliable.

'Is everything ready?' Charlie asked him.

'All done, sir, as per your instructions.'

Charlie had given up telling Pat to stop calling him sir and use his first name instead. The man was a law unto himself and sometimes it was best just to leave things. He took a seat as the boat pulled away from the dock.

The sea was relatively calm for this stretch of the coastline, which meant that the journey to the island would take no more than fifteen minutes. He looked at his watch. 11 a.m. Still early. The others would arrive in dribs and drabs during the course of the day. All but one of them was coming from London, which was a good four hours' journey away, but Charlie had told them to get to the jetty by 6.30 p.m. at the latest, so they didn't have to make the crossing in the dark. He was banking on the fact that they all had too much to lose not to come, but you could never tell, even though every one of them had responded to his invitation with a yes. Still, he'd be a lot happier when they were all together behind closed doors. Then, finally, they could discuss murder.

The island loomed up in front of them – a ten-acre sloping rock jutting out of the sea a mile and a half out from the long, deserted stretch of bay that it partially protected. It had once belonged to an eccentric English lord who, having returned from the horrors of the First World War, wished to cut himself off as much as possible from civilization. He'd built a large, rambling house tucked into the lee of the rock, facing back towards the mainland he wished to escape from, and planted a small pine wood on the gentle incline that ran down to the water. He had spotted the island for sale in *Country Life* magazine five years earlier, and wanting to find a place in which he could truly escape from the pressures of work, he'd bought it outright for the bargain price of nine hundred grand. Diane had been mortified. She too had wanted a second home, but had her hopes set on Provence or Umbria, not a windswept rock off the coast of west Wales. But Charlie had been insistent, which was something he was very good at, and he'd never regretted the purchase, even though he knew it would be a bugger to sell. This was his place and its isolation would serve him well this weekend.

The boat slowed as it approached the tiny wooden dock that stuck out from the narrow stretch of sandy beach where Freddie and Tamsin liked to play when the family came here in the summer, and Pat cut the engine as they pulled alongside.

Charlie stood up, grabbing the side rail for support, and climbed out of the boat. He turned to go over the instructions with Pat one more time, but the caretaker was already turning the boat round. Charlie wasn't concerned. Pat would know what to do. You only needed to tell him something once. He was efficient and, more importantly, discreet. Charlie knew that Pat could ruin him if he wanted to, which was why he paid him double what he was worth to look after the house, but he also knew that one day there might have to be some kind of reckoning between them.

With a deep breath, he headed for the path that wound through the thick wall of pines up to the house. As far as the world knew he was here alone for the weekend to work on his memoirs. If anyone – family, friends or, God forbid, colleagues – had any idea what the real reason was, it would shock them to the core.

Karen Thompson had hoped this day would never come. She was a firm believer in karma, and that whole concept of divine justice, but felt that she'd been punished enough already for that one terrible mistake in her youth. In truth, she'd been paying for it for the past twenty-one years.

Karen had always been a worrier. It was a legacy from her mother, who'd spent her entire life incapable of seeing the bright side of anything. But over time she'd learned to manage her fears, as well as the guilt. She'd built a decent career for herself in the Department of Transport, had finally got married to a nice guy after several less-than-ideal long-term relationships, had given birth to a daughter who'd been her world, and then – bang, just like that – it had all been taken away from her. In a way, it was the punishment that a part of her had always expected – perhaps even hoped for – as a means of expunging her sins.

It had taken her a long time to get some semblance of her life back together after Lily's sudden death and even now, just thinking about her daughter could reduce her to tears in a second. Surely, God, it had been punishment enough.

And yet it hadn't been, because now the past looked like it might finally be catching up with all of them.

With a deep sigh, she picked up her overnight bag and looked in the mirror. The woman who stared back at her was thin and exhausted, with deep bags under her eyes. There were still a few vestiges of the looks that had turned heads all those years back, but it was clear they were facing inevitable defeat against the worry lines that seemed to grow deeper every day.

Bastards, she thought. Why did I ever get involved with them?

Well, you did, said the voice that always lurked in the back of her mind. And now you've got to stay calm and deal with it. Because if you don't . . .

She shuddered, knowing only too well the consequences of failure, as she headed out into the dangers of the outside world.

'Listen, John, I'm going to be uncontactable from lunchtime until Sunday afternoon, period. So you're just going to have to run the meeting yourself, OK? You've got all the relevant figures and you're a big boy, so sort it then mail me the good news.'

Marla Folgado ended the call without waiting for his response. John was one of her best sales consultants and could easily close the deal on his own, but a lot of the time he acted like a puppy round her, always wanting her input. Her approval. Even at forty-two, Marla was still able to use her sexuality with devastating effect. Most of the time it was a power she loved wielding. Occasionally though, like today, it was just plain annoying.

Marla closed the front door of her two-bed Chelsea flat behind her (bought for £350k ten years ago, now worth a nice, round million) and strode down the street towards where her Boxster convertible was parked in a residents' bay opposite the coffee house. As she passed the newsagents, she forced herself to glance at the paper stand outside.

It had been more than three weeks since Danny Corridge's face had first appeared on the front pages staring out angrily at the world, and plenty of other front pages covering different stories had appeared since. Even so, it still scared Marla to look at the papers in case there'd been some new revelation about the case in the intervening period. Or that, of course, he'd come back seeking revenge. The other day she thought she'd seen him walking on the other side of the King's Road, watching her. Instinctively, she'd turned away from his gaze and when she'd looked back, he'd disappeared. She knew she was being paranoid. She hadn't seen the guy in twenty years and she'd barely glanced at the photo in the papers. As her father used to say (at least behind closed doors), they all look the same anyway. It could have been any middle-aged black man staring at her. Jesus, men stared at her all the time.

As she got in the car, she looked at the note with map attached that had been posted to her by Charlie a week and a half ago, inviting her to his island – his bloody island, for Christ's sakes – in some godforsaken part of Wales. She didn't want to go. She didn't want to see any of them again – not now – but it was clear from the tone of the note that failure to turn up was not a viable option. She read it again, concentrating on the last sentence. 'It's in all our self-interests to be there because if we don't present a united front, we are finished.'

Suitably dramatic language from one of Parliament's most flamboyant speakers, but unfortunately also very true.

She started the car and pulled away.

Under normal circumstances there was no way Luke Jacobs would kick a hot 29-year-old out of bed at 11.30 in the morning, especially while she was going down on him, but these were anything but normal circumstances.

This one was called Claire, and Luke had met her a couple of weeks earlier on Tinder. On her profile, she'd said she was only looking for men between the ages of twenty-five and thirty-five, which was some way south of forty-two, but Luke prided himself on not looking his age, which was why he pretended to be thirty-six whenever he met a new girl. They'd slept together on the second date, and last night had been the third. Luke had cooked her chilli con carne, plied her with mid-priced red wine, and taken her to bed. He had the day off today, and she wasn't starting work until 5 p.m., so they'd slept late, eaten breakfast in bed, and carried on from the previous night.

As a general rule, Luke loved his life. He had a relatively easy job in software sales that paid a decent salary but didn't require long hours. He rented a nice one-bed flat in Balham, had a good social life and got laid frequently. He'd never quite understood the whole concept of marriage. Why settle with one woman when you could have many and stay as free as a bird? It was the same with kids. Luke loved kids – he really did – but he didn't want his own. They drained your money, your time and, worst of all, your sex drive. Luke had seen some of his male friends reduced to husks of their former selves by the demands of their new families.

No, adulthood had been a real breeze for Luke Jacobs.

Until now.

'I'm sorry, babes, I've got to go,' he said reluctantly, carefully extricating himself from Claire's mouth and silently cursing that arsehole Charlie Williams for making him traipse all the way to Wales for the weekend. He'd never liked Charlie that much at uni, and liked him even less now that he kept seeing him on TV the whole time, looking full of himself. He also didn't like the way Charlie was organizing this whole thing, like he was the one who had to be in charge. Acting all cloak and dagger with his instructions: no contacting each other by phone or email; all correspondence on paper with no copies, and burn everything as soon as it's memorized. He'd even insisted that everyone drive themselves to Wales and not take public transport, because it was essential no one on the outside knew they were meeting. Luke half wanted to turn up on the train just to piss Charlie off, but he was sensible enough to know there was no point. Charlie might have been an arsehole but he was a cunning one and, right now, like it or not, they needed him.

Claire gave him a vaguely irritated look as he stepped off the bed. 'Don't you like me or something?'

'Course I do,' he said, suppressing a sigh as he pulled on his shirt, 'but you know I've got to go. I have a stag weekend and I need to be at Waterloo Station for 12.30 otherwise I'm going to miss the train.' He'd already told her the lie twice but clearly it wasn't getting through.

She started to say something else but Luke was no longer listening. He was thinking about the phone call he'd received yesterday from a DCI

Johnson. Apparently, the police had already called round twice at Luke's place, missing him both times, and were very keen to have – in Johnson's words – a chat about Rachel Skinner.

'You're the first of the group I've approached,' he explained. 'I thought you might be able to shed some light on things.' The implication was obvious. Luke was being given a chance to cooperate. If he said something now, it might help him further down the line.

He'd been caught off guard by the call, even though he'd been preparing for it ever since they'd released Danny Corridge. A big part of him had wanted to spill his guts on the spot and blame the others, but in the end he'd kept his options open and made an appointment to go to the police station on Monday, by which time he'd have had plenty of time to work out how to play things.

Luke knew he was involved in a very high-stakes game. How he played his hand over the next seventy-two hours would determine whether he continued to live a charmed, hassle-free life, or whether he spent a significant portion of the rest of it in prison.

Louise Turner dreaded seeing any of her former group again. She'd not kept in touch with any of them, which was hardly surprising under the circumstances, and she'd spent the past twenty years asking herself what she'd actually seen in any of them in the first place. They'd been a pretty narcissistic bunch – all just after a good time, and not really interested in each other, let alone anyone else.

Louise had changed immeasurably since then. After twelve successful years as a family lawyer, she'd had two children with her long-term partner, Ian, and become a full-time mum, setting up home in a village just outside St Albans. She loved her new life. Her younger son, Finn, was still in pre-school and, at three, he was undoubtedly a handful, but she felt blessed to be able to spend so much time with him. Nor did she miss the London rat race. Ian still had to commute into the city every day, leaving the house at 6.30 and often not getting home before 8, and Louise longed for the day they could afford for him to take a position more locally. All in all, though, they were a pretty happy family leading a pretty happy life.

And then, twenty-seven days ago, the authorities had released Danny Corridge from prison after twenty-one years behind bars with an official pardon, apologizing profusely for the terrible miscarriage of justice he'd suffered. And now, as the saying went, all bets were off. Corridge was officially innocent of the murder of Rachel Skinner, which meant two things. First, someone else was guilty, and so the police had no option but to reopen the case and start digging for the truth. Second, Corridge was likely to be a very angry man. She remembered from the trial that he had connections to some pretty nasty types, and frankly the prospect of him on the loose, looking for the people whose evidence had helped put him down, terrified Louise. She even thought she'd seen him driving past their house a couple of days ago. It might have just been paranoia, but it definitely looked like the man who'd been all over the news these past few weeks. The thing was, it wasn't herself she was worrying about. It was the kids. If anything happened to her they'd be torn apart.

Her mum was walking up to the front door and, as they caught sight of each other, Louise grinned and picked up Finn so he could wave to her. Her mum was a huge help with the boys. They seemed to give her a purpose now her dad was gone.

'So, are you ready for your weekend away, love?' asked her mum as Louise let her in. 'You need it. You never get away. It's just a pity Ian's not going with you.' She took Finn from Louise and began bouncing him up and down. Finn cooed delightedly.

'It's a university reunion, Mum. He'd just be bored.'

In truth, Louise wished she was taking Ian with her. She desperately needed his input on the whole situation but of course she couldn't say a word to him about any of it. It was her secret. No one else could, or would, ever know about it, not even the man she considered her soulmate. Thankfully he believed the reunion story too, which made things a lot easier.

'Freddie's got after school club tonight so he needs picking up at five, and Ian's said he's going to be back about seven.'

Her mum laughed. 'Don't worry, we're going to be just fine. Aren't we, Finn? Now go and have fun with your old friends.'

The Costa Coffee on Paddington Station's concourse was busy as Crispin Neill sat drinking his skinny latte and picking at a limp-looking salad, pondering on how his life had come to this: eating crap food alone while waiting for a train to take him into a past he'd hoped he'd left behind long, long ago. He didn't even have a car to arrive in, as had Charlie requested. It was all such a far cry from his youth. Crispin was a dreamer. He'd always wanted to be a writer and at school he'd been told by a succession of teachers that he had a rare talent for story-telling, and when he'd gone to university, he'd been filled with hope and ambition. Even after the incident, he'd still been optimistic that he could put events behind him and move on – maybe even use it as a kind of grim inspiration.

But life has a habit of never going the way it's meant to. There's no logic to it, Crispin thought bitterly. He'd lost the girl he'd thought of as his true love and had never replaced her; and though he'd managed to get stuff published in magazines, no publisher had taken the three books he'd written. All that sweat and effort and it had come to nothing. In total, he'd earned a paltry £1,335 from writing – less than sixty quid a year when he dared to make the calculations – and now, at forty-two, he was a drifter with no real home, back living with his mum after a five-year stint in Perpignan where he'd scraped a living waiting tables and painting houses, planning but never quite managing to write that fourth novel that was finally going to bring him success. He couldn't stay at his mum's much longer. It was a living hell listening to her wonder constantly why he couldn't just get a proper job like everyone else. Luckily he had a friend who'd agreed to hire him as a manager of his bar in Ko Samui, so he was flying out there next week, the plan being to leave the UK for ever. He'd considered not turning up at Charlie's place this weekend. After all, the best way to deal with this new development with Danny Corridge was for them all to just keep their mouths shut and carry on as before, which would be a hell of a lot easier for Crispin as he was going to be six thousand miles away.

In the end, though, he'd decided it would be better to find out what Charlie had to say. Anything was better than spending another weekend at home with his mother, and he had to admit that he was intrigued at the idea of seeing Karen again. He wondered what she looked like now and whether he'd still have any residual feelings for her. It had been twenty years since they'd last seen each other and he remembered that final goodbye – the passion, the rage, the terrible frustration. Nothing had ever been quite the same again.

He shook his head, trying to banish the memory, and drained his coffee.

Which was the moment two men in suits sat down opposite him, wearing cold smiles.

Crispin's first thought was that they were police officers, but there was something not quite right about them. Somehow they looked too cocky.

'Hello, Crispin,' said the older of the two in a cold, Estuary accent. 'We need to have a word.'

1

So there we were in the dining room of Charlie's island retreat – a suitably imposing structure with impressive views towards the wild Welsh coastline. Five friends who'd parted company all those years ago, hoping that they'd never see each other again.

But in the end, of course, we should have known. The past was always going to come back to haunt us.

It had been strange seeing them again after all those years. Even stranger that none of us had really changed that much, either to look at or in their mannerisms. Marla still looked unbelievably hot for a woman in her forties. She still had that thick, jet-black hair that was naturally curly but which she'd always straightened religiously, and the most alluring brown eyes I think I've ever seen. Weirdly, she'd always looked at me as competition which, I think, was why we'd never got on that well, but I could never work out why. I'm not being self-critical, but looks-wise she'd always been way out of my league.

Then there was Luke – still the big, bluff and handsome rugby player, his naturally blond hair unsullied with grey, as if the stress of what had happened had never affected him; and Louise, far more serious and distant than I remembered, dressed conservatively, with her ash-blonde hair tied back in a severe bun – and trying to make the effort to be friendly but not quite managing to hide her distaste at being here. Then there was me – poor, gaunt Karen – torn up with worry and forever tarnished by tragedy, but doing my level best to hide it. And Charlie, still just being Charlie.

He was standing at the head of the table now – every inch the big politician – as if he was at the dispatch box about to make one of his impassioned speeches. He was still handsome in a soft, boyish way, but the fat that he'd been staving off since uni looked like it was in danger of winning the war. He looked out of shape and pale, but that wasn't really surprising. Of all of us, I suppose he was the one with the most to lose.

'Well, we can't wait all night for Crispin so it's best we get started,' he said. 'Thank you all for coming. I appreciate it.'

'We didn't really have a lot of choice, did we?' said Marla, flicking back her lustrous black hair just to make sure everyone noticed it. There was a vague irritation in her voice that I remembered had often been there, as if the whole world was an inconvenience to her.

'No,' said Charlie pointedly. 'None of us had much choice. We've got to sort this whole thing out now once and for all.'

I'd been the last of the five of us to arrive and in the two hours since, we'd all tried our best to avoid each other, and when we had been forced to socialize, it had been awkward small talk, with everyone deliberately avoiding the subject at hand as if it was something toxic – which, of course, it was.

Charlie had tried to make everyone feel at ease, pouring drinks, asking what we'd all been up to, even though I'm sure he knew every detail, and generally acting as if this was some real uni reunion and not a clandestine meeting. Needless to say, it hadn't worked. The atmosphere was tense and a little unpleasant, as we threw sideways, distrustful looks at each other – as much combatants as old friends – and I was glad to finally get down to business.

Charlie took a theatrically loud breath and began talking. 'So, the background. Danny Corridge was released just over three weeks ago with a full pardon. He's always protested his innocence of the murder of Rachel Skinner, but then, to quote Christine Keeler, 'He would say that, wouldn't he?' Anyway, here are the facts: Corridge had a long criminal record before Rachel's murder. He had convictions for robbery with violence; GBH; assault on a police officer; and crucially he'd also been charged with rape.'

'He was acquitted though, wasn't he?' said Louise, her tone as severe as her hair, sounding just like the lawyer she was.

'Yes, but on a technicality. Either way, this man was, and probably still is, a very bad egg. At the time of her murder, Rachel was Corridge's ex-girlfriend. She'd finished with him two weeks earlier and he wouldn't accept it. He turned up at the house Rachel shared with Karen and me, tried to knock down the door, and was subsequently arrested for harassment, during which time he put one of the arresting officers in hospital.

'Danny Corridge was also the last the person to see Rachel alive. He admitted inviting her round to his flat, and a witness saw her turn up there. After that, as far as the world's concerned, she was never seen again.' He paused. 'Rachel was reported missing the following night by Karen and me after she failed to return home, by which time we hadn't seen her for well over twenty-four hours. The next morning, before he was questioned by police, Corridge reported his car stolen. It was discovered abandoned on a country lane later that day and, although there were signs it had been hotwired and driven without keys, a forensic examination found traces of Rachel's blood inside the boot. Three days later, a dog walker discovered her body in a shallow grave in woodland less than three miles away. She had major injuries consistent with being beaten with a blunt instrument, and traces of Corridge's semen were found inside her. Corridge – a man well used to police interrogations – vehemently protested his innocence.

He claimed that he and Rachel had had consensual sex and that he'd dropped her off around 10 p.m. at 23 Worsley Court where you guys' – he motioned to Luke, Marla and Louise – 'and Crispin lived, claiming she was attending a gathering there with friends. There were six of us in the house that night – the six who'll be here this weekend – and as we told the police afterwards, Rachel never arrived that night. No one else came forward to back up Corridge's story that they'd left his flat together and driven to Worsley Court, and so the police concluded that he was lying and he was charged with Rachel's murder.

Charlie sighed. 'It was, as we all know, a controversial trial. The case against him certainly wasn't watertight. There were no signs of a struggle in his flat, and the murder weapon was never found, but he proved to be an unreliable and volatile witness, and I'm sure we all remember the time he jumped out of the dock and tried to attack me while I was giving evidence.' He shrugged. 'Anyway, that's history. The jury found him guilty and the judge ruled he should serve a minimum recommended term of twenty-five years. That should have been the last we ever heard of him if his case hadn't been taken up by a firm of human-rights lawyers who specialize in dealing with so-called miscarriages of justice.'

It was ironic, I thought, how Charlie seemed to spit out these last words, as if he couldn't understand how these lawyers could act in such a low, underhand manner, even though he knew, as we all did, that a huge miscarriage of justice had indeed taken place. But that was Charlie for you; he was driven by a sense of his own superiority.

'The problem is,' he continued, 'they were successful, and now Corridge is out, the case is live again, and it's only a matter of time until attention focuses on us. To be honest, there have been rumours floating about that we may have been hiding something, but I've always managed to keep a lid on them with the threat of legal action. However, it's going to be open season now, particularly with my involvement.'

'I'm afraid Corridge might come after us,' said Louise. 'I think I might have seen him drive past my house.'

'I thought I saw him the other day too,' said Marla. 'On the King's Road.'

I hadn't seen him, but the thought that he might come after me made my stomach turn over. I remembered him from the trial, bug-eyed and wild, screaming abuse at us, being wrestled to the floor by half a dozen struggling prison officers.

'If any one of us hears anything from him, or suffers any harassment, we have to report it immediately,' said Charlie, who was still standing at the head of the table. The man who always had to be in charge. 'And remember, we've all got to keep to the same story we told all those years ago. This weekend we're going to go over everything so we've got it watertight. Now, has anyone been approached by the police to make a new statement?'

I shook my head, as did the others.

'What about the press?'

'I was approached a couple of years ago, when all this stuff about a miscarriage of justice first started surfacing,' said Marla. 'I kept to the script and told them that Rachel never turned up that night. Period.'

'Christ,' said Luke. 'I never thought it would come back to this.' He glared at Charlie. 'We should have gone to the police straight away rather than listening to you.'

Charlie gave him a withering look. 'Don't be stupid. You were the one in bed with her, Luke. You would have been the prime suspect. I don't remember you arguing about it back then.'

Although Luke was twice Charlie's size, and had always had a reputation as a bit of a hard man, his only reaction to the dressing down was a grunted, almost childlike, 'I didn't kill her.'

'How do you know? You were off your face when you went to bed. We all were. Any one of us could have killed her.' Charlie looked round the table then, his eyes settling on me for just a heartbeat too long.

I looked away. An image of Rachel laughing appeared right at the front of my mind then. Perfectly clear. God, she'd been so pretty.

'I'm not a killer,' protested Luke, banging his fist on the table, his actions again reminding me of a big child, and it struck me, rather unkindly, that he was a perfect cliché for the male equivalent of the dumb blonde. 'I'm just an ordinary bloke who got involved in something . . . something horrible.'

'Is it safe to be talking in here?' demanded Louise. 'If anyone had a bug . . .'

'It's safe,' said Charlie. 'I've got an advanced bug finder and I've run it over the room twice today. Anything that's said in this room stays between us.'

Louise took a gulp of her wine and put the glass down on the table, her eyes scanning the rest of us like a lawyer surveying a jury. 'Well, I want to know who killed her, because it wasn't me. And whoever it was has ruined my life.'

'That's not the purpose of this meeting, Louise,' said Charlie. 'The purpose is to make sure we all go back to our lives knowing we're all singing from the same hymn sheet.'

'You had a motive, Charlie,' said Luke, draining his glass and refilling it with wine. 'Corridge beat the shit out of you because Rachel told him you'd tried it on with her. Apparently, you were pretty pushy with her.'

Charlie's face reddened and he glanced across at me. I remembered Rachel telling me about it. It had happened at the house the three of us shared, although I'd been out that night. She was really angry when she told me about it the next day, claiming that Charlie had pawed her breasts and tried to kiss her. She said he was like a rooting dog and she'd had to slap him to get him to stop, although she admitted she'd been hopelessly pissed at the time. I confronted Charlie after that and he'd been hugely apologetic. He claimed he was hopelessly pissed too, and that he'd thought she was up for it.

I got him to make a grovelling apology to Rachel, which she seemed to accept. Except clearly she didn't, because at some point during the next couple of days, she told her boyfriend, Danny Corridge, what had happened and when he next turned up the house he battered an unsuspecting Charlie, punching him to the living-room floor before laying into him with a series of kicks until the two of us finally managed to pull him off. I always remember Rachel saying, 'He's not worth it, baby,' to Corridge as she ushered him out, leaving a dazed, bleeding Charlie lying there humiliated, tears in his eyes. The comment infuriated me at the time because I could see that a part of Rachel actually enjoyed the cruelty of the whole spectacle. To be honest, it still infuriates me now.

For a second I saw the depth of Charlie's humiliation in his eyes. Then he turned away. 'I may have had a motive, Luke, but it wasn't much of one, was it? Kill a woman because her boyfriend had assaulted me. You, however, had the opportunity. And others here had the motive too. You had some big arguments with her, Karen, if you recall. You did too, Louise. And I remember that screaming match stroke bitch fight you had with her, Marla. You hit her hard, and made some pretty ugly threats –'

'Oh bullshit,' snapped Marla, her dark eyes hard and angry. 'We had a fight, yes, and I slapped her a couple of times but that's a hell of a lot different to caving her head in with a hammer.'

'How do you know it was a hammer?'

'Oh, fuck you, Charlie.'

'Look,' said Charlie, exasperation in his voice. 'It doesn't matter who killed her. It's in the past. It's gone. And if we all stick to our story, then we're home free.' He sighed. 'Now, shall we eat dinner?'

2

So, what can I say about Rachel Skinner? Well, as you can probably tell by now, she wasn't the easiest of girls. But she was fun; she was full of life; and she had moments of real kindness. When I lost my grandma, a woman I was very, very close to, Rachel took me in her arms on hearing the news and stroked my head as I cried on her shoulder, telling me that everything was going to be OK. I remember being surprised that she could be so kind, and we ended up talking deep into the night.

But she was a volatile girl too, capable of ferocious rages, like the time she fought with Marla. The argument was about nothing really, but there'd been always been a rivalry between Marla and Rachel – I think Marla saw all women her own age as potential rivals – and, as was so often the case in those days, there was drink involved. One minute they were laughing; the next they were attacking each other like savages. Marla had the better of her, but as we pulled them apart, it was Rachel who was screaming and spitting, with utter hatred in her eyes.

Rachel was also manipulative and selfish. On more than one occasion, she slept with someone else's boyfriend (and girlfriend), and it never appeared to bother her in the least that she was potentially wrecking a relationship. And probably most destructive of all, she dated a violent thug like Danny Corridge, pandering to his worst side as she showed him off like some kind of twisted status symbol.

But in the end, whichever way anyone cares to look at it – and I can assure you I've looked at it many, many times – Rachel Skinner did not deserve to die.

The night it happened will always be a blur. It wasn't a party so much, or even a gathering. It was just a crappy video night at the other guys' house. We'd rented out *Jurassic Park* of all movies, because Luke and Crispin wanted to watch it on the new surround sound system Luke had put in at the house. In the end, no one really paid much attention to it because we were too busy smoking dope and caning the booze which, as I've mentioned before, wasn't that unusual for us.

It was Rachel who turned up with the ecstasy and the coke, which she'd got from Corridge. She knew enough not to bring him in the house – after all, she wasn't even meant to still be going out with him – but she was in a generous mood that night because she had a hell of a lot of gear on her and she was doling it out like candy.

We got absolutely wrecked. I was seeing Crispin at the time, and I have vague memories of me and him kissing and making out on one sofa, and Louise on the other sofa making out with Luke, though I'm still not sure about that last bit, because Louise denied ever touching him the next day, and anyway, Luke ended up in bed with Rachel that night. I do remember Rachel and Marla doing a sexy dance together, and Charlie trying to get involved, which was typical of him, and being rebuffed, which was also typical (at one time or another he tried it on with all us girls, without any real success), and of us all having a real good laugh – all rivalries and petty squabbles having faded in the drug and drink-fuelled haze – before finally the night descended into the deep, empty blackness of memory loss and sleep

And then the noisy, bright awakening on Marla's bedroom floor – the inside of my mouth dry as a bone – with her calling out for me to wake up, panic in her voice, the tears streaming down her face.

'It's Rachel. She's been hurt . . .'

3

Dinner was parma ham with figs, followed by a rich chicken stew served with vegetables and crusty bread. It would have been delicious but, to be honest, I wasn't hungry. I've never been much of a foodie and I also tend to lose my appetite when my routine gets broken, and I'm in places I don't want to be. Like Charlie Williams' dining room.

I also hadn't realized – even though I should have done – what an uncomfortable night it was going to be. With the possible exception of Charlie, no one wanted to be there and it showed on all their faces, just as I suspect it showed on mine. I was also disappointed that Crispin hadn't shown up. Not only did it make the purpose of the weekend redundant if he wasn't a part of it, but in truth he was the only one I wanted to see again. Crispin had been my first true love, and we'd been together over a year at university. Who knows what would have happened if Rachel hadn't died? Maybe we'd still be together now, with a couple of kids and a house in the country. But the pressure caused by the circumstances of her death, and our collective part in it, had destroyed any hope of that.

The only way I could tolerate the evening was by drinking and, as I refilled my glass from the rapidly emptying bottle of pinot grigio in front of me, I noticed my hand was shaking. Marla noticed it too and raised an eyebrow – a gesture I ignored.

Charlie was asking Louise about her kids in the way a politician does – oozing fake sincerity – while harping on about his own offspring. It angered me that he seemed to be taking all this in his stride, as if the whole thing hadn't really affected him at all. Luke just looked bored, and Marla was pointedly ignoring the conversation.

She looked at me. 'Charlie told me about what happened with you, Karen. I'm very sorry for your loss.'

How many times had I heard those words, always uttered with the same desperate sincerity? Far too many, and yet they never ceased to hit me like hammer blows. My loss. It was so much more than that. It was a huge black hole in my life that would never be replaced. And yet a part of me was disappointed that Marla hadn't even heard about it – after all, I'd kept tabs on her life – although really I shouldn't have been. Marla had never been that interested in me. We'd been part of the same circle, but of all of them she'd been the most distant, and even now I still felt vaguely intimidated by her.

'It's OK,' I said. 'It was a few years back now.'

She sighed. 'Still, it stays with you.'

How the fuck would you know? I thought.

The others had turned my way now, putting me on the spot.

'Yeah, I heard about it too,' said Luke, who looked relieved to have something to talk about. 'Really sorry.'

Louise didn't say anything. She'd heard about it at the time and had sent me flowers along with a note saying that if I ever needed to talk to someone, she'd be there for me. I'd never called, and she hadn't called me, but at least it was a gesture of sorts.

'I hope you don't mind me telling the guys, Karen,' said Charlie. 'I just thought it best they knew.' At the time he'd bought me flowers too, and had even made it to the funeral.

'No, of course not,' I said, fiddling awkwardly with my wine glass. 'But you know, I'd rather not talk about it.'

Everyone nodded to show they understood, and predictably the conversation immediately ground to a halt.

Thankfully, we were all rescued by a loud knocking on the front door.

Charlie stood up. 'Let's hope this is Crispin.'

Luke got to his feet as well, looking pleased. He and Crispin had been good mates back in the old days, even though they were both very different people. Crispin the thoughtful, creative one; Luke the hard-drinking, hard-playing jock. I'd once asked Crispin why he and Luke got on so well, and he'd said it was because, unlike a lot of people, Luke was straight down the line. What you saw was what you got. The answer had never really satisfied me because my memory of Luke was different. He might not have been the brightest of sparks, but he could be ruthless and calculating when he needed to be. After all, he'd been the one who'd stolen Danny Corridge's car and used it to transport Rachel's body.

And then there he was in the room. The man who'd been my first love. Taller than I remembered, and still in possession of the lean, rangy features that I'd been so attracted to, but now they made him look thin and unhealthy. His face was lined and drawn, and his eyes had lost their spark. This was someone who, like me, had been affected deeply by the events of that dark and terrible weekend all those years ago.

Luke embraced him with real passion. 'Mate, good to see you. It's been too long.'

Crispin smiled, but it looked forced. He kissed Louise on both cheeks but seemed to flinch slightly as Marla moved in on him, greeting him with two kisses. She'd always fancied Crispin. I think he was a challenge to her because he'd never shown any sexual interest where she was concerned, and I wondered if she'd try it on with him this weekend. I didn't trust her.

I stood up and caught Crispin's eye over the other side of the table. His face seemed to light up a little and I knew then that the connection we'd had was still hidden away there somewhere. I came round the table and we embraced awkwardly. 'Good to see you again, Crispin,' I said, and he nodded and said it was good to see me.

I wanted to say more but it would have to wait. The others were watching us and I had no desire to share my thoughts with any of them. I sat back down.

Charlie asked Crispin if he wanted anything to eat.

'I don't feel like eating,' he said, sinking into a spare seat next to Charlie and directly opposite Marla. 'I need a drink.' He grabbed a wine bottle and filled up his glass. 'I'm sorry I'm late but I had a visit today.'

That got everyone's attention. 'From whom?' asked Charlie. 'The police?'

Crispin shook his head. 'No. They were private detectives. They said they were working for Rachel Skinner's father.'

Charlie frowned. 'Brian Skinner's a powerful man. It doesn't surprise me that he's asking his own questions about the murder, now that Corridge has been acquitted, but he's got no reason to suspect any of us.'

'Well, clearly he does,' said Crispin, taking a big gulp of wine. 'Because these guys were very aggressive with me. I told them that I'd told the police everything I knew at the time and I didn't have anything to add, but they said that now the police had reopened the case, attention was focusing on us, and that we were all suspects.'

'Jesus, this is all we need,' said Marla. 'More people snooping around, digging up dirt.'

'They said that they knew one of us had killed Rachel and covered it up. They even named each of us as suspects and said they'd get to the bottom of it eventually. They offered me the chance to cooperate now, saying it would save me a lot of trouble later.'

'And you didn't tell them anything?' said Luke.

'Of course not. But they really didn't want to take no for an answer. I wasn't at home either. I was in a café so it was obvious they'd been following me. Even when I got up and left they followed me.' He shook his head, looking flustered. 'I literally had to run off.'

'That's harassment,' said Charlie, striking the table. 'You can sue them for that. I tell you, if they try that with me I'll have them in court in a second.'

'There's no way they followed you here, is there?' asked Louise.

Crispin shook his head. 'No, I was careful.'

'They came to see me, too,' I said in the silence that followed. 'Yesterday, at home. They were waiting for me outside when I got back from work. I told them the same thing Crispin did – that I'd said all I knew at the time – and when they started to get heavy I threatened to scream. So they left.'

In truth, a part of me had wanted to unload everything. To let them know my suspicions about which one of us had killed Rachel, because – rest assured – it was one of us. To get the whole damn thing off my chest and face the consequences. But of course there was no way I could do that because the consequences meant, at the very least, a spell in prison followed by public opprobrium over the fact we'd let an innocent man spend close to half his life in prison for a crime he didn't commit.

I felt the guilt weighing me down more heavily than ever as I looked round the table at my old friends. Which of them felt the same as me, and which had let the guilt slip away like an unwanted smell? Charlie had no guilt, I could see that. I'd always thought he was a bit of a psychopath, incapable of empathy with others, and nothing that had happened since had made me change my mind. Luke probably felt bad about what had happened. He'd been pretty shocked at the time, as you would be if you'd just woken up next to a girl with her head based to a bloody pulp – although that didn't mean he wasn't the one who killed her – but either way, he'd never been the type to dwell on anything too much. Marla was hard. She always had been. Whether it be fickle boyfriends, poor exam results, a death in the family, or even murder, she was able to move on. Louise I wasn't so sure about. She too had been pretty cut up at the time – and if I recall correctly, had been the one most vocal about calling the police when we'd found the body – but had since done a pretty decent job of putting it behind her, what with her high-powered career, and now her perfect marriage and children.

'This has got to end,' said Crispin, his voice deep with emotion, and I knew he'd suffered as much as I had.

'And it will end,' said Charlie, calm and smug as ever. 'All we have to do is ride the storm and in a month's time this will all be over. We've all made it this far, and we're all going to make it a lot further.' He lifted his wine glass, a fleshy smile on his face. 'To us,' he said. 'To the survivors.'

Which was the moment Marla screamed.

'What the hell is it?' demanded Charlie as Marla jumped to her feet.

'I saw a face at the window,' she said, pointing, her beautiful face shocked and white. 'Just now.'

We were all on our feet now, looking round. Charlie went over to the window. 'I can't see anything.'

'I'm not making it up. I definitely saw someone.'

'Did you get a look at their face?' I asked, my heart hammering in my chest.

'No, he had something covering it, a scarf or something. And he was wearing a hat so I only saw his eyes. But he was there, I promise.' She looked how I felt. Spooked.

Charlie sighed. 'It must be Pat. He's just dropped Crispin off so he's probably still about. And there's no one on the island except us.'

'Did he have a scarf and hat on when he dropped you off, Crispin?' I asked.

Crispin shrugged. 'He definitely had a hat. I can't remember about a scarf.'

'Well, if it is him, he shouldn't be spying on us like that,' said Marla. 'Pull those curtains, Charlie. And if you see him, put a rocket up his arse.'

'We don't want him listening in to anything either,' said Louise. 'Not when we're raking up all this crap.'

'He's going to the mainland now and you won't see him again until you leave, I promise.'

Charlie pulled the curtains, blocking out the night, and slowly we all sat back down.

Six of us round the table. The survivors, Charlie had called us.

But it turned out that we were anything other than that.

4

One of my bad habits is smoking. I ration myself to half a pack a day unless I'm have a particularly bad one, then I give myself a bit of leeway. I hadn't smoked all evening, mainly, I think, because no one else was, and I didn't want people to see that even at forty-two, I hadn't managed to kick the habit. So I smoked two in a row as I stood at the open window of the bedroom I'd been given by Charlie. It was at the back of the house facing out across a surprisingly small manicured lawn that ended abruptly in the steep rocky hill that acted as a break against the westerly wind coming off the open sea on the other side of the island.

I stared out into the night with the lights out. It hadn't taken me long to calm down after the scare with Marla and the face at the window. I was pretty sure it was Pat, the taciturn caretaker who'd brought me out on the boat earlier. He'd seemed a nice guy – good-looking too in a weather-beaten, slightly used way – and we'd struck up a half-decent conversation about the outdoor activities in these parts. I'd even attempted a bit of flirting, without much success, and I definitely didn't see him as the peeping Tom, lecherous type.

I still had a vaguely uneasy feeling about everything, though, as I pulled the curtains and locked the door. Firstly, I'm a cynic. I've had too much experience of the terrible things people do to each other. Secondly, I didn't trust Charlie as far as I could throw him. He'd brought the five of us here to this island in the middle of nowhere. Each of us could ruin him just by opening our mouths to the wrong people, and I was reminded of that old Sicilian saying: 'Three can keep a secret if two of them are dead.'

I told myself to stop being so melodramatic as I slipped between the sheets and switched out the light. Out of habit I went to check my phone for messages, but of course there was no service, and I remembered Charlie telling us earlier that he didn't have a wireless network in the house either, as he thought it was better for his whole family to escape technology when they came here.

I put the phone down and looked at the old-fashioned digital clock on the bedside table. 11.36 p.m. Downstairs I could still hear movement. After dinner, we'd retired to the lounge where Charlie had poured brandies and tried once again to lighten the mood.

It hadn't worked. First Crispin had gone to bed, having hardly said a word to me (which, I have to admit, grated me a little); then Marla shortly afterwards; and I'd gone a few minutes after that, partly I suppose to check that Marla wasn't using her exit as an opportunity to try it on with Crispin (she wasn't), leaving the other three talking.

I shut my eyes and tried to imagine how different my life would have turned out if Rachel Skinner had never been one of our group. If she'd just made a different choice on her university application form. It was a day dream I often indulged in, with various different endings, all of them one hell of a lot better than reality, but tonight I drifted off to sleep before I could really get going.

I awoke to the complete silence of the countryside. Even the wind had dropped to nothing. I looked at the clock. 1.51 a.m. Another broken night's sleep. The story of my life. I decided to take one of my herbal sleeping tablets but for that I needed water and I didn't have any. After a short mental battle between the lazy me and the more proactive me, I slipped out of bed and unlocked the door.

The main light on the landing was on and everyone's door was shut as I tiptoed down the stairs and into the gloom. Stairs creaked underfoot and I could hear the steady ticking of the grandfather clock in the hallway. The atmosphere felt vaguely spooky as I went into the kitchen and poured myself a glass of water, taking a big gulp to get rid of the dry, stale alcohol taste in my mouth, before heading back out into the hallway. As I passed the big oak front door, I saw it was bolted from the inside, which was a comforting thought, and then, just as I was about to climb the staircase, I glanced quickly into the lounge where we'd been drinking the brandies earlier and could just make out through the darkness a figure asleep in the chair. It looked like Louise.

I thought about leaving her there but it struck me that it would be good to have a quick chat with her on her own about the situation if she was up for it. And if she wasn't, then she'd probably want to be woken anyway rather than sleep in a chair, so I tiptoed into the living room.

She was lying away from me and I leaned forward and tapped her on the shoulder.

She didn't move.

I tapped her again. Still no movement. So I tugged at her blouse, turning her towards me.

And gasped in shock.

During

5

For a good minute I stared, unblinking, at the huge knife jutting out of Louise's chest, the shock striking me in powerful, intense waves, just as it had that terrible morning when I'd first seen Rachel's battered corpse. I wanted to cry out, to be sick, to throw open the front door and run away, but I was unable to move. I could feel myself shaking as a panic attack began, and knew that if I didn't do something soon I'd succumb to it.

'Help!' I yelled, my voice reverberating round the house as I finally broke free from my torpor. 'Get down here now! It's Louise!'

And then, for the first time, the fear factor kicked in as I realized that the murderer could still be here. What if he'd killed everyone already and was just about to come for me? I swung round fast in case he was sneaking up on me, already yelling some more, but the room was empty, and it was clear that people were still alive because I could hear the sound of doors opening upstairs and then rapid footfalls on the staircase.

The first one through the door was Charlie and he immediately switched on the main light, making me squint against the sudden brightness. He was dressed in old silk pyjamas and was pulling on a dressing gown like something Hugh Hefner would wear. He was closely followed by Luke in a T-shirt and boxers.

For a couple of seconds neither of them seemed to compute what had happened but then, as I stepped out the way and they both caught sight of Louise in the chair, their mouths gaped open in shock.

'Oh, Jesus,' said Charlie as he approached the body. 'What happened?'

'Fucking hell,' said Luke, moving in behind him.

I stared down at her too. She looked like a waxwork dummy, her eyes half-closed, a blank expression on her face. The knife jutted out of her chest like a stage prop, only the handle and an inch of blade showing, surrounded by a single uneven stain of blood no bigger than the size of a man's hand. I thought of her two children and it made me want to throw up.

At that moment there was a commotion in the doorway as Marla came in dressed in a baggy nightshirt, skimpy white panties and pink socks, somehow managing to look incredibly sexy for someone who'd just leaped out of bed. She put a hand to her mouth and let out a muffled scream. Behind her a sleepy Crispin trailed in wearing the clothes he'd arrived in. The sleepy expression vanished as soon as he saw what we were all staring at.

Charlie leaned down and – rather unnecessarily, I thought – felt for a pulse before shaking his head and retreating.

The five of us stood there, scattered about the lounge, keeping a distance from our murdered friend and for several minutes, maybe even longer, no one spoke.

It was Crispin who finally broke the deafening silence, his voice shaky. 'It looks like she's been dead a little while. The blood looks pretty dry and there's not much of it. I read somewhere that the heart stops pumping blood the moment it stops beating, which means she must have died very quickly.'

'That knife looks like it was plunged straight into her heart,' said Charlie. 'By someone who knew what they were doing.'

'Fucking hell,' said Luke again, seemingly unable to tear his eyes from Louise's corpse.

'Do you think it was the same guy I saw at the window?' asked Marla, looking round anxiously. 'He could still be here.'

'We need to check the house for any signs of forced entry,' I said, fighting to stay calm. 'He didn't come in the front door. It was bolted from the inside.'

'He didn't come through the windows here either,' said Crispin. 'They're all locked.'

'All the windows automatically lock when they're shut,' said Charlie. 'There are only two doors in and I bolted them both after Crispin arrived, so no one got in that way.' His words had lost all their usual power and he looked pale and drawn. He seemed devastated by what had happened to Louise, but for all I knew, it could have been an act. Charlie was a politician so he was used to lying for a living.

He saw me watching him and looked away. 'We'd better take a look round the ground floor and see how he got in.'

I wondered who Charlie meant by 'he' since he'd made a big deal about the fact that Pat had gone back to the mainland and we were alone on the island, but I didn't say anything. Instead I followed Charlie as he led us out of the room in a long, fearful line. En route he picked up a bronze sculpture of an African tribesman, which he clutched in front of him like a club, in what I suppose for him passed as an aggressive pose but which I couldn't help thinking was unlikely to scare any cold-blooded killer in our midst.

He found the open window quickly enough. It was in the downstairs toilet and, although it wasn't the biggest opening in the world, it would have been easy enough to get through. There were streaks of dirt on the toilet seat that looked like they'd come from the sole of a boot.

When we'd all taken turns to have a look, Charlie shut the window and we retreated to the dining room well away from Louise's body.

'I'm getting a nasty sense of déjà vu,' said Marla as we stood round the table. 'Seeing Louise like that reminded me of Rachel.'

'We need to call the police,' I said. 'I'm assuming you've got a landline here.'

Charlie nodded. 'I have, but let's not be hasty about making any calls.'

'What do you mean, don't be hasty?' I demanded, trying not to lose my temper. 'Our friend's just been murdered in your house. We have no idea who her killer is, or even if he's still here in the house somewhere.'

'Do you think I don't know that? I was just talking to Louise about her kids . . .' Charlie's voice was a hoarse shout. 'The problem is if we call the police, we risk having to explain what we're all doing out here. Don't you think it'll look extremely suspicious coming just after Danny Corridge has been released from prison?'

'Right now that seems to be the least of our problems,' I said. 'There's a killer on the loose. We can say we were just here for a reunion. The timing might be iffy but it's not proof we did anything wrong. What do you think, Crispin?'

'I think we should call the police,' said Crispin.

'So do I,' said Marla. 'Luke?'

'I don't know. Charlie's right. We need to think about this.'

Marla looked aghast. 'Our friend's lying dead with a knife in her heart and you need to think about it?'

Crispin looked thoughtful. 'I don't see who could have killed her. The only other person on this island is Pat. How well do you know him, Charlie? He looked a bit of a strange guy.'

'He's worked for me for three years. I know him well. I can't see why he'd suddenly turn into a murderer and kill a woman he's never met before. And he shouldn't even be here. He was going back to the mainland.'

'Well, who the hell does that leave?' said Marla.

No one said anything for a moment. Then I spoke. 'One of us,' I said simply.

Everyone looked at me and the room seemed to grow colder as we all took that rather grim statement on board.

'Look, someone broke in,' said Charlie, but he no longer sounded like he believed it.

'That could have been faked easily enough,' I said, a new authority in my voice. I was scared – God, I was scared – but I was also angry because it was probable that someone in this room was Louise's killer. 'Who was the last person to see her alive?'

'Charlie was,' said Luke. 'I left the two of them down in the lounge. That was about half past midnight.'

Charlie nodded. 'It's true. We carried on talking for about another ten minutes or so. I finished my drink before she did and told her I was turning in. She said she'd make her own way to bed, and when I left her she was sitting where you found her.'

Luke looked puzzled. 'Why would one of us want to kill her?' he asked, aiming the question at me.

'God knows,' said Charlie.

I looked at them both. 'Well, it wasn't random, was it? Louise was murdered for a reason and it looks like she was taken completely by surprise, before she could cry out. And from the position she was sitting in, she would have been able to see anyone she didn't know coming through the door, so there's no way they could have crept up on her. Which means she would have had time to cry out or at least make a break for it, and she didn't.' I paused for breath. 'So I think she knew her killer.'

When I'd first started speaking, I don't think I truly believed that one of us had murdered our old university friend, but now that I was laying everything on the line, it was becoming more and more obvious that someone in this room had done it. I looked at each of them, trying to prise out any signs of guilt, but the faces that stared back at me were full of shock, confusion and, of course, fear.

'And you were the last person to see her alive, Charlie,' said Marla, glaring at him. 'You could easily have done it. Louise wouldn't have stood a chance.'

Charlie looked exasperated. 'But why? What would have been the point?'

'Because it's one less witness to worry about,' I said.

'You organized this whole weekend, Charlie,' continued Marla. 'Almost immediately someone ends up dead and, lo and behold, you were the last person to see her alive.'

We were all looking at him now and he took a step back.

'If you're fucking us about, Charlie, and you killed Louise, then you are a dead man,' said Luke, leaning forward threateningly.

Charlie cringed away from him. 'I didn't do anything, I promise. I invited everyone here to get our stories straight. That's it. I'm no killer. I'm just a bloody politician.'

'And someone with a lot to lose as well,' said Marla. 'Remember, it was your idea to cover up Rachel's murder all those years ago.'

'Hold on,' said Crispin. 'We were all involved and we all agreed to the cover-up.'

'But it was still Charlie's idea,' continued Marla. 'And let's not forget: one of us in the house that night twenty-one years ago killed Rachel. Now I know I didn't do it. And I know I didn't kill Louise tonight. I'm innocent and I'm prepared to stand up in court and say it too because I've had enough of this, and there's no way we can cover up two murders. Let's call the police, like Karen says. Now. I'm not staying in this place any longer than I have to.'

Luke cursed. 'Jesus, what have we got ourselves into?' He turned to Crispin. 'What do you think we should do, Cris?'

'Marla and Karen are right. We've got to phone the police. Where's the phone, Charlie?'

'In the hall,' he answered reluctantly.

'I'll make the call.' Crispin walked past him, displaying an authority I hadn't seen in him before, and disappeared into the hallway.

I followed him out, watching as he turned on the hall light and located the phone before dialling 999 and putting the handset to his ear. He frowned then looked down at the keypad, pressing more numbers, and I felt a growing sense of dread.

'What is it?'

He put down the phone. 'The line's dead.'

The others had come out into the hallway now. Charlie grabbed the phone from Crispin and tried dialling himself with precisely the same result. 'Someone must have cut the wires,' he said shakily.

I could hear my heart beating rapidly in my chest and I followed the advice my therapist always gave me by silently telling myself to stay calm and take slow, deep breaths. But how the hell was I meant to keep calm when I was trapped in a house with a dead body and four other people who were all suspects in her murder?

'I'm scared,' said Marla.

I took a long, deep breath, then another, but it wasn't making me any calmer and I could feel the panic bubbling away inside me like the contents of a slowly boiling kettle. 'There must be some way off this island,' I said. 'Surely you can't just rely on your man Pat to come and pick you up, Charlie? What if the two of you had an argument?'

'I've got a RIB – an inflatable boat – down in the boathouse near the jetty for emergencies. We can all get across in that. But it's best to wait until the morning. The crossing to the mainland can be pretty hairy at night.'

'No way,' said Marla. 'I want off this place. Right now.'

'Look, it's too risky. We'd do better to stay here now. All the bedrooms have got locks on so no one's going to be able to hurt any of you. And if it makes anyone feel safer they can take a kitchen knife up to bed with them. There are plenty to go round.' Charlie sighed. 'Please. It's the best way.'

The room was silent while we digested this suggestion. Like Marla, my gut feeling was to get off the island as soon as possible, but I didn't like the idea of doing it at night in a glorified dinghy. Plus I didn't want to go out into the night just in case I was wrong and the killer wasn't one of us but a stranger waiting for us in the darkness. 'OK, let's stay here,' I said, and there were murmurs of agreement from Luke and Crispin.

Marla sighed. 'All right, but I want a knife, and if it's any of you who's the killer, you won't find me such an easy target.'

'No one's killing anyone tonight,' said Charlie, trying to keep tempers calm.

There was a slight smell of decay out in the hallway, and straight away I knew what it was. 'We're going to have to move Louise,' I said. 'We can't leave her sitting in a chair in the living room.'

'The police will be pissed off if we move the body,' said Crispin. 'They don't like . . .'

'I don't give a shit what they like. I'm not leaving her like that. Is there anywhere we can store her?'

'We could use the woodshed,' said Charlie. 'It's just round the side of the house. There's room there.'

I nodded slowly. 'Let's do it, then. Have we got anything to wrap her in?'

It was awful going back in the lounge and looking at Louise again. She'd been so alive only a few hours ago, and what was so terrifying was that it could just as easily have been me. I'm not the kind of person who fears death. On a few occasions these past years, when the guilt's been weighing me down, I've actually embraced the thought of it. But that was when it was still only a vague, distant presence. Now it lay taunting me with all its terrible power, and it was taking all my self-control to deal with it.

Luke and Crispin lifted Louise gently out of the chair and wrapped her in a double bed sheet. Marla was standing in the doorway sobbing silently while Charlie stood watching the scene, his face pale, although I noticed that his hands were steady. Could he have killed Louise? Easily. He had to be the most likely suspect. The question of why was harder to answer, though. If his plan was to get rid of the other people involved in the Rachel Skinner murder, wouldn't it have been far easier simply to poison our food or drink? Then we'd all be out of his hair at the same time, instead of which we were now all on our guard and his opportunity to pick off the rest of us was severely diminished.

So maybe he'd killed Louise for another reason. Or maybe it hadn't been Charlie at all.

Then who could it be?

I didn't want to think too much about that particular question, so instead I waited while the men took the body out. Then, with a grunted goodnight to the others, I climbed the staircase to my room, a long, sharp carving knife gripped in my fist, ready to begin the long wait until morning.

6

Not surprisingly, I barely slept a wink that night. For a long, long time I lay under the covers, the knife next to me, listening for anything that sounded out of place, determined not to be caught out by the murderer. The bedroom door was locked, as was the window, but I still didn't feel safe. Locks can be picked. If Charlie was the killer, he might have spare keys. I managed to push a small chest of drawers in front of the door to slow down any advance, but it was hardly foolproof.

In the end, though, even the fear gave way to exhaustion and I drifted off sometime around dawn, awaking with a start at 9.16 a.m. I felt like crap but there was a real sense of relief too. I mean, if nothing else, I was still alive. Sunlight drifted in through the narrow gap in the curtains and I pulled them open, squinting against the brightness. I don't normally smoke first thing in the morning but I made an exception today and had a cigarette out the window. The wind had picked up substantially and, even with the shelter provided by the rock, it was still powerful enough to make me shiver. It wasn't going to be the easiest crossing in a RIB but, quite frankly, I was prepared to take on a tsunami if it meant getting away from here.

When I'd dressed and moved the chest of drawers back roughly to its original position, I picked up the knife and unlocked the door, stepping out onto the narrow landing. All the bedroom doors were closed but I could hear the sound of talking coming from downstairs.

There was a large bay window above the staircase affording a view across the sea towards the rugged crags of the mainland a couple of miles distant and, for a good few seconds, I stood staring out. Whitecaps appeared in the swirling water, but the view still comforted me. In the gleam of a bright new day, home seemed so much closer than it had done in those grim early hours when I'd discovered Louise's body.

The voices downstairs belonged to Crispin and Marla. They were sitting at the kitchen table drinking coffee from a cafetière. There were empty plates in front of them and it was clear they'd made themselves breakfast. They were sitting quite close together as well – too close together for two people who hadn't seen each other in twenty years, and I immediately felt a pang of jealousy. I was also surprised by how relaxed they looked considering what had happened the previous night, and they didn't appear to have armed themselves with knives.

They both looked up as I came in, giving me the same tight, sympathetic smiles of people who knew they were meant to be feeling very emotional about what had happened, but who weren't quite able to manage it.

'Hey, Karen, how are you?' asked Crispin. 'Do you fancy a coffee? It's freshly brewed.'

I nodded and sat down, putting my knife down on the table but well within reach as I poured myself a cup from the cafetière.

Marla looked at the knife but didn't say anything. 'Did you sleep OK?' she asked.

'As well as can be expected. Where are the other two?'

Marla shrugged. 'We haven't seen them yet. I suspect they're still in bed.'

'Marla and I have been talking,' said Crispin, watching me carefully. He looked more relaxed and less tired this morning, as if he'd slept well.

I couldn't help feeling there was something about the two of them that didn't feel right, but I didn't say anything and waited for him to continue.

'We've decided that as soon as we get to the mainland we go straight to the police and tell them the truth about what happened back in 1994 with Rachel. I know it means we're all going to get in a lot of trouble – especially after everything that happened to Corridge – but I can't see how we can avoid it now that Louise's dead. The longer we put off the inevitable, the worse it's going to be.'

'The thing is,' added Marla, 'the three of us aren't as involved as Charlie and Luke. I mean, remember it was Charlie who said we had to cover Rachel's murder up? And remember how insistent he was about the whole thing?'

'Yes,' I said. 'I remember.' And I did. I remembered everything about that day. The terrible shock of seeing a dead body for the first time, made all the worse by the fact that it was someone I knew, and by the gruesome manner of her death. Then the nausea. Seeing Rachel lying naked on the futon mattress with her head a gruesome claret pulp, the blood caking her blonde hair, the smell in the hot, airless room almost unbearable, made me throw up immediately. And finally the fraught meeting in the house's poky little kitchen as the six of us tried to come to terms with what we'd just seen, while we worked out what to do. Luke was in a state of near-catatonic shock. He'd been the one in bed with her at the time and now he was staring straight ahead, mumbling to himself, tiny flecks of blood still peppering his face. Louise was crying hysterically, saying we had to call the police. It was harder to remember how I felt myself. I think I must have been totally shocked too. The whole incident had seemed so surreal. Things like that just didn't happen in my life. I hadn't known what the hell to do.

And then Charlie had taken over, rallying the troops, saying we couldn't go to the police, that we'd all be in trouble . . .

Crispin lowered his voice to barely a whisper and leaned forward in his chair. 'In hindsight, we can see how he pushed us to do things, and because of the way he acted back then it's possible – maybe even probable – that he committed Rachel's murder himself and was using us to help cover his tracks.'

'I still don't see why Charlie would have killed Rachel,' I said. 'He and Rachel both lived in the same house as me and, apart from that time when Corridge came round and beat him up – which, yes, he was very upset about – they got on fine.'

'It doesn't matter whether he had a motive or not.' Crispin shrugged. 'As far as I can recall none of us had any real motive to kill her, but she still ended up dead. The fact is Charlie was the driving force of the cover-up. It was his idea to set up Danny Corridge for the murder. And Luke played a big part too. He was the one who stole Corridge's car, and it was him and Charlie who got rid of the body. All we three did was keep quiet about something we should have spoken up about.'

'We were young,' said Marla. 'That counts in our favour.'

I looked at them both. 'You guys really have been talking, haven't you?' The thing was, I didn't like it. It was as if they were a team, and everyone else was on the outside of it. They were asking me to be a part of whatever they had planned but the fact remained I didn't entirely trust them. And now that they'd laid their cards on the table, it scared me. 'I hate the idea of going to jail for a crime I didn't commit, and I hate the idea of the whole world hating us for what we did to Corridge.'

'Ditto,' said Crispin. 'I was going to Thailand next week to start a new life. The last thing I need is a criminal record and an angry public, but we've got no choice. This thing's gone way out of control.'

And that, of course, was the decider for me. This had to end.

'OK,' I said. 'I'm in.'

There was no point hanging round the island now and it was with a heavy heart that I left Crispin and Marla in the kitchen and went upstairs to rouse Charlie. I tried to imagine what my family and work colleagues – what few good friends I had – would say when our terrible secret came out into the open. My mum would disown me. I'd lose my job. My liberty. I'd lose everything. And yet finally perhaps I'd be able to start making amends for what I'd done. I'd be able to wipe the slate clean, and start again.

I stopped at Luke's door and put my ear against the wood but couldn't hear anything, then continued on to Charlie's door at the end of the landing. Still holding the knife in my hand, I knocked hard and called his name.

Nothing.

I knocked again, and this time when I called his name, it was near enough a shout.

Instinctively, I tried the handle and, as the door clicked open, I experienced that now all-too-familiar feeling of dread.

The bedroom was empty, with the bed roughly made and the curtains open, and I felt an immediate sense of relief. There was a small en suite attached and I poked my head inside. The large power shower unit was completely dry so it didn't look like he'd used it this morning. Frowning as I left the room, I knocked hard on Luke's door, and almost immediately got a grunted, exhausted response telling me to hold on.

A few seconds later he came to the door, looking dishevelled, still wearing the boxers from the previous night.

I asked him if he'd heard anything from Charlie this morning. 'He's gone missing.'

Luke rubbed his eyes and shook his head. 'No, nothing. I've been flat out.'

Marla and Crispin had come up the stairs now and I told them what I'd just told Luke. 'How long have you guys been up for?'

'I was up at eight,' said Luke.

'And I was about ten minutes after that,' said Marla. 'Charlie hasn't shown his face during that time.'

I looked at my watch. 'It's almost ten o'clock now, so he's been gone a hell of a long time.'

Marla gave a decisive nod. 'He said the inflatable was down in the boathouse. Let's go down there ourselves and take it.'

Luke frowned. 'We're not planning on leaving Charlie on the island, are we?'

'Why not? He was the one who get us into this mess.'

'He clearly left his room voluntarily,' I said. 'The curtains are open, the bed's half-made, and there are no signs of a struggle.'

'Shit,' said Marla. 'Do you think he left here without us and went back to the mainland?'

'Why would he do that?' said Luke.

'Because, apart from you, the rest of us wanted to call the police after what happened to Louise. If he leaves us here without any way of communicating with the outside world, we can't talk to them.'

'But we'll be able to talk to them eventually. He can't leave us on here for ever.'

'Why not? If the inflatable's not here we've got no way of getting off.' Marla's voice had risen an octave and, like me, she looked panicked at the prospect of being stuck on the island.

411

'Look, let's all stay calm,' said Crispin. 'Charlie might just be taking a walk, or sitting on the beach contemplating the world and thinking about how his island retreat's just been destroyed by a murder. We don't know. So let's just get all our stuff together and head down to the boathouse together. If we can't find Charlie, then we'll go without him.' He looked at the three of us. 'Agreed?'

Everyone nodded.

Twenty minutes later – and with still no sign of Charlie – the four of us left the house through the back door, leaving it unlocked so we could get back in.

I have to admit I was getting more and more nervous by this point. Charlie had been gone more than two hours now and, whether he'd been taking the time to contemplate the world or not, he should have been back before now. Which left three alternatives. One, he'd left the island, as Marla had first suggested. Two, something bad had happened to him, although God knows what it could be. Or three – and I liked the thought of this the least – he was hiding somewhere, planning to murder us one by one, thereby getting rid of all the people who could incriminate him for the murder of Rachel Skinner.

As we walked the two hundred yards or so along the narrow path that wound through the pine wood down to the jetty, we all called his name and looked about us, but there was no answer, nor any sign of any other human presence. All was silent, bar the sound of the wind blowing through the trees, and the odd snippet of birdsong. It was as if this dark, rocky island had swallowed Charlie up altogether.

The jetty was empty, the speedboat that had brought us here nowhere to be seen. Thirty yards further along the beach, and partly obscured by a large weeping willow that looked out of place among the pines, was the boathouse, a single-storey wooden structure with double doors.

We stopped in front of it, standing in a row on the narrow strip of sand and pebbles.

'It doesn't look like he's left the island,' said Crispin. 'The doors are shut and there are no drag marks from the boat.'

'They're unlocked, though,' said Luke, gently pulling on one of the handles. The door opened with a long whining creak to a curtain of darkness beyond. 'Has anyone got a torch?'

'I have,' said Crispin, pulling one free from his backpack.

Luke opened the door as far as it would go then did the same with the other one, revealing an empty room that smelled vaguely of engine oil. 'There it is. On the wall there.'

Crispin shone his torch up to where Luke was pointing. The inflatable boat was little more than a dinghy and didn't look like it would hold six people. There was no engine attached and it didn't even appear to have been properly inflated.

Then the torch picked up the deep slash marks running symmetrically down each section.

'Oh, Christ, what's going on now?' said Marla, staring up at the damage.

'This is getting bad,' said Luke quietly. He no longer seemed big and strong. Now he looked pale and scared and the expression in his eyes – that of a man frozen in the path of an oncoming locomotive – was exactly the same as I remembered it being immediately after Rachel's murder. 'What the fuck are we meant to do now?'

It was Crispin who answered him. 'We don't panic. That's essential. We stay calm and we work out what to do next.'

Marla frowned. 'Who did this? Surely it wouldn't have been Charlie. Because that means he's trapped himself on the island. What about that man I saw at the window last night? Could it have been him?'

'But Charlie thought that was Pat,' I said, 'and his boat's gone.'

'Maybe he waited here overnight and took Charlie back,' said Crispin, shining his torch round the floor space, its beam picking up a couple of boxes in one corner.

I shook my head. 'No. That doesn't make any sense. He's . . .'

'Jesus Christ!' Crispin's words reverberated through the gloom like gunshots.

We all looked where his torch was pointing.

Marla made a long moaning sound that seemed to come from deep within her. Luke let out an almost childlike cry and began to retch.

I simply stood stock-still, unable to react in any way at all.

Perched up on an otherwise empty shelf that ran the length of a far wall, like a grisly trophy, was Louise's freshly severed head.

7

Her eyes were open and staring vacantly into space, her long, wavy blonde hair flowing down on either side of the pale, lifeless face. When we'd wrapped her body in the sheet, her hair had been tied in a ponytail, which meant that the killer must have untied it in yet another act of defilement. There was something in her mouth too. A rolled-up piece of paper sticking out like an oversized cigarette.

Marla ran out of the boathouse sobbing while Luke fell to his knees with his head in his hands. It sounded like he was crying too.

I could feel myself shaking as I tried to compute the full ramifications of what I was seeing. Someone on this island had not only murdered Louise but had deliberately and carefully chopped the head from the corpse and left it in a place that we would see it. To be the target of such hatred is a terrifying prospect at the best of times. But when you know you're trapped and that it could be your murder next, it's a thousand times worse.

Out of the corner of my eye I saw Crispin watching me with something like sympathy in his eyes. He said something but it sounded faint and far away and I couldn't make out the words.

Finally, he moved the torch light away from Louise's head then, as I watched, he walked slowly over and gently removed the rolled up piece of paper from her mouth. Turning away, he put an arm on my shoulder and I didn't resist as he led me outside, telling Luke to follow.

When we were all back on the beach and Luke had shut the doors, Crispin unrolled the paper and flattened it with his hands. I watched him carefully. He looked scared but nothing like as scared as the rest of us, and I was surprised by his ability to stay calm under such pressure. I'd always had him down as the most sensitive and vulnerable of all of us, yet he was now undoubtedly the man in charge.

'What does it say?' I asked, speaking for the first time since I'd seen what had been done to Louise, my voice weak and close to cracking.

Crispin didn't answer so I asked the question again, louder this time.

Marla, who'd been pacing up and down a few yards away, stopped and glared at him. 'Come on, Cris,' she said. 'Tell us.'

He swallowed audibly, and for a moment he looked like he might lose it. But then he seemed to compose himself. 'I don't think you want to read it.'

'Give it to me,' I said, knowing I had to see what was written there, however grim it was. He handed it over.

It was a simple, made-up poem typed out in block capitals.
Six devastating lines that sounded like my worst nightmare.

> JUSTICE EVENTUALLY COMES TO ALL,
> AND NOW ONE BY ONE THEY FALL.
> LEAVING THE VERY WORST TILL LAST,
> AS THEY PAY FOR THE SINS OF A DISTANT PAST.
> MY KNIFE IS SHARP, BLOODY AND TRUE,
> AND VERY SOON IT WILL COME FOR YOU.

The page shook violently in my hand and it was Marla who took it from me. I heard her curse as she read it too but I was already turning away and walking rapidly down the beach, ignoring the shouts of the others.

I broke into a run, sobbing as all the emotions that had been swirling round me these past hours – these past weeks, indeed these past years – suddenly erupted within me. As I reached the empty jetty, I jumped on to it and sprinted right to the end, thinking for a moment of throwing myself into the sea, going under, and never surfacing again.

But I stopped myself, the need for self-preservation still too strong to let go entirely, and stared down at the eddying grey water. In front of me the mainland was close enough to make out clearly – a mile, maybe two miles away, but no more. The sea was choppy and there were no boats out there today. No one who could help me. I wasn't a strong swimmer. I'd never make the distance. I probably wouldn't make a hundred yards.

I was trapped.

I heard footsteps behind me and swung round as a sudden wave of panic hit me.

It was Crispin. He approached gingerly. 'Are you OK, Karen? We've got to hold things together.'

He looked so lean and handsome, standing there in the wind, that my panic was replaced with a deep sadness. 'Why did it all have to go wrong, Crispin?' I sobbed, refusing to call him Cris like all the others did. 'Why did we ever have to meet that bitch, Rachel?'

'Whoa, hold on. This isn't about her.'

'It is. She's infected everything. If she'd never been part of our group, you and I would still have been together, don't you understand? We'd have travelled the world, got married. Had kids . . . Had a fucking life!' The words were pouring out of me now. I no longer had any control over them. Over anything. 'But instead it all went to shit. Someone killed her and it was never the same again, and I've been punished ever since. I lost you, and I married a man I didn't love, and then, when I finally did have something beautiful in my life, I lost her too.' I pictured Lily, with her round soft cheeks and infectious little laugh – only five months old when she died. 'I lost my little girl, Crispin. My child. Haven't I been punished enough already without all this?'

As the knife I'd been holding all this time clattered to the decking, he took me in his arms and held me tight. 'It's OK, Karen,' he whispered. 'It's going to be OK.'

I wished he hadn't called me Karen. I wished he'd called me 'little chick' or 'baby' or any of the other pet names he'd used when we were seeing each other. Karen seemed so formal. But I tried not to think about that and held him back just as tightly, my head buried in his shoulder, taking in his scent, soaking up our memories, allowing his presence to calm me.

My sobbing stopped as the grief temporarily subsided. 'What are we going to do, Crispin? We've got to find a way off this place.'

He nodded. 'I know, and we will. But first things first, we need to get back to the house. It's dangerous out here.' He looked around.

'It might be dangerous back there too. We left the back door open, didn't we?'

'We've still got knives.' He pulled his from his backpack. 'And there are four of us and one of him, so the odds are in our favour.'

'What do you think's happened to Charlie? Surely he can't have done this?' It was impossible to imagine a man like Charlie – out of shape from too much good living, and looking like Bertie Wooster in his silk pyjamas and slippers – deliberately severing the head of a woman who'd once been his friend, and using it to taunt us.

Crispin took a deep breath. 'God alone knows. Nothing would surprise me after what we've just seen. Come on, let's go back to the house.'

I could see the other two waiting on the beach, and I picked up my knife and walked back along the jetty with Crispin, pulling out my cigarettes and lighter from the sleeve of my hoodie and lighting up. Right now, I didn't care who saw me smoking.

'I didn't know you smoked as well,' said Marla as we reached the other two. 'Can I have one?'

'I didn't know *you* smoked either,' said Crispin, with a half-smile, aiming the comment at Marla, and once again I was uncomfortably aware of an intimacy between them. 'All right,' he continued, 'back to the house, everyone, keep your eyes peeled and your knives out. As soon as we're back we'll lock the place up and work out our next move, and remember: whoever's doing this can't touch us if we all stick together.'

The wind was picking up now and the earlier blue sky was all but gone, replaced by a swathe of grey-white cloud. I looked up at the ominous wall of pine trees that led back to the house, and I felt the fear kick in again. Somewhere in those trees was a man waiting for his opportunity to pick us off one by one. Right now, we were still four and, as Crispin had pointed out, there was comfort in numbers.

But if we started losing more . . .

We walked two abreast along the narrow path, each person no more than a yard from the trees that rose up on either side of us, shutting out the sky. Although they'd been planted in careful rows, tangled bushes and clumps of ferns and heathers had grown up in the gaps, offering numerous places to hide, and we all scoured the surroundings with an intensity born of fear, keeping close together. Marla had somehow managed to make sure she was the one leading the way with Crispin, while Luke and I brought up the rear.

I asked Luke if he was all right. He was still very quiet, although thankfully he seemed to have shaken himself out of his earlier catatonic state.

'I'm fine,' he whispered tightly, without taking his eyes off the wood. 'Concentrate on keeping watch. He could be right on us.'

I narrowed my eyes, keeping focused, my hand gripping the knife so tightly it felt numb, wondering if, even now, we were being watched by an unseen killer. I prayed that we'd make it back to the house safely. That whoever it was had decided against killing the rest of us, and had already left the island.

Something moved.

Behind one of the trees, maybe twenty yards in, partly obscured by a thick holly bush.

And then, without warning, a hooded figure – his face obscured – appeared, holding something out in front of him. It was a crossbow and it was aimed right at us.

'Run!' I yelled, immediately bolting in the other direction, my head down low as I knocked into Luke. I heard something whistle past my head; heard a scream; and then I was gone, into the trees away from our attacker, running for my life. I pulled off the backpack containing my stuff, not wanting to slow myself down, and threw it into some bushes. I zigzagged between the trees, charged straight through undergrowth, never once looking behind me. Even when I stumbled and fell, dropping my knife in the process, I was back on my feet and moving in an instant, picking it up as I sprung away, all the while ignoring the terrible burning in my lungs.

I don't know how long I ran for but it was probably no more than three or four minutes and then the woods ended abruptly, to be replaced by a wall of rock a good thirty feet high and, at least at the point I was looking at it, totally insurmountable. I ran down alongside the rock wall for about thirty yards as it tapered off before finally giving way to a short but sheer cliff that looked down on the rock-strewn, bubbling sea below.

I thought about following the cliff round until I eventually came back to the beach, but decided against it. There was no shelter for me there, plus the killer might expect me to go that way. I stopped and crouched low behind one of the last of the trees, and forced myself to look back.

There was no one there. I couldn't hear anything either.

I crouched there, panting for a few minutes while I got my breath back, wondering if the others were all right. It wasn't a surprise I couldn't hear them. Like me, they'd be trying to keep as quiet as possible. But I remembered hearing a scream so it was possible one of them had been hit. It had sounded like it had come from a man and, with a jolt of fear, I wondered if it was Crispin. That would be the worst blow. Of all of us, he was showing the most resilience.

I continued to scan the trees, thinking about my next move. I couldn't stay here. I'd be trapped if the killer approached through the woods. Again, I wondered if it could have been Charlie. It was impossible to tell from the glimpse I'd got of him but, as unlikely a murderer as he made, it had to be a strong possibility. I wondered what he'd do if he had me here at his mercy. Could I possibly get through to him? We'd been good friends once. Of all the girls in our group, I'd probably got on with him the best. It was almost impossible to believe that someone I'd known so well would kill me in cold blood, but then if he'd thrust a knife into Louise's heart while she sat facing him, he could probably just as easily do it to me.

In the end, I knew I had to try to make my way back to the house. As I cautiously stood and took a couple of tentative steps into the woods, keeping in the shadows of the nearest tree, it began to rain.

I moved slowly and quietly from tree to tree. A few yards a minute, never out in the open for longer than a couple of seconds, my ears straining against the wind that blew through the wood in a life-or-death effort to hear the slightest noise that might indicate an ambush. Because that's what this was. Life or death. The fear that I might be dead within the next few minutes almost knocked me over with its sheer power and it took every inch of a willpower I didn't even know I had to keep going.

I was moving at what I hoped was a rough forty-five-degree angle through the wood in the direction of the house, avoiding the path for obvious reasons. One way or another, the house represented my best chance of safety now that I knew for certain that neither Crispin, Marla nor Luke was the killer, because I guessed all of them would be heading there too.

The rain was getting harder now and I shivered against the cold, resting for a second in the shadow of one of the pines.

That was when I saw him. Dressed all in black, a ski mask almost completely obscuring his face, creeping quietly between two lines of trees, holding the loaded crossbow in front of him as he scanned the woods for his prey. No more than ten yards away and getting closer.

I pulled my head back sharply behind the tree and kept my gasp of shock inaudible. Had he seen me? I didn't think so.

But what if you're wrong? said the nagging little voice that was always there. What if he's coming towards you right now, finger tensing on the crossbow's trigger, ready to fire a bolt through your brain and ending everything you've ever felt in an instant?

Run.

Stay put.

Run.

Stay put.

I held my breath, not daring to move a muscle, feeling the pressure build in my lungs.

I heard a twig break. Nearby.

It was taking all my self-control not to bolt for it.

Slowly, ever so slowly, I turned my head and saw him, almost touching distance away, creeping past the tree I was hiding behind, his face turned the other way as he prowled for victims.

As he turned round in my direction, I jerked my head back, still holding my breath, and inched my way round the other side of the tree, praying he hadn't seen or heard me because otherwise I was dead. I'd had barely a second to observe him – not long enough to confirm whether or not it was Charlie, but I was pretty sure it wasn't. This man moved like a hunter. I'd never seen Charlie move like that.

I counted to ten in my head, every second seeming to drag like an eternity of pure, ice-cold fear, before slowly exhaling and immediately sucking in a deep breath of air, and holding it in.

I counted to ten again and finally risked a glance round the tree.

He wasn't there. My eyes scanned the woods but there was no sign of him.

I didn't like this. He'd been moving slowly. He wouldn't have got more than twenty or thirty feet in the time I'd been counting in my head, but he'd disappeared completely.

Was this some kind of trap? Was he waiting for me a few yards away so he could take me down like an animal with his crossbow? But I couldn't stay here. Eventually he'd come back and discover me. He had all the time in the world. I had none. I couldn't be more than a hundred yards from the house. If I could get there, I was safe. At least that was what I was telling myself. The little voice that was always there was telling me to run. Now. As fast as I could. And hope for the best.

I didn't want to look behind me – Jesus, I didn't – and I had to force myself to slowly turn my head, knowing that whatever was behind me could well be the last thing I ever saw, and it was an incredible relief just to see the empty line of pines.

I made a decision. Taking one last look in the direction the crossbowman – whoever he was – had gone, I peeled myself off the tree and crept as quietly as possible past a fan of mature ferns, using them as cover, until I got to the next tree, then did the same again. The lines of pines had now given way to a sprinkling of oak trees as the woods thinned, and I could see the vague outline of the house through the undergrowth, no more than thirty yards away.

I looked back. Still no sign of my pursuer. For the first time, I felt a thin ray of hope. I took a step backwards, then another, manoeuvring round the tree trunk to make myself as invisible as possible.

And touched something. Something that felt very human.

The shock made me jump forward and I swung round fast, looking straight into Charlie's cold, staring eyes.

He was skewered to the tree by two crossbow bolts. One had been fired through his chest – the entry point very similar to where the knife blade had been thrust into Louise the previous night. The other was jutting out of his throat. There was a lot of blood. Thin rivulets of it ran from both corners of his mouth in long lines, mixing with the thick drying stain that covered his throat and chest, and I immediately recalled what Crispin had said about Louise hardly bleeding at all because the knife thrust into the heart had killed her instantly. This was very different. The killer must have shot him in the throat first, – probably at point-blank range, and let him choke on his own blood before finally finishing him off.

I couldn't help it. Instinctively, I cried out, the sound far too loud in the natural quiet of the woods.

Then, as I tore my gaze away from Charlie's corpse, I saw him standing twenty yards away, the crossbow to his shoulder as he pointed it right at me in a marksman's stance. The man who'd murdered my two friends.

For a second I didn't move. I don't know if, in that moment in time, I'd resigned myself to my fate, but it was almost as if I was waiting for him to fire.

But he didn't. And that hesitation on his part was enough for me.

I dived round the far side of the oak and temporarily out of sight just as a bolt flew through the air, reverberating as it hit a nearby tree. I was on my feet in an instant, tearing through a tangle of brambles, ignoring the pain as the thorns slashed at my face and body, staying low and trying not to keep to a straight line.

I ate up the ground, the house taking shape now. I snatched a look over my shoulder. Saw him running too, the crossbow reloaded, a couple of trees back but keeping me in sight. I turned forward again, almost hit a tree, dodged it at the last second, stumbling on something but somehow managing to keep my balance.

And then I was out of the wood and running across the front lawn. At the last second, I remembered that the front door would be locked and I darted down the path round to the back of the house, flinging open the side gate which clattered shut behind me, praying that the door there would still be open.

Panting, I reached it and yanked the handle.

It was locked.

There was no longer any point in trying to be quiet so I hammered on the door, pushing my face against the glass. The back hallway was empty but there had to be someone in there because we'd left the door open when we'd left barely half an hour ago.

I kept hammering, the glass shaking from the blows, screaming for them to let me in. 'Help me! Help me!' But no one was in there. No one at all. Surely they couldn't all be dead. But what if they were? What if I was the last one left alive on this godforsaken island with a killer who was hunting me down like a dog?

Which was when I heard the side gate clattering again.

He was here.

After

8

I still had my knife and I knew that if I moved fast I'd just be in time to stab the crossbowman when he emerged round the corner into the back garden. But that's the kind of thing that brave, decisive people – or those who aren't afraid of death – do. I wasn't one of those people. I was just a scared forty-something woman flung into the middle of a waking nightmare and the fear was crippling me.

He was coming. Jesus, he was coming.

And then I heard the back door being unlocked from the inside and saw Crispin's face in the window.

'Let me in! Now!'

He released the final bolt and pulled the door open and I pushed past him to get inside. 'Lock the door for God's sake!' I yelled, stumbling against the washing machine but, as he went to lock it, a shadow appeared through the glass.

I screamed.

'Fuck, it's Luke,' said Crispin and let him in too before flinging the bolts across and turning the key in the lock.

Luke looked scared and relieved, which I'm sure was pretty much how I looked. I noticed he didn't have his knife. Crispin's was sitting on top of the washing machine – a long paring knife with a good, sharp blade – and he grabbed it now.

'Did you see anyone behind you?' I asked Luke. 'I was being chased by the guy with the crossbow.'

He shook his head. 'No, I didn't see him.'

I wiped sweat from my brow and walked through the utility room and into the kitchen. The rain was coming down hard now and the back lawn looked forlorn and bedraggled, and thankfully empty. I pulled the curtains shut and switched on the light, before grabbing an empty glass from one of the cupboards and pouring myself a glass of water.

The other two followed me in.

'What happened to you and Marla?' I asked Crispin.

'We just ran, same as you guys, then doubled back through the woods.'

'You managed to stick together, then.' I was conscious of the note of accusation in my voice.

He nodded, ignoring my tone. 'Yeah, we did.'

I pulled my pack of cigarettes and lighter from inside the sleeve of my hoodie and lit one, taking a long, much-needed drag. 'Sorry, but under the circumstances, I'm not going to smoke outside.'

Crispin gave me a half-smile. 'It's fine. Have you got a spare one?'

I lit one for him, ignoring Luke's dirty look. 'Is this place secure?'

Crispin nodded slowly and once again I found myself surprised by how calm he was. 'As secure as it was when we left, but it's not impregnable. The good thing is there are four of us, and a crossbow's not going to be much use to him in here.'

'He's got all the time in the world,' said Marla, who'd appeared in the doorway. 'He can pick us off one by one. I mean, it's not as if we're going anywhere, is it? Do you think it's Charlie? It's almost impossible to believe it could be him . . .'

I took another drag on the cigarette, beginning to get my breath back. 'It's not Charlie.'

'How do you know?' demanded Marla. There was an accusing tone in her voice too.

'Because I saw his corpse.'

That shut everyone up.

'It was pinned to a tree with crossbow bolts.' I told them how I'd discovered it.

Marla put a hand to her mouth. Crispin frowned deeply. Luke, though . . . he looked sceptical.

I glared at him. 'What? Don't you believe me?'

'Well, it's funny that of all the places his body could have been hidden in that wood, you managed to find the exact tree.'

'What the hell are you insinuating? That I'm making it up? Why the fuck would I do that? I saw him clear as day. He had a bolt through his throat and one through his chest. If you don't believe me we can go down there and take a look. It's not very far away.'

He didn't say anything.

'Come on,' I said, shouting now. 'Let's go and have a look.' I don't think there was any way I'd have gone back out there but I was genuinely furious at being treated this way, after everything I'd been through.

'OK, I'm sorry,' he said. 'It's just it's difficult to believe that Charlie's dead too. I think I'd convinced myself that he was behind all this. You know, he had the opportunity to kill Louise. Somehow it's easier to think of him being the killer.'

'It must be the man I saw at the window last night,' said Marla.

I nodded. 'It's got to be Pat. Charlie was dressed when I found him so he obviously went outside voluntarily. Maybe he went to meet Pat.'

'That's all well and good,' said Crispin, 'but Charlie said that Pat had left the island. So why would he go out to meet him if he didn't know he was there?'

I shrugged, trying to come up with a viable theory. 'Maybe he went for a walk and ran into Pat. Pat threatened him with the crossbow, took him into the woods and shot him.'

'But what's Pat's motive?'

'I don't know. The note we found makes clear the motive's revenge, and that must mean revenge for what happened to Rachel. Maybe Pat found out about what happened and decided to act.'

'It's a bit unlikely, isn't it?' said Crispin. Which, to be fair, it was.

Marla shook her head dismissively. 'I can't see Charlie just going out for a morning stroll when he knew Louise had been murdered and didn't think it was one of us who'd killed her. He'd have been too scared.' She frowned. 'There's something else too. When I went to the toilet last night during dinner, I was sure the window was shut, and I've checked again and it definitely locks automatically if it shuts, so I don't see how the killer could have got in.'

'Why didn't you say anything before?' I asked.

'Because I was still in shock, and at the time I wasn't entirely sure, but now I've had time to think about it, and I am.'

Crispin sighed. 'Which brings us back to the fact that it could be one of us who killed her. Except we know it can't have been because we all saw the man in black back in the woods.'

The room fell silent as everyone tried to work out what was going on. If no one had broken in last night then one of us must have killed Louise. Charlie had been the obvious suspect but now he was dead, so there had to be another killer.

Luke eventually broke the silence. 'It doesn't really matter, does it? What matters is that we get the hell off this island.'

'That's a lot easier said than done,' grunted Marla.

'I don't care. I'm going, even if I have to swim for it.' But I noticed Luke was making no move to go.

'Come on, Luke,' said Crispin. 'You've seen the sea out there. It'll be impossible to swim it, and the water will be freezing. Even if you don't drown you'll die of hypothermia.'

'Well, I'm not fucking staying here!' He shouted the words and hit the wall so hard, the crockery on the dresser rattled. I remembered that he could be aggressive sometimes. Something of a hard guy, or at least he thought he was. He'd talked about going after Danny Corridge when Corridge had beaten up Charlie, but he'd never managed to put his words into actions, and looking at him now, he reminded me of a frightened and frustrated little boy.

'We could set alight to the house,' I said. 'Then climb up on the rocks. They're bound to see the fire from the mainland.'

'That's a real last resort,' said Crispin. 'It's very risky and we could end up being sitting ducks.'

'Have you got any better ideas?' said Luke.

'Yes. Right now, let's stay put. The place is pretty secure, and we've got food, so we can play a waiting game too. The only way the killer will be able to get us out is if he burns this place down, so let's make sure we draw the curtains, seal off the letterboxes, and wet some towels so we're ready for any eventuality.'

Crispin's coolness under pressure seemed to galvanize everyone. He was the leader now and everyone recognized that. His words should have made me feel better but, as I went through to the lounge to pull the curtains, my heart beating in my chest as I passed the spot where Louise had been murdered, I thought back to the horrors I'd witnessed that morning. Louise's severed head with the note sticking out of her mouth; the man in black with his loaded crossbow, stalking me; Charlie's ruined corpse pinned to a tree. But there was one thing that stuck in my mind above any other. Those five words the killer had written.

LEAVING THE VERY WORST TILL LAST.

He'd had me in his sights. He could have killed me earlier. Easily. But he hadn't. He was leaving me alone. But that wasn't what frightened me the most.

What frightened me the most was how he knew I was the worst.

9

The rain rained and the day dragged.

Crispin's plan was for us to stay together downstairs and make sure that no one was left in a room on their own, but it didn't quite work out like that. People got restless. They moved around. It's impossible to relax when you're trapped with individuals you haven't seen for years in a house in the middle of nowhere, knowing that outside is someone who wants you dead for something you were involved in over two decades ago. Someone who, it seemed, was able to sneak into the house and murder Louise without her making a sound or making any effort to escape.

At one point, I fell asleep on the sofa, out of pure exhaustion, and when I woke up I was alone in the room. I found Luke in the dining room peering out through a gap in the curtains, a long kitchen knife in one hand. He turned my way when I came in but didn't say anything, and I left him there.

I looked for Marla and Crispin but I couldn't find them anywhere downstairs. In the end, I felt a bit of a panic coming on and I stood at the foot of the stairs and called their names.

They appeared a minute later, fully clothed, and Crispin told me they'd been watching over the wood from upstairs and apologized for disappearing like that. 'You were fast asleep,' he said. 'And we didn't want to make too much noise and disturb you.'

'No problem,' I said with a forced smile.

But there *was* a problem. The fact was I was jealous. I didn't like the way they were acting with each other. They were intimate. Close. It made me wonder how often they'd seen each other since uni and what their relationship was. In my paranoid state it also made me wonder if they had something to do with all this. Either one of them could have killed Louise. And by the same token, either or both of them could have led Charlie outside this morning and killed him, without Luke or me being any the wiser.

Unfortunately, the theory fell apart the moment you took the man with the crossbow into consideration. But maybe the three of them were in it together? It was hard to believe, of course, especially as Crispin had once been my boyfriend, but then this whole situation was hard to believe, and that didn't mean it wasn't happening.

'Have you searched the loft?' I asked him.

'I had a look up there earlier,' he said. 'Right now, this house is as secure as it's ever going to be and there are no bad guys hiding anywhere.'

But I wasn't convinced. For much of the rest of the afternoon, I explored the downstairs rooms, looking for hidden entrances, hidden passageways – anything that might explain how Louise and then Charlie had been killed. I tapped walls, lifted up paintings, ran my fingers along acres of skirting. But in the end, I found nothing.

Eventually night fell and, to take our minds off things, Marla suggested we all cook dinner.

'Sounds like a good idea to me,' I said and followed her into the kitchen. We found a large joint of beef in the fridge as well as plenty of vegetables. I quickly located the potatoes and vegetable oil and we started preparing a roast. Crispin and Luke sat down at the kitchen table and cracked open a bottle of red, filling glasses for all of us. You wouldn't call the mood convivial – not with two of our number dead – but it's amazing how a bit of cooking can add a sense of normality to any situation.

We got through the first bottle of wine in barely twenty minutes, and I located Charlie's wine store and dug out a 2011 Fleurie. The alcohol was giving me a much-needed warm feeling. To be honest, I'd had a problem with alcohol in the past. I became too dependent on it in my twenties, managed to wean myself off it when I was pregnant with Lily, and then when I lost her I kind of went off the edge of a cliff and was a full-on drunk until finally my mother dragged me to rehab. Since then my relationship with booze has been calmer, and more off than on, but tonight I truly thirsted for its embrace, even though it was the last thing any of us needed.

The Fleurie lasted longer than the first bottle, but it still wasn't that long until we were on to number three.

'Does anyone know where the gravy is?' asked Marla.

'In here,' I said, pulling a tub of Bisto from one of the overhead cupboards.

'You seem to know where a lot of things are, Karen,' said Marla, and there was no mistaking the suspicion in her voice. 'I've been noticing it ever since we got here. You haven't been here before, have you?'

I laughed. 'Of course not.' But I didn't look at her as I spoke and I could hear the lie in the words myself. It must have been the alcohol. It was making me lax. Everyone else could hear it too.

'Karen,' said Marla harshly. 'You have been here before, haven't you?'

I turned to face her, preparing to lie again, but the intensity of her stare stopped me. Out of the corner of my eye I could see the other two staring at me too. I swallowed, paused.

Marla's dark eyes flashed with anger. 'Tell the truth.'

'All right, I have.'

The three of them expressed various levels of shock and Marla demanded to know when, and why I hadn't mentioned it before.

'I had an affair with Charlie,' I said reluctantly, pulling out my cigarettes and lighting one, knowing I couldn't tell this story without a smoke. 'It started at the funeral. For my daughter, Lily. Charlie attended. I wasn't expecting him and when he did turn up, it was the first time I'd seen him since we'd left uni. We had a quick chat back at the house afterwards. I was in a state of complete shock, just numb really, and Charlie said that if I ever needed to talk then I should call him. He gave me his business card.' I sighed. 'Things were going bad between Jeff and me at the time. They had been even before Lily passed, but they just got worse after that. I called Charlie a few weeks afterwards. He suggested we meet for lunch, so we did and we talked for hours. He was sympathetic and I really did literally cry on his shoulder. In hindsight I know he was just being predatory, but I was in a very fragile state and I guess I just fell for it.' I paused, took another drink of the wine. 'The affair didn't last long. No, that's a lie. It probably lasted six months, but we didn't see each other that often. Charlie let it be known that he wouldn't be leaving his wife and, to be honest, I didn't want him to. I don't think I even knew what I was doing. I just wanted comfort, some kind of intimacy, however snatched and fake it was, and Charlie was just in the right place at the right time, and, like all charmers, he knew which buttons to press. Eventually, though, I came to my senses and finished it. It was all very amicable. In fact he was pretty relieved and I didn't see him again until last night, but yes, I came here with him once. I hated it then. And I hate it now.'

I drew on the cigarette, blowing out smoke towards the ceiling, relieved that I'd finally got it out in the open. It had been weird seeing Charlie last night and not being able to make any mention of our shared time together, however brief and unfulfilling it had been.

But the reaction I got was nothing like I'd been expecting.

It was Marla who spoke first, her tone cold. 'Well, that explains a lot.'

I frowned. 'What do you mean?'

'You're the one who things keep happening to. It was *you*' – she emphasized the 'you' – 'who discovered Louise's body. It was *you* who saw Charlie impaled against a tree – no one else – and it was *you* who got chased by the man with the crossbow but somehow managed to outrun him.'

I looked at her aghast. 'What on earth are you insinuating? That Charlie and I are behind all this?'

'It's definitely a theory.'

'You've been keeping very calm today,' said Luke accusingly, getting to his feet. His cheeks were pink and I noticed he'd been caning the wine. 'Especially after everything that's happened. You even fell asleep.'

'That's because I was fucking exhausted. Just because I had a brief thing with Charlie five years ago when I was mourning the death of my baby daughter does not mean that I'm now in cahoots with him, planning to murder you all.'

'Then why didn't you mention your affair with him?' demanded Marla.

'Why should I? You didn't mention that you and Crispin have obviously been seeing plenty of each other.'

'I don't know what . . .'

'Oh, please. It's fucking obvious.' My voice was loud and I was beginning to sound hysterical, even though I was more in control of my emotions now than I had been all weekend.

'All right, all right, that's enough.' It was Crispin speaking now. He was on his feet with his palms stretched outwards in a gesture of calm. 'Yes, Marla and I have been in contact. We met up again a few years ago and we've stayed friends since then, although we don't see much of each other.'

'Why didn't you ever stay friends with me, Cris?' asked Luke, sounding hurt. 'I tried getting hold of you a couple of times. You never got back to me.'

Crispin turned towards him but he never got a chance to answer because a second later the kitchen window exploded and something flew through the room, striking the far wall.

Instinctively, we all ducked and I felt on the worktop for my knife, holding it close as I stayed low in case something else came hurtling through the window.

But nothing did. The curtain flapped wildly in the wind and the room felt cold but there was no further assault.

Crispin crawled under the kitchen table and retrieved the missile. It was part of a house brick with a note attached by two rubber bands. He tugged the note free and, still sheltering under the table, inspected it.

'What does it say?' asked Marla quietly.

This time Crispin didn't try to hide anything. With a resigned sigh, he read out the contents of the note.

'I HAVE TAKEN TWO LIVES NOW
BUT MY BLOODLUST HAS YET TO BE SATED.
RACHEL SKINNER DEMANDS ANOTHER KILL,
ALREADY THE TRAP HAS BEEN BAITED.
THERE IS NO ESCAPE. IT IS FAR TOO LATE.
LOOK THROUGH THE WINDOW TO SEE YOUR FATE.'

'Oh, Jesus,' whispered Marla. 'What's he done now?'

'Don't look,' said Crispin, crumpling up the note and throwing it on the floor. 'Anyone who puts their face up to that window is going to be an obvious target.'

'We're all targets in here,' hissed Luke. 'He could throw a petrol bomb in here and we'd all be burned alive.'

'Why's he doing this?' Marla's voice was cracking under the pressure now. 'I didn't kill Rachel. I never touched her. I never touched her!' she screamed, her voice filling the room, the words clearly aimed at the killer, wherever he might be.

The bad voice in my head was shouting at me to panic. To jump up, unlock the door and run for my life. Or just to run the knife I was clutching across my throat and end this whole damned nightmare for ever. I was shaking with fear but I fought to control it. Stay in adult, I repeated to myself, using a phrase my therapist always used. Do not let the anxiety consume you.

'I never touched Rachel!' shouted Marla again.

'Shut the fuck up!' I hissed, feeling an intense and sudden burst of rage.

She looked at me, saw something that clearly had the desired effect, and shut her mouth immediately.

'Quiet, everyone,' snapped Luke. 'He could be standing right outside the window.' He lowered his voice so that it was barely audible. 'We've got the wet towels in the hall. If he throws anything in, we can put out the flames. Now it's time to take the fight to him.' He slipped out from underneath the table and switched off the light, then crawled along the floor until he was between Marla and me. He reached up to the hob and lifted the saucepan of boiling water that was going to be used for the vegetables, before creeping out of the room with it.

I heard him go upstairs, his footfall quiet, followed by a great splash of water outside the kitchen window as he upended the saucepan.

A minute later he was back in the kitchen. 'If there's anyone out there, then they're badly scalded now,' he said quietly.

'The note said to look out of the window,' said Marla. 'Did you see what's out there?'

'He's just taunting us.'

'Did you see anything?'

'No. Now we need to wet some more towels. Marla, you and Luke do that. As many as you can. I'll get the beef out of the oven. Karen, can you grab some cutlery and plates? We're going to eat in the lounge on the floor.'

I'm not sure how many of us actually had an appetite after what had just happened but I think we were all happy to have someone taking charge of the situation, even though, as I've said before, I would never have guessed it would be my Crispin. Within a few seconds, we were all following his instructions.

My whole body was shaking as I clambered round in the gloom, collecting together the plates and cutlery, but I did it, and it was almost with surprise that I found myself alone in the kitchen. I looked at the curtains flapping in the draft caused by the hole the brick had been made.

THERE IS NO ESCAPE. IT IS FAR TOO LATE.
LOOK THROUGH THE WINDOW TO SEE YOUR FATE.

I knew I shouldn't look. The killer could be only feet away from me right now, waiting for me. But that voice in my head was insistent. I had to see what fate was in store for me. I had to. Because I knew Crispin was lying. He'd seen something. And it had shaken him. He'd hidden it well but I'd noticed, even if the others hadn't.

Just one look.

It was madness, utter madness. But it was as if I couldn't help myself. I had to see what new horror awaited and so, with trembling fingers, I inched open the curtain and stared out into the rain-smudged night.

There they were in the middle of the lawn, nothing more than faint silhouettes in the darkness, but unmistakeable nevertheless.

Two severed heads sitting atop long stakes.

Louise and Charlie.

10

That night in the lounge we made a plan. Tomorrow morning, just before first light, we would dress in as many layers as possible using clothes from Charlie's wardrobe, so we were well insulated and at least had some protection against a crossbow bolt. Charlie owned a whole range of outdoor coats so there would be no shortage. Crispin had also found some bike helmets in the loft so we would wear them too. As soon as dawn broke we would set fire to the house and, when we were sure that the flames would take hold, we would exit the front door, armed with our knives, make a bolt for the sea along the path, staying together, then wade into the water until we were almost out of our depth and stay there until help arrived. If nothing else, we'd be able to see the killer coming from a long distance away and it would make his task far harder if he had to wade into the waves to get a shot at us.

To be fair, we all knew the plan was full of holes but it was the best we could manage, and no one wanted to remain trapped in the house any longer. It was, as Luke said in that slightly hackneyed way of his, 'shit or bust'.

No one mentioned anything more about my affair with Charlie, or Marla and Crispin's own 'friendship'. Or even what it was that the killer had wanted us to see outside the window. It was all business, the mood tense yet productive. Together at least we had a chance, and I think we all belatedly realized that.

We decided to keep watch through the night in pairs. I think Crispin and Marla wanted to do one shift but Luke and I both vetoed that one. Luke wanted to go with Crispin, his old uni mate who'd somehow neglected to keep in touch with him, but so did I, and because it was more effective to have a man and a woman in each shift, Luke and Marla took the first one, Crispin and I the second, beginning at 2.30 a.m.

I slept fitfully on one of the sofas, only feet away from where Louise had died, my knife at my side. When I did dream, it was about my daughter. My poor, long-gone daughter. In the dream, Lily was sitting in my arms, still a baby, just as she'd been on the day I'd discovered her dead in her cot, aged four months and twenty-two days, but now she was talking like an adult, telling me how she was really looking forward to going to university and making new friends and broadening her horizons. Her dad was in the room with us, stroking my hair, and I think Charlie was there too, saying something, but I couldn't really hear what and anyway I was only interested in my darling, beautiful Lily, the apple of my eye, my life, my world . . .

And then I was being shaken awake by Marla and I had a sudden, vivid memory of that bright, terrible morning all those years ago when Rachel was lying in Luke's bedroom with her head bashed in.

Luke. Luke. Still the most likely suspect to have killed Rachel. Don't forget that.

'It's 2.30,' said Marla. 'You were dreaming then, weren't you? You were flapping and shaking about.'

I grunted something and rubbed my eyes, not bothering to give her a proper answer. Crispin was already up and awake, drinking from a glass of water, while Luke had taken his place on the sofa and was trying to get comfortable. I got up and Marla lay down where I'd been.

'Did anything happen while I was asleep?' I asked her.

'Nothing. Totally quiet.' She shut her eyes and was out in seconds, which made me think that, when you're that tired, you can sleep through pretty much anything.

Still yawning, I made tea for Crispin and we sat on the floor out of sight of the window and away from the other two. I offered him a cigarette.

'I shouldn't,' he said, but he took one anyway.

'I think the long-term health risks are pretty irrelevant right now,' I said, and lit us both up, noticing that my supply was coming to an end. I'd only brought a single pack, as lately I'd cut my intake down to eight a day, but now that there were only four left, I wished I'd brought more, even though they wouldn't survive the drenching in the sea we were planning for a few hours' time.

'I'm so sorry to hear about what happened to your daughter,' he said, and I could tell from the expression in his eyes that he meant it. That was the thing about Crispin. There was a real kindness about him, and it made me wonder how I could ever have suspected his involvement in this.

I sighed. 'It was the most horrible thing that's ever happened to me in my whole life. Including this, believe it or not. At the time I genuinely didn't think I could get through it. I just wanted to die. And I felt like that for a long time afterwards, but the thing is, you do get through it. You survive, and you carry on.'

'I'm sorry about Marla and Luke earlier, too. You know, the fact they didn't believe you about Charlie. I know you were telling the truth.'

'Is that because you saw what was outside the window?'

He frowned. 'You looked?'

I nodded.

'So you saw the heads. I'm glad you didn't say anything to the others.

I don't think Marla especially can handle much more of this.' He drew on the cigarette, blowing smoke towards the ceiling. 'It's funny, isn't it? When we were at uni, I always felt that Luke and Marla were the strong ones. And now look at us.'

'You're strong, Crispin. I don't know about me.'

'Jesus, Karen, you've survived everything that life's thrown at you, including being the one to discover the murdered bodies of two of your friends in the last twenty-four hours, and you're still keeping your head. You, my girl, are a strong woman.'

He smiled at me then and, even in the midst of this nightmare, I felt a warm glow.

I took his hand, gripping it hard, and I think I would have tried to kiss him but I saw his smile fade a little at the prospect. Whatever I might have liked to think, Crispin was Marla's man.

I removed my hand and took a sip from the rapidly cooling tea. 'So, how did you and Marla meet up again?'

I could tell he wasn't keen to talk about it but I wasn't going to let him off the hook that easily now that I had him alone. I needed to know.

'It was pure coincidence really. I was at a bar in the West End – I can't even remember which one now – with some mates, and Marla walked in with a bunch of her friends. We spotted each other, got talking and stayed in touch afterwards.'

'How long ago was that?'

He looked at me sadly. 'A long time. Maybe fifteen years.'

I worked hard to suppress the hurt. 'And you've kept in contact ever since?'

'No.' He paused for a moment, presumably wondering how much to tell me. 'I'll be honest. We hit it off and, even though we were both in relationships, we started seeing each other. I finished with the girl I was with but Marla was married at the time, so it was harder for her.'

'You had an affair.'

'Don't judge, Karen. I'm not that kind of man, you know that, but things . . . things just went out of control, like they did with you and Charlie. Eventually, after about a year, Marla left her husband and we moved in together.'

He waited for me to say something. But I didn't. I let him talk.

'We lived together for about a year. It might even have been longer. We were going to get married, too, once her divorce came through, but I suppose it wasn't meant to be because things didn't work out and we finally split up. We stayed friends, but I moved to France after that so we hardly saw each other. Last night was the first I'd seen of her in a couple of years.'

'But the spark's still there, eh?'

He shrugged.

'And did you . . . did you ever sleep together while we were seeing each other?' I asked, wondering why I always had to be so masochistic.

'Of course I didn't,' he said, but I spotted the lie in his eyes. He had.

The bitch. I hated Marla then. Always thinking she could get any man. Messing with people's feelings. Just like Rachel had when she was alive. What was it about these bloody women?

We talked some more – mainly about him and his travels; a little about my life too – and smoked the rest of the cigarettes. But to be honest I'd lost the appetite for the conversation. Too much water had passed under the bridge between us. We were no longer two former lovers reminiscing. We were just two individuals trying to take our minds off the bloody reality of our situation.

And at some point during the night I made a terrible mistake.

I closed my eyes.

11

I opened my eyes slowly and the first thing I noticed was daylight behind the drawn curtains.

I frowned. Our plan was to get ready half an hour before dawn at 5.30 a.m. I looked at my watch. It was now almost 7.30.

I'd fallen asleep sitting against a wall and my body was at an uncomfortable angle, so I propped myself up and looked around. Luke and Marla were still asleep on opposite sofas but there was no sign of Crispin and I couldn't hear him anywhere.

I noticed something else too.

My knife was gone.

Slowly I got to my feet and checked on Luke and Marla. Luke was snoring lightly so there was nothing wrong with him, and Marla was breathing softly, a peaceful expression on her face. I couldn't see their knives either.

I thought about waking them up but instead I crept into the hallway, listening out for Crispin. I wasn't unduly worried. No one could get in the house and, even if by some mischance they'd managed to, they would have killed us by now. We were safe. We were fine. We'd just overslept.

But where was Crispin? The house was totally silent, the doors still locked. Nothing moved. There was no sign of him.

Yawning, I realized I needed to pee. I needed coffee as well if I was going to function, but peeing came first.

As soon as I started to open the downstairs toilet door, the odour hit me like a slap. My heart leaped and I began shaking as the full realization of what lay beyond the door dawned on me. I didn't want to look. Oh God, I didn't want to look. But it was as if my body was operating independently of my brain and, almost in spite of myself, I put my head round the door, inch by bitter inch.

The killer had sat Crispin on the toilet in a final act of humiliation, with his head propped back against the windowsill. A clear plastic bag had been forced over his head, sticking to his face like a second skin as he'd sucked the air out of it, and his mouth was wide open, as were his eyes, in a classic expression of desperation. It was debatable whether asphyxiation had killed him, though, because his throat had been torn right open along its entire length, emptying its contents all over his shirt, which was now almost entirely crimson. Protruding from his groin, like a thin metallic dick, was my knife.

My poor, poor Crispin. Ruined and mutilated. Gone for ever.

I cried out then and backed into the hallway, a hand covering my mouth as I tried to work out the logic of what I'd just seen. Someone had taken and killed Crispin without him having a chance to make a sound, then come into the lounge and stolen each of our knives, yet without making any attempt to kill any of us. It didn't make sense. None of it did. And how on earth had the killer got in here?

A hand grabbed me roughly on the shoulder and I swung round fast.

It was Marla, looking concerned and alert. 'What's going on?' she demanded. 'Where's Crispin?'

She saw the look on my face and her eyes widened. 'He's not . . .'

I nodded slowly. 'He's . . . He's dead. In the toilet. Someone stabbed him.'

She took a step back, breathing rapidly. Then her expression changed, and she hurried past me, put her head round the toilet door, ignoring my protestations, and let out an ear-piercing scream, before racing back out into the hallway.

'I don't know what happened,' I explained. 'I must have fallen asleep.'

But Marla wasn't listening. She walked around me, keeping as far away as possible, never once taking her eyes off mine. 'You killed him, didn't you?'

The accusation was like a physical blow. 'No. No. Of course I didn't. Why would I do that?'

'Because you're the killer. It's you and Charlie. You're working together. And now you've murdered Crispin, you bitch. But don't try it with me, because if you do, I will fucking kill you.'

As she backed away towards the lounge, Luke appeared in the doorway, rubbing his eyes. 'What the hell's going on?'

Marla pointed at me. 'Crispin's dead. She killed him.'

'I didn't,' I said desperately. 'I just found him now. I fell asleep . . . I . . . Someone must have broken in.' The words were falling out of my mouth in a desperate blur but I could see that neither of them believed me. They stood together, mistrust pouring off them. And anger too.

'You killed Cris?' said Luke, aghast.

'No. I didn't.'

'She did. She fucking did. It's her knife sticking out of him. It's her and Charlie. They planned this whole thing to get rid of us.'

'I don't know what you're talking about. I'm nothing to do with this. And Charlie's dead, remember? If you don't believe me, take a look outside. The killer put his head on a pole next to Louise's.'

Doubt appeared – at least on Luke's face.

'Go on!' I shouted. 'Look!'

Marla ran past me into the kitchen and pulled the curtains open. 'Where?' she demanded, staring out. 'Where are these heads meant to be?'

'On the back lawn. Right in front of you.' But even before she closed the curtains with an angry flourish, I knew that the heads had been moved. Because whoever was behind this was deliberately trying to taunt me, and no one else.

Just me.

'They were there, I swear it.' But I could hear the doubt in my own voice.

As I was speaking, Luke put his head round the toilet door and let out a low keening sound, not dissimilar to a wounded animal, and when he turned back to look at me, his face was a mask of fury.

'What have you done?' he yelled, his voice reverberating round the whole house.

'I haven't done anything. Why would I kill Crispin? Or anyone?'

Marla pointed an accusing finger at me. 'The two of you are doing it to get rid of everyone else involved in Rachel's death. That way it's only you guys left.'

'Bullshit.' I pointed at Luke. 'He's got more of a motive than me. He was the one who hotwired Corridge's car and helped bury Rachel's body. And it was his room she died in. I was just in the wrong bloody place at the wrong bloody time. And Jesus, I've paid for it since.'

Marla snorted. 'Oh, yeah. Poor little innocent Karen. You think I don't know about your dirty little secret?'

'What secret?' demanded Luke.

'Why don't you tell him, Karen?'

'I don't know what you're talking about.'

'You were just as implicated as Luke. Maybe even more so. Because you were sleeping with her, weren't you?' A cruel grin twisted across her lips. 'Crispin told me. He said you were obsessed with her, and that the two of you almost broke up over it.'

'That's a lie!' I yelled.

'So you're a lesbian?' said Luke, more surprised than angry, it seemed, by this sudden revelation.

'Are you saying you never slept with her? Is that what you're saying, Karen?'

I hesitated. It was enough.

'You killed Rachel, didn't you? Didn't you, you fucking whore?'

'No!' I screamed, lunging forward and striking her hard round the face.

Which was when Luke punched me in the side of the head, knocking me down.

I cried out, hoping it would stop him from hurting me any more, but he pulled me to my feet by my hair and twisted an arm up behind my back.

At the same time Marla rushed into the kitchen, pulling open drawers until she found what she was looking for – a serrated chopping knife. She marched up to me and held the blade close to my face.

I tried to struggle free of Luke's grip but he pushed my arm even higher up my back, making me wail with the pain.

'Admit you killed Crispin,' hissed Marla. 'Admit it now, or I will cut you into fucking pieces.'

'I didn't. I swear I didn't.'

She pressed the blade against my cheek and behind me I heard Luke's sharp intake of breath. I thought he was going to say something – tell her to calm down or something – but he didn't.

'Please . . .' I was weeping now, unable to quite understand what was happening to me.

Marla stood there breathing heavily, her eyes full of rage, and I wondered whether or not she had it in her to carry out her threat. I wondered too whether she was actually the killer and was trying to put the blame on me, but that didn't make sense either.

And then I saw the faintest flicker of doubt cross her face, and she moved the knife away. 'We've got to get rid of her,' she said to Luke. 'I don't trust her.'

'Let's lock her in the woodshed. Then we can get the fuck out of this place.'

'No, please,' I begged.

But Luke was already marching me towards the back door, one hand pulling my head back by the hair, the other hand continuing to keep my arm right up my back. The pain was excruciating but still I tried to struggle, desperate not to be sent outside where I knew the killer lurked.

'Don't fight or I'll break your fucking arm,' he hissed in my ear, pushing my arm even higher so it felt like it was going to snap. 'Open the door for me,' he told Marla, moving aside to let her through.

She unlocked the door and Luke dragged me out on to the back patio, manoeuvring me towards the woodshed.

I wasn't going in there. Not with Louise's rotting headless corpse, and where I'd be at the mercy of the man who was intent on killing us all.

I couldn't. I had to survive.

Luke momentarily eased the pressure on my arm while he went to unbolt the shed door, and I thrust my free hand between his legs and grabbed his balls, twisting hard. He yelped in pain, his grip immediately slackening, and I pulled myself free.

'Bitch!' he yelled, but I was already running.

He was quick to recover though, and I only just managed to throw open the side gate and run through it before I heard him right behind me. I accelerated, sprinting across the front lawn, heading for the safety of the trees. Except it wasn't safe. This was where I'd seen Charlie's ruined corpse. I desperately wanted to try to reason with Luke – to ask him why, if I was the killer, hadn't I murdered him and Marla when they'd been fast asleep in the lounge? But I knew it was too late for that. He was only a yard or two away from me now, breathing heavily like an animal as he tried to run me down.

I hit the tree line, tore straight through a ragged tangle of brambles, ignoring the thorns as they slashed my skin. Ignoring, too, the pressure building in my lungs. I just had to keep going, lose him in the woods then plan my next move . . .

I stumbled on something and was suddenly yanked backwards as Luke grabbed me by the hood of my top. The momentum sent us both sprawling to the ground, but he still had hold of me and, in one swift movement, he flipped me over so I was lying on my back, and jumped on top of me, his knees pinning down my arms. The murderous brutality of his expression told me there'd be no mercy from him, and there wasn't. He placed his hands almost carefully round my neck and began squeezing.

His grip was vice-like, cutting my air off immediately. I was utterly helpless beneath his weight, and within seconds my vision began to cloud round the edges. Luke was going to kill me. He was actually going to kill me! I felt myself passing out, which was when I had a sudden chilling realization.

Luke was definitely the killer. It made so much sense. He'd always been the most heavily implicated in Rachel's murder, and now he was getting rid of the witnesses to the crime, just as Marla had accused me of doing.

'You bastard!' I thought with a mixture of fear, anger and resignation as I began to pass out. 'You fucking treacherous bastard!'

And then, just like that, his grip loosened and, as my vision began to clear, I saw why. Protruding from his mouth, like a long, forked tongue, was the end of a crossbow bolt. Blood collected in a pool on his lower lip before dripping down on to my face. He made a horrible gurgling sound like an old man choking on phlegm, and his body began to sway slowly from side to side.

More blood poured out of his mouth now, in a continuous flow. Sickened, I pushed his hands away and shoved him off me, adrenaline surging through my body.

The killer stood in the shadow of a pine tree no more than ten yards away, blocking the way down to the sea. He was still dressed in black from head to toe, his face covered by a ski mask, just as it had been the previous day, and he was reloading the crossbow, his movements almost leisurely, as if he had all the time in the world.

Scrambling to my feet, I ran back the way I'd come. Clearly the house wasn't secure but I had a better chance of defending myself inside than I had anywhere else. I prayed that Marla would let me back in because, if she didn't, by the time she realized her mistake I'd be dead. My only other alternative was to make a break for the rocks, start climbing and hope for the best, but right now I could only think a few seconds ahead.

I ran back through the side gate and round to the back door. I couldn't see Marla through the window, and I was certain she would have re-locked the door, but I tried the handle anyway, not expecting it to open.

It did.

I was inside like a shot, locking and bolting the door behind me as I called Marla's name.

No answer.

I ran through to the hallway, looking round wildly.

And that was when I saw her emerging from the lounge, holding the knife with the serrated blade she'd threatened me with earlier.

Something was wrong. Her expression was vague and distant, as if she was puzzled by something.

Then I saw the long thin slash of red opening up along her throat and, as if by some off-stage cue, a curtain of blood poured out like something out of a horror film, engulfing her neck and chest. She began to topple, managed to put a hand against the banister to steady herself, then fell face first to the floor and lay still, the blood seeping out from under her, staining the floorboards the colour of claret.

The killer stepped out from behind her, a bloodied machete in his hand, staring at me from behind his ski mask, cold contempt in his eyes.

For an interminably long moment I stood there, unable to believe my eyes. How on earth could he have got in? He'd been behind me when he'd killed Luke and he couldn't have got in through the front door, which was still bolted from the inside.

But in the end none of this mattered. What mattered was that I got out. As he raised the machete I turned and bolted back the way I'd come, scrambling to unlock the back door before it was too late.

As I threw it open, I stole a rapid glance over my shoulder and saw him walking steadily towards me, not even bothering to increase his pace.

And then as I ran outside on to the patio, a shadow appeared in the corner of my eye and I was grabbed from behind in a tight chokehold and, before I could even properly compute the fact that there were two masked killers, not one, I blacked out.

12

I awoke in a room with bookshelves lining the walls and a long teak desk at one end. This was Charlie's upstairs study. I remembered it vaguely from the time I'd come with him for the weekend all those years ago, although the room had been much more cluttered then.

Sitting on the desk facing me, arranged in a neat row and draped over a white beach towel, were the severed heads of Louise, Charlie, Crispin, Luke and Marla. All had their eyes open as they stared vacantly into space, and for some reason they didn't look real to me, or maybe it was because I'd seen so much horror these past thirty-six hours that I'd become inured to it. Instead, I focused on the video camera that was pointing at me from a central position between Crispin's and Luke's heads, trying hard not to wonder why it was there, before turning my gaze to an empty chair standing in front of the window. A length of rope with a noose attached hung down above it from a purpose-built metal joist in the ceiling.

It took me a few moments to realize that I was secured to a chair myself, with my wrists bound behind my back and two further loops of rope securing my arms to my side. I tested the bonds. They were pretty tight but I had a tiny bit of wriggle room, although that wasn't going to help me much unless I could free my hands.

Before I had a chance to dwell too much on what was being planned for me, the door to the room opened and the man in black walked in, still wearing his ski mask. He appeared to be unarmed, which gave me at least a tiny bit of relief.

He stood in front of me and, as I got a better look at the eyes behind the mask, I realized that, even though I hadn't seen him in over twenty years, I knew exactly who it was.

Danny Corridge pulled off the ski mask with a flourish and gave me a sadistic smile. 'Remember me, Karen?' he asked, bringing his face close. 'The man whose life you wrecked?'

'I'm so sorry,' I said quietly, because in the end what else could I say?

His laugh was loud and empty. 'Yeah, I fucking bet you are.'

'I am. I never wanted it to be like this.'

'Shut the fuck up or I'll cut your eyes out.'

I stopped speaking as cold fingers of dread crawled slowly up my spine.

'You know what's going to happen now, don't you?' continued Corridge, his face so close to mine that I could smell the acid in his breath. 'We're going to hang you. But it ain't going to be a nice quick snap of the neck. Oh no. Not for you. For you, it's going to be nice and slow. The knot's positioned so it'll throttle you slowly, and while you're choking out your last pathetic breaths we're going to film the whole thing.'

I wondered who the 'we' he kept referring to was, and the question was at least partly answered for me when a second man walked into the room.

So there had been two killers. It seemed almost too much to believe.

And then he too removed his mask and my shock deepened as Charlie's caretaker, Pat, was revealed.

'Thank God for that,' he said, chucking the mask on the floor. 'I was getting bloody hot wearing that the whole time.' He gave me a playful half-smile, no longer the taciturn man who had brought me here by boat. Now he seemed confident and in control. 'So, how have you been enjoying your weekend, Karen?'

For what felt like a long time I didn't say anything. It was all just too much.

'What's wrong, Karen?' asked Corridge with a grin. 'Cat got your tongue?'

They were standing next to each other now, watching me like a couple of sadistic school bullies.

'You know why you're here, don't you?' said Pat. 'Why you're the last one left alive?'

'No, I don't. Please. I didn't do anything . . .' There were tears in my eyes now as fear and despair engulfed me. I was throwing myself at their mercy even though I knew it wasn't going to do any good. These men were the most horrific kind of killers, yet what else could I do?

'You killed Rachel, Karen,' said Pat. It was a statement, not a question. 'And the reason that I know that is because Charlie told me.' He smiled. 'I can see I'm going to have to start at the beginning, aren't I? You see, it was Charlie and I who set this whole thing up. He knew a while back that Danny here was going to get released, him being a big politician and all. He also knew that, even though he'd never admit a thing about what happened with Rachel, he couldn't trust one or more of the rest of you not to fold under questioning and implicate him. He was scared he'd lose everything, and Charlie couldn't have that. He had big plans for himself, even one day being Prime Minister and lording over the country.' Pat gave a dismissive grunt before continuing.

'The plan was simple. He and I would get rid of you one at a time, incinerate the corpses, and bury whatever was left on the island. Because the whole weekend was going to be kept secret, and no one knew any of you were here, suspicion would never fall on him. But that was Charlie for you. A clever man but not half as clever as he thought he was. The plan would never have worked, but I wasn't going to tell him that. So I let him kill Louise on that first night, even though I really wasn't sure he could go through with it. He insisted, though. He actually *wanted* to kill her – I think the thought of it turned him on.' He shrugged. 'And credit to him, he did the job well. All that shit he used to give in Parliament about being a principled man standing up for morality and decency, and he stabbed a mother of two through the heart when she was least expecting it, all to save his own filthy skin.'

I felt sick. This was the man I'd had an affair with. And, sadly, I was certain that Pat wasn't lying.

'The plan was for Charlie to leave the house early yesterday morning, which he did, so we could then pick the rest of you off. He didn't want to do it that way, of course. If he'd had his way he'd have poisoned you all at dinner on the first night, because he's a coward, but I wasn't having any of that, and because I've spent a lot of time in the army, he knew he had to listen to me. So, anyway, he came out to meet me yesterday and that's when I introduced him to Danny here.' He chuckled. 'You should have seen the look on his face when they came face to face after all these years and he realized I'd set him up. So we killed him – nice and slowly – and after that we had all the time in the world to toy with the rest of you. And that's what we've been doing. Toying with you. Paying you back for the sins of your past.'

'How did you kill Crispin?' I asked. 'We had the house completely secure.' It was a pointless question under the circumstances, but I couldn't help it. I had to know. And the longer I kept the conversation going, the longer I stayed alive.

Pat looked pleased with himself. 'I was in the house already. There's a separate crawl-space in the loft, shut off from the main part. I was in it all day and evening yesterday, just waiting for the right moment to strike, and I've got to be honest here, it wasn't hard.'

'But what I don't understand is why did you of all people want to kill us? I can understand him doing it,' – I motioned towards Corridge – 'but not you.'

Pat sighed. 'Rachel Skinner was my step-sister. I grew up with her, and even though I didn't see much of her after my dad divorced her mum, I still loved her.'

I vaguely remembered Rachel telling me that her mum had remarried for a few years after she'd divorced Rachel's dad, but she'd never gone into any details.

'I was gutted when I found out she'd died,' continued Pat, a dark cloud of emotion crossing his face, 'but I thought when Danny was found guilty that at least some semblance of justice had been done. I went off to the army, served in wars, and I suppose I forgot about it. But Rachel's dad, Brian, didn't forget. Nor was he ever fully convinced that Danny was guilty, and the more he looked into it, the more he felt that there'd been a major miscarriage of justice. In fact it was he who helped get Danny's case taken up by the court of appeal. He also became convinced you six had covered the murder up to suit your own ends.' He paused. 'So when I was discharged from the army, Brian approached me with a proposition. He wanted me to get close to Charlie and find out what I could about his involvement. At the time I had nothing. No money, no prospects, so I changed my name and moved down here after Charlie bought this place. It didn't take long to get myself on his radar and he ended up hiring me to run this place while he was away. But I was a lot more than a caretaker. I became his confidant. He trusted me completely. So much so that he even told me about Rachel, and you know what? He was always convinced you were the killer. He said you slept with her a number of times, and he told me how jealous you became when she went back to Danny. And when she slept with Luke that night . . .' He whistled through his teeth. 'Well, that would have been the final straw, wouldn't it?'

'It's bullshit. That's what it is. Just because I slept with her doesn't mean I killed her.'

'It took me a long time to get all the evidence we needed to act,' continued Pat, ignoring my protestations as if he hadn't heard them, 'and by that time it was obvious Danny was going to be released. So as soon as he got out, I made him an offer. Earn some serious money and get revenge on the people who'd destroyed his life.'

'And I'm glad I did,' said Corridge, 'because making you bastards suffer for what you did to me has been worth every penny. And this is the bit I've been looking forward to most. Watching the one who started it all die.' His face contorted into a snarl of pure hatred as all those years of pain were relived. 'But I'm going to hurt you first.'

'Don't forget, Danny,' Pat warned. 'No obvious injuries on her. She's the one who's going to be held responsible for the murders when someone finally turns up here and discovers all this.'

'That's right,' chuckled Corridge. 'We're going to make your death look like murder-suicide so that your family know you're nothing more than a sick, twisted killer. Or what's left of your family anyway.' He leaned forward, grinning. 'I heard about what happened to your kid. I'm fucking glad the little brat died. I hope it was painful.'

I felt a wave of anger then. If I had to die, so be it. I'd sinned in the

past and now I was being made to pay for it. But to bring my daughter –
my poor, beautiful, innocent Lily – into this was a deliberate affront to
everything that was good and decent in the world.

I wasn't just going to sit here and beg for my life. One way or another,
I was going to resist.

That was when it occurred to me that my lighter was still tucked into
the sleeve of my hoodie. Using my fingers I managed to slip it free. If I
could somehow burn the rope binding my wrists . . . It was a ridiculous
plan, of course. I was totally helpless and one way or another they were
going to kill me. But there was no way I was going to waste any more
breath begging for mercy. I wasn't going to give these pieces of shit the
satisfaction.

It was then that a very strange thing happened. As Corridge continued
to goad me – his words nothing more than a single blurred noise that I was
now shutting out – Pat came up behind him, slipped an arm almost leisurely
round his neck and dragged him back into a chokehold.

Corridge's eyes widened then almost immediately closed and he went
limp in Pat's arms.

'That's enough, Danny,' said Pat, winking at me as he dragged Corridge's
body over to the chair with the noose hanging above it. 'The problem with
civilians is that they're just too damn confident in their own abilities. And
yet so many of them are idiots. You know you can't afford to be an idiot
in the army, Karen. If you are, you die. But Charlie, and Danny here, they
went to their doom never realizing how much they were being played.' As
he spoke he sat Corridge in the chair, lowered the rope, and placed the
noose carefully around his neck, tightening it so it was a nice snug fit.

I knew I only had one chance. 'Why are you doing this?' I asked, at the
same time touching the lighter to the rope binding my wrists and flicking
it on.

Pat reached round behind the desk and untied the other end of the rope
before giving it a hard pull. Corridge's body straightened in the chair as it
was lifted upwards and his eyes began to flicker open. 'There's no way
anyone will believe that you managed to kill all five of your friends, and
particularly that you decapitated them. But they'll believe that Danny
Corridge – former violent criminal hell-bent on revenge would have. No
one will know how he got on the island or how he managed to do it, but
that won't matter. The police will have their victims and their perpetrator,
and that'll be enough. And if you're wondering what the camera's there
for, it's to record your confession followed by your dying moments.' He
kept pulling on the rope, lifting Corridge to his feet so that only his toes
were touching the floor.

I could smell burning and I knew that any moment Pat would be able to as well, but I could also feel the rope giving.

Corridge's eyes opened properly now and, as he belatedly realized what was going on and grabbed at the noose, Pat gave another big tug, putting all his weight into it. Corridge's feet left the floor and he bucked and kicked wildly but Pat held on tight, his face reddening with the effort.

I felt the lighter scalding my skin and the next second the rope burnt through and my hands were free. I tried to wriggle out of the ropes binding my body but they were too tight. I managed to lift my forearm a few inches so that the lighter was close to the bottom of the two ropes and I flicked it on again.

Corridge was making horrible gasping sounds now as his face went a mottled purple. His thrashing got worse then began to subside as the life was sucked out of him. The smell of smoke was really obvious now and for the first time Pat glanced my way, a puzzled expression on his face, and I knew he smelled it too, but he was holding the rope that was throttling Corridge and he was in no position to do anything about it.

I could feel my back burning and knew that I'd probably set fire to the hoodie as well but I ignored the pain. All that mattered right now was escape. And I was inching ever closer to it.

Corridge stopped moving. His body went limp and almost immediately a strong smell of shit filled the air, temporarily masking that of the smoke.

'What are you doing over there?' snarled Pat. 'If you try anything I'll make your death slow as well.'

The bottom rope split, leaving only one left and, as Pat reached round to re-tie the other end of his hangman's noose now that Corridge was dead, I managed to pull off my hoodie, giving me enough wriggle room to slide down the chair and free myself from the last length of rope still binding me.

I was on my feet in an instant as the adrenaline surged through me. Hope. I finally had hope. The door was still open and I charged through it and along the landing, taking the stairs three at a time.

He was right behind me as I leaped the last five steps, landing in a squat. The front door was bolted and the key was no longer in it. I had to use the back door or nothing.

It was then that I remembered something. Turning a sharp left I ran into the lounge and over to the grand old fireplace, silently thanking God, or whoever it was protecting me today, that what I was looking for was there.

The door slammed shut behind me and I could hear him in the room.

Crouching down, I grabbed the ornamental poker and swung round just in time to see him running towards me – a long-bladed, bloodied knife in his gloved hand.

With a bloodcurdling scream, I swung the poker as hard as I could in a tight arc, putting every ounce of strength into it.

Pat tried to throw up an arm and get out of the way at the same time but he'd miscalculated and he wasn't fast enough. The poker caught him right in the throat, knocking him to one side. He stumbled into a footrest and fell to the floor, managing to keep hold of the knife while clutching his throat with his free hand.

I didn't hesitate. As he rolled round to face me, I lifted the poker above my head and hit him a second time, the blow making a sickening crunch as it struck the bridge of his nose, shattering bone and cartilage. Then I was hitting him again and again, a cloud of rage, euphoria and power swirling through my mind and, in that moment, I was transported back to that dark bloody night all those years ago. I'd used a hammer then but the feeling was exactly the same. Complete and utter release. Blood splattered the floorboards, the furniture, even the walls. But still I didn't stop until Pat's head was nothing more than a pulped, bloody mess and he'd finally stopped breathing. Only then did I drop the poker and step back from his body.

I'd felt the same way when I'd killed Rachel. Sated. At least for the first few seconds. Then reality had set in, followed by regret, because I genuinely hadn't wanted to kill her. It's true. I was obsessed with her. I think I'd had a crush on her right from the moment we'd moved into the same house but then, after she'd seduced me one night, it moved from crush into far deeper, darker territories. We had a brief relationship. It was our secret. I didn't think anyone knew about it, especially not Crispin or Charlie. I loved Crispin but I was infatuated with Rachel and when it became obvious that she didn't feel the same way – that, as far as she was concerned, I was just another notch on her bedpost – it made me angry. Angry and jealous. I hated the way she toyed with people, and that night, when she'd started getting off with Luke in front of me, my rage had become uncontrollable. I confronted her in the toilets and she'd dismissed me like I was nothing, telling me to, in her words, 'get a fucking life'.

But I didn't get a life. I took one. More sober than the rest of them, I'd waited until she and Luke were comatose in his room and then I'd crept in, naked, with the hammer, and killed her. How Luke didn't wake up I'll never know, but he didn't, even though he was splattered with her blood.

After I'd finished I washed myself, washed the hammer, put it away in the cupboard I'd got it from and went into Marla's bedroom and lay on the spare mattress on her floor, wondering what I was going to do, until eventually I fell asleep.

I'm glad I've told you everything. The guilt's haunted me over the years and, as you know, I've been paid back many times for the sin I committed that night. I'm sorry Rachel's dead. I always have been. I'm sorry the others are dead too.

On the way over in the boat, I'd offered Pat a smoke and he'd taken it, so I searched through his pockets now, and struck lucky, finding a half-full pack of Rothmans and a box of matches, as well as a bunch of keys. I found the one that opened the front door, then, as my breathing slowed to normal, I lit a cigarette and used the rest of the matches to set fire to the lounge curtain, before wandering round downstairs, setting more fires.

Only when the flames began to really take hold did I leave through the front door and, with barely a look behind me, I started the walk through the trees down to the beach and the jetty, finally enjoying breathing in the fresh country air.

It was time to begin the rest of my life.

FIND OUT MORE ABOUT
SIMON AND HIS BOOKS ONLINE AT

www.simonkernick.com

 /SimonKernick

@simonkernick

dead
good

*For all of you who find
a crime story irresistible.*

Discover the very best crime and thriller books, handpicked by our editorial team so you have tailored recommendations to help you choose what to read next.

We'll introduce you to our favourite authors and the brightest new talent. Read exclusive interviews and specially commissioned features on everything from the best classic crime to our top ten tv detectives, join live webchats and speak to authors directly.

Plus our monthly book competition offers you the chance to win the latest crime fiction, and there's DVD boxsets and devices to be won too.

**Sign up for our newsletter at
www.deadgoodbooks.co.uk/signup**

Join the conversation on: